FROM
THE GRAVE
OF THE GODS

THE AUGMENT SAGA: BOOK ONE

ALAN K. DELL

ACKNOWLEDGEMENTS

First things first, I must give thanks to my wonderful family. Especially my long-suffering wife, Emma, who has had to endure my rabbiting on about this book for the last couple of years, from its very first inception, through each successive edit and rewrite; through my own lack of patience, rising insecurities, anxiety and second-guessing; through working on supplementary material, and finally to publication. She has begrudgingly helped me with phrasing and proofread my work to ensure it makes sense.

Then, to my children, Oliver and Eulalia, who have similarly had to endure Daddy burying his head in his writing. This first part of the project has taken a lot of work to put together, and it could only have come together with their support.

Next, I need to give a special thanks to my incredible beta readers, who took the time to read through my manuscript and provide valuable feedback which inevitably led to important changes—including wholesale rewrites of entire sections—shaping the book as it is today. Without these individuals, this book would surely look very different, and would perhaps never have seen the light of day. Thank you for all your comments, thoughts, critiques, suggestions, home truths, and most of all, for your support.

Adam Sadler
Kane Ridley
Drew Wagar

In fact, I owe a particular debt of thanks to Drew—who is the author of the official Elite Dangerous novels, *Reclamation* and *Premonition*; the official novelisation of *The Lords of Midnight*; and of *The Shadeward Saga*—for taking the time out to help this random fan and Twitter follower achieve his first published novel.

And finally to you, my dear readers, thank you. I hope this first part of the Augment Saga ignites in you the same excitement and wonder at the future as it did in me when I dreamt up this series in imaginary play as a child. The themes have certainly matured with me, but the sense of optimism and adventure remains as vivid as it ever was.

'It was sometime afterward when the thought flashed upon my mind that the disturbances I had observed might be due to an intelligent control.'

—Nikola Tesla, Talking with the Planets, 1901

PROLOGUE

THERE WAS A STRANGE SOUND. It was deep and muffled, with an urgent cadence. Somewhat recognisable, but drowned out by another, an obnoxious ringing in my ear. As both sounds grew in volume and intensity, even in the darkness of my mind I began to differentiate them. One was a klaxon, a blaring alarm warning me of some impending danger. The other was a voice calling my name, becoming clearer by the second.

'Mum? Please, no, I don't want to wake up yet,' I mumbled.

It wasn't my mother, but nevertheless I felt like I needed more sleep; my head was heavy and my eyes were locked shut. After what seemed like several minutes, but in truth could only have been a fraction of a second, the fog in my mind cleared and I opened my eyes with a blink. There were blurred lights all around me; red, flashing LEDs. As I lifted my head, I saw a huge expanse of brightness and swirling colour filling the view before me.

The urgent voice assaulted my ears again. 'Lieutenant Fowler! Goddammit, James, come in. You need to pull up

1

right now!'

I mumbled again: 'Pull up? What does that mean?'

Soon after, my eyes and head cleared a little more, enough for me to remember that I was a pilot, usually a damn good one: Flight Lieutenant James Fowler, Royal Air Force. But I had made a huge mistake this time. I'd climbed at too steep an angle, stalled my aircraft and blacked out. I should have known better.

Reflections danced off the inside of the visor before my eyes, and the oxygen mask covering my mouth felt uncomfortable. Odd, to feel stifled by the very thing keeping me alive. The helmet pushed down upon my head with an oppressive weight and I was immobile, trapped in the pilot's seat by tight restraints.

I looked around, taking in my surroundings. There were toggles and switches all about me and a flight stick between my legs. At the sight of the stick, I snapped back to my senses and I felt an attack of severe vertigo as the view out of the cockpit became clearer. In truth, the vertigo wasn't inside my head; I was in freefall. I had woken up with the aircraft in a nose-dive, the tons of state-of-the-art machinery tumbling through the air, plummeting towards the ground.

'Fowler, you need to stabilise and pull up right now, do you copy?' came the voice of the controller through my helmet radio.

My eyes widened and my heart pounded. Beads of sweat poured down from my sodden hairline as fear took hold, flooding my system with adrenaline.

'I don't want to die!' I blurted out in a raspy voice.

My hands shot forwards as if by themselves and grabbed the flight stick. I wrestled with the aircraft for control, pulling this way and that. The spinning hunk of metal and plastic seemed to have a mind of its own.

I took a deep breath

Now, fully cognisant of my impending doom, I pulled the thrust control back to zero. In a practised movement, I set the ailerons to their neutral position and turned the rudder left, opposing the plane's chaotic spin. All that was left was to push forwards on the stick to bring the wings out of their stall.

'Copy that, Control. Pulling up.'

The plane flew out of its spin, but it was getting very low to the ground. I pulled back on the stick and prayed I wasn't too late.

'This is gonna be a close one, lads.'

* * *

'No, this is not the right one; sweep it again.'

There was another voice, one I didn't recognise, with an unpleasant, grating rasp. Was it a voice? It echoed around my mind. It wasn't Control, it didn't come through a headset, but seemed to rise up from within, as if my thoughts themselves were being invaded. The fog returned, filling my head, and I could no longer see.

Where did my plane go? Did I hit the ground? Wait… That was a memory. A memory from a lifetime—no, several lifetimes ago.

A second, distorted voice with a distinctive whine replied in protest, 'But its neural processes are erratic and transitory!'

'I don't care how hard it is; sweep it again and again until you find the right entry point!' the raspy voice shouted.

A horrible pain rushed through me and a dreadful scream emanated from somewhere in the room.

Did that come from… me? Everything feels so detached.

Raspy piped up in an apologetic tone, as if speaking to someone new, 'We need to be careful. We don't want to kill this one. Others of its kind have already expired, and we have tested other beings far stronger that were not as… fragile.'

'Yes, but this one is different. It is resilient and its mind is like a fine banquet. Continue the neural sweep,' a third, menacing voice growled.

The clunk of boots on metal grew louder, approaching my position. Seconds later, there was the deep rattle of laboured chest movements next to me and I could feel my captor's warm, putrid breath on my cheek.

'You will reveal *all* to us,' Menacing whispered, his mental voice permeating my skull.

Now I remember, I was captured. You'll get nothing from me.

I felt him stand up, but the horrible smell lingered for a few seconds more. I heard a scuffing noise as he turned on his heel and the clanking of his boots receded as he strode away.

I can't speak. If only I could reply…

'Restarting neural sweep,' called Whiny.

A sharp pain hit my body all at once and what little I could perceive went dark and silent.

* * *

The room faded into view and I began to tremble. I wasn't prepared; I hadn't had the time—that was what I'd been telling myself anyway, and anyone who would listen, anything to justify not studying. As I sat at my small wooden desk, I looked around the room; it was large and filled with rows of single-seater desks just like mine. It wasn't that long ago

4

that this hall had been full of gymnastics equipment, but in this configuration it was far more intimidating and felt much larger. Footsteps and indecipherable murmurs echoed across the hall as others filed in and took their seats.

I looked back down at the desktop in front of me and ran my hands over its rough surface. The wood was old and worn from the decades of students who had sat here before me. It looked as though many had got bored, picking and chipping with their fingernails, gouging chunks with their pens, scribbling and carving nonsensical symbols. I imagined that there would be a plentiful variety of chewing gum stuck under the worktop, but I didn't fancy checking. Following in the footsteps of all the nervous and jittery secondary-schoolers who'd come before, I started picking at my name tag, which was stuck on the top right corner of the desk, just above the channel meant for holding pens.

The corner of the paper began to peel and tear as my other classmates took their seats around me. Some of them were in the same boat as I was: hadn't studied. I knew for a fact that was the case for Felix. Served us right for staying up drinking all last night at his place. He had raided his dad's cabinet early in the evening while his parents were out and brought us the strong stuff. This was the 'important work' that meant we didn't have the time to prepare, but I was suffering for it now. My head pounded, but at least the evening had been fun.

Come on, Felix. Where are you?

I hadn't seen him on the way in this morning, and he wasn't in the line when we all entered the hall. He must have overslept. I didn't even want to think about the bollocking he'd have got from his dad after his parents kicked me and the other guys out in the early hours.

Ah well, he wasn't going to study history at college anyway. One fail can't hurt, can it?

The invigilators glided around the hall, distributing exam sheets on all of the desks—throwing them down in passive-aggressive protest—before returning to their stations, where they watched over the hall like stalwart sentinels. I straightened the paper and saw the space on the front to write my name. I picked up the pen and wrote 'James Fowler, Candidate Number 2611'. Twiddling the pen around in my fingers, I read the rest of the front page. There was a bunch of colourful exam board logos, administrative information and the title, which read, 'GCSE History, Paper One, Summer 2001'.

The chief invigilator cleared her throat and I looked up. The second hand of the clock on the wall above her head ticked closer to twelve.

'You may begin… now,' she bellowed, and I turned the first page.

* * *

'What are you doing?'

I came around and everything was black again, the same horrid voices from before echoing around my brain and the unbearable discomfort rushing back.

'This is still not right; this is too early in its history. You would dare serve this to the Inquisitor? There are no answers here. Run the sweep again. Curse these disorganised creatures and their tiny, unordered brains!' cried Raspy, slamming something fleshy down onto a metal surface.

Good. Failure.

Whiny replied, 'Do not concern yourself. It is necessary for calibration. Unless *you* want to explain to the Inquisitor why it expired before we could extract its important memories?'

Raspy huffed and grumbled, 'I fear the Inquisitor is over-confident in this one's resilience.'

A machine whirred to life, spooling. It sparked and crackled. Then there was another loud scream and the smell of burning flesh. The pain built up within my body, coursing along my entire nervous system. I writhed and fought. This one was much worse than the last. Mercifully, it didn't last long, and the blackness swallowed me once more.

* * *

I opened my eyes with my face pressed against the floor; a thin blue carpet, scratchy and scattered with debris. A sharp pain shot through my head as though a knife had been jammed in behind my eye. My arms trembled and gave way as I tried to lift myself up. The room spun about me and my ears rang with an uncomfortable high-pitched squeal. I lifted my soot-blackened hand in the low, flickering light to wipe the dampness away from my forehead. Pulling my hand away, I saw on my fingers not sweat but blood, mingling with the dust and dripping down my wrist. With a grunt, I forced myself up, overcoming the weakness in my arms, and came to a kneeling position. There was a dull pain in my abdomen and I wrapped my arm across it. With my other hand, I reached out and grabbed the back of a nearby chair. The singed fabric crackled under my weight. As I shifted my legs and staggered to my feet, I scanned the room. It was dark; fire and choking black smoke billowed from consoles and terminals. Sparks flew from openings in the ceiling and wires hung down all over the semicircular room. Muffled explosions sounded off in the distance behind me.

People lay on the floor, good people. Some writhing in pain, some motionless. Others limped and hobbled, battered and bruised, supported by the less injured. One man lay on his front ahead of me, unmoving, his limbs splayed at strange angles like a ragdoll in a burned United Earth Confederacy uniform. He'd been thrown forwards in the crash; it was the last thing I saw before blacking out. The ringing in my ears faded and I stumbled over to him, faltering and tripping. Others, to the left and right, were struggling to pull themselves to their feet, with the floor buckled and uneven, and a whole section slanting downwards. I dropped next to the man and checked him over. Blood poured from under his head and his eyes were open, giving his face a blank expression. The usually brown skin on his cheeks was seared and blistered. I moved my hand to his neck and felt for a pulse, but all was still. I heaved a great sigh and closed the lifeless eyes of my first officer.

'You deserved so much better, my friend. Your family will know you died a hero,' I said, coughing and struggling once again to my feet.

'Captain Fowler, are you alright?' came a voice from behind me.

I spun around and saw the terrified face of Lieutenant McDowell. He looked relatively unscathed; one of the lucky ones.

'I'll be fine, Lieutenant,' I replied. 'We need to evacuate. Now.'

He turned around and shouted to the others, 'Okay, everyone! Captain's orders: move out.'

The muffled explosions continued to sound outside, and I looked back towards the front of the bridge. The viewing window was gone, smashed in the impact.

At least the plasma windows are still holding; otherwise we'd be exposed to hard vacuum.

Ganymede wasn't a nice place for a stroll outside, a fact I knew from experience.

I made my way to the rear of the bridge and pressed an intercom button on the wall. 'All hands, this is the captain speaking. Make your way to the cargo bay airlock as quickly as you can. The city will provide us with shelter.'

I took one last, longing look back at the bridge that had been my home for so many years and, with a sigh, turned to leave through the rear door. As I hurried along the darkened corridor behind my surviving bridge officers, more crewmembers poured out of side rooms, many of them limping and injured, bleeding and dejected. Some carried the bodies of their friends who had been killed in the assault. Security officers argued with them, telling them to leave the dead and evacuate, but the crewmembers were so distraught they couldn't bear to stop dragging their friends along.

There was an ensign sitting with his face in his hands in a doorway on the left. He was covered in blood which was not his own and sobbing to himself. I leant down and grabbed him under the shoulder, pulling him to his feet.

'Move, Wyatt! I'm not having you die here too,' I said, pushing him out in front of me as we hurried along to the cargo bay.

All of a sudden, another explosion rocked the stricken starship. It was much louder and closer than the previous ones, indicating a cascade failure. The lights flickered and officers cried out, almost losing their footing.

'Go, now!' I cried at the top of my lungs as I regained my footing. We continued along the corridor at a faster pace until it opened out into the cargo bay.

Most of the surviving crew were already present, waiting by the airlock. I could hear the panic in their voices as I moved through the crowd towards the door. Some noticed me and stepped aside of their own volition, while others needed to be pulled out of the way. As I reached the door, I peered through the window.

Thank goodness, the docking tunnel is attached.

Turning around to face the jostling crowd, I said, 'Okay, people, let's keep this orderly. There will be medical teams waiting for us on the other side.'

Facing the door once again, I pressed some buttons on the panel in the frame and the airlock pressurised with a hiss. As soon as the light on the panel turned green, I pressed another button and the door opened with a whoosh.

* * *

'This is better, Operator. Much closer. You just need to tune in to the right waveforms,' crackled Raspy, addressing the whiny-voiced operator.

'It was closer, certainly, Supervisor,' replied the operator. 'But its brain is snapping to its strongest traumatic memories. It is making it more difficult to home in on its origins.'

'Try targeting the spikes that correspond to formative memories, and filter for noise.'

The operator raised his voice and became more distorted: 'But I cannot account for its inherent randomness. There is a high probability of generating spikes based on its *current* emotional state. Look! It is bleeding from its facial orifices as we speak. Its anxiety is overwhelming and creating a spike right now.'

'Excellent,' laughed the supervisor. 'This could be exactly

what we need. Lean into it with the sweep and see what it reveals…'

A surge of white-hot pain shot through my body, causing me to convulse in my solid restraints. I felt my consciousness begin to fade away yet again.

* * *

I awoke once more standing on the bridge of a starship, staring out of the front window. My eyes widened and my heart pounded in my chest as I looked, helpless, upon the scene unfolding before my eyes. This was a different starship, a later memory. My ship's dorsal hull stretched out in front of the bridge, and beyond it, among unfamiliar stars, appeared an entire fleet of abominable, dark, eldritch warships. Their asymmetrical space-frames were covered in spikes and writhing growths of tentacles. More ships, of varying sizes and configurations, materialised before me in the deep, silhouetted by the infernal glow emanating from the wormhole. An unsettling reddish-orange and white light came from the centre as though the very gates of hell itself had burst, tearing the fabric of spacetime asunder and burning it in some unholy fire.

I stood, transfixed, as the numbers continued to increase. There were thousands—no, tens of thousands of Harvesters. Each in itself was an unknowable cosmic horror; together, their predatory appearance awakened my deepest, most primal fears. Yet I was enraptured, staring in awe and reverence at the emergence of this terrible, malevolent force.

Tearing myself away from the scene, I looked at my first officer. His mouth flapped open and closed, telling me something about the dreadful event, but his speech was inaudible, the fog of terror and guilt obscuring the facts about their numbers and capabilities. My eyes moved from him and rested on each crewmember in turn; they stared at me, expecting orders, instructions or maybe a plan.

That's a laugh…

I stumbled towards the captain's chair, longing for the comfort of its familiar and reassuring softness, and all I could think was, *What have I done?*

* * *

'Far too recent!' shouted the supervisor, his voice echoing once again around my mind like a gong. 'That has disrupted the waveform tuning entirely.'

I awoke with a start and the intense pain returned. Still unable to see or move, I could feel myself sweating—or perhaps bleeding—all over.

'Wait, there. Right there,' said the supervisor. 'I believe this is our way back in after that mind-quake. Target that pathway and sweep it again. Push even harder. We may be able to force it to relive the correct parts.'

My heart rate increased and my breathing quickened. I tried shouting and protesting, but my captors either wouldn't listen or couldn't understand me—if I even spoke at all!

All of a sudden the already unbearable pain became unlike anything I had ever felt before, as though my body was about to tear itself apart. Another convulsion hit and I felt my blinded eyes rolling into the back of my skull. The pain overloaded my senses and became like white noise inside my mind, infinitely loud and distracting. After what felt like hours, the pain blurred as I faded out yet again, falling back through my own memories. As I tumbled, my mind lingered on one scene in particular and a wave of fondness washed over me.

* * *

I sat looking up at an unfamiliar night sky. The landscape of distant mountains and sweeping countryside before me was lit by the sky's deep, red nebulosity and the twinkling of thousands of young, hot stars. Closer, strange alien grasses and flora swayed in the breeze of the cool night air. The stars here shone much more crisp and clear than anywhere on Earth, thanks to the lack of light pollution and atmospheric haze. The view was spectacular. I lifted my arm and took a swig of the beverage in my hand; it tasted sweet with a hint of bitterness, not unlike a fruity cider. But it was not like any fruit I'd ever tasted; it was somehow much more refreshing despite the high alcohol content.

I leant back in the wicker chair, which creaked under my movement, and took a moment to examine the bottle. It was of pearlescent glass and had an innovative shape unsuited for human mouths. It didn't matter; if there was a way to enjoy alcohol, humans would figure it out, no matter how awkward.

My companion sat next to me in his own chair. This was his veranda, attached to his summer home. He noticed me inspecting the container and chuckled.

'We should have done this years ago, James… When we weren't trying to kill each other, of course.'

I took another drink. The guilt over my own actions still hadn't gone away despite the passage of time. I thought for a moment about all the times I should have taken some leave to come and visit.

'You won't get any arguments from me,' I replied. 'Maybe

if you'd told me the view on P'horesh was this good…'

I trailed off and moved my bottle to tap the side of his with a clink. He looked at me with a confused expression as I cried, 'Cheers!'

Laughing once more, he turned his head back to face the countryside. 'You humans and your strange rituals.'

* * *

The memory faded, but the longing remained as I continued to fall through my past. Fragments of memories lit up around me as if on miniature screens. Some good, some best left forgotten. As I looked with my mind's eye around the swirling vortex of white noise, I felt myself be drawn towards a scene. There was a primitive spacecraft, long and slender. It had two large habitation rings, which turned slowly. Crude thrusters hissed, bringing it into orbit around the Red Planet.

Then the scene changed. A long blade glinted in the low light, and someone screamed. My body, my very soul, went cold with dread as the worst day of my life played out before my eyes.

Not this… Anything but this!

A faint cackle from the operator echoed around inside my head, calling out, 'This is it! The memory we need.'

'The Inquisitor *will* be pleased,' replied the supervisor, its grating rasp reverberating through the vortex.

All of a sudden, my mind accelerated towards a bright light and I heard the operator say, 'Begin recording.'

I.

CHAPTER ONE
THE MAGNUM OPUS

6th March 2025

STARS COVERED THE SKY IN ALL DIRECTIONS, their true splendour and clarity witnessed by only a precious few in all of human history. A hundred million miles out from the Cradle of Life—a vantage point thus far given only to lifeless robotic sensors—their apparent brightness was multiplied. Strands of interstellar dust streaked the sky, interspersed with fluffy nebulae of all shapes, sizes and colours: the grand arc of the galactic centre displayed in all its wonder and mystery. It made for the most magnificent of backdrops. At this distance, the Earth was a miniscule azure spot, and its rufescent cousin took its place, interrupting the astronomical mise-en-scène with its proximity.

After seven long months of travel in the void, the *Magnum Opus*—the largest spacecraft constructed in the history of humankind—loomed close to the Red Planet, the retrograde thrusters of its state-of-the-art engines firing, pushing hard against its forward momentum. Once it had slowed enough to enter a stable Martian orbit, manoeuvring thrusters all over the gargantuan vehicle's flimsy frame burst into life, turning the spacecraft and bringing its port side—housing the Martian Excursion Module between its two rotating habitation rings—to face the planet.

Commander James Fowler floated along the spacecraft's central tube, past exposed cables and conduits secured down by pieces of tape, pulling himself along using the handles on the walls. He wore a simple grey t-shirt and tracksuit bottoms that looked as though they were in desperate need of a wash. All this time in the black with only a limited set of clothing and rationed washing facilities meant he and the rest of the crew couldn't be concerned by things like body odour and stains. In a way it was rather freeing. He moved towards the Command Module to check in with Major Zhu O-Huang, who had piloted the craft and positioned it in orbit.

The Command Module of the *Magnum Opus* was designed to detach from the rest of the craft for controlled re-entry upon the crew's safe return to Earth. Unlike the rest of the craft's hodgepodge of tanks, containers and mismatching parts, the Command Module was sleek and stylish, with a smooth, aerodynamic frame; a white space-plane emblazoned with space agency logos and black heat-shielding on its ventral hull.

'Magnificent, isn't it?' said James, staring out of the cockpit window from the rear hatch and marvelling at the alien world before him. 'How're we going, Major?' he asked as Zhu flicked a few switches.

The major, unfazed by James's sudden appearance, looked around at him and replied, 'I've parked us in geosynchronous orbit over the impact site, sir. We should be able to commence imaging whenever you and Yula are ready.'

Major Zhu O-Huang had been top of the CNSA's shortlist

of pilots for the project and had excelled in all her simulation training. Her skill in the Chinese air force was widely known, even outside of China, but wasn't something she ever brought up in conversation. Her appearance was somewhat unassuming: a slender figure with sharp facial features. Her skin was a warm beige, she wore her hair in a short brown bob and her eyes had a look of innocent, youthful optimism.

'Excellent work. I'll let the captain know,' said James. He went to move away, but stopped, turned back and patted her on the shoulder. 'Hey, I can't believe we're finally here.'

'Yes, sir,' Zhu replied with a grin. 'It's good to have something else to look at out there.'

James smiled and gave a short laugh. 'Yeah, sure is.' And with that, he floated off back down the long corridor.

After a short while travelling along the passage, he passed a thick join in the wall and its diameter widened. The whole section could be seen turning slowly, if one stayed still long enough. James held on to one of the handles in this spinning area, causing him to match its rotation. He continued along and reached an opening off to the left side. Having turned himself around, he went through feet first, grabbed the rungs in the wall and climbed down the ladder. The *Magnum Opus*'s rings—named Hab-1 and Hab-2 respectively—were spaced evenly along the ship's hull and connected to its slender central tube by several of these long spokes, each of which contained a ladder. When he reached the bottom, he stepped off the final rung, careful about planting his feet on the floor. The rotation of the habitation ring simulated near-Earth gravity and it could be disorienting to go from zero-G to a standing position. James took a moment to compose himself and then walked along the inside curve of the ring— so large that his immediate vicinity seemed flat—over to the bunk room, where Captain Austin Queen lay on his bed reading a magazine in silence.

Austin was a stout, muscular man from Van Buren, Arkansas. He wasn't much shorter than James, but at forty-two, was nearly three years his elder. He had brown crew-cut hair with hints of grey coming through above his ears and his eyes were very dark; in truth they were brown, but at first glance they appeared to be pitch black. It was only after looking into them for a short while that anyone could notice the subtle difference in tone between his iris and pupil. It was a good thing that Austin was brimming with confidence and excellent at maintaining eye contact. His square jaw and tanned peach skin completed the look, giving him the appearance of an 'all-American hero'. It wasn't his appearance, though, that had made NASA choose him to command the *Magnum Opus*; he also had a keen scientific mind and had pushed hard to gain the coveted position.

The bunk room was small and low, with some steps leading down into it. There was barely enough room for the bed but space enough for clothes and some personal effects in the storage compartment above, and a desk and chair at the foot end.

These individual bunks in the habitation ring had been home to the crew for the duration of their journey, so it was no surprise they had personalised them. Captain Queen had put out a picture frame on the small desk—next to his work laptop—with a photo of his dog in it. On the overhead storage compartment, he'd hung a great big American flag, something which everyone agreed was a tad too much.

'She's parked, Captain,' said James as he bent down and leaned his head into the bunk room.

Austin peered over his magazine. 'Great news. Go tell

Yula she can start imaging; I'll be heading to the CM in a moment. Where's Grant?'

'Gone for his morning run around Hab-2, sir.'

The captain nodded and went back to his magazine, and James moved off to find Cosmonaut Yula Merkulova. He walked further along the ring from Austin's bunk and peered into Yula's, but she wasn't there.

Probably already in the imaging lab...

He jogged over to the nearest ladder and ascended back up to the main concourse and its zero-G environment. The imaging lab was towards the rear of the craft, behind the two habitation rings and affixed to the outside of the corridor. It was adjacent to one of the ship's sets of huge solar panels, which stuck out like wings either side of the central tube.

As he floated along the corridor, he passed through another rotating section and could hear rapid footsteps coming from Hab-2, echoing up the ladders. He shook his head and moved on, eventually coming to the doorway for the lab on the right.

James drifted through the doorway and into the room. Yula was there, facing away from him and getting the imaging equipment ready. She was so involved in what she was doing that she didn't notice him. This morning, she wore small, loose-fitting pyjama shorts and a grey tank top with a *Magnum Opus* mission patch printed on the back. Her skin was smooth and soft, a pale pink with cool undertones. After seven months in space, her shoulder-length black hair was now routinely tied back in a tight bun, and errant strands poked out all over.

'Now, how did you know we were ready to start taking pictures?' said James, breaking the relative silence and causing her to jump.

'You startled me, James,' she replied, spinning around in

the microgravity to look at him. 'It is simple. I felt Zhu turn us about.'

James smiled and let loose a small laugh. 'Alright. I know you've spent more time in space than the rest of us combined, but there's no need to show off.'

Yula couldn't help but smile. When she had first joined the crew for the final stage of mission training prior to the launch of the *Magnum Opus*, she had kept her distance, as this was the first time she had been part of such a diverse international team. She had done a few stints on the International Space Station already, but it was as part of an all-Russian expedition. However, having spent the journey cooped up with the likes of Captain Queen, the laidback southerner of NASA, and Commander Fowler, the East London boy of the ESA, her demeanour had softened and she'd felt able to let her guard down, happy to join in with—and instigate—the banter.

'Just because ESA does not train astronauts properly...' she teased, trying to keep a straight face.

James's first impression of Yula was that she was ultra-cool and professional, but aloof. However, he soon found out that they had a lot in common and that her coldness was just hiding her nerves. The two of them had become the best of friends during the trip.

A soft beeping sound came from the imager. Yula looked and then turned herself back around before flicking a switch on the machine.

'All done,' she said.

'Brilliant. Let's have a butcher's at this thing then,' James replied, pushing himself towards her.

A moment later, Austin and Zhu floated around the corner. They remained levitating in the doorway next to one another, holding on to one side of the doorframe each.

'Status, please, Yula,' said the captain.

'Imaging of surface has begun, sir. It will take some time.'

'Ah! Sounds like it's about time for breakfast.'

'But, sir, should somebody not monitor cameras to ensure nothing goes wrong?'

'Nonsense, it'll be fine. We've got a long day ahead of us and we could all use a bite. Hey, Jimmy you coming?'

'Yes, sir! Would kill for a full English right now; shame it's just rations,' said James.

All three crewmembers looked over at Yula. She stared for a few moments, and in the silence between them came the distinctive sound of a stomach growling. The three smiled at her, and she tried to feign ignorance, but she had woken up before everyone else and got right to work on diagnostics and calibration, not even taking the time to get dressed, so she was famished.

Relenting, she said, 'Very well, I shall meet you in Hab-2 soon.'

The others nodded and moved off towards the second habitation ring, to find Specialist Grant Oliveras, hoping to recruit him to their 'breakfast club'.

By his own admission, Grant had been at a little bit of a loss during the trip to Mars. His role on the team wasn't to begin until they touched down on the surface. A geologist by trade, he had been appointed mission specialist, in charge of collecting rock and soil samples from the remains of the mysterious comet and around the impact site. His days on board had, for the most part, been spent taking long post-wake-up jogs around the habitation rings or spending time in the ship's poor excuse for a gymnasium. He was short, shorter than Austin, and had a small head compared to the rest of his muscular body. His face was round, with green eyes and ears that stuck out a little, and he had a brown shadow where his hair would have been if he didn't shave it every morning.

By the time James, Austin and Zhu found him, he had finished jogging around Hab-2 and was busy lifting weights in the gym. He didn't look at them as they walked over to him, and only replied with a grunt and a brief pause in his reps when Austin invited him to join them for breakfast in the Hab-2 mess hall.

Grant hadn't spent a lot of time with the rest of the crew, opting instead to be alone in his bunk whenever the others were being social. When he was with them, however, he wasn't shy about offering an authoritative opinion about things, whether they were in his particular area of expertise or not. But that didn't stop Austin and Yula from trying to include him in their leisure activities. James had long since stopped, however, as Grant wouldn't even give him the time of day, despite their having trained alongside each other. It was only through quiet conversation with the others that James had found out that Grant had a particular dislike for British people. His parents were from Seville, and after their divorce, his father had emigrated to Montpellier. Flitting between these two tourist hotspots in his youth, Grant had seen the behaviour of many British tourists. This made him resentful of them, particularly for how disrespectful they could be towards his father.

Grant joined the others a few minutes after they had sat down at the dining table in the mess hall, just down from the gymnasium. For all his grouchiness, he always made sure to put the equipment away properly. The others were tucking into their rations and having an animated conversation full of banter when he sat down in silence adjacent to James.

24

'So… what about you, Grant?' asked Zhu, leaning forwards on the table. 'We were just talking about our plans for after we get home.'

'Oh, I haven't seen my father for a while,' he replied, putting his spoon down into his ration packet. 'He runs a small bakery in the south of France, and it was starting to get a bit much for him the last time I saw him.'

'So you plan to help him out while you're on leave?'

'Yes. As much as I can, anyway.'

James finished a big gulp of his breakfast and said, 'Bet he taught you a thing or two, eh?'

Grant shot him a look that said he didn't quite understand the meaning of his words and neither did he like the sound of them.

'I—I just meant,' sputtered James, swallowing another spoonful of his rations, 'that you must've learned a lot from him; the family business, you know?'

Grant nodded and replied, 'Ah, yes. In another life I would have been a baker. I just like rocks more than bread.'

'But then you wouldn't be out here on the adventure of a lifetime!' Austin interjected. 'So James, I'm guessing you're gonna be making plans to propose when you get home, right?'

'Absolutely!' replied James with enthusiasm. 'I've got Ange this ring with a big ol' diamond on it, and I will definitely propose as soon as we're back home.' He riffled in the pocket of his tracksuit and pulled out a small black box. He opened it and passed it around for everyone to have a look.

As it passed to Yula, who had changed into her blue jumpsuit before breakfast, she said, 'Wait, you brought ring *with* you on mission? On *ship*?'

James laughed and scratched the back of his head. 'Uhh,

yeah, ummm, yes. I keep it with me wherever I go. Truth is, I've had that thing burning a hole in my pocket for the last two years. Been waiting for the perfect moment to pop the question.'

In fact, James had bought the ring nearly two and a half years ago and had tried many times to propose to his girlfriend, Angela Marie-Stewart, but had found himself unable to for a variety of reasons. Those reasons included being interrupted and called away by work, random things going wrong—like the time he tried it in a country park at sunset but knelt in goose poo by accident—and just simply bottling it. Sometimes it felt as though his 'perfect moment' would never come.

'So,' said Grant, handing the ring back, 'what you're saying is that you kept getting cold feet. Did you ever try taking her to Andalucía? I feel it is maybe more romantic than London, no?'

James laughed. 'Funny story. We did come round by your neck of the woods, but…' He paused, this time rubbing the back of his neck. 'I misplaced the ring that whole weekend.'

The whole table erupted with laughter and Yula was sent into a fit of giggles. When it had died down, she wiped her eyes and tried to speak through calming her breathing.

'Oh, James! You mean to tell us ring is safer in, in depths of space—on Mars—than… than is in your pocket in Spain?'

The thought made her start giggling all the more, and she struggled to regain her composure.

Austin had already finished his food and was disposing of his packet. Still smiling from the absurdity of the confession, he came over and slapped a hand on James's back, making him recoil.

'Hah! Don't worry, my man, I'm sure you'll work yourself up to it when we're home and being hailed as heroes. That'll give you a confidence boost.'

James replied, catching his breath, 'Actually, I did try again recently, but then I was told about this mission, so I decided that wasn't the right time either.'

Austin sat back down at the table and sighed. 'Well, I don't have any of that garbage to worry about; just got my Poochie waiting at home for me, and that's all I need.'

'I think we've all seen the picture frame on your desk, sir,' replied Zhu. 'Who's looking after her while you're out here for fourteen months?'

'My sister and her husband are taking care of her – taking her out for walks, getting her fur cleaned, pampering her like crazy. She won't wanna come back home with me after all that.'

'Is this the same brother-in-law who was on that talk show with Guy Furious… Alex Hayes, right?' Grant asked.

Austin scoffed, 'Yeah, that's him.'

'Wait, what talk show?' James interjected, looking between Austin and Grant.

'You ain't seen it?' Austin asked.

James shook his head. 'No, sir.'

'Ah, well. Back in August of 2019, he was one of the first people to observe the pair of comets out by Jupiter. He insists he was *the* first, but he was just one of hundreds to call the IAU that night. Damn near crashed their reporting systems.' Austin leaned back in his chair with a sigh and continued, 'Y'know, I was with him when he spotted them. Did any of you guys ever see them?'

The crew around the table shook their heads in unison. The memory of the incident five years ago was still stuck in their minds. It had been another landmark moment in history. Everyone remembered where they were when the

Comets of Jupiter arrived.

Only visible through telescopes, their arrival was sudden and scientifically remarkable, but it was the aftermath that had really caught the public's imagination. After the third night of the comets' trip through the solar system, observatories the world over watched as the lead object of the two went down on Mars, gliding through the atmosphere as if it were designed for atmospheric entry. It impacted the planet in the Arcadia Dorsa region in the northern hemisphere, sliding along the ground for several kilometres before coming to a halt near the edge of the Milankovic Crater.

The second object was just as much an oddity as the first, as it slowed down, turned its trajectory ninety degrees and disappeared from the solar system in a streak of light.

'It was damn mesmerising, I tell you,' said Austin. 'A pair of small, bright lights moving about through the telescope, and the occasional flash passing between them. Like they were dancing.'

'I was still a flight lieutenant in the RAF at the time,' said James. 'But anyway, if your brother-in-law was just one of hundreds, how did he get on this talk show?'

Austin gave a hearty laugh and leaned forwards onto the table. 'Alex has connections with some studio execs. It wasn't too hard for him to weasel his way onto the show. He found out they were going to have Dr Renard on to make the big announcement for NASA. I think he just wanted to sit next to her and look important.'

'I'd be interested in seeing that, sir,' James said.

'I've got a recording saved on my phone if you want it? Here, I'll upload it to the *Magnum*'s computer.' Austin pulled out a small device from his pocket and unfolded it. After a few taps on the screen, he nodded and said, 'All done.'

After a short moment, Yula leaned in towards the captain and said, 'So, decorated US Navy captain, mission commander, animal lover *and* very single? Eligible prospect, sir.'

'Nah, nah…' Austin looked down at the phone in his hands and placed it back in his pocket. He began playing absentmindedly with some ration packet detritus on the table. 'I'm not really interested in all that. I am perfectly happy just me and my pupper.'

'Fairy nuff,' said James. 'Here, Major, you taking any leave when we get back?'

'No,' replied Zhu with a large grin. 'When we get back, the CNSA has me staying on the ISS. I am very much looking forward to it.'

'We are on a trip to Mars—where no human has gone before—and she is most looking forward to staring at the Earth from the Space Station?' exclaimed Grant, wringing his hands. He got up, disposed of his ration packet and continued, 'Well, it has been a pleasure, but I am going back to the gym. Yula, would you let me know when you have something for me to analyse, please?'

While the remaining four stayed in the mess hall, clearing up, they heard a faint alarm coming from the direction of the imaging lab. Austin looked up at Yula with some concern on his face, but before she could respond, James spoke up.

'Ah, sounds like we've got something to look at. We'd better head over to the lab. Will you be joining us, Captain?'

'Sure, I'll come take a looksee.'

The four departed from the mess hall, heading up the nearest ladder to the central corridor. Here they parted ways with Zhu, who went back to the Command Module to see if any orientation adjustments were required, with James joking that it was just an excuse to stare out of the window at the view. Austin, James and Yula drifted along to the lab and entered the room. The imaging machine looked thoroughly unremarkable by itself; the casing was a simple box with some controls on it, not unlike an office photocopier, and was set against the back wall of the small lab. Inside, however, were the automated control units for a vast array of cameras that deployed from a bay on the outside of the module. On the adjacent wall was a computer terminal hooked up to the imager with a set of three screens of varying sizes attached to the wall. A green LED on the control unit of the imager blinked as the alarm sounded. Yula floated over to the imager and pressed a button, cancelling the alarm and sending the data over to the terminal, which started to load up pictures on the screens. Many of the photographs of the impact site were extremely zoomed-in images taken with the craft's long-range camera in a variety of wavelengths, and a few had wider fields of view. The images were all in need of processing, but there was enough information in the initial photographs to give a good idea of what the site was like.

As Yula zoomed in on one of the images taken in the visible spectrum, her eyes widened and she gestured for the others to come over. Austin and James drifted across the lab to join her, holding on to some of the equipment to steady themselves as they floated either side. James looked at the image for a moment and went as white as a sheet.

He leaned in for a closer look and muttered, 'Well, bugger me…'

Austin punched the wall, shouting, 'Damn it!' and he turned away from the screen. Without saying another word, he left the room in the direction of the Communications Module, which was further towards the rear of the ship, leaving James and Yula examining the images.

'How?' said Yula. 'How is this even possible? James, how did we miss this?'

'They were right. Those goddamn conspiracy theorists.'

James moved over to the doorway and called out down the corridor for Zhu to come and see, while Yula radioed for Grant to make his way to the lab.

'Grant, we have something for you. You will want to see this.'

Minutes later, both appeared through the doorway and James gestured for them to look at the monitors.

* * *

Austin arrived in the Communications Module. It was a small, cramped room with a single screen and webcam, with a keyboard attached below. The walls were covered in colourful, loose wiring and there was a seat in the middle. He strapped himself into the chair and set up the comm system to broadcast a message to Mission Control. The screen flickered to life and Austin could see the view of his own face as taken by the wide-angle webcam. He composed himself, adjusted the seat so that he was in the middle of the view and hit a button on the keyboard with a loud clack.

Austin cleared his throat and said, 'Howdy, Control. This is Captain Queen coming at you live from Mars orbit. First things first, we have arrived safely and the major has put us in geosync. As per the morning's schedule we started taking pictures at 0800 and we've just got the results back. My team are processing them as we speak, but I gotta say…' He paused and sighed, looking around the room. 'It wasn't what we expected at all. After we've done a detailed analysis, I'll send a data burst your way, but… It's not a meteorite or a comet. What we're seeing appears to be engineered. Goddamn, Control, I can't believe I'm about to say this, but it looks like a fuckin' huge *nonhuman* spacecraft. I repeat, it looks like something of extraterrestrial origin. Media's gonna have a field day with this. I'm sure I don't have to tell you to be careful who you share this intel with. Don't want it getting into Guy Furious's hands again. Anyway… Queen out.'

CHAPTER TWO

ANALYSIS

'Now, I'm not saying it's aliens... but it's totally aliens!' came the excitable voice on the screen. The man waved his hands up and down and leaned forwards on the edge of his seat. His eyes glinted in the studio lights, revealing a mix of determination, glee and just a hint of madness. This guy was deep in the rabbit hole with no turning back. His rambling and convulsions were fascinating to watch, which was perhaps why he had been invited as a guest on this particular mid-week talk show.

The host had introduced him by his online handle, 'Guy Furious', and had brought him in as an entertaining counterpoint to his other guests, the first of whom was Austin's brother-in-law, Alex Hayes, who was simply introduced as a local amateur astronomer. The other guest was acclaimed, popular astrophysicist and official NASA representative Dr Louise Renard, who had spent most of the evening sitting on the sofa next to Alex, frowning and shaking her head.

Guy Furious had long, slick black hair tied high in a pony-tail and a straight, bristly goatee that resembled a paintbrush growing from his chin. His skin was pink and flushed, and he had a small, pointed nose upon which were indents where his glasses would have sat. But for this show he had to make sure he looked presentable, and so he wore contacts.

'These advanced aliens,' he continued, spreading his arms out in front of him, the sleeves of his claret velour blazer riding up past his wrists, 'contacted me in a dream. They told me that they were coming to take back the rogue lizard people that have infiltrated governments all over the disk…' He paused for effect. '… of the Earth.'

The studio audience fell about with laughter, but Guy either didn't notice or didn't care as he was having the time of his life, shouting and raving to an audience of unprecedented scale, and all served up to him on a silver platter. Never before had he been able to reach so far with his message; it was the largest debate he'd ever not prepared for. Not that he needed any of that 'preparation' nonsense; he knew his mind, and that was sufficient.

As the audience howled, Guy stood and held up his colour-ful necktie, which was tied around his neck instead of under the unbuttoned collar of his white shirt. He waved it around, pointing to the conspiracy-related phrases printed on it, such as 'Water finds its level' and 'Buoyancy, not gravity'.

Dr Renard buried her face in her hands and then stared with incredulity at the host, who was gazing, transfixed, at Guy and rubbing his hands together with mirth like a king with his court jester.

Within days of the Mars impact, the looping footage of the second object's mysterious disappearance had been leaked on the internet by an unknown source, and had become prime content for internet conspiracy theorists and armchair physicists around the world, of which Guy Furious was one of the most prominent. Guy and his ilk began referring to the event as an 'alien incursion' that was being covered up by the governments of the world. This perception was not helped by the fact that world security organisations—fearful of the potential impact of the leak on the public consciousness—classified the footage and tried to get it removed from the internet. They even went so far as to locate and arrest the source, a Swiss researcher by the name of Jan Huber.

The video that got Guy Furious his invitation to the talk show, however, was a time-stamped comparison of the footage alongside data from the LIGO gravitational wave detectors, which showed an anomalous wave detection at the same moment the object shot off into the night.

'But,' continued Guy, after the audience had calmed, 'the top-secret government Space Force operating out of Area 51 went up there in their battleship—stolen from the Roswell aliens—and shot the second object down on Mars!'

'And that's what you think the two objects are?' asked the host.

Guy sat back down and put his hands together. 'Exactly. The one that went down on Mars is an alien warship, see? And the one that disappeared was flown by our very own men in black, using their classified warp tech to blip out of sight and return to Earth.'

All of a sudden, he leaped from the chair, grabbed one of the cameras with both hands, planted his face close to the lens and shouted, 'The problem is, they did such a lousy job that the warship's now sitting there on Mars out in the open for anyone to see!' He let go of the camera and turned and glared at Dr Renard. 'That's why I think NASA are gonna send another team to finish the job. Get rid of the evidence before someone takes a picture of their little secret.'

Dr Renard rolled her eyes and crossed her arms as Guy sat and reclined in his chair.

Without moving from his own relaxed position, Alex piped up, 'Yeah, uhh, I've got a question just for you, Guy.' He raised his hand as if to ask permission, but continued regardless, 'You are one crazy son of a gun, totally, and I respect you, but why does it have to be aliens? I don't buy it… Right, so, these aliens crash-landed on Mars. What, are they planning an invasion or something?'

The audience fell silent as Alex looked on, waiting for Guy's response. There was a smattering of coughs and mumbles from the stands.

Guy's expression was deadpan as he leant forwards and looked at the astronomer. 'No, *Alex*,' he said. 'The aliens will have died from exposure by now if they weren't killed on impact. And *why* aliens? You look at the footage and tell me that's a natural phenomenon. We all know rocks don't move like that.'

After a few seconds, the host tapped his flashcards on his desk and—half laughing—said, 'Thank you, Guy, for your *incredible* insights! Let's have a round of applause for Guy Furious.'

The audience erupted in cheers, and Guy stood up and gave an ostentatious bow before returning to his seat.

After the applause dissipated, the host continued, 'Now, Dr Renard. We've heard from Guy. What about you? What's your take, and NASA's, on these objects?'

The astrophysicist was red in the face. She had been approached by the network and was under the illusion that she would have a serious debate with learned individuals and be given the chance to inform the public of the latest scientific theories. That was right up until she was sitting on the sofa and saw Guy walk on set after the host introduced him as the other debater. At that point she knew it was all nothing more than a glorified circus.

'Well,' she began, 'I think it's safe to say that neither I nor NASA nor the scientific community as a whole subscribe to Guy Spurious's ridiculous hypothesis.'

At this, shouts and howls of laughter erupted from around the studio audience and Dr Renard allowed the tiniest of smirks to appear on her face.

'Of course you wouldn't,' Guy interjected. 'And real mature on the name there, Louise Ret—'

'Hey, hey!' The host cut Guy off and there was a sharp intake of breath from the audience. 'Please continue, Dr Renard. And try to lay off the name-calling; this *is* a family show.'

Dr Renard shifted in her seat, adjusting her navy-blue dress and crossing her legs. 'The fact of the matter is that we don't know a lot about these objects. However, we do know that they were very likely interstellar visitors, possibly a pair of large, unstable comets that were ejected from their own star system. Just like Oumuamua and Borisov, they followed a parabolic trajectory, which supports the extrasolar comet theory.'

'So in a sense Guy's correct in that they are "alien visitors"?' asked the host.

'I guess so. And he's also correct that we intend to continue researching the remaining object in detail. We've never seen anything like these two objects before, and they indicate that the universe is far stranger than we previously thought.'

'What has NASA got in mind then?'

'Satellite imaging can only get us so far. Our current satellites aren't equipped to deal with the level of detail we're looking for. On top of that, we'd really like to get hold of some samples for analysis. This impact gives us an unprecedented opportunity to study an extrasolar visitor extensively over a long period of time, something we couldn't do with the others.'

'Got it. So they're putting together another rover?'

Dr Renard cleared her throat and smiled. 'No, not this time. We've talked a lot in the past about a crewed mission to Mars. Well, this impact presents the perfect opportunity to make that a reality in the near future.'

Guy scoffed and interrupted: 'I knew it. Destroying the evidence.'

'How near future are we talking here?' the host asked, leaning forwards and narrowing his eyes.

'Five years,' Dr Renard replied. 'We're aiming to launch the first crewed mission to Mars in the second half of 2024.'

The audience gasped and fell silent as the host pressed for more information. 'That's gotta be a massive undertaking, no?'

'It's still going through the initial funding stages, but the intention is for it to be a collaborative project with the ESA, CNSA and Roscosmos. There's nothing official yet—pending federal funding approval—but we're hoping that international co-operation will lessen the financial strain across the board, given the size of the spacecraft, which is looking to be the largest ever constructed in the history of mankind.'

'Oh, really?' said the host. 'That's incredible news. Where is this spacecraft being built?'

'Just like the ISS, it'll have to be built in space, in stages. The Space Station will receive the modules and put it together so that it ends up docked there. Then it will launch from low

Earth orbit, hopefully on time.'

Guy gave the audience a knowing look as Dr Renard was speaking and Alex looked at her in awe.

'Well, thank you for that incredible info-drop, Doctor. You heard it here first, folks. We're going to Mars!'

The audience erupted once more and gave a standing ovation. After a few minutes, the host motioned for them to quieten down, and once they were finished, he looked over at Guy Furious.

'Guy, do you have something you would like to add before we finish?'

'As a matter of fact I do,' he said, standing up. 'Get ready for a whole bunch of bad CGI of rocks covering up the real alien crash in the next five years. I'm telling you, they're gonna destroy the evidence. The public's not ready. It's never gonna be ready. They don't want you knowing about the lizard people that control your lives and manipulate you into thinking we live on a spinning ball!'

The host laughed. 'Well, folks, sadly that's all we have time for this afternoon. What an utter bombshell to end on. A round of applause for our special guests, please. Until next time...'

* * *

James paused the recording and stared at the screen, his mouth agape. Yula and Grant floated either side of him in the imaging lab, both in stunned silence.

'Captain Queen's brother-in-law is a complete moron,' said Grant after a few seconds.

James looked over at him, incredulous. 'Really, Grant? That's what you're taking from this?'

Grant shrugged as Austin floated through the door behind them.

'Commander, report,' he said, gripping the handles either side of the frame. 'Wait, why're you watching my brother-in-law's greatest hits at a time like this? You're supposed to be running analysis on the images.'

James spun around to face him, stopping himself with the ceiling handle. 'Yes, sir. We've actually completed the analysis and were watching the talk show to see if there were any clues as to why Guy Furious seemed to know so much about this object back then.'

'Turns out he's just a moron too,' Grant interjected.

James rolled his eyes.

Yula gave Grant a stern look and mouthed, 'Stop being such an asshole.'

Austin either ignored Grant or seemed not to notice as he continued, 'Okay, about this analysis then. What are your findings?'

Hours had passed since the crew of the *Magnum Opus* had discovered the true nature of the object on the surface. Yula, James and Grant had run a detailed analysis of all the images and done some limited post-processing. They had discovered that the object was over eight hundred metres in length. The bulk of it lay at the end of a deep trough from when it had ploughed through the land during its descent. The main body was a beige cuboid shape with slopes and curves. Amongst the various tears, cracks, fractures, scratches and dust was evidence of markings—lines and dots in green and purple emblazoned on the hull. There were other constructs—buildings and towers, strange green orbs and pylons—dotted over its topside. Further back from the semi-intact mass were broken parts of varying sizes strewn about the trench, with the largest parts—resembling engines—looking like they had been ripped from either side of the main body.

Grant had determined that the hull was made of some kind of unknown composite that was over two metres thick in places, and James had annotated images, circling mechanical structures which resembled gun emplacements. There were two large openings on each side of the midsection of the craft which housed enormous slender structures. James theorised these could be the ship's heavy ordnance and may have been the cause of the streaks of light that were reported in the night sky. Yula had examined images of the nose of the ship, which resembled a flat cone and had sustained the brunt of the impact. Much of it was buried in the Martian dirt and it was bent at an odd angle. Infrared images showed the ship was still emitting heat, even after five years.

All three agreed on the same thing as they discussed and made their report to Austin together: that the spacecraft was not an exploratory vessel, not made for scientific investigation or scouting. They concluded that it was most likely a ship of war.

Following the analysis, Austin sent both raw and processed files, as well as their reports and findings, to Mission Control over several data bursts. In turn, after a lengthy delay, they relayed instructions to him on how to proceed.

The crew gathered in the briefing room in Hab-1. It was no bigger than Hab-2's dining room, but it had large angular windows to one side from which the crew could see Mars periodically as the ring rotated. The room was darkened and a thick curtain on the inside wall blocked out the light from the ring's corridor, allowing the crew to focus on the projector screen on the wall.

On one side of the screen, the final images from the site were displayed in a loop. On the other, the leaked footage from the Swiss Observatory was playing. It showed the first object appear to pull further away from the second, which slowed to a crawl, came close to a stop and then made an impossibly sharp turn. As the first object went out of the field of view, the second travelled a short distance in its new direction and vanished in a flash of light, leaving a streak behind.

Austin paced back and forth, looking down at the pad in his hands, as the others took their seats around the table in the middle of the room. He held a control in one hand and turned the screen to his first slide.

'Okay, people. I know the last few hours have been pretty intense and we're all still processing our thoughts on the situation, but we've received an update from Mission Control,' said Austin.

'They're scrubbing the mission?' Grant interrupted with a smile on his face.

'No,' Austin replied. 'Not at all. Mission Control wants us to continue as planned, despite the drastic change in scope.'

Zhu leant forwards on the desk and said, 'So they want us to land anyway?'

Austin nodded.

Incredulous, Grant said, 'I did not sign up for this! I'm no xeno-expert. I say we turn around—'

James slammed his palm down on the desk, interrupting Grant and making the others look up at him. 'And do what? Come on, Grant. It's taken us seven months and millions of dollars to get here. There's no way we're abandoning the mission now.'

'The commander is right,' said Austin, putting his pad down

on the table and leaning on the back of a chair. 'Our orders are to make the landing, investigate the crash site and take samples.' He turned towards the screen, changing the image to a topographical map of the area with annotations on it.

'This,' he continued, pointing at a marked area of the map, 'is our landing site, south of the impact trench. It's about ten kilometres from the big boy. Once we've made our descent in the MEM we'll have to travel to the site in the rover. From there we'll try to find a way inside.'

'Going *inside*?' asked Yula, her eyebrows raising. 'Spacecraft still has power, so there may be survivors. Have we got any weapons?'

Austin shook his head. 'We weren't exactly expecting to meet any aliens on this trip.'

'Well, those conspiracy theorists were right about the spacecraft,' offered James. 'That Guy Furious thought all the aliens would've died in the crash or from exposure to the Martian atmosphere, so…'

Austin put his hand to his face. 'I can't believe we're sitting here taking some idiot like Guy Furious seriously now. Anyway, once we're inside, all bets are off as to what we'll find in there, so it's probably best if we try not to wander off alone.'

Yula had placed her head in her hands and was staring into the middle distance. 'Maybe it has armoury,' she mused.

The others turned in their seats and stared at her.

'What? If it is warship, then surely it will have armoury, no?' she said, looking around at the group.

'We're not shooting the aliens, Yula,' Austin groaned.

'And,' said Zhu, 'how do we know they even have arms? Or that we'd be able to operate any of their technology?'

Yula looked down and played with her fingers. 'I just…

do not like idea of being defenceless down there.'

'The major makes a good point, though. How *do* we know we'll be able to operate any of their systems? What if we can't interact with anything down there, sir?' asked James.

'I think we gotta go down there with the assumption that we *can*. If we assume otherwise, we might go in underprepared,' replied Austin. 'In either case, we document everything. We'll be taking cameras, so I want us to take detailed photos and videos of anything we come across. Mission Control will need as much data as we can give them.'

'What about the possibility of salvaging some of their technology, sir? They're clearly more advanced than us if they're building warships in space with weapons that size and fighting through our solar system.'

'We have a limited capacity for bringing back samples of their tech, so we're gonna have to see what's down there and if necessary make choices about what to prioritise. I'd rather not go over-mass on the MEM.'

'I volunteer to stay behind and pilot the *Magnum*,' said Grant. 'I'll be useless down there anyway.'

'No, Zhu's the pilot; she'll keep us afloat.'

'But—'

'No buts. You're the mission specialist, you're coming with us. At the very least you can analyse the effect that the impact's had on the surrounding land, or take samples of the hull material,' said Austin. 'Oh, that reminds me. Mission Control also want us to make a TV broadcast before we make the landing.'

He saw their already sullen faces drop even more. 'Hey, remember, guys, this is still a historic moment for mankind—the first humans on Mars! But we should take care not to mention any of this stuff about the alien ship. Just the landing. Got it?'

CHAPTER THREE
REVELATION

THE CREW'S EVENING MEAL TOGETHER in the mess hall was marked by solemn silence, as they ate their rations and kept to their own thoughts. After they cleared away, the time came for the television broadcast. The crew had done a few of these during the journey; they usually spent fifteen to twenty minutes talking viewers through a day in the life of an astronaut, what it was like travelling to Mars and their expectations, and they would take the camera around the spacecraft on a mini tour. The broadcasts were supposed to be live, and so the further they travelled away from Earth, the more they had to compensate for the time delay.

This time, the length of the delay would be much longer, around thirteen minutes, so the organisation had to be precise. And this time, whereas the crew's collective consciousness should have been on their impending descent and its gravitas— their original plans had included explaining the descent process to viewers at home—they found themselves distracted.

James headed back to his bunk room after dinner, in what little free time he had while Austin got everything ready for the broadcast. He walked down the steps and sat on the bed. His leg bounced up and down as he leant forwards on his knees, staring at the floor.

Incredible. Aliens. Real life aliens. A whole other species living somewhere out there in the galaxy, on an alien planet, around an alien sun, looking up at an alien sky…

A smile erupted on his face and he shot up from the bed. He leant over to his desk and opened the lid of his laptop. His desktop background was a picture of him and Angela, all dressed up from when they went to the Shard back in London; another of those times he had tried and failed to propose to her. He stared at the picture and sighed, pulling out his chair and sitting on it. He opened his personal mission diary and began to type:

Ange… I wish I could tell you what's going on. It's like a dream come true. Shame this will probably get classified. The others haven't said anything since the captain relayed our orders from Mission Control, but I can tell they're taking it a lot harder than I am.

James paused for a moment and thought about his other team members, then starting typing again.

Yula's clearly scared, which is understandable; we don't know what we're going to find down there. But Grant, well, he seems to be even more miserable than usual, if that were possible! I reckon the whole thing is making him feel small. Might do him and his massive head some good. The captain and the major, though… I can't read them at all; seem to be taking it in their stride. If I'm honest, even though I'm excited, it's hard seeing the others look to me for guidance as their first officer. I think the major is doing a better job than I am at being stoic about it all.

He stopped typing, clicked save and closed down his laptop. A moment later he heard Austin's voice come over the ship intercom.

'We're live in five, everyone. We're gonna start this off in Comms, so gather round, kiddos. Queen out.'

The five gathered outside the Communications Module, having set their jumpsuits straight and made themselves more presentable for the camera. Austin looked at his watch and counted down the seconds to the time he had organised with Mission Control, then turned on the camera and hit record.

* * *

'Is it just me, or do they seem a bit bored to you?' asked Alex, his eyes fixed on the TV screen as the crew of the *Magnum Opus* proceeded to talk viewers through their descent plan.

'Mmhmm, abshlutley,' replied his wife, Emily, stuffing a handful of popcorn into her mouth. She swallowed and continued, 'Well, not so much bored, just… elsewhere.'

Alex shifted on the sofa, turning to face his wife. 'You know, I still can't believe I never actually heard back from the IAU about all this.'

'I know.'

'To think I should've got my name to—'

'*I know.*'

'But *I* discovered this stuff.'

'And?' cried Emily, folding her arms. 'Stop complaining. You got to go on that show and sit next to that hot doctor woman!'

'But—'

'Dad!' piped up a small voice. 'Are you gonna say that *every* time Uncle Austin comes on TV?' said Hayden, reaching over and grabbing some popcorn from the bowl his mother was holding and proceeding to spill some down between the sofa cushions.

'He's right, honey. You've said it with every single broadcast for the last seven months. It's getting tiresome. The whole thing was five years ago; you need to drop it,' said Emily.

Alex just grumbled and crossed his arms as his family went back to watching the broadcast.

Cory and Hayden—Alex and Emily's two boys, aged six and eight respectively—had been fascinated by the Mars mission ever since it had been announced that their uncle was going to be leading the team, and after they watched the launch together, they had insisted that they watch every broadcast live as a family.

At first, Alex didn't want to; he was still holding a grudge because the International Astronomical Union hadn't got back in touch with him about his 'discovery' and had in fact credited somebody else with being the first to see the 'Comets of Jupiter'.

'You'd think they'd be more excited about seeing a crashed comet on Mars for the first time,' said Emily as her brother moved on to interviewing Specialist Grant about his role.

'Mommy, why does Mr Grant sound so sad?' asked Cory. 'He's got the most awesome job in the whole wide universe.'

'I don't know, sweetie.'

'Something's definitely off here. You think they had a falling-out?' asked Alex. 'You know your brother can be a bit cantankerous.'

Emily just shrugged, and so Alex got up from the sofa

and went into the kitchen to make himself a coffee. They were about ten minutes into the broadcast, with Major Zhu giving an interview about her role as pilot and showing viewers around the Command Module. All was going well and Zhu was describing in detail how she would monitor the descent.

'But of course we're not expecting to find anything alive down there,' she said. 'Although that alien spacecraft is certainly big enough—'

The screen went black as the broadcast feed disconnected and a 'Please stand by' message card appeared on the television. Emily and the kids looked at one another with confused expressions.

Moments later, there was a loud crash.

The family turned around and looked over the back of the sofa to see Alex standing there, mouth agape and staring at the TV screen, with a ceramic coffee mug smashed to smithereens on the floor around him and hot coffee spreading out on the tiles.

'Mommy?' said Hayden after a few seconds. 'Why did the pilot lady say "alien spacecraft"?'

* * *

'Damn it, Major!' shouted Austin, switching off the camera and glaring at Zhu's horrified face. 'I said to keep it about the landing for crying out loud, and now because of the delay we won't know whether anybody saw that and how much trouble we're in for the next thirty minutes.'

'I'm so sorry, sir, it just slipped out—'

'If that goes through, then everyone, *everyone* on Earth will know there's an alien spaceship sitting on Mars!'

Zhu looked around the Command Module for a second, then offered a solution: 'I could try to backtrack? Or perhaps say I was—'

'It's too late now, Zhu; I've cut the feed. We can't continue the interviews until we know for sure whether that got broadcast.' He paused and let out an exasperated sigh, placing a hand on his hip. 'If it did, at least we're going to be out here for another seven or eight months, so we won't have to see *the entire goddamn world flying into a panic.*' Austin slammed a fist against the wall, growled and floated off back to the Communications Module grumbling about how it might be the last broadcast they'd ever be allowed to do. James put a hand on Zhu's shoulder and Yula floated in from the side to give her a hug.

Later that evening, after the excitement of the day's events had abated, the crew received the devastating news from Mission Control that Zhu's final words had indeed been broadcast to millions of people watching from all over the world. Control commended Austin's swift action in cutting the feed, but it had been too late, and the extra delay between Earth receiving the transmission and sending it out to home televisions hadn't caught it in time either. The consequence for the crew of the *Magnum Opus* was that their other scheduled live TV broadcasts for after the Mars landing had been cancelled. The landing itself was also supposed to have a live feed, but the crew were instructed to make a recording instead and send it via data burst to Mission Control for vetting.

'Thankfully, Control haven't scrubbed the mission,' said Austin, having called a briefing in Hab-1 to discuss the fallout. 'We're still on track to go down there in the morning.'

James chipped in, 'Well, all the technical preparations for tomorrow have been completed, sir, and we'll board the MEM at 0800 hours.' He looked over at Zhu, who appeared downcast. 'Are you okay, Major? You know, this could've happened to any of us.'

'I'll be fine, sir. We have a more important job ahead of us and I'd prefer to focus on that. It's a historic event, after all.'

'Well, I'm glad to hear that.'

'No one blames you, Zhu,' said Yula, leaning across the table and gripping her hand for a moment.

'Except maybe Captain Queen,' Grant interjected with a shrug.

'You don't speak for me, Grant,' Austin shot back. 'I don't blame you, Major, and for the record, I agree with Commander Fowler. We're all out of our depth here.'

Zhu looked around at them all with a smile and said, 'Thank you for your support, everyone.'

A contemplative silence fell amongst the group for a few minutes, as each stared out into the middle distance. James sighed heavily and leant back in his chair. Grant slumped forwards on the table with a groan, placing his head in his arms, and Yula looked at Zhu with a worried expression. The stillness was broken by the sound of Austin's chair scuffing backwards across the floor.

'Right, people, let's get our beauty sleep. Big day tomorrow, come what may,' he said, getting up from his seat. Everyone else murmured in agreement and followed suit, heading to their respective bunks.

CHAPTER FOUR
Descent

A T 0800 HOURS, AFTER PULLING ON their bulky white spacesuits, the crew of the *Magnum Opus*—minus Zhu—opened the airlock and filed into the hangar bay, which housed the ship's Martian Excursion Module. There was a small balcony with two gangways leading away from it, one of which led down a long boarding tunnel.

As he floated above the metal surface of the balcony, James looked around the space. He had only seen technical specifications and concept drawings for it before; he had never been inside. The airlock for this area had remained sealed for the duration of their trip. The hangar itself was a large rectangular hall, and every sound echoed off its huge, flat walls. The sight of it made James stop and stare with wide eyes, causing him to fall a little behind the others as they moved off towards the tunnel.

'This is amazing,' he said under his breath.

The room was spacious enough for the large, conical

landing craft to fit inside, with plenty of room around it for the crew to have access to make repairs and adjustments. To that end, there were walkways around the MEM proceeding from the second gangway and some bays full of tools on the walls. A huge, folded robotic arm was attached to the inside wall of the hangar, with a sturdy clamp at one end that gripped the top of the MEM, ready for deployment. On the outside wall were expansive bay doors that were sealed shut and filled the length and height of the hangar.

James caught up with the others, and the team pulled themselves through the boarding tunnel, which was attached the MEM's open access hatch, with Captain Queen leading the way. The tunnel had a transparent canopy, providing the group with a constant view of the imposing vehicle as they drew nearer.

The Martian Excursion Module was an incredible feat of engineering, with a design that harked back to the Apollo programme's Command Module, except much larger. It featured ablative heat-shielding on its curved underside and a powerful set of reaction-control thrusters able to slow the final descent after its parachute phase enough for a soft touchdown. There were retractable landing legs stowed underneath the heat shield that would deploy after the shielding had burned away. Once it landed, large portions of the craft were designed to detach in order to construct a surface habitat that could be used as a base camp for as long as two weeks.

Austin went through into the MEM first, followed by Yula, then James and finally Grant. Inside the dimly lit module, there were four seats positioned close together, facing inwards around the centre. James pulled himself into his seat and locked down his straps. He looked around at the others, who were at different stages of strapping themselves in. Austin was flicking switches on the arms of his seat, which featured a small joystick on the right side. He then moved on to pressing buttons on the control console just above his head. For such a large descent craft, the interior felt small and cramped, because the top half of the capsule, including the cockpit, comprised the ascent vehicle for their return to the *Magnum*. The chairs were tilted back and each of the team had a similar console to Austin's, complete with a screen—displaying the craft's telemetry—above their heads.

After a couple of minutes, the capsule's batteries turned on with a low hum. Aside from the colourful backlit buttons and controls, the inside of the MEM was very stark and grey, with flat, segmented wall panels going up at an angle, following the exterior cone shape. Near to the floor of the MEM were locked compartments containing all of the equipment the team would need for their trip, and there was a single small, reinforced circular window in one of the walls.

After the MEM's systems had come online, Austin drifted around the cockpit checking on the crew's restraints, before finally strapping himself down.

'I hope this tin can holds up,' said Grant with a worried look on his face as he gripped his restraints.

James laughed and replied, 'Don't worry. They've tested these things rigorously.'

'Things!' Grant shot back. 'What happened to the others?'

Laughing again, James just went back to looking at the telemetry screen above his head.

In the five years of preparation that the participating nations had to make the mission a reality, the MEM unit had been the one thing they tested more than any other, even going so far as to drop one from the International Space

Station with a human test pilot inside. The first test was an abject failure, as the RCS thrusters didn't engage. The test pilot survived the splashdown, and it was a miracle that there were no injuries. However, by the fourth test, the ESA—the primary agency working on the MEM—had almost perfected the capsule.

As the team prepared—Austin still carrying out preflight checks and Yula setting up recording equipment for the descent—Zhu spoke over the intercom to check in with the intrepid adventurers.

'All systems on the *Magnum* are ready for your descent, Captain,' she radioed.

'Copy that, Major,' replied Austin as he finished the preflight checks. 'By the look of things in here, we're about ready to go as well.'

'Okay, remember, Captain, the parachutes are set to deploy automatically at around eleven thousand metres. You have the controls to manually engage them if they don't. You'll need to begin thruster navigation control from around fifteen hundred metres to guide you in to the landing zone.'

'Copy that. See you on the other side, Major.'

James smiled and said, 'Good luck, Major. Try and keep the seats warm for us while we're gone, eh?'

Ignoring him, Zhu said, 'Depressurising MEM hangar bay in three, two…'

There was a loud hissing sound from outside the MEM, which faded into silence.

'Okay, helmets on, people,' said Austin.

The team lifted their arms and pressed a small switch on the front of their spacesuits. There was a whirr of tiny motors as their segmented helmets—which had been retracted into the back of their suit collars—came up and over their heads and their visors locked into place.

'Opening hangar bay doors,' came Zhu's voice over their suit radios.

A dull thud reverberated through the capsule from outside, and a second later the MEM began to vibrate with the muted grinding sound of the hangar bay doors opening. A few seconds later another dull thud knocked the capsule, and then all was still.

'Deploying MEM,' said Zhu.

The craft jolted, causing Yula to grab on to her restraints in surprise. Then the vibrations started up again. James looked up at the porthole and saw the bay walls move and give way to the darkness of space.

'How're you feeling, Grant? Excited yet?' James teased.

Yula leant across and slapped his leg as Grant gave him a dirty look and went back to staring at the ceiling. James knew that Grant had always hated the descent training back home.

After a couple of minutes, the vibrations stopped with another jolt.

Zhu's voice came over the radio once more: 'Commencing descent cruise phase in five… four… three… two… one.'

The clamps disengaged and the thrusters on the top of the MEM pushed it away from the *Magnum Opus* with a hiss. The craft fell, drifting through the vacuum towards the Red Planet, the crew inside feeling nothing more than the usual weightlessness.

They waited, taking in the tranquillity of the moment and anticipating the next phase like they were on a rollercoaster hanging over the edge of its biggest drop. The wait seemed like a lifetime, and in the wider context of humankind, this moment had indeed been anticipated for a lifetime. Many sensitive robotic probes had made this dive before over the last couple of decades and survived. But now it was the turn of humanity to take the plunge and be the first non-robotic feet on the planet.

The craft plummeted at its descent angle for around seven minutes before the silence inside was broken by Austin checking the telemetry. 'Entering Mars atmo'. Hold on to your seatbelts, kiddos, this is gonna get rough.'

The descent craft jostled and shook as it slammed through the thickening ether, before settling into an uncomfortable vibration. Hurtling through the upper atmosphere, the underside of the MEM began to heat up rapidly from the drag—and glow, first a dull red, through orange and yellow, before finally settling on a blinding white. The ablative shielding did its job, burning off its outer layers as a gas and dissipating the heat away from the vehicle. Through the solitary window the crew could see only a glimpse of this iridescence, which lit up the interior in a golden hue.

As the descent continued, Grant and Yula tightened their grip on the restraints, turning their knuckles white. They screwed up their faces and kept their eyes closed, while Austin held on to the seat arms. James seemed to be the only one of them having fun, laughing and whooping throughout.

After only four minutes, which seemed like an eternity, the glow from outside faded and the vibrations settled down as the hypersonic phase of the descent came to an end.

For the benefit of the recording, Yula continued narration where Austin had left off. 'Entering aero-braking phase. Current velocity: thirteen thousand seven hundred kilometres per hour. Altitude: fifteen thousand metres.'

The automated guidance from the RCS thrusters turned the MEM to a shallower angle, allowing the atmospheric pressure to slow the craft even further. This phase of the descent was thoroughly disagreeable for all inside, and even James fell silent as the G-force increased from the rapid deceleration. Austin moved one hand near to the release switch for the parachutes, while the other gripped the flight stick, and he watched on the screen as their altitude continued to decrease.

Fourteen thousand metres.

Thirteen thousand metres.

Twelve thousand metres.

The seconds passed by as if in slow motion, and the tension was tangible.

Eleven thousand metres.

As they passed by the target altitude, lights began to flash and alarms sounded.

'Parachutes have not deployed. Captain Queen commencing manual deployment,' said Yula.

They were careening towards the surface at nearly seventeen hundred metres per second. Austin was prepared, and he reacted quickly—he'd had intense reaction training for just this sort of eventuality—pressing the manual deployment button resting under his clammy index finger.

There was a sudden jolt as the parachutes deployed at ten thousand metres, and the descent craft slowed to a fifth of its previous speed. Yula was still narrating the process for the recording while Austin concentrated on the task at hand. By the time they reached an altitude of seven thousand metres, the parachutes had slowed them to just one hundred and twenty metres per second, but not enough.

'Commencing RCS burn,' he said.

Engaging the map view on the screens, the captain increased the thrusters' power until their velocity slowed at an acceptable rate, judging it by eye until they reached three thousand metres. Austin gave James the go-ahead to extend the landing legs. The team heard three small bangs coming from below, followed by three thumps as the legs descended and locked in place.

'Deployed,' said James.

The RCS burn continued as the craft dropped past the thousand-metre mark; Austin had slowed them enough for landing. He eased back on the power and used the flight stick and maps to guide the MEM to the landing site, slowing them even further and hovering above the surface, trying to avoid any large boulders. Once Austin had found a suitable position for landing, he gently lowered the vehicle down to the surface, displacing dirt and dust with the thrusters.

A few moments later, the Martian Excursion Module had completed its touchdown on the surface and the engines disengaged.

'And… we're down. Safe and sound. Engines off. Phew! What a ride,' Austin exclaimed.

A few of the crew let out a sigh of relief, and they all looked around at each other. The small cabin pressurised, and Grant and Yula pushed up their helmet visors.

'We're on Mars,' shouted Grant. 'We're actually on Mars!'

'Smooth landing, Captain,' said Yula.

'Hey, thanks. Almost didn't make it for a moment there. I'm gonna have to run some diagnostics on the MEM to see why the parachute's auto-deployment failed.'

James unbuckled his restraints and rose from his seat. The sensation of Martian gravity was strange; it didn't feel natural. Not zero-G like the *Magnum*'s central frame, but still much less than he was used to in the habitation rings, which simulated near-Earth gravity. At the same time, the whole drop from leaving the *Magnum* had taken only thirteen minutes but had caused a real strain on his body, fun as it was. He could feel bruises on his chest and sides from the vibrations and it took a moment to compose himself.

The others appeared to be in much the same condition. Austin unstrapped himself and stretched, then turned back to the controls on his seat to make sure they were still connected to the ship in orbit and that the recording had been sent to the Communications Module.

'Zhu, are you reading us?' said Austin.

The sound of static came over their suit radios, before fading into a familiar voice. 'Loud and clear, Captain. Congratulations, you are now officially the first humans on Mars.'

While Austin breathed a sigh of relief, James, Yula and Grant crouched down to the storage compartments in the walls and started unlocking them. The thin metal panels came away easily and clattered as they were placed on the floor. It took them a few minutes to pull all of the crates and equipment out and stack them up in the cockpit ready for taking down to the surface.

James lifted his helmet visor and wiped his brow. 'So… external inspection time. Who's going down the ladder first?' he said.

'Surely the captain, no?' replied Grant.

Yula shrugged. 'First boot-prints on Martian surface; whoever is descending ladder needs something suitably momentous to say for recording.'

'Wait, did no one else plan a pithy saying?' said Austin with the slightest hint of disappointment in his voice.

James raised his eyebrows and looked over at the captain. 'You've got nothing, sir?'

'Nah, I always thought if I were the first man on Mars, I'd just wing it… Y'know, like Neil Armstrong; he thought of his in the LEM.'

'Well, here we are.' James said.

The others stared at Austin expectantly.

'Oh, damn it all,' he muttered.

The group sat discussing who should go down the ladder and what kind of thing they should say. Options ranged from aping the famous Moon Landing phrase through the inappropriate to the outrageous.

After the group had fallen silent, having exhausted most of their ideas, James spoke up. 'You know what? I think I've got something…'

'So, what is it?' asked Austin.

James just tapped his nose and gave a wry smile. The others rolled their eyes and mumbled that he might as well just go for it, as they hadn't thought of anything else in the last half an hour. And so it was decided: Commander James Fowler would be the first to descend the ladder, and he would say whatever he would say.

The hatch on the side of the lander had a small compartment just below it which contained a telescopic ladder. James walked over to the door and pressed the controls to extend the ladder down to the ground. The group locked their visors back down and Austin depressurised the cabin. There was a great clunk as the hatch unlocked, and the door swung open slowly, almost reverently. Seconds later, James stuck his head through the opening. He looked and saw for the first time, with his own eyes, an alien world.

The morning sky, a mixture of pinks and reds with a band of fading blue towards the horizon.

A vast rust-coloured desert strewn with dark rocks of all sizes across the plain.

The sound of wind rushing past his helmet. Familiar,

yet otherworldly.

He stared for a few moments, taking everything in, from the smallest grey pebbles below to the peaks of small hills in the distance. It was eerie, yet peaceful. He raised himself out of the MEM and turned around, gripping the small handles either side of the door. He placed his feet upon the top rung of the ladder and looked at his comrades. He was nervous, and his crewmates could tell. They offered him looks of encouragement as he began to step down, rung by rung. Yula pulled out the camera to record footage of his historic descent.

James's mind raced. Did he really have the right thing to say? Was it grandiose enough? Did it truly convey the gravitas of the moment? As he continued downwards, he looked at the outside of the MEM; it was covered in scratches and small dents, but nothing out of acceptable parameters. Halfway down, he cleared his throat and began to recite the words of Edward Young:

'So much a stranger, and so late arriv'd,
How can man's curious spirit not inquire,
What are the natives of this world sublime,
Of this foreign, unterrestrial sphere,
Where mortal, untranslated, never stray'd?'

Coming at last to the final rung, with nothing left between him and his first steps on the Red Planet, he stretched out his boot and lowered it onto the Martian soil. The dust gave way a little under his boot and felt smooth apart from the crackle of small stones. It was not unlike standing on fine beach sand. He took a moment in silence to appreciate the familiarity of the texture, then he removed his other foot and stepped off the MEM.

He turned around and looked out at the pinkish sky and

mounds in the near distance. His viewpoint had hardly changed, for the hatch of the MEM was only a short distance above him, but the feeling of standing on the surface with his own two legs was very different. He sighed, closed his eyes and continued his recital:

'O ye, as distant from my little home,
As swiftest sunbeams in an age can fly!
Far from my native element I roam,
In quest of new, and wonderful... to man.'

CHAPTER FIVE
Excursion

'RIGHT THEN,' SAID JAMES, clapping his padded space-suit gloves and rubbing them together, 'that looks to be about it.' He stood back, looking in triumph at their new surface habitat, at last unpacked from the MEM, which sat a couple of hundred metres away. It was a small collection of large, fabric-domed tents supported by an internal structure of lightweight metal rods and arranged in a cruciform shape. It looked like a scaled-up version of a set of interconnected children's play tents, without the bright colours.

Nearby, the rest of the team were working by the Mars Roving Vehicle. Like the MAV and the habitat, the vehicle was for the most part coloured white. It had six rugged wheels with segmented tyres and the roof was flat, carrying an array of solar panels. The cockpit was large enough for them all and was rounded at the front, with a trapezoidal panoramic windshield. All the other windows to the sides were small and triangular. At the rear was a long storage compartment, from which Austin, Grant and Yula were unloading crates. As large as it was, it had still taken several trips to bring everything over.

'Can we get going now?' James asked.

The others stopped what they were doing and looked at him. James couldn't see the team's faces because of the reflections on their visors, but their body language showed they were a picture of bewilderment.

'Bit eager,' grunted Austin into the suit radio, and went back to moving boxes.

The large aluminium crates were filled with different types of equipment. Some were self-contained units that could be opened out into solar panel arrays to provide power for the habitat. Others housed weather monitoring stations, soil-sampling machinery and computer terminals. Regardless of the contents, all of the crates from the MEM's storage compartments were crucial for the mission, and the team had wasted no time in starting to load them onto the MRV before transporting them over to the habitat. Still, the job was very far from complete.

'Uh, yeah, bit eager…' James chuckled, kicking some dust up with a light tap. 'I just meant that I want to get out there and see the spaceship.'

'Maybe we could go over there sooner if you were helping us with these crates!' Grant shot back.

Turning red inside his spacesuit, and glad that no one could see his face, James cleared his throat and rushed over to help Grant pull the next crate out of the vehicle; the waste collection system.

Charming.

Despite not being able to smell anything but the clean,

neutral odour inside the suit, and his hands and body being protected by several layers of state-of-the-art fabric and insulation, James wrinkled his nose while carrying the hefty commode. After the two had connected the waste unit to the habitat, Grant moved away without a word to open up the soil-sampling equipment.

'You're welcome,' called James into his suit mic, staring at Grant as he walked away. Grant threw up his middle finger—as best as he could in his bulky gloves, but well enough to be recognisable—and James shook his head.

Prick.

With a sigh, he then went to assist Yula in setting up some solar panels. Opening the units themselves was a simple matter of pressing the release button on the front, lifting the lid and pulling on the central handle inside, which brought up and unfolded the panels all at once. Yula had already done this with the first set of panels and was busy connecting them up to the ship, so James did the same with the second set: gripping the square-edged handle, he felt the movement of the unit's internal runners as he pulled, and the blue panels unfolded from their cocoon like a butterfly's wings and clicked into place. He then set about connecting the cables up to an outlet at the side of the habitat. James walked back to the crate, turned it on and began calibrating the units, ensuring they were set at the correct angle to auto-matically track the sun during the day. The buttons were quite clear and there were instructions on the inside of the lid, so he was done in no time. Yula gave him a thumbs-up as she moved on to the next task.

It was around noon and the sun was shining in a sky that was clear but for some wispy, high-altitude clouds. The astro-nauts were glad of the insulation of their spacesuits, as the midday sun did not have the same warming effect as on Earth and the outside temperature was a brisk ten degrees. Nevertheless, they were sweating. The hours of work, from pulling the MRV out of its storage bay and setting up the habitat, through to ferrying and setting up the equipment, meant James and the rest of the crew had worked up quite an appetite, as they had not eaten since earlier that day on the *Magnum Opus*. So once the last of the crates had been unloaded, Austin called time and they all headed inside the habitat for lunch.

After a weary and silent meal, the four astronauts filed out of the habitat and walked towards the MRV. James led the group with gusto, rushing up to the left side of the vehicle. He turned the recessed circular handle to unlock the door and swung it open. He clambered into the cockpit and moved all the way to the right. Inside the cockpit, the lightweight seats were three abreast at the front, with a fourth on the right behind them. The driving apparatus was in front of the central seat but attached to the dashboard by a rail, which meant it could be moved across to any seat and locked in place. It consisted of a horseshoe-shaped box with a hand throttle on one side and a stick on the other that could be pulled towards the driver and fixed in a comfortable position.

Yula climbed into the vehicle after James and sat in the middle, followed by Grant, who took the rear after loading some cases of equipment into the back and glaring at James. Finally, Austin sat in the left seat, closing and sealing the door behind him. Yula reached across to the dashboard and toggled a switch, unlocking the controls, before sliding them across to Austin.

'You get to do the honours, Captain,' she said.

After Austin had adjusted the controls, he flicked a few

switches, turning on the batteries and starting up the vehicle, but paused on the final one.

'Standby for pressurisation,' the captain ordered. He waited until everyone was strapped into their harnesses before flicking the switch.

There was a hissing sound as the small cabin filled with air. A green light appeared on the dashboard, and everyone unlocked and slid up their visors.

'Thanks to the prime location of the landing zone, our target is due north of here,' explained Austin as everyone listened. 'The journey should take about an hour depending on the terrain. Once we get there, our first objective is to examine the outside of the craft and maybe check on some of the debris.' He turned his head as far as he could to look at Grant and continued, 'That'll mostly be your job, Grant. And it might be worth James going with you; I'd like you both to take a look at that thing that looks like a broken engine.' Facing the front once again, he addressed Yula: 'You and I will try to find a way in.'

The three murmured in agreement. Yula activated the on-board cameras, and Austin eased the throttle forward, allowing the vehicle to pull away.

The journey north was rough. Though it was the largest lowland region on the planet, the Vastitas Borealis was far from a flat plain at ground level. The terrain was rocky, scattered with medium to large boulders that needed to be avoided, and with numerous dips and humps along the way. It made for an uncomfortable ride and slowed the MRV's progress considerably. There was also the occasional small impact crater to navigate around, and these were difficult to spot. Just one mistake would strand the vehicle.

Despite the difficulties, Austin managed to keep the

buggy averaging half speed, and the view out of the front windscreen and triangular side windows was second to none. James pressed his face up against the side window with wide eyes and mouth agape, watching the Martian landscape whoosh past and taking in the varied surface features of this alien world. The views were nothing spectacular in the traditional sense—no incredible picture-postcard mountains or valleys; they had landed in the northern plains, after all—and the scenery was fairly repetitive, but the very experience of traversing alien topography was fascinating enough to keep the journey from being tedious.

Even Grant appeared to be having a good time.

As the team continued along due north from their camp, something began to loom over the shortened Martian horizon; a gargantuan structure, silhouetted against the bright sky. From a distance, the astronauts could see that it was tipped downwards towards the west and looked uneven in places, buckled and broken. Its intimidating presence on the skyline interrupted the excitement of the journey. James stared out of the front window at the structure. Despite his enthusiasm, even he began to feel uneasy, and he could only imagine what the others—especially Grant and Yula—were feeling. As the behemoth continued to rise up on their slow-but-sure approach, questions began to flood James's mind.

Where did it come from? Why did they come to our solar system? Are they still alive in there?

'By Ares's sweaty jockstrap! Would you look at that thing,' exclaimed Austin as he slowed the buggy to a crawl, staring through the windscreen at the immense wreckage—still quite a way off in the distance—its sheer scale sinking in.

As they drove closer, the structure towered over them like a skyscraper. Their eyes adjusted to the exposure of the silhouette, which occupied most of their view and obscured the bright sky, revealing smaller, detailed structures littering the surface. Boxes upon boxes, shorn metal, exposed innards, as if a giant monster had ripped through an industrial estate.

'Definitely seen better days,' said James.

Yula unstrapped her harness while they were still moving and leaned towards the windscreen for a better view. 'To think someone built that. It makes the *Magnum* look tiny.'

Austin brought the buggy to a halt on the port side of the craft, the vehicle skidding a little on the fine Martian dust. The captain then instructed everyone to prepare to head outside. Once all four had fastened their visors, Austin depressurised the cabin again and opened the door on his side. James waited while the others got out, then shuffled along the seats and stepped back out into the harsh Martian environment. From outside he could get a much better look at the huge beige wall that was the ship's hull; it was like standing across the street in a city centre and looking up at the high-rises during an apocalypse.

To the right of where the team were standing was a heavily damaged section, where an entire portion of the ship had been ripped off during the impact. Large conduits, pipes, structural beams and internal machinery of unknown purpose were sticking out of the gaping hole, having been pulled towards the rear. To the left, the near face of the ship's front cone was flattened to form a sort of aerofoil, and there was evidence of darkened tiling on the underside, similar to the ceramic heat-shielding on the underside of the *Magnum*'s Command Module. The wing tip had been twisted and bent in the impact and most of the tiling had broken off.

'That is probably what stopped ship from burning up,' said Yula.

James noticed that the wing tip was embedded in the ground. 'And it looks like it might be our way up,' he said, pointing over at the wing.

He turned his attention to the wall in front of him. It was huge and flat, and the detailing of the scratched and scuffed panels of its armour plating was visible. Aside from the seams, the surface was almost completely smooth. Some of the sizeable panels had been bent open, and underneath he could see the internal structure of the armour, which was a more natural metallic grey. Beams and conduits crossed and intersected, but otherwise there were no breaches significant enough to give access to the inside of the ship.

Further up, James noted some large worn markings in a greenish colour. Pointing at them, he said, 'What do you guys think of that? Name of the ship? Its designation?'

'Impossible to tell,' replied Austin. 'Could even be the captain's favourite poem for all we know.'

'Or route number,' said Yula. 'Like bus or train.'

Austin turned to his crew and said, 'Okay, people, with a craft of this size, it's clear we're gonna have to use the MRV. So we'll stick to the plan. James and Grant, I want you to take the buggy over to the ship's back end and along the impact trench. Yula and I will walk over to that wing and see if we can get up on top.'

'We will need equipment from MRV,' said Yula, turning to James. 'I will unload now, then you and Grant can go.'

James replied in the affirmative and watched as she walked over to the vehicle's storage bay and pulled out a couple of small equipment cases. She set them down, opened one and picked up a harness and camera, which she then fixed to the mountings on her suit.

James glanced at Grant once the two of them had sat down in

the MRV and—after pressurisation—slid up their visors. He looked pale and a little green, like he was about to throw up. Grant had remained silent for almost all of the excursion so far; he had never believed in aliens. James knew that while Grant acknowledged the possibility of aliens on a microbial level, he had always denied intelligence, particularly advanced intelligence. In fact, he was vehemently against the idea, and had made that known during one of the few group discussions he had participated in over the last seven months.

'Incredible, isn't it?' said James as he pulled away in the MRV, driving eastwards towards the rear of the vessel. 'I mean, look at all this machinery; I've never seen anything like it,' he continued, pointing at the destroyed section.

Grant grunted and carried on staring out of the window, facing away from James, who decided it was best not to push the matter any further.

As they passed the spacecraft's stern, they took a wide turn to the left in order to get a better look at the rear. On the far left and right were large structures like rocket nozzles and thrust chambers.

Hmm, they seem a bit small to move such a big ship. Boosters, perhaps? Better not ask Grant...

As James looked out the window, his eyes darting all over the craft. There was damage here, but not like the rest, and the most striking feature was the gaping hole complete with radiating scorch marks to the top left.

Okay, there is no way that came from the crash.

The large hole was amorphous and the damage to the surrounding armour pointed outwards, suggesting an explosion. Some of the burn marks on this part of the hull looked like the scorching on a material from a magnifying glass held up to the sun. As James continued to survey the back of the ship, he noticed similar scorch marks in great streaks, and some secondary blast holes further along to the right.

Urgh, looks like I'll have to…

'Hey, Grant, I know you don't want anything to do with this, but I feel like I need a second opinion here,' James said, turning to Grant, who was once again sitting in the rear seat, as far away from James as he could get. 'I'm thinking these holes and burn marks are what caused the ship to go down; possibly damage inflicted by the other ship before it left. What do you think?'

Grant rolled his eyes, then got up and moved to get a better look. 'So we're making the assumption that the second object was also a spacecraft now?' he said. 'If that were the case and it was hostile to this one, then I suppose this damage would be the result of weapons-fire. It's inconsistent with the other impact damage.'

'But look at the burn marks; do you think they used some kind of particle weapon?'

'What is it that the captain says? "All bets are off"? This is way outside my remit.'

And with that Grant slumped back in his seat.

James frowned, then moved the MRV off again on its original heading, passing much closer to the edge of the impact trench.

* * *

Austin and Yula came to the end of the wall and noticed that this part of the ship was rhomboid in shape; the western surface was roughly triangular, not just sloping upwards on the top but also downwards on the bottom towards the middle. The western wall itself was not a flat plane like the southern one but housed an enormous grill.

'A Bussard scoop perhaps?' Yula said, looking the grill up and down. 'Or maybe an exhaust vent?'

Austin scoffed, 'Your guess is as good as mine there. But if I had to choose, I'd guess the scoop. I don't care what species you're from, it wouldn't make sense to put an exhaust port on the front of a ship. Now scooping fuel, on the other hand...' He trailed off, peering deeper inside the structure.

There were large holes and breakages in the grill rack, and inside there was a further honeycomb structure, but beyond was shrouded in shadow.

They continued on and saw that James was right: the wing tip on this side was jammed into the ground and looked like a viable way up. In fact, the whole front cone had suffered heavy damage, having taken the brunt of the impact. It hadn't broken off completely, but it was twisted towards the ground on this south side. Most of the damage was buckling, like crumple zones on a car. Friction had stripped swathes of ceramic plating off the underside, but some tiles were still visible on the portions that hadn't come into contact with the ground. This plating gave way at the very front to heavier armoured segments around the front rim.

As they moved along to survey the bow of the craft, they noticed that there was a large ovular inset in the front of the cone which housed hundreds of broken masts and antennae of varying lengths, as well as copious amounts of Martian soil. Right in the centre of this inset was a hole which was filled with dirt.

'Definitely not getting in through there,' said Austin, pointing at the caked opening. 'Let's give that wing a try.'

And so they walked back to where the wing was stuck in the ground. Austin placed his boot on it first, testing its stability, then began to climb, with Yula following.

'Good thing this is so scratched-up; this surface is really slippery,' said Austin with a hint of surprise in his voice, reaching down to rub his glove over an unscratched portion of the hull.

'Less admiring, more climbing… sir,' Yula grunted.

Laughing, Austin continued moving up the wing, which was steeper than he had anticipated. After some time and a little scrambling, they finally made it to the top of the cone. They found that it had an extra piece of hull plating on the top at the rear, which was bent upwards like a car bonnet, creating a large gap in the hull. Austin looked down into the hole. It was a sheer drop that went quite far down, and he could just about see from the little sunlight shining through that it was full of debris and dirt.

'This one's a no-go too,' he said, and moved away.

Yula took a moment to peer down the hole herself before joining Austin on the edge of the broken section.

From their vantage point on top of the hull, the symmetry of the ship was apparent. To the front, facing east, they could see the surface that should have been flat, complete with the broken remains of a turret, leading along to the slopes, which in turn led up towards something that looked like the bridge of a seafaring warship and was the highest significant point on the vessel. On the right-hand side—the top of the rhomboid main hull—one of the ship's colossal artillery was half-raised from its bay. It was an intimidating sight: the largest gun they had ever seen. It led down towards some kind of rotating jacket mechanism and ended at the main body and trunnions, affixed to a turret mount. Most of the cannon was a dull metallic grey, but the jacket parts were bright blue and slightly translucent, glinting in the sunlight. On the left side, the muzzle of an identical weapon extended from its half-open bay.

Austin lowered his gaze from the topside of the hull and looked down. There was a large gap in the connecting space between the cone section and the rhomboid main hull where it had been torn asunder. Near the bottom of the gap, he could just about see an opening large enough for them enter, in the side facing them, and some flickering lights coming from the inside.

* * *

James and Grant had reached their first target, a rectangular object around four hundred metres in length that had sustained heavy damage. Based on the amount of tearing and broken machinery on its north-facing side, it looked like it was one of the pieces that had been ripped from the main hull in the impact.

'Seems like it rolled a few times from the momentum,' said Grant into his radio.

He had got out some equipment to analyse the wreckage and he broke off a loose fragment of the hull material to take as a sample for further study back at the habitat. Having placed it inside a container, he then wandered around taking samples of scorched Martian dirt and rock from the impact trench.

James was busy inspecting all the debris with his camera, providing commentary for the recording and taking the occasional detailed still image.

'... mostly composed of hull fragments, but the occasional smaller piece of machinery is present. The large wreckage here looks to be some kind of engine pod. It's possible the main ship had one of these attached on each side and they

provided the main forward and reverse thrust for the craft...'
He continued wandering and talking, documenting everything he could see around this area of the wreckage.

After working for a while, they got a call over their radios, complete with plenty of static.

'Hey, uh, guys... Yula and I have found a way into the ship. Get here as soon as you can,' said Austin.

'But we've only just started!' replied Grant.

'We'll have plenty of time to come back later. Right now the priority is to head back to camp, check in with Zhu and report to Mission Control. The ship still has power. We don't want to rush in half-cocked.'

James replied before Grant could get the chance to retort. 'Yes, sir. Just need to pack our gear away and we'll be back over your way in a jiffy.'

CHAPTER SIX
TRESPASS

THE MRV ROLLED UP TO THE HABITAT in the late afternoon after an uneventful return journey from the alien wreck. James and the team filed out of the vehicle and trudged across to the main tent where they had eaten just a few hours before. Once through the airlock, the team removed their spacesuits, and Yula got to work setting up the communications equipment to check in with Major Zhu. Meanwhile, Austin and James tinkered with the long-range transmitter for the message to Earth. Grant spent a few minutes flitting in and out of the habitat bringing in the samples he had taken from the crash site. Once he was done, and the airlock closed behind him a final time, he moved over to his lab station, which contained an array of devices for analysing geological samples. Without a word to the others, he sat at the computer terminal there and began to process what he had collected.

Yula flicked a switch on her device and, holding headphones to one ear, spoke close to the microphone: '*Magnum Opus,* come in. This is Mars base camp, Cosmonaut Yula Merkulova calling for scheduled check-in at 1700 local time. Major, are you there? Over.'

Radio static hissed for a few minutes, causing James and Austin to look up from calibrating their transmitter.

Yula tried again, pressing and turning a couple of dials on the device. 'Major Zhu, come in. Repeat, this is Mars base camp for scheduled check-in.'

Austin and James looked at one another with concerned expressions as the static continued. After a moment, the hiss grew in intensity and a familiar voice broke through.

'Yes, Mars camp, this is the *Magnum* reading you loud and clear. It's good to hear your voice, Yula; I was getting worried,' said Zhu.

Yula sat back with a smile and a sigh, then looked to the captain. 'Connection established, sir. It's all yours.' She offered him the headphones and scooted to one side on the bench.

Austin smiled and sat next to her, leaning close to the microphone.

'Howdy, Major,' he said. 'Hope you're keeping my ship tidy?'

'Not a thing out of place, Captain. Minor attitude adjustments; otherwise orbit is stable. I trust all went well with setting up the hab and the excursion?'

'That's a big affirmative, Major. No problems our end. All the equipment made it down intact, even though we very nearly didn't. Wish you could have been down here with us. The ship is a helluva sight to see… Anyway, how're we looking for weather? These Martian summers can be unpredictable.'

'I'm picking up a minor dust storm on the sensors, but it's around thirty kilometres east and receding from your current position. Forecast data still indicates you'll be free and clear for the rest of the mission.'

'Good work, Major. Depending on what Mission Control says, we're likely to be heading inside the wreck next visit, so we'll be out of comms range for a while. We'll check in again at 2200 local. Queen out.'

Austin cut the feed and set the headphones down on top of the machine with a sigh. After a moment, he looked up and said, 'Yula, get us a connection with Earth. Time to find out what Mission Control want us to do.'

Yula wasted no time at all establishing a connection through the long-range transmitter and moved aside so that Austin could send his message.

'You think they'll want us to go in there?' asked James in a hushed tone, sidling up next to Yula as Austin spoke into the microphone. 'I mean, you confirmed the ship still has power. How is that possible after all this time?'

'I do not know,' Yula muttered in reply, leaning against the dining table. 'But if power systems survived crash, who knows what else could have survived?'

'You're right, they'll probably scrub the mission. We're not equipped to go in there and make first contact... Especially if they're not friendly.' James then scoffed, nudging Yula with his elbow, 'Hey, if there are survivors, at least Guy Furious would be wrong about *something*, right?'

'That is what I am fearing.'

Austin stopped talking, got up from the device and walked over. 'Alright, I've sent the transmission,' he said to Yula. 'I told Mission Control that we found a way in, and that the ship still has power.' He looked at James and continued, 'I've also told them what you and Grant found at the rear. I'm thinking it'll be about an hour before we hear anything back, factoring in time for consideration.'

'Yes, sir,' James replied. 'What are your orders in the meantime?'

Austin looked between James and Yula, then sighed, placing his hands on his hips. 'James, you go help Grant with his analysis. Yula and I will get the equipment ready to go back out there.'

Yula's expression fell and she stammered, 'You are expecting to go back, sir?'

'Yeah… Remember the millions of dollars? Huge waste if they don't have us investigate the inside, even with the power on. We'll have to be careful. No unnecessary risks.'

* * *

Two hours later, the four astronauts stood together on the precipice of the broken section of the ship, looking down at the small opening in the wall below—at the light flickering in the exposed corridor. Mission Control had returned their verdict in line with Captain Queen's expectations, and so with trepidation, and the decision made for them, the team had returned to the crash site.

'How the hell are we supposed to get down there?' asked Grant, his voice raised and trembling.

'Carefully,' said James.

Yula looked around the area below them, then pointed to a few promising places. 'There! And there! I see some damage that we can use as footholds.'

'Doesn't look particularly secure…' replied James, craning his neck to look over the edge.

Austin interjected, 'Well, we'll just have to take it slow. It's our only option, far as I can see.'

'No unnecessary risks, right, sir?' James said, looking glum.

Austin patted James's shoulder, then stepped towards the edge without a further word. He knelt down and hung his leg over the side, placing his boot down on the first damaged section. After waiting a few moments, he shimmied along the narrow metal ridge until he got to the next handhold, which he used to step down a few metres, like a ladder. However, on the final makeshift rung, his boot slipped and he fell with a shout.

'No!' both James and Yula cried as Austin slipped straight downwards.

He managed to grab the former foothold with his right glove. He hung there, sweating and panting, his heart pounding in his ears, and closed his eyes, breathing a sigh of relief that he hadn't missed the hold.

'Uhh, guys, I can't hold this much longer. Suggestions, please,' Austin cried, opening his eyes again. He knew a fall from this height, even with a third of Earth's gravity, would do him serious injury, perhaps kill him.

'Anywhere you can swing to, Captain?' asked James.

'I can't see. Goddamn suit's in the way,' Austin replied, wriggling his body as he tried to look around. 'Hold on—ah, damn it, my helmet's fogging up. I think there's a recess in the wall to my left. Don't have much choice here.'

'Sir, I can see platform to your left also,' cried Yula. 'Be careful!'

'I'm going for it,' Austin grunted, and he swung with his free arm as hard as he could, praying his fingers wouldn't slip. His hand went into the dent and he closed his fingers around a protrusion inside it. He then raised his left leg as high as he could, trying to find the platform.

'More left,' Yula shouted.

Austin brought his leg down, panting with the strain,

then, holding his breath, swung it out once more, this time a little further. His boot caught the top edge of an outcrop and he shuffled his foot to get a better purchase.

'Got it,' said Austin, releasing his breath.

Gripping hard with his left hand, he removed his right hand from the other handhold and transferred it quickly into the same dent as the other. He shuffled and manoeuvred his left boot further along the outcrop so he had room for his dangling right foot, and once it was in place, he moved on to more stable holds until he reached a ridge that he could shimmy along. He dropped to his hands and knees once he had room, and waited to catch his breath.

'Christ almighty, that was hard,' said Austin, panting into the radio.

James replied, 'Well done, sir. You had us worried for a second there.'

'Don't be singing my praises yet, Commander. Still gotta get across that bridge.'

When he reached the metal support beam, the ridge had widened enough for him get down and crawl on his hands and knees across it. It was a very long way down. He crawled, placing his hands on either side of the thin grey girder.

Eventually, he came to the other side and was able to stand. He was only a few hundred yards from the corridor, and the metal platform that went across to it was wider and looked more secure. Along the wall there was a lot more exposed machinery that he could use for handholds.

He clapped his gloves together and, with renewed determination, he grasped a bit of pipe that was sticking out from the wall and raised himself up onto the foothold, keeping his body close to the wall. He shimmied along, grabbing at anything he could through the holes in the wall. About half-way along the wall, he held a thick black cable. The force of his grip pulled it free and the wall erupted with a crack. A volley of bright electrical sparks covered his helmet and he yelped, falling away from the wall. He reached out and grabbed another protrusion, stopping himself.

'Are you alright, Captain?' asked James. 'We saw a flash.'

'I'm fine,' Austin replied. 'Just some sparks. No damage to my suit, but it scared the shit out of me.'

After a short break, he continued along the wall, this time testing every handhold before committing to it. A few minutes later, he had traversed the distance between the girder and the exposed corridor. He grabbed the edge of the opening, pulled himself around the corner with effort and threw himself onto the secure floor of the corridor.

A moment later, a loud, distorted sound erupted in his ear, and he looked up to the others on the ledge. They were jumping up and down, waving their arms around; the sound was their collective cheering. After he had caught his breath for a few moments, he spoke over the radio to the others.

'That... was *not* my best idea!' he panted. 'You guys oughta be careful on your way down here. Don't, whatever you do... don't follow my lead, alright?'

'You got it, sir. And for the record, this was Yula's idea—ouch!' James laughed.

The weary captain looked up at the group on the ledge and saw Yula smack James's arm. Austin sat down in the mouth of the flashing corridor and closed his eyes—resting from the stress of his recent foray into extreme rock-climbing—while he awaited the others. It wasn't long before they joined him without incident.

'Heh, must've learned from my mistakes, eh?' said

Austin as the group came through the opening one by one and into the corridor.

The three nodded in agreement, mumbling variations on, 'Yeah, pretty much,' before falling silent and looking down at Austin, who was still on the floor. James and Grant helped him to his feet and they could finally survey their surroundings.

* * *

The corridor was long and dark. The main lights in the ceiling were the cause of the flickering, but there was also low-level emergency lighting that cast everything in a blueish hue. All along the passageway were broken panels and fallen support struts. The floor was uneven in places due to buckling underneath and there were doorways leading off to different rooms. Debris and dirt covered the walls and floor, and Martian dust hung in the air, illuminated by the flashing lights, twisting and turning in the light breeze. Cables dangled from panels in the ceiling, sparking and scattering incandescent particles on the floor.

'Alright, torches out, people,' said James as he pulled out his own. He switched it on and ran the beam of light over the walls in his immediate area. They looked to be a pure white under the layers of dust and they were covered with intricate detailing—carvings of unfamiliar symbols and iconography—reaching all the way up to the ceiling, which was not that much higher than in an Earth building. The tops of the walls curved seamlessly into the ceiling, but at the bottom was a much harsher corner. On the floor there was a dark-grey, thin, carpet-like material with a deep-red stripe running down the centre. It was enough to dull his footsteps, but he could tell it was resting on a hard metal surface.

'This place almost looks like it could've been made by humans. It reminds me of a hospital,' James murmured.

The others lit up their torches and they picked their way along the corridor together, climbing around or over fallen beams. As they moved along the dark passage, Yula's light beam passed over something strange on the left-hand wall: a short smear of a dark-blue gelatinous substance. She walked up to it to take a closer look.

'What do you think this could be?' she asked. 'It looks like some kind of congealed liquid.'

James came over and examined the substance. 'That is weird. Could it be... blood?'

'But it is *blue.*'

James shrugged. 'Octopuses have blue blood, as well as a few other animals. I'm no astrobiologist, but if this *is* alien blood, they may also breathe oxygen.'

As they continued to creep along the corridor, it began to bear to the right. An open panel in the ceiling rained a constant stream of sparks. James walked beside Yula, with Grant just in front and Austin leading the way. Though the whole group's pace was cautious, Grant seemed particularly jumpy and flinched at every loud crackle. He hugged the wall, too busy watching the sparks to notice much else about his surroundings.

As they crept past an open doorway to a pitch-black side room, Grant slipped on something, causing James and Yula to stop dead behind him. Grant pointed his torch at the floor to see what he'd trodden on. He shrieked and jumped away, knocking into Austin.

'What in the hell are you doing, Grant? You nearly gave me a heart attack!' Austin hissed.

Grant pointed at the object lying on the floor without

saying a word. James and the others shone their lights on it in unison.

'Is that what I think it is?' asked Yula.

James couldn't see her face very well through her helmet, but he could tell by her tone that she was disgusted. He stepped over and gingerly picked up the strange-looking yet familiar form from the small, dark pile of metallic dust. He turned it over in his hands. The object was long and pale beige in colour; it was semi-translucent, and covered in a fine, transparent down. At one end it there was a large mass of bone which was covered in the blue liquid they had seen before. The other end gave way to a palm and three slender, sharpened fingers which were knobbly and curled.

'Well…' said James with similar disgust in his voice. 'At least now we know they have hands.'

Grant turned away to avoid looking at the appendage as James laid it back on the floor. In unison, the group now turned their attention to the lurking darkness of the room beside them. Austin shone his light into the room. It appeared empty at first glance, so he stepped inside. Yula opted to remain in the corridor with Grant, and bent down to take photographs of the severed arm.

James followed the captain inside. The darkness of the room was oppressive, but when he pointed his torch forwards, all he could see was a metallic surface in front of him.

Wait, the captain must be in here somewhere, surely?

He ran his torchlight across the surface and saw an opening on the left side. The metal surface was leaning down at an angle from the ceiling but only blocked off the right two-thirds of the room. As he edged around the metal, he could hear Grant hyperventilating through his suit radio and whispering, trying to reassure himself that Guy Furious was right and all the aliens were probably dead.

'But what if they're not?' he blurted out.

James stifled a giggle. He found this whole excursion exciting and fascinating, and he didn't understand why Grant was having a tough time processing it. Much as he disliked Grant, he hadn't set out to be mean, but at the same time he couldn't help finding it amusing to see Grant's self-assured bravado disintegrate like this.

James continued into the rear half of the room and saw Austin waving him over. The walls were the same as in the corridor, white with carved symbols, and they reflected the torchlight, giving the room a little lighting. There was a terminal of some kind on the back wall with a giant flickering screen and a sloped desktop in front of it at around hip height. On the desktop was an array of indented symbols that spanned the entire length.

Could this be a keyboard? Their alphabet? More symbols here than any human language.

As he moved to join the captain, James heard Yula's voice over the radio. 'Grant, I do not like this any more than you, but this whole section, maybe even whole ship, is depressurised. They are surely dead.'

Trying to reassure him in her own way. That's Yula alright; hard as nails, great sense of humour and very kind, but zero bedside manner. He'll be over the moon she's comforting him like that... God, he's so jealous. I've told him there's nothing between us.

Austin tapped James on the arm and pointed down at the floor. James pointed his torch and gasped. There, at his feet, lay the owner of the severed arm. He ran his torchlight over the corpse. Its form was larger than the average human, and it was clad in some kind of white, plated body armour covered in the same strange symbols from the walls. It was impossible to tell the creature's true body shape because of the armour, but from the geared joints in its dog-like legs, it looked like the suit was also mechanised.

Not just a spacesuit then. More like an exosuit; probably enhances their natural strength.

Moving the beam of light up the body, James could see that it had been impaled through the abdomen by a fallen pipe, the same blue blood emanating from the wound. The creature had two sets of arms: one long like a chimpanzee's and connected at human-like shoulders, and one short—almost vestigial—tucked in close to the chest. There were large technological constructs around the wrist of the longer right arm, but the left one stretched out and ended in a stump against the metal surface—a fallen ceiling panel—that had obscured it from outside. James looked at the stump and saw that the armour had reformed over the severed end.

'Amazing, ain't it?' said Austin, leaning against the keyboard. 'It's so… different.'

'Guys, come take a look at this,' James said into his suit radio. 'We've found it.'

He continued to pass the torchlight up the alien's body. The armour was much denser at the neck, but its head was uncovered, with no helmet to be seen.

The sight of the alien's face made James recoil.

Its features were those of an apex predator. The wide-open, lipless mouth contained long, sharp black teeth and a strong jaw. Its head was large and kite-shaped, and covered with the same pale-beige skin that was on the arm. The skull had bony structures at the top and some colourful, recessed skin in between, similar to the frill of a dinosaur. Its lidless eyes were ovoid in shape, similar to a human's but three times the size and pitch black. There was nothing on the face that could be counted as a nose, and only some small holes in the side of the head where a human's ears would be.

James heard Yula and Grant scrambling into the room, trying to find their way around the ceiling panel, so he turned and walked back towards them. He saw Yula come around the corner first and he reached out his hand to grab her shoulder, which startled her.

'Sorry, it's just me,' said James.

She breathed a sigh of relief and asked, 'Where is Captain Queen?'

'Hey, over here,' said Austin, waving his torchlight around.

James then directed Yula to view the alien corpse. Grant filed into the room behind her and proceeded no further, staying with his back to the wall.

Yula bent down and reached out with her gloved hand to touch the corpse. She rested her palm on its chest, just below the pipe wound, and then pulled her hand away and lifted the camera to record footage of the alien.

'I think we're done with this room. Let's move,' said Austin.

He made his way past Yula, James and Grant towards the doorway. Grant followed close behind and James stayed while Yula finished up with the camera. As she stood up, James could see her visibly shaking and he put his arm around her shoulders.

'You okay?' he asked. He could just see her head through the helmet nodding back at him.

'Thank you,' she said and hugged him back.

The two of them made their way back out of the room and into the corridor, where Austin and Grant were waiting.

They continued along, ducking and climbing around the debris, and after a few minutes they came to a large, circular atrium area with other corridors leading off from it. In the centre of the room was a huge curved symbol, crossed and dotted, set into the carpet. The deep-red stripe on the floor joined in the middle with more coming from the other rooms. James raised his finger and counted the different directions they could take: six corridors in total, all with the same dim and dingy blue hue and flickering white overhead lights.

'Sir, the sun will be going down soon,' said Grant. 'Maybe we should turn back before night falls, head to the basecamp and analyse what we've got so far?'

Austin checked the built-in watch on his suit and tilted his head left and right before replying, 'Ah, you're right, we can always come back tomorrow morning. Alright, every-one, let's turn around and move out.'

As they all turned to go back down the corridor they had come from, the bulkhead door slammed shut in front of them with a reverberating clang.

'Oh, shit!' shouted Grant, running at the door and banging on it. 'What are we going to do now?'

James swore under his breath and told his panicking colleague, 'We'll be fine, mate. We have enough air to last us a good long while yet. We can just push on and find another way out.' He turned to Austin, who was staring in horror at the closed door a foot from his face. 'Sir, which direction should we go now?'

'Uhh, umm…' Austin gulped and stammered. 'I, err… James is right. We need to press on if we're gonna get outta here before our air runs out… *Fuck*.'

There was a sudden hissing sound all around them.

They turned back around to face the atrium. After a few minutes, the sound abated and the atmospheric pressure sensors on their suits lit up, indicating the presence of a breathable atmosphere.

I knew it! thought James. *They're oxygen breathers.*

The four looked at one another, variously frowning or raising their eyebrows in confusion. How was this possible? Was it a glitch in their suits? Perhaps the ship had scanned them and adapted the environment to their physiology? There was only one way to be sure.

Amid objections from the other three, James raised his arms to unlock his visor and retract his helmet. Tentatively, he gripped the sides of his visor with both hands and closed his eyes, crumpling up his face. After a few seconds, he pushed. His visor clicked and slid upwards into the helmet. From there, James held the sliding toggle switch around the neck of the segmented helmet and retracted the whole thing behind his head. He took a deep breath and sighed; the air smelled stale, but it felt better than having his head stuck in a bowl for the entire trip.

'Small mercies.'

The others saw that James wasn't suffocating and followed suit, retracting their helmets. Yula closed her eyes and breathed in deeply through her nose, and Austin took the opportunity to wipe the sweat from his brow. Grant took a big gulp of air and ran over to one of the walls, where he doubled over and vomited on the floor. James walked over, patted him on the back and helped him up, while Austin continued surveying the room.

'Six possible routes; four of us…' he pondered, weighing the options for a few moments.

Grant recomposed himself and James put an arm around him and brought him back to the group.

'Look, guys and gal, I can't see any other option…' started Austin. 'I think we're gonna have to split up.'

'What? No!' protested Grant, shoving James away. 'I refuse to go wandering this ship on my own.'

'No, what I mean is we split into two groups to minimise risk and increase our chances of finding a way out.' Austin held up his fingers. 'Two of us take one corridor, the other two take another and we keep in radio contact.'

'Like a buddy system,' said James.

Austin nodded. 'Exactly. And remember, people, this ain't just about getting out. We still have a job to do, and we don't have to worry about air anymore, so let's seize the opportunity. Document *everything*. See if we can't find out more about who these aliens are and what they're doing in our solar system.'

James nodded and Yula murmured in agreement. Grant frowned and crossed his arms, grumbling under his breath.

CHAPTER SEVEN
The Buddy System

'JAMES, YULA, YOU GO RIGHT. Grant and I will go left,' said Austin, gesturing to each side of the room. 'That makes three corridors each. Pick one and go together.'

James cast a glance at Grant, who wore a look of defeat on his face. He then turned to Yula and motioned for her to have the first choice of corridor. After a few seconds, she pointed to the left one closest to the middle of the room, as the lighting there looked the most stable.

'Come on, Grant,' said Austin as he walked towards the middle corridor of their three.

Grant said nothing but skulked away after the captain.

'Have fun, kiddos. And remember, maintain radio contact.' Austin waved as they disappeared from view.

James and Yula walked together into their chosen passageway, putting their torches away in their belts. The corridor was much brighter than the one they had first come through and it was easier to see the white, clinical aesthetic.

'Do you think all this was carved by hand?' asked James, looking around at the symbols on the walls.

'I find that unlikely,' said Yula. 'Would have taken them years. Was probably machined.'

This corridor was much the same as the first: a long, winding route with rooms off to either side, all in different states of damage. This section was deeper towards the centre of the ship, so had sustained much less destruction than their entry point. There was still the occasional loose panel, but for the most part the corridor was clear.

James and Yula had continued on for what seemed like a long time when they came to a darkened section of the passage. The lights and ceiling here had been broken, and there was severe denting to one of the walls. It wasn't long before they came across the reason for it. Lying face down on the floor in the middle of the corridor was another dead alien in full armour.

'It's wearing the same suit as the other one,' said James.

Yula knelt down beside it, checked it over and replied, 'Likely standard issue. Workers perhaps? I do not see any weap—' She leapt back with a yelp as a long, wide blade erupted—metal scraping and grinding—from a section of the armour on the back of the right forearm.

James caught her as she jumped up and stumbled backwards into him.

'Thanks,' she said, trying to catch her breath from the shock. 'I must have knocked button of some kind when I examined it.'

James moved over to take a look at the blade. It was straight, thin and double-edged, about a metre in length and ten centimetres wide. A double fuller ran down the middle and its ultra-sharp edges tapered towards a point at the end.

No doubt it would have been incredibly heavy to carry but for the mechanised suit of its bearer. The metal itself was dull, matted, and had an interesting pattern, similar to Damascus steel. At the bottom of the blade, below the fullers and just poking out of the hole from which it emanated, a small curved symbol—similar to the shapes on the walls—was carved into the metal.

'I'm not so sure these are just spacesuits...' said James, turning to face Yula.

'Really? Was it sword that gave it away?' she replied, gesturing at the blade. 'Not worker, *infantry.*'

'Soldiers? I guess that fits with the warship theory.'

James stood back up and motioned for them to continue along the dingy hallway. Yula nodded in agreement.

As they walked, Yula said, 'So... what is with you and Grant anyway?' she asked.

'Hmm? What? Is this really the time to talk about something like that?'

'Please, James, this place gives me creeps and I need distraction. The two of you do not get on. Why?'

James shrugged. 'He's told us all before about how tourists have made his dad's life a living hell...'

'That is not what I mean,' Yula shot back. 'And you know, this goes beyond simple xenophobia. He seems really not to like *you.*'

'Look, I have nothing against the bloke. We trained together for the mission, and I found him likeable enough at first. Maybe he's just a miserable bastard.'

'So you not do anything to him? No teasing, bullying? You sleep with wife, maybe?'

'No way! Wait, he's married?'

Yula shrugged and continued grilling him: 'There must

be *some reason* he dislikes you.'

'Yeah, he's a miserable cu—'

'Apart from that!' groaned Yula.

The two of them stopped, their path blocked by fallen debris. A section of ceiling, complete with supports for the deck above, had dropped down. Broken girders, metal tiles, active electronics and the flooring of the upper deck were piled high in front of them. They could see the flickering lights of the deck above through the opening in the ceiling, but there was no way to climb up.

'Dead end,' said James. He looked around for a few moments, assessing options. 'I can't see a way around.'

'There is gap here,' said Yula, pointing to an opening in the left side of the heap.

'It's a bit small… Maybe if we weren't wearing these bulky suits.'

Yula stepped forwards and started picking up small bits of debris and moving them aside. 'Come help,' she said, motioning to James.

He joined her and the two of them spent the next few minutes lifting as much stuff out of the way as they could. Despite their clearing the smaller, loose pieces, the hole was only a little bigger, still not enough for them to fit through.

They turned their attention to a large, heavy lump of metal and wires at the lower edge of the hole, both gripping either side of it.

'If we can get this free, it should make the hole big enough for us to fit through,' said James.

Yula nodded and braced herself. 'Lift on count of three. One. Two. Three.'

The two companions heaved the lump with great strain, and after a few moments it came free. It was quite a bit heavier than James expected, and they soon dropped it down next to them with a loud clang. Panting, James turned back to the blockage and looked at the hole, which was now big enough for them to fit through one at a time.

He clapped his hands together and moved to go through, but Yula grabbed him by the arm just as the corridor shook and more debris from the sides caved in with a crash. James and Yula covered their faces and turned away as dirt and dust flew up towards them. They waited a few seconds for it all to settle, and then lowered their arms and looked again at the blockage.

The hole was gone.

James sighed and kicked a small metal chunk. 'So much for that idea. Should we head back and try a different route?'

'We could try one of these side rooms,' said Yula, looking around.

James rubbed his chin, giving the doors nearby a cursory glance, then shook his head. 'Most of these are jammed shut or caved in,' he said.

Yula looked to the door immediately right of the blockage and then walked over to it and ran her gloves around the edges.

'There is gap here,' she said. 'Big enough for fingers. Help me try and pull open.'

James joined her once again and, standing behind her, put his fingers in the door gap either side of hers. 'I don't see what good this will do,' he said, bracing himself.

The two of them pulled on the door, and it began to move in fits and starts, grinding along the top and bottom edges. After they had pulled it halfway open, it slid the rest of the way with ease, taking them by surprise and causing Yula to fall on top of James.

They helped one another up and peered into the now

open doorway. The inside of the room was well lit, a stark contrast to the darkness of this part of the hallway. As they moved into the room, they noticed that it was undamaged, and so they were able to get a much better idea of how the ship had looked while in full working order.

The interior was large and spacious, and here the ubiquitous white of the corridor walls gave way to a stark grey. The floor was a deep red, with a white circle in the middle of the room. Inside the circle was a large lime-green symbol, different to the one in the atrium.

There was a computer terminal at one end of the room, with a large blank screen embedded in the wall and the same long keyboard they had seen earlier on a slanted part of the wall below the screen.

There were closed, built-in storage compartments all along one of the longer walls, and in the far corner was a glass floor-to-ceiling container where a transparent violet liquid bubbled away. There was a button pad next to it, a door in the side and some equipment—concertina pipes and what looked like medical apparatus—on the inside, suspended in the liquid.

'Crew quarters?' said James. 'No bed to speak of, though.'

'Is very empty,' Yula replied, pointing at the strange fluid-filled device. 'Maybe they use container as bed?'

James shrugged and continued moving through the room. He noticed that on the same short wall as the strange receptacle was a doorway. Yula moved to pull the door open, but James pressed a button next to the door frame and it opened with a whoosh.

This room was much the same as the last, except reversed.

'Adjoining rooms,' muttered James. 'So they're not big on privacy.'

Yula pointed to the far corner and said, 'Look, door back to corridor is open.'

'Lucky.'

The two of them hurried across the room, through the door and out into the passage. They looked back and could see that they had come out on the other side of the blockage. James turned and, raising his torch, continued to move along the dark corridor.

Yula skipped up alongside James with a mischievous smile on her face. 'So…?' she urged.

'Wha— No, I told you,' James started in protest, before throwing his head back and letting out a loud groan. 'Fine! I'll tell you.'

He remained silent for a few moments.

Do I tell her that he's jealous of our friendship? Nah, he's a proper creep, and I'm not his matchmaker. If he wants to get rejected, he can do that himself.

Yula tutted and gestured for him to get a move on.

'Well, alright. You know how Grant can be a bit of a busybody, yeah? Like, he butts into conversations as if he's the foremost authority?'

'Yes,' laughed Yula. 'He *is* mansplainer.'

'Exactly. Well, very early on in our training, when we were just getting to know each other, I kind of called him out on it. He was trying to tell some women engineers—y'know, the ones who built the bloody thing—how the *Magnum*'s engines operate. It was embarrassing. He's hated me ever since.'

It's not a lie. I didn't make a very good impression on him. He was expecting me to back him up and be his wingman.

'Oh… that's all?' replied Yula, her smile fading.

James just shrugged. 'Now you know why I didn't want to say anything.'

* * *

It was dark inside the room that Grant and Austin had located. Unlike the rest of the ship, which was bathed in the blue glow of the emergency lighting, this room was pitch black. This wasn't just because of the lack of lighting; the walls themselves were black and plain, without the characteristic carvings of the corridor. As far as they could tell from their torchlight, the area was spacious, with a ceiling which curved upwards to form a dome. On the floor in the middle of the room, under the dome, were concentric circles traced in gold radiating outwards to the walls. In the very centre of the circles was a dainty white pedestal that had a small computer console that resembled a lectern sitting on top of it. The sloped top glowed with its own backlight, and to one side was a small sphere, no bigger than a ping-pong ball, embedded halfway into the surface. There was a faint, oscillating hum in the room that came from all around them, but the clunking of their boots was deadened, as if the room were soundproofed.

Austin had placed his camera into a holster on the chest of his spacesuit, in order to free up his hands. He crept over to the pedestal and examined the surface.

'Hey, could you shine your flashlight over here for me?' he asked, switching off his own and placing it into a compartment on his waist before removing both his gloves and putting them down on the floor.

Grant shone his torch over the console so the captain could see what he was doing, and Austin placed the tips of his fingers on the ball. It had barely registered his touch when the rest of the surface lit up as a screen with some lime-green glyphs, similar to those on the walls in the hallway, arranged in a list.

'Sir, that thing you are touching looks like a trackball to me. If you move it, you might be able to scroll through the text on the screen,' said Grant, proud of his deduction.

Austin rolled his eyes and said, 'Gee, thanks, Grant. I couldn't've figured it out without you.'

As he rotated the ball towards himself, a small strip around it lit up white, registering the movement. It was responsive enough, and the text on the screen scrolled, but the language was indecipherable. Still, he continued to look through the alien menu on the table in front of him, but he soon stopped when he noticed a glyph he thought he recognised.

'Take a look at this.' He motioned to his torch-bearing companion. 'Does that look like a galaxy to you?'

Grant stepped over and looked down to where Austin's finger was pointing, at a squashed spiral shape with a large dot in the middle.

'Maybe, but I don't see how it could be. The rest of the letters do not look like pictograms to me.'

'I'm gonna press it.'

'Is that really a good idea, sir?'

'Nope! But I'm gonna do it anyway.' Austin pressed his finger firmly down upon the glyph. There was a confirmatory ping and the glyph's colours were inverted.

All of a sudden, the darkness above their heads erupted in a dazzling display of brightness, bathing the room in colour and light.

'Dios mío!' exclaimed Grant as he stumbled backwards and onto the floor, dropping his torch in the process.

Austin spun round, squinting and shielding his eyes from the sudden brightness. Slowly, his eyes acclimatised and he lowered his arm. His eyes widened in amazement as he looked up. With his mouth agape, he backed away from the middle of the room to get a wider view of the incredible sight. Thick lanes of dust, pinpoints of colourful light—reds and blues, browns and yellows—all spiralling out and rotating slowly around a bright central point. A three-dimensional holographic projection of exquisite detail and incredible scale, depicting the intricate structures holding together nearly four hundred billion stars.

'This… this is *our* galaxy!' exclaimed Austin as he looked over the familiar structures of the Milky Way, from the warped barred-spiral disc to the tiny representation of the Orion Molecular Cloud Complex. 'This must be some kind of astrometrics lab.'

He jumped back over to the control console and began turning the trackball in different directions while looking up at the galactic map overhead. As he rolled the ball, the projection moved in tandem, panning left, right, forwards and backwards.

There must be more ways to control this. It's not very useful to see the whole thing at once.

He noticed that the screen was no longer displaying the list but instead showed different glyphs segmented into groups. He pressed down on one of the glyphs and rolled the trackball, all the while looking to see how the hologram would respond. This time it zoomed in towards the centre of the projection.

Austin pressed a different glyph and rolled the ball, which tilted the galaxy around an axis. He pressed another of the buttons on the screen, but before he could scroll, the hologram zoomed in rapidly to a familiar-looking area of space, with one star-system flashing in lime green.

'Looks like you've found the "You Are Here" sign, sir,' said Grant.

'Certainly looks like us alright,' Austin replied. 'Yeah!

See if I zoom in a little further, we can see the solar system coming into view, and the marker is on the fourth planet.'

'This is really advanced stuff,' replied Grant in wonder, creeping forwards.

Austin laughed. 'And here I thought you hated this place.'

The two of them continued to investigate the holographic galaxy map and its controls for some time, and they discovered an overlay which displayed the ship's prior course in a long, winding line, covering a significant portion of the galaxy. They deduced that these aliens had come from far out near the edge of the Milky Way in the constellation of Cygnus, but it was impossible to tell how recent the route plotting was, or how far back in time it went.

'The one thing I can't get this map to show us,' Austin said, 'is *why* these aliens came through our system.'

Grant examined the route line and pointed to where it passed close to the Witch Head Nebula. 'The movement here is erratic. Everything else is straight.'

'You're right. Could be where they met the second object, and it chased them all the way here.'

'That's a long way, sir. About a thousand light years. A long time too.'

'Well, I guess that means they can travel faster than light then. Either that or this ship is truly ancient.'

Before Grant could reply, there was a sudden rattling noise in the direction of the door, and a flash of light as it opened and closed. It had all happened so fast, but the noise had made the two stop dead.

After a few moments of silence, Austin spoke with a chill in his voice: 'We're not alone...'

* * *

James and Yula came at last to the end of their corridor. Jammed half open in front of them was a large set of double doors, the frame filling the height and width of the hallway. These were similar to the doors to the other rooms they had passed on the way—crew living quarters, they assumed. However, these doors, while consisting of the same dull grey metal and equally lacking in embellishments, were twice the size and opened diagonally, the left-hand door to the upper corner and the right to the lower corner. The gap between them looked just large enough for the two companions to squeeze through. They could see through the gap that the space beyond was much darker than the corridor; yet again it had the oppressive blue emergency lighting and intermittent flashes of sparks emanating from unseen electronics. Both of them approached the doors and peered through the gap, shining their torches into the room.

'Doesn't look like any of the other rooms,' whispered James.

'Hard to tell from here, but looks like there are consoles and seating,' Yula replied, darting her beam of torchlight around.

After a few moments of looking, James stood and began placing one leg through the gap in the doors.

'I reckon there's nothing else for it. We need to get a good look inside,' he said.

James struggled to get his spacesuit through the narrow gap owing to all the gadgets and equipment that kept getting snagged on the door. He twisted this way and that, compressing the suit in the right places for him to squeeze through. After a minute of writhing, pushing, grunting and swearing, he managed to heave himself into the room. He stood, dusted himself down and then turned, motioning for Yula to follow him.

Before long both astronauts were through the doorway and inside the mysterious dark room. It was much larger than they had thought. They appeared to have entered from the right-hand side of the front wall, as much of the seating in the central area was facing towards them. As they moved forwards into the centre of the room and turned around, they saw a large flickering screen covering the wall, stretching the width between the door they had come through and a similar door on the other side. Aside from this one, flat wall, the rest of the room was circular, with concentric gold rings emblazoned on the ceiling in between rings of light fittings. Immediately in front of them, facing the screen and either side of the centre line, were two large consoles with chairs. Further back, in the very middle of the room, was a single chair with some elaborate devices on the armrests. Around the edge of the back half of the room were another eight seats with their own, much-larger terminals, all turned to face the central chair. Still more computer terminals, with their strange alien keyboards and other peripherals that neither of the companions recognised, were embedded in the round wall of the room.

The damage in here was minimal, just a few fallen ceiling panels and light fittings dotted around the place—with the exception of a large pipe emanating from a break in the floor behind the central chair, piercing it and impaling its occupant. More worrying were the burn marks on some of the chairs, as if the terminals in front of them had exploded. There were more corpses lying on the floor, some positioned near walls or underneath chairs with limbs sticking out at odd angles. It appeared to James and Yula that the crew in this room had been thrown around like ragdolls by the impact and killed. A few crewmembers were wearing the now-familiar white exosuit, but others were wearing form-fitting lime-green jumpsuits.

James pointed to one of the corpses in a jumpsuit and

said, 'Looks like they're just as hench as their suits make them look.'

Yula looked around with a confused expression and said, 'This looks like bridge.' She turned to James and continued, 'But we have not gone up to top deck we saw from images.'

'You're right, we haven't gone up at all; we're on the same level we started on,' he replied, inspecting the console in front of him.

'Is sensible, I think,' she pondered, running her hand over the back of the chair to her left, 'having bridge this deep in middle of ship. Protected. Top deck is viewing platform perhaps?'

'Could be... Gah! These blasted consoles are absolutely cream-crackered. There's no way we're starting any of them up.'

James walked on, further around to the right side of the room, examining the terminals and strange peripherals. Nothing seemed to have any power.

All of a sudden he saw movement out of the corner of his eye. Yula was over on the other side of the bridge, but the movement didn't come from her; it came from behind her. James turned to see a huge shadow rise up from the darkness. All he could see was shadow upon shadow, and his torchlight was too diffuse for the distance.

'Yula!' he shouted as the figure lunged at her, just missing her as she turned. She stumbled backwards onto the floor and scrambled away from the figure. It made an angry hissing sound as it dragged itself along the ground in her direction, scraping the floor with its armour.

She screamed and panicked, backing away. James bounded around the room and grabbed her under the arms, pulling her to her feet. They continued to back away as the creature once again rose to its feet and hobbled towards them. As it passed into the light they saw that it was one of the white-armoured aliens, the top of its head glowing and pulsing a deep orange, its sharp black teeth bared. It reached over its shoulder with one of its mechanised arms and pulled a long object—an assault weapon—away from its magnetic mounting.

Struggling and exhausted, it raised the weapon towards James and Yula, but stumbled and fell to one knee. The weapon discharged a bright flash of white-hot plasma into the wall, burning a large hole where it hit.

James and Yula shouted and dropped to the floor.

The alien groaned, having given the last of its strength, and looked up to the ceiling. The vibrant orange glow from its cranium faded, then the creature convulsed and fell face down on the floor, motionless.

Yula and James were both huddled together, leaning against the wall, shaking and hyperventilating. James tried to slow his breathing and calm his nerves. After a few moments, Yula rose up and strode over to the now-dead alien. She reached down and picked up its weapon. Her eyes were wide and angry. Breathing raggedly, she scanned the room, then looked down at her attacker and gave it a kick.

'This,' she huffed, holding up the plasma rifle with effort, 'is mine now, *chertov ublyudok*!' She spat on the corpse and walked over to James to help him up off the floor.

'Cheers. Hey, are you okay?' asked James, dusting himself off.

'I will be fine,' said Yula.

Just then their radios crackled to life and they heard Austin's voice. 'Yo, heads up, people: we're not alone in here. Grant and I just saw something leave the room we're in.'

CHAPTER EIGHT
SEPARATION

S TILL IN A STATE OF SHOCK, James and Yula searched for a way off the bridge. James leaned against a panel in front of one of the inward-facing chairs, and the screen, which had been flickering, lit up with a view of the outside world. The sudden brightness caused both James and Yula to look up with a start. The view on the screen seemed to be from a camera on the front of the ship; some of the broken outer structures could be seen encroaching upon the image.

'Wow, it is miracle this is even working at all,' said Yula. 'I wish we had cameras this tough.'

'Well, it's definitely night-time now,' James said, pointing at the screen.

The landscape before them was lit only by starlight filtering through the thin Martian atmosphere. It was as Grant had feared: even if they made it out of the ship alive, they would have to contend with a night-time return to the habitat, treacherous even for the MRV given the uneven terrain. Overlaid on the image on the screen was a heads-up display showing information in the alien language. The ship's remaining operational sensors knew that the craft was planet-side and so an augmented-reality attitude indicator was displayed in the centre, perfectly adjusted for the Martian horizon.

'I thought terminals had no power?' said Yula.

'Looks like it was just a case of finding the right panel, preferably one that hadn't exploded,' James replied while shining his torchlight around the room some more.

The beam of his torch rested upon a door in the centre of the back wall of the bridge that they had not noticed before.

'Ah, we've got a choice: exit through this door and push further in, or take the other door at the front and essentially go back the way we came,' said James.

Yula hoisted her weapon higher and replied, 'I am fine to continue onwards.'

They both crept towards the rear door of the bridge, and James stopped. Yula looked back at him with a confused expression on her face.

'What is problem?' she asked.

James pointed at the door and said, 'Where's the control panel? How do we open it?'

'Maybe motion sensor?' said Yula, and she moved closer to the door to stand in front of it. After a short time, she looked back at James, frowning.

He walked to the door and ran his hands around the edge and along the wall. Yula stepped forwards and did likewise on the other side. After checking all the way down to the floor, she stood up and took a step back.

'So much for carrying on. Shall I just blow door open?' she asked, raising the heavy rifle and aiming it at the door.

James stopped examining the wall and turned to face her. 'What? Bloody hell!' he cried, jumping away from the door. 'Do... do you even know how to use it?'

Yula smiled and shrugged. 'No better time to find out.'

The plasma rifle was huge and bulky. It had a triangular barrel with a single large muzzle. Underneath the barrel was a series of tubes that led back to a round generator at the rear of the weapon. There was a hand-hold under the piping, uncomfortably close to the muzzle end of the rifle, and at the rear, what appeared to be a trigger and some switches were embedded in the receiver. The weapon had no shoulder stock or underslung grip, but rather it appeared to be designed to be held low down for hip firing. As such, the firing hand wrapped around a grip at the top of the receiver with the trigger itself on the underside of the grip; all too easy to pull accidentally, but for a safety catch further along with the rest of the controls. As for the size of these parts, they were designed for the larger alien hands, so Yula had difficulty wrapping hers around the grip and reaching the controls. She propped the muzzle end down on the floor while she disengaged the safety switch with her free hand, and picked it back up again. Aiming from the hip, she squeezed the trigger. The weapon powered up with a whirring sound, but nothing happened.

Yula turned her head and looked at James. She started to ask him a question and absentmindedly removed her fingers from the trigger. There was a loud blast and a flash erupted from the end of the rifle, sending a volley of plasma at the door and burning a large hole right through the middle. Some of the remaining energy from the blast shot down the corridor on the other side and hit the ceiling. Yula stumbled back in shock, scraping the barrel of the weapon on the floor.

After her surprise had worn off, she laughed. 'Okay. Now

we know it is *release* to fire.'

'Yeah, right ol' giggle, that,' said James, recovering himself.

They waited a couple of minutes for the burns around the edge of the hole to cool down, then they went to take a closer look. The hole was just big enough for them to climb through. Yula went first and took point on the other side of the door while James struggled to get his suit through the opening and fell in a heap on the other side.

The corridor was well lit and short enough for them to see it ended in another door, which curved outwards into the hallway.

'At least there's a panel on the wall for that one,' said James.

Yula nodded and pressed on along the corridor.

As they walked, she pointed out two rooms, one either side of the passage. The doors were open and they could see both were similar to the crew quarters they had come across earlier, except much larger and with more facilities. There was a large office area in one, with a long desk and several chairs around it. A screen was embedded in the wall at one end of the table.

'I've seen this episode,' joked James, peering in. 'This is a briefing room for the bridge crew.'

Yula rolled her eyes and shook her head. 'This is not one of those American sci-fi shows. Although...' She looked around the room some more, then sighed and muttered, 'You may be right.'

They left the briefing room and continued on towards the end of the corridor. When they reached the door, James saw that the panel on the wall was flat and, unlike the control panel in the crew quarters, there were no buttons. He stared at it for a moment, then removed one of his gloves and pressed his fingers to the panel. The glass was cold to the touch and smooth. It was responsive and lit up at his touch, opening the sliding door with a whoosh.

They stepped through and stood inside an enclosed circular room, big enough for a few of the armoured aliens to fit in but still very small in comparison to the quarters. James turned to face the doorway and noticed that there was another panel on the wall to the right-hand side of the door frame, this one lit with some alien glyphs. He cleared his throat and leaned across Yula to touch one of the glyphs on the panel at random.

'Excuse me,' he said, and stood back in position, putting his hands behind his back and staring straight ahead. After a brief delay, the door closed and they felt the room move upwards.

Yula smacked James on the arm and said, with a smile, 'Is this part of famous dry British humour?'

James just smiled back and stood straight in silence.

They weren't moving long before the lift jolted to a stop, throwing them off-balance and making the lights flicker. The lift door opened a crack, just enough for them to see where they were. Yula peered through the gap and saw that they had stopped just short of the terminus for the upper deck. The corridor outside was much the same as the ones on the floor below. Sparks were erupting from broken panels on the walls and there were some collapsed beams hanging down from the ceiling. The floor level was up to their knees and they would have to force the door open in order to climb up out of the lift.

A crackle came over their radios. 'Status report, please, guys. Haven't heard anything from you in a while. Over,' said Austin with a measure of concern in his voice.

James held the button down on his radio and responded, 'Yes, sir, thanks for the heads-up about the sighting. We located the bridge in the ship's central body. Unfortunately, nothing was functional other than the external cameras. We also encountered a live alien, and that thing was *not* happy to see us.'

'It attacked you? Are you alright?'

'Yeah, we're fine. It died of its injuries and Yula nicked its weapon. We've moved on from there and are currently one or two decks up, trapped in a lift.'

'Are you in need of assistance?'

'Nah, we should be able to get the door open one way or another.'

'Okay, well… watch out for yourselves, kiddos. We caught up with our little friend and have been tailing him. He's weedy, injured. Not in a suit like the others. Seems to be searching for something. We'll keep an eye on him.'

James thanked Austin and ended the conversation. He and Yula grabbed the open edge of the door with both hands and pulled as hard as they could. After a few seconds and with great resistance, the door opened a little. Once they had created a gap wide enough for them to fit through, Yula slid the plasma rifle along the floor of the corridor; it clattered on the uneven tiles. She climbed out of the lift on her hands and knees, then turned and grabbed James's hand to help him up through the gap and pulled him to his feet. There they stood, in a brand-new corridor on a completely different deck, but you wouldn't know it by looking; it was ruined in almost exactly the same ways as on the lower deck.

Yula retrieved her weapon from the floor, and she was just about to say something to James when there was a loud creaking sound and the twang of steel cords snapping one after another. They spun around with the final snap and watched the lift they had been in plummet down the shaft.

James leaned through the doorway and looked over the edge. After a minute or so, they heard a loud crash of crushing, twisting and shearing metal reverberate back up the shaft. James gulped and looked with wide eyes at Yula, who had gone as white as a sheet and was trembling. She looked him in the eye, tightening her jaw, trying to compose herself.

His expression softened. He stepped forwards and put his arms around her, holding tight as she broke down, sobbing into his shoulder. She stayed that way for a short while, making his suit wet with her tears, then pulled away.

'Thank you,' she said, taking off her gloves and wiping her face.

'Yeah, that was a bit *too* close, wasn't it,' he replied with a small laugh.

Yula sighed and placed her hands on her hips. She looked up at the ceiling and whispered, 'I hate this place.'

The two companions moved on from the lift shaft and began exploring side rooms. Many of these appeared to be science labs of varying kinds, and none of them had doors. They came back out into the corridor together and stopped.

'There's a lot of stuff in these labs. Stuff that's probably worth looking at in more detail,' said James.

Yula pursed her lips, tutted and replied, 'Yes, it will take time to go through everything…' She swung the rifle up to rest on her shoulder and put one hand on her hip. Thinking out loud, she said, 'We may cover more ground if we split up.'

'As in, you take the left, I take the right?' enquired James.

'Mmhmm,' said Yula. 'Is all open here. Rooms lead on to one another. Should be fine, *da*?'

'Okay, let's do that then. We'll move along a bit and meet back in the middle.'

So James moved off into the lab on the right, leaving Yula to investigate the one on the left. The room was dark; even the emergency lighting wasn't working properly. Only the occasional spark from some broken equipment and the odd working emergency bulb provided any light. From an initial survey with his torchlight, James could see that the lab appeared to be dedicated to mechanical engineering, especially relating to the alien exosuits and weaponry. There was a long desk along one wall with computer terminals and screens all over it. Some of the screens were working; a couple displayed wireframe schematics of the suits, while others flickered with images of the ship's main artillery and some ground vehicles. In one of the corners of the room was a plinth with an unoccupied suit which had fallen to the floor.

At the end of the long desk was a strange, intricate mechanical device, similar to a 3D printer, and some unbroken jars containing a metallic powder. James walked over to the terminal nearest this device, attached his camera to his chest and started pressing on the screen, trying to bring up whatever information he could. Despite the indecipherable language, he managed to pull up a schematic which showed a rotating, spider-like robot with a triangular body. James pressed on the screen some more, and the powder in one of the jars came to life. The jar began to shake and the powder swirled around inside, as if being stirred by an invisible spoon. There were some new icons on the screen and so James pressed one. The swirling in the jar continued for a moment before stopping dead. However, the powder was no longer in a pile but had formed into the shape of a small section of armour plating.

Of course. The suits are nanotech! That's why the severed arm was sitting in this powder; it must've lost connection to the suit when its wearer died.

He pressed a pictogram on the screen and the armour piece lost cohesion, turning back into powder once again.

James turned away from the desk. There was an open

doorway in a transparent wall to his left, leading into the next part of the lab. He walked through and looked around; it looked more like an armoury than a laboratory. In the middle of the large oblong room was a shooting range with small lime-green targets at the end. To the right and left were weapon racks containing plasma rifles like the one that Yula had acquired, all standing upright side by side in their holders. James also saw smaller sidearms in the form of pistol-like weapons, as well as knives of varying lengths and designs. He picked up one of the sidearms and looked it over, surprised at how light and inconsequential it felt to hold. He bobbed the weapon up and down, transferring it from one hand to the other and back again.

I wonder if they hold these in those little vestigial hands of theirs...

The whole weapon looked as though it were a single, smooth piece of chromed metal, each part of the gun merging seamlessly into the next. There was a single muzzle at the end of a short barrel which blended into a handle towards the rear. The grip had a guard that came out diagonally underneath it and joined back up with the muzzle in a triangular shape. Just like on the plasma rifle, the trigger was on the underside of the grip, but there were no other controls.

Out of curiosity, James stepped up to the shooting range and raised the firearm towards the targets. There was no clear way to aim with this weapon, with no sights along the barrel, but he did his best to point it at one of the targets. He squeezed the trigger, expecting the weapon to be just like the plasma rifle and only fire upon release, but he was wrong. As soon as the trigger was depressed, the weapon fired; not a plasma projectile like the rifle but an invisible stream of high-energy particles. James only knew this from the effect it had on the target he was aiming at. The beam—which was sustained for the length of his hold on the trigger—had burned a sizeable hole clean through the target. There was a sound that accompanied the firing, emitted from the weapon itself, like a high-pitched hum. James looked once more at the weapon and thought that the sound effect completed its resemblance to a child's toy ray gun.

Why would you use this when you can't see the beam? They do have very strange eyes; maybe they can *see the beam.*

All of a sudden, a piercing scream shattered the stillness. It was hard to tell which direction it had come from, owing to the reverberations, but it was followed by the booming discharge of a plasma rifle.

Yula!

He looked over to his left, through the open door of the laboratory and into the corridor, and rushed out. His heart pounded and he felt a horrible cold sweat come over him. His boots squeaked on the floor as he skidded and ran through the nearest doorway on the left side.

He stopped, panting, his eyes darting around the room.

Shit. Not here.

There was a door ahead of him, so he ran through, the clomping of his boots echoing off the walls. This second room was pitch black. He fumbled for his torch and darted its light around the walls and floor.

Not here either. Fuck.

'Yula!' he called, breathing heavily. His voice became more high-pitched than usual. 'YULA!'

As he hurried through a third dark room and into a fourth, he was met by the sound of heavy breathing and grunting.

'Yula?' he called.

'James!' Her reply was breathless and raspy.

He followed the sound of her voice out of the fourth room, back into the corridor and left through another doorway.

'Help me! I am stuck. Can hardly breathe!' she cried out.

The room was dark and smaller than the other labs. It appeared to be a storage room for a hydroponics laboratory, housing strange plants that favoured darkness, most of which were strewn over the floor with smashed receptacles around them. The shelving units that lined the walls were almost bare, and there was no emergency lighting at all. James pointed his torch at the middle of the floor and saw the corpse of an armoured alien lying face down with a hole burned through its abdomen, still smoking.

There was movement underneath the otherwise lifeless heap and James could see Yula struggling to get free from the weight of the alien on top of her. Her weapon was a few feet away on the floor and she was pushing on the alien's shoulders with both hands but could barely move it.

'James!' she said, spotting him there. 'Get this thing off me.'

He knelt down and put his hands around the alien's left shoulder and tightened his grip.

He looked at Yula and said, 'Right then, after three, you give it a good push on this shoulder and we should be able to roll it off you. You're going to be fine.'

They counted down together. 'One. Two. Three!'

They heaved together with all their might and eventually rolled the immense dead weight off Yula, flipping the alien onto its back. Free at last, Yula shuffled away and sat up against a wall, taking big gulps of air and leaning her head back.

'Monster,' she said, breathless and wiping the sweat from her face. 'Was staring at me from corner. When I shined light, it advanced. Was so fast, it is miracle I was able to get off shot.

Hit it in chest.'

'Yeah, I can see your shot burned right through its armour. Those weapons are potent. I've picked one up for myself,' said James, brandishing the particle gun. 'Anyway, looks like it's *my* turn to help you up off the floor now.'

James extended his hand, clasped Yula's outstretched arm and pulled her to her feet.

CHAPTER NINE
The Lab

James helped Yula out of the storage room; she had her arm around his shoulders, which he held in place, and he supported her movement with his arm around her waist. They limped a little further along the dark corridor, the combination of the darkness, flickering lights and debris making it difficult. After a short while they came to a doorway on their right which led to another laboratory. This one was better lit than the others, as the lights were not flickering, and while there was some damage, the room was relatively tidy.

They decided to stop and rest for a while to allow Yula to recover. A shiny grey metal box was on the floor at the base of the nearest wall. It was a unit of some kind that had tipped over onto its face. James pointed it out to Yula, who decided it would be good to use as a bench.

He helped her lower herself onto it and placed her weapon on the floor nearby. He then stood up and looked around the room. It had the same clinical white walls of the corridors and appeared to be a computer lab, monitoring different kinds of ship diagnostics with operational workstations. There were touch-panel screens recessed into the walls, as well as the now-familiar keyboards made up of glowing glyphs embedded in the long single desk, and a number of strange peripherals sitting on top. The desk with workstations stretched all the way to the far end of the room. There were also some vertical glass touch panels arranged in the middle of the floor at intervals which seemed to be used as tactical displays. All but two of them were smashed and the pieces littered the floor around their pedestals.

After a moment, James heard a rumbling noise and looked down at Yula sitting on the makeshift bench. She looked up at him, her cheeks flushed, and held her stomach. He gave a short laugh and remembered that he too was very hungry. He hadn't thought about eating since they boarded the ship, but they had been exploring for goodness knows how many hours and their last meal had been back at the habitat before they set off. All he knew was that it was night and they had missed their evening meal.

'Luckily,' James said, rustling in a small pouch on his waist, 'I brought some provisions with me.' He pulled out a couple of energy bars and waved them about in front of Yula.

Her eyes widened and she looked up at him with a smile.

Never one to pass up the chance for mischief, he smirked and said, 'What? You mean you didn't bring anything with you? What *are* you going to eat?'

Yula's face fell.

James chuckled to himself and handed her one of his energy bars. Yula took it gratefully and then kicked him lightly in the shin.

'You bastard,' she said, returning his smirk and undoing

the wrapper.

'*Cheeky* bastard, thank you very much,' James replied as he squatted down next to her and took a bite of his bar.

For the next few minutes, they sat in silence tucking into their rations and resting. James stared off into the distance, thinking about all that had happened to them so far. He had sat down with his arms resting on his knees and his head in one hand. He let out a small yawn. The ship was quiet, except for the slight hum of the computer terminals along the walls. James hadn't realised quite how quiet the ship could be when there were no sparks flying, debris falling or giant aliens lunging at them. A rare moment of tranquillity.

Yula had her eyes closed as she chewed her food. James turned his head in his hand and looked at her. They had been through so much together in a short space of time and he considered himself lucky to have been paired with her. What it would have been like with Grant didn't bear thinking about. James thought of the captain and pitied him.

He understood what Grant saw in Yula; she was very beautiful. But he didn't think well enough of Grant to credit him with looking much deeper than that. She had much more incredible—and important—qualities besides, all of which had made her become one of James's favourite people. Back on Earth, he had introduced her to Angela, and he'd been concerned at first that Angela might feel threatened or jealous, but the two of them had seemed to hit it off long before James got to know Yula.

After what seemed like an age, Yula broke the contemplative silence. 'You are staring, Commander,' she said with a smile.

She opened her eyes and looked at him.

James laughed. 'Sorry, I was just thinking about home. You never did say what you were planning on doing after this mission.'

Yula sighed. 'Well, I go where I am told. Roscosmos will assign me something, I am sure.'

'I just mean I wouldn't want to lose touch with you.'

'Hmm. Are you forgetting you are taken?' she said softly.

James blushed and sputtered, 'What? No... I'm flattered, but that's not what I mean. I just mean, when all this stuff is over, it would be great to hang out together. You, Angela and me.'

'It still sounds like you are coming on to me,' she laughed.

James frowned and grumbled, and Yula pushed him with her boot.

She yawned and stretched, placing her hands behind her head. 'Do not worry; I tease. You are great friend, and I would like nothing more than to come to your wedding.'

'Wedding?'

'Yes. You are going to propose to Angela as soon as we are home, are you not?'

'Well, yes. When I find a way—'

'No!' she chided. 'You are to do it immediately. Waste no time, or I swear I will beat sense into you.' She leant forwards and jabbed him in the back with her finger.

'Ouch! Leave off,' he said, batting her away. 'Alright, I'll do it the moment I lay eyes on her after we land.'

'Good.' Yula smiled and gave an approving nod.

James looked around the room once more. He had got somewhat used to the ship over the last few hours, but talking of home made it all seem so alien again.

'You know,' he said, leaning back against the box, 'it's hard to believe that only yesterday we thought this was just a meteorite. We were more excited about being the first humans on Mars than anything else. But all this...'

Yula made eye contact with James once again and replied, in quiet exasperation, 'They are so alien, yet their ship is so human. I do not understand.'

James lifted his head out of his hand and said, 'Yeah, I was just thinking that. But I guess they're not so different from us really, when you think about it.' He motioned to the room. 'They breathe the same air, have eyes, arms and legs… they bleed and die… and I guess the environment of space encourages certain design choices.'

Yula also took a moment to look around the room. Her gaze stopped on the terminals and she replied, 'I wonder how they have dealt with zero gravity?'

'Hmm. That's a good question,' said James, perking up a little more. 'I mean, they are so much more advanced than us. I just hope it's not beyond our understanding. The *Magnum* is very different to this, primitive even, but it still seems plausible for a species like us to build this.'

As Yula stared in silence at the terminals, her expression turned to one of sadness. 'I hope Zhu is okay.'

James looked down at the stark grey floor of the lab, which was beginning to feel cold through his suit, and replied, 'Probably doing better than us.'

'She has not heard from us for most of day. We have missed check-in after check-in. She is probably very worried.' There was a slight tremble in Yula's voice and her eyes began to water.

James saw she was starting to become upset again and patted her knee. 'Hey, first thing we'll do when we get out of here is check in with the major. But we have to focus on getting out first.'

Yula sighed and wiped her eyes. She looked at James and nodded, then patted her hand on his—which was still resting on her leg—and mouthed, 'Thank you.'

'What are friends for?' he replied, smiling.

'Are you able to stand?' James asked. Yula nodded and rose to her feet without aid.

'I am feeling much better now, thank you,' she said. Pointing at the terminals, she continued, 'I would like to look at some of these computers.'

The two of them walked over to the nearest screen, which was scrolling through detailed ship schematics, showing the extent of the damage to the ship's systems. James moved to the computer on Yula's left. Both of them tapped on the screens and made educated guesses on which glyphs to press on the keyboards embedded in the desk. The language barrier made it very difficult to decipher any of the information on the screens, and impossible for the pages that displayed only the alien text. There were, however, some pages with information laid out graphically which were much easier to decipher and helpful in their investigations.

'Looks like ship is never flying again,' said Yula. 'Extent of damage is incredible—not only from impact; it looks like other ship destroyed main engines.' She continued to flick through pages of damage report schematics. 'As suspected, this part of ship was best protected. Although…' She trailed off and moved closer to the screen, examining the graphics further. 'Life-support power has been rerouted to these few decks recently.'

'We know that already. Remember when the bulkheads closed and the whole place filled with air?' James said without looking up from his own terminal.

'Yes, but I mean it was not automatic. It was done *manually*.'

James's interest was piqued. He looked up from his screen at Yula and said, 'You think Austin and Grant's survivor turned on the life support?'

'Is most likely. But ship crashed over five *years* ago. How could any oxygen breather have survived that long without functioning life support, and why turn it on *now*, just as we arrive?'

'I don't know,' said James, slumping back in his seat.

He glanced over at Yula's screen as she continued to cycle through the damaged systems on the map. He noticed something towards the rear of the ship that made him sit up again, a large, undamaged room that spanned several decks and contained thousands of small dots.

'Hold on a moment,' he said. Yula stopped and looked at him as he pointed at the screen. 'What is that room? It's huge. Any way of finding out what's in it?'

'Why?'

'Just humour me.'

Yula rolled her eyes and navigated over to that section of the ship. After a little fumbling, she managed to enlarge the view to an isometric wireframe with a scrolling list off to one side. There were countless capsules in the room, stacked on top of one another from floor to ceiling, with walkways and ladders connecting them in a grid. The room was full of these strange devices, and the screen reported that most of them were operating at full power.

'What are these?' Yula muttered, frowning at the screen.

'Thought so… Knew this place seemed a bit empty.'

'What do you mean?'

James pointed at one of the functional capsules. 'See if you can get it to show us information on one of these devices. If I'm right, you'll see.'

Yula tapped on the keyboard, but nothing happened. She thought for a moment, then touched the capsule on the screen. A new overlay opened, showing a schematic of the capsule.

It had curved sides tapering off at the top and bottom, and a door on the front with a circular window about three quarters of the way up. Next to the schematic was a list of glyphs and a display of what looked like vital signs.

'*Kriokonservatsiya*,' Yula whispered, leaning back in her chair.

'Exactly,' said James with a triumphant grin. 'The majority of the crew are in some kind of suspended animation.'

Yula's eyes widened and the blood drained from her face. She looked from the screen to James and back again. 'There is whole army of them.'

She exited the view of the capsule and began to move on from the room's page, but hesitated.

'What is it?' asked James.

Yula pointed at a row of pods near the front of the schematic; they were reading as damaged. She tapped on one, bringing up the detailed view, and it showed the occupant as deceased. Then she navigated back and tapped on another pod in the row. When it came up on the screen, it showed as working but open and unoccupied.

'Look at this,' she said, her voice filling with dread. 'Is only open chamber in row. Other occupants are dead.'

James drew a sharp breath and stared at the screen before getting up from his chair and placing a hand on her shoulder. 'Come on,' he said. 'We'd better not stay here too long.'

She complied and rose from the chair, and scooped her weapon up from the floor as they exited the room.

Once they were out in the corridor, Yula stopped and said in a trembling voice, 'Explain.'

James halted and turned to face her, coming close in the darkness. 'I think the ship detected our presence as intruders when we arrived. My hypothesis is that the ship knew we were here and woke up one of the crew to deal with us. Likely some kind of security response. Then that security officer—the captain and Grant's survivor and the owner of that single open pod—went and activated the life support.'

'So why was it in room with them? Why not kill them there?'

'The captain said the creature wasn't in one of those exosuits. It could probably survive long enough without one to activate the life support, but then... well, my next priority would be to send a distress call. After that, it'll probably go looking for a suit and a weapon.'

'And where would it go for that?'

James rubbed his face with his hand and paced back and forth. 'I don't know. Here. Maybe? I found a suit in a lab and a bunch of weapons back there in a sort of shooting range. So if it's making its way up here, we'd better go.'

He turned to continue walking away, but Yula grabbed his arm. 'Okay. Explain other two survivors to me. How have they survived five years with no air?'

He shrugged and said, 'Maybe their species is just really hardy?'

'Then we need to tell Captain Queen. They may be in danger,' Yula replied.

James nodded and activated his suit radio. 'Captain? Grant? Check in, please. Over.'

There was a moment of tense silence as the two companions stared at one another. Then James breathed a sigh of relief as the radio crackled and Austin's voice came through clearly.

'Yeah, we're fine, Commander. Got some good news and some bad news for you, though.'

'Great to hear your voice, Captain. We were getting worried. What have you got?'

'I'll lay the bad news on you first. We lost sight of the alien

131

a while back, and when I said it was looking for something… yeah, that was a suit. Last we saw, it entered a room and then left wearing one. It didn't spot us, though. We tried following it, but with the suit on it was just too damn fast, and it disappeared through a maze of rooms.'

'Shit… What's the good news?'

'We found a map room. Grant's trying to get it working now. He thinks we can get it to track the bastard.'

'Well, we've got some news too,' said James. 'We— err—*I* think that your alien friend is part of the ship's security response. The rest of the alien crew is in some kind of stasis at the rear of the ship, but there's one empty pod. It's likely the one you've been tailing came out of there. We thought you might be in the line of fire, as it were. By the sounds of it, you're probably in the clear for now. But it may be making its way up towards us.'

'Alright, we'll check that, soon as we can.'

Just then Yula chipped in, 'Sir, I have located airlock on this deck.'

James looked at her in confusion and she shrugged, taking her fingers off her transmitter. 'What? It was on early schematic. I meant to say, but we started looking at pods.' She then pressed her radio again and continued, 'There is large laboratory at end of corridor. If we pass through, we come to airlock.'

'Excellent work, Yula,' Austin said. 'We'll make our way over to you. You're one deck up, right? Ah, never mind, we'll find you on the map, *if Grant ever gets it working*!'

James heard the faint sound of Grant groaning.

'Roger that, sir. We'll head to the airlock and hold down the fort till you get here.'

After they had finished speaking with Austin, the two

companions stood in the darkness of the corridor. The flickering overhead lights lit up their faces in sharp relief. James had been excited about meeting aliens at first, but now it was more like a horror story and he wanted nothing more than to leave and get home to Angela.

Yula stood there in front of him; the flashes of light showed her eyes were red and damp. 'James, I am scared,' she said.

'Me too.'

'What if you are right? What if it *is* coming and we cannot hold it off?'

'Well,' James said, 'I hope I'm wrong. But... we've got weapons of our own, so we *will* hold it off—I have to believe that—and I will fight tooth and nail to make damn sure we get out of here.'

Yula dropped her gun to the floor and hugged James. They remained for a few moments more in the relative quiet, each comforting the other and calming their nerves. Yula let go and dried her eyes as James did the same.

'Airlock is this way,' she said, sniffing and picking up her rifle again. She marched past James and he followed her lead.

A short way down the corridor, Yula pointed out a set of double doors unlike any they had seen on the ship so far. These matte grey doors had a slender, scimitar-shaped window each side of the seam. The top of the door frame was curved, but the bottom widened out, giving the frame a triangular appearance. As they approached, the doors slid open automatically for them with a whoosh.

James and Yula stepped through together and raised their torches in unison, moving the light beams around the large room. Shadows danced under flickering lights and sparking wires, revealing rows of beds stretched out along the walls. Attached to each bed was a metal stalk with an adjustable arm and trays full of strange utensils. The room smelled vile, vaguely of rotten flesh. James's nose crinkled and he coughed. He considered putting his helmet back on for a moment but decided against using his suit's oxygen supply, reasoning that he may get used to the pungent odour. Their footsteps echoed as they crept towards the middle of the room, which was clear. There was a domed ceiling with the same concentric golden rings they had seen on the bridge spreading out from the centre, a pattern which was repeated on the floor.

James moved his torchlight to the left and saw a gap in the row of beds in which sat a large cylindrical chamber with an open door surrounded by a vast console of lit buttons and dials. He moved closer to one of the beds; it was covered in alien blood and there were restraints to either side of the metal frame, which looked primitive and out of place.

A loud clatter of metal on the floor caused James to spin around. Yula looked back at him, having dropped some of the terrifying utensils out of the tray she had been examining on the other side of the room.

He sighed and said, 'You gave me a fright there.'

'Sorry,' she said, placing the tray down on another blood-stained bed.

'I guess that's the exit,' he said, pointing to a door at the far end of the room, where the light of a corridor shone through the crescent windows.

'Yes.'

They continued moving along at a careful pace until they reached the very centre of the room, when their radios crackled to life and Austin's familiar drawl came through their suit speakers.

'Status report, people. You copy?' he said.

James pressed the button to reply. 'Reading you loud and clear, Captain. We're in the lab Yula mentioned, just heading through now. It looks like what passes for a medical bay or surgery around here. There's blood everywhere and it smells awful. I don't think it came from the crash, though.'

'Okay, well, Grant is making progress on the map, and we've picked up one or two things to bring back to the habitat that might be of interest to the folks at home.'

James heard a pinging sound come over the speakers.

'Ah, sounds like Grant's got the map working...' Austin continued. 'Shit. You said before that Yula's armed, right?'

'Yes, sir. Me too. There's an armoury up here.'

'Well, I don't wanna alarm you, but—'

Just then Grant interrupted in a panic, shouting into his suit mic, 'You need to get out of there. It's approaching your position *right now*!'

CHAPTER TEN
TERMINUS

T HERE WAS NO TIME. The moment that Grant spoke, James and Yula heard a whooshing sound from the doors behind them. They spun around and saw, standing in the doorway and silhouetted by the emergency lighting of the corridor, a huge figure. It stood tall, much sturdier than the weakened crew they had seen before. A brief flash from the lights in the medical bay illuminated the form of the alien. It was clad in armour, similar in style to the other aliens' but a deep blue. Its head was uncovered and its cranium glowed and pulsated with bright-orange luminescence as it stared at James and Yula. A hissing sound came from its expressionless mouth and its sharp black teeth glinted in what little light the room provided.

The two earthlings started to back away, trying not to make any sudden movements.

The alien warrior advanced towards them at an incredible pace. Its mechanised legs moved faster than it looked like they should and its heavy boots made a loud, reverberating clang with each step.

'Shit!' cried James.

He drew his sidearm from his waist and swung it upwards to point it at the alien. He pulled the trigger but all too late. The alien's remarkable augmented speed brought it upon James before he could aim true. It grabbed him and threw him aside just as the invisible beam emanated from the weapon, burning a streak in the ceiling behind it.

James stumbled backwards as the alien continued to advance on him. He swung his arm around again to take aim at the alien. It too swung its left arm hard and shoved James away. His weapon clattered to the floor and the force of the push sent him flying into the open cylindrical chamber to the side.

As soon as James hit the back of the chamber, the doors closed down in front of him and locked tight. The machine whirred to life and steam started to rise on the outside as power flowed into it. James could only watch, banging on the sealed, transparent doors, as the creature stomped towards him.

The alien warrior clenched its left hand into a fist and a giant blade erupted from its forearm mount. James could see his weapon on the floor next to the alien.

Gotta dive for it as soon as it opens the door.

But just as he considered his ridiculous plan, he heard Yula shout something from behind the creature. A moment later, she fired her rifle in their direction, sending a volley of hot plasma into the wall on James's right, missing the creature. The alien soldier paused, turned on its heel and marched at Yula. James continued banging on the doors, trying to gain its attention again and give Yula more time.

It was all for naught, as Yula fired again and clipped the alien's right shoulder, causing it to stagger but doing only minor damage. It moved to the left and circled slowly around her until it was blocking the escape route to the airlock. Glaring at it, she lifted her rifle in an attempt to fire into the creature's abdomen, but it grabbed the barrel of the gun with its right hand and moved it aside, causing the shot to fly across the room. In the same movement, it thrust forwards with its sword.

'NO!' shouted James as he watched the alien bury the blade in Yula's chest.

She screamed in pain and struggled against the brute force, grabbing the edge, trying to pull away.

The alien hissed, threw the rifle to the floor and grabbed her by the shoulder. As James banged on the door, shouting and crying, he heard the cracking of bone and the tearing of fabric as the alien forced the great sword through Yula's body.

James couldn't hear himself anymore, but he was sure he was still shouting and screaming. He banged so hard on the chamber that his fists went numb and bloody.

In a display of strength, the alien lifted Yula clear off the floor and held her up to its head height. Her legs dangled and blood dripped from her boots onto the floor. It moved its face close to hers as the life drained from her eyes. As she drew her final breath and fell limp, the alien became aware of James's presence once more.

When he saw that Yula was dead, James banged hard one final time on the chamber doors and slumped to the floor, glaring at the alien with tears in his eyes. He knew at that moment it was over. He had broken his promise to Yula: neither of them would be getting out alive.

Still holding Yula's lifeless body aloft, the alien looked at

James encased in the chamber. It walked towards the control desk and reached out with its right hand. The creature pressed buttons and turned dials with surprising dexterity.

James watched from the chamber floor with gritted teeth, clenching his fists and trembling with rage.

Come on! Open this fucking door. Open it. I fucking dare you.

He glanced out at the pistol on the floor and back at the monstrous creature. He started to bang on the door in a deliberate rhythm, spattering the toughened glass with his blood, willing it to open, or break.

'Goddammit, open the door!' he roared.

However, the door did not open.

All at once, several spider-like drones inside the chamber dropped down in front of James and crept towards him. The chamber started to fill from the bottom with liquid as the robotic spiders crawled onto James's suit. He stood and backed up, trying to bat away the drones with frantic movements. The infilling of liquid was fast and within seconds it had reached his chest. He ran out of space at the back of the chamber and lifted his fingers to press the controls on his neck. His helmet shot over his head and sealed down. Instinctively, he took a deep breath as the liquid covered his head. However, the robotic spiders, which were now all over him, ripped holes in his suit, allowing the violet liquid to seep in. He writhed as they crawled inside and latched themselves on to his skin. He looked up and saw one on the outside at the neck of his suit. There was a crack and his helmet disengaged and liquid flooded his face. Then, as the drones' needles plunged into him in unison, he screamed.

II.

CHAPTER ELEVEN
Awakening

JAMES OPENED HIS EYES. Everything was blurry, a wash of indiscernible brightness. He blinked a few times to clear away the bleariness and looked directly in front of him. His eyes pulled the white blur into focus.

Ceiling tiles? What?

All of a sudden he could feel softness below him and that his head was being propped up by a lump of material. His body was covered by a sheet and he started to hear a soft beeping sound.

I'm lying in a bed... But this isn't my bunk on the Magnum.

Then his head started throbbing and his eyes ached, so he closed them again.

Memories began to filter into his mind, though in no sensible order. He felt a strong wave of conflicting emotions and his eyes began to water, but he couldn't identify why. Something welled up inside him, an overwhelming feeling of grief, but for whom? An image flashed in front of his eyelids, as clear as if he were looking right at it. A darkened room, a claustrophobic chamber, a giant armoured creature and… his best friend, hanging from a blade.

James jolted up, his eyes wide and his heart pounding. He was breathless and he had come over in a cold sweat. He darted his eyes around the area he was in. Perplexed, he saw all the makings of a room on a hospital ward: magnolia walls, clean floors, diagnostic equipment and even some synthetic flowers on a moveable table at the end of his hospital bed. He looked down and saw that he had wires and monitoring pads attached to him, and he had a cannula in his hand which was hooked up to an IV drip.

'Yula!' he shouted. His throat was dry, his voice strained and crackly. 'Yula!'

He began to sob and continued shouting through the sudden release of emotions. Sadness, rage, guilt, grief and fear all came flooding back at once. His shouting and crying alerted those outside the door that he was awake. Seconds later, the door flew open with a crash and four nurses came rushing into the room. Two of them grabbed his shoulders and restrained him, pushing him back down on the bed. He struggled hard against their combined force.

'Yula! Let me see Yula. Where is she?' he roared.

The other two nurses advanced and injected something into his cannula. James felt his vision blur and his head became foggy. He tried to carry on the struggle but felt the energy drain from his body and dizziness take hold. His protestations grew quieter, and then everything before his eyes faded to black.

* * *

When James woke again, the raging tempest of emotion was gone and all was calm. He opened his eyes and blinked a few times, allowing the fog in his mind to dissipate. As he lay on the bed, taking in the ambiance of the room, he became aware of a presence next to him.

'Hello, James,' came a gruff male voice.

James turned his head to look at the figure sitting beside his hospital bed. An older gentleman with kindly eyes behind round, thin-rimmed glasses looked back at him with a smile on his face. He was of average build and clean-shaven, and had a bulbous red-tipped nose. His hairline had receded and the remaining tufts either side of the forehead were a deep grey. Overall, his appearance reminded James of an old professor he'd once had at school, but this man wore a pristine white lab coat instead of his teacher's vomit-coloured patched sweater.

'I'm sure you have a lot of questions,' he said with compassion in his voice. 'First things first, my name is Dr Hales.'

'Where am I?'

Dr Hales smiled and said, 'You are in the Royal London Hospital.'

'I'm… I'm back on Earth?' replied James, confused.

'Ah, that's good. You remember. Yes, you are back on Earth. Now, can you tell me your full name?'

James shuffled up a little in the bed. 'Commander James Mark Fowler, astronaut for the European Space Agency. Umm, can I sit up, please?'

'Certainly,' replied Dr Hales, reaching for the bed controls. 'Tell me when.'

The doctor pressed a button on the control unit and the bed began to move to put James in a sitting position. James indicated that he was comfortable, and the doctor stopped the

145

bed's movement and placed the controller back in its holder.

'So… how long have I been here?' asked James.

'Before I answer, James, I must warn you that this may come as a shock, so please be prepared.'

James nodded and took a slow, deep breath.

'You have been in a coma ever since your accident on Mars. Your fellow astronauts looked after you as best they could on the return journey, and you were admitted here.'

'Seven months?' cried James in disbelief.

'No,' replied Dr Hales. He inhaled slowly and paused before continuing. 'Today is the 1st of October 2026. It has been one year since you were admitted into our care. From the reports of your comrades, we're looking at around nineteen months since your accident. In fact, you spent the first two months after your return in a quarantine ward. Once we were satisfied that you were not carrying any extraterrestrial pathogens and were in relatively good health despite the coma, you were moved here.' He chuckled and gestured around the room. 'And here you have remained.'

James's eyes widened and he stared at the doctor in silence as his mind raced.

A year and a half of my life just… gone?

More and more questions rushed around in his mind; he didn't quite know where to start. Before he knew it, his mouth was blurting out a question.

'What happened to me?'

Dr Hales considered the question, not breaking eye contact. 'Evidently, you were caught in a cave-in, dear boy. You and the Russian cosmonaut. Sadly, you were the only survivor of the two of you.'

James became agitated. 'What? That's not what happened at all. Yula was murdered by that damn alien; there was no

146

cave-in aboard that ship!'

'Aliens? There was certainly no mention of alien survivors in the news reports, and they were quite clear about the cave-in.' Dr Hales leaned over, looked closely into James's eyes and examined his head, pushing it around with his hand. 'Well, you have been through an exceptionally traumatic event and that can play havoc with the mind. Comas are tricky things and hallucinations are not uncommon. After your comrades told us you had been comatose for several months already, we thought it highly unlikely you were ever going to wake again.'

'Hallucinating? No, there's no way that's the case.'

'Well, I can't say for certain; you were on an alien space-craft, after all. But hallucinations in coma patients can feel very real indeed.'

James fidgeted on the bed. His head hurt from trying to think about Yula's death. 'Presumably you ran tests on me to see why I was comatose?' he asked.

'Yes. Oh my, yes, we ran several. EEG, MRI, blood tests and many more besides. Most patients who remain in this state for over a year transition into a persistent vegetative state, but you did not. Your abnormal brain activity remained constant. It was as if your coma were medically induced and all we had to do was find the right drugs to bring you out of it, but we had no idea what was causing it.'

'So I came out of it on my own?'

'Yes, evidently. Ah, I mentioned blood tests… We found some abnormalities in your blood, which led us to your bone marrow and eventually caused us to run a genome test. We're not sure what the effects are—whether they're benign or severe—but something has changed in regard to your genetic makeup. Only time will tell.'

James felt like his eyebrows were going to escape into his hairline. 'My genes are different? Have I got cancer?'

'Heavens no, my boy. We don't think it should be anything to worry about. And other than that, you are in remarkably good health. Little to no muscular atrophy, in fact.'

Doesn't sound like a normal coma to me.

James sighed and rubbed his eyes. Keeping his palms pressed to his eyelids, he said, 'Can I have visitors? I want to see Angela.'

'Certainly. She has already been notified, I believe.'

Dr Hales got up from the chair to leave. He stopped, glanced back at James and said, 'Your case has been a very interesting one, Commander. Once you are discharged from the hospital's care following a full physical evaluation, I think you would benefit from speaking to a psychotherapist.'

'You think I've gone mad?' asked James. 'Because of the alien thing?'

'No, no, not at all. It's just that traumatic experiences such as yours can leave mental scars that are best worked through with a therapist.' Dr Hales pulled out a white business card and fiddled with it for a few moments. 'To tell you the truth, Commander, I am here in a consultant capacity. I actually work out of a private hospital, and we have a counsellor in our employ whom I highly recommend.'

He handed James the business card. James turned it over in his hand and read the name, *Dr Antonio Volpe, Psychotherapist*, and the contact details underneath.

'I can personally vouch for Dr Volpe,' said Dr Hales. 'And my hospital is willing to fund your therapy. Please do consider it.'

And with that he left the room, closing the door behind him.

Nurses came and went on a regular basis over the course

of the next few hours, performing check-ups and other tests on James. Despite his excellent physical condition, moving around for the first time in more than a year made his joints ache and he tired out faster than he had anticipated. Being prodded and poked by the hospital staff didn't help either, and after they finally left, he slumped back on his bed feeling drained. As he lay staring up at the ceiling tiles, he reflected on his conversation with Dr Hales. The doctor's words about Yula's death weighed on his mind.

Did I really imagine her murder? Could it have been a cave-in and my mind has conjured up something different to cope with it?

He closed his eyes and tried to remember anything about a cave-in, but all that came were vivid flashes of moments from the incident. He recalled with perfect clarity the sound of the alien warrior's boots clanking on the floor of the med bay, the glint of the blade as it shot out of its forearm, the crack of bone and Yula's blood-curdling scream.

James woke with a start and sat bolt upright, covered in sweat. He looked at the clock on the wall above the door and saw that it had advanced an hour.

'Close my eyes for half a second and I fall asleep? Urgh…' he muttered, wiping the sweat from his face. 'That cave-in story is absolute nonsense, I'm sure of it. No way I could've imagined all that.'

His thoughts jumped to the last conversation he'd had with Yula and his eyes began to water as he was overcome by an intense feeling of crushing guilt.

'James, I am scared.'

'Me too.'

'What if it is coming and we cannot hold it off?'

'*... We* will *hold it off... I will fight tooth and nail to make damn sure we get out of here.*'

What a joke. What arrogance. I couldn't save her; I was just tossed aside like a ragdoll and she died trying to save me.

James was so consumed with introspection, staring once again at the ceiling, that he barely registered the sound of the door to his ward opening and closing.

It was the sound of someone clearing their throat from over by the door a few moments later that brought James out of his tearful brooding. He frowned, unsure that he had really heard what he thought he had heard, and lifted himself up onto his elbow. He looked over towards the door and saw a woman standing there. She had piercing blue eyes and tears were rolling silently down her soft pale-pink cheeks. She looked at James and moved a lock of her long flame-red hair out of her mouth to behind her ear with the rest. She interlinked her fingers and held them down, playing with them. She wore ripped jeans, and a black t-shirt emblazoned with a griffin logo above a spacecraft flying towards a polyhedral star-port which James recognised as one of his own. He choked back an awkward combination of a sob and a laugh, making a strange, guttural sound.

Then he cleared his throat and gushed, 'Angela?'

At this, she whimpered and placed a hand to her mouth. James moved to get up out of bed, but Angela rushed forwards and embraced him, pulling him close so his head rested between her breasts. She buried her lips in his hair and made the top of his head wet with her tears. He put his arms around her, feeling her slim figure through the t-shirt. All at once, tension that he hadn't even realised he'd been holding in his muscles released, and for the first time since waking he felt himself relax. Her embrace pushed all of the guilt and regret from his mind, and he finally had some brief respite from the horrifying visions that had plagued him. He held on tight, taking in her divine scent, her warmth, and ran his hand over her lower back, as if scared that missing even a single detail would mean she was imaginary, and he began to weep.

I'm home… I really am home.

After a while, they released one another a little. James looked up at Angela's smiling face, gazing deep into her eyes as she rested her hands behind his neck.

'Sorry for making you worry, love,' he said.

Her lips quivered; she held back tears and shook her head. 'No, no,' she whispered. 'It's alright. Everything's alright.'

'I've missed you so much, Ange.'

She sat on the bed in front of him and the two sighed, resting their foreheads together. She moved in and rubbed her nose on his, and their lips connected. He moved his hand up to touch her cheek as they kissed, and their tears mingled. Pulling away, James dried Angela's tears and she held his hand to her cheek.

'I was so scared you wouldn't remember me. You have to tell me *everything*,' she said.

James snorted, '*You* have to tell *me* everything. I must've missed loads.'

'Alright, we'll take it in turns.'

'Great, you go first, love,' he said with a wry smile.

With a sigh, she proceeded to tell him all about her experiences of being a famous astronaut's girlfriend over the last two years. Angela had followed the mission's progress at home every step of the way, tuning in to the live broadcasts from the *Magnum Opus* and inviting their friends and both of their families over to watch. They became quite the little soirees, with Angela providing buffets, drinks and a play space for her young nieces and nephews. They were, in fact, all together having one of these parties when they heard from Major Zhu about the alien ship, a revelation which shocked them and left some scared while others scratched their heads. Angela's elderly father offered the suggestion that the message had somehow been lost in translation because of Zhu being 'foreign', despite her speaking perfect English for every broadcast.

The parties weren't always wonderful hosting events, however, as a couple of times during the broadcasts, a few (more distant) relatives noted how pretty Cosmonaut Yula was—much to Angela's chagrin—and how close she and James seemed. This put a dampener on Angela's enjoyment a little, especially since she and Yula had got on so well during the last phase of James's training. Angela had been quite happy to see Yula open up and become more laidback during each progressive broadcast, and she didn't appreciate the spurious insinuation that James had a wandering eye. She had also met the other crewmembers once or twice. Major Zhu and Captain Queen were a good laugh, but she had only seen Grant from afar.

The actual landing event on Mars drew the biggest crowd to Angela's house yet, and she struggled to provide enough of anything, but she found it thrilling to follow the historic landing.

She paused in her story and looked down at James, resting on her shoulder. 'Y'know, I think I should get some credit for your little speech on Mars,' she teased. 'You only knew that poem from *my* copy of *Night Thoughts*.'

He laughed. 'I knew I'd read it somewhere.'

'Yeah, straight off my bookshelf! Imagine, my boyfriend: courageous astronaut, first man on Mars… plagiarist.'

They both giggled, and then James spoke up with a question that had been on his mind while Angela recounted her story. 'So, how did people take it, the alien spacecraft thing? I mean generally around the world. We never did get to hear the fallout.'

'Well… several governments actually had the gall to try covering it up, the US and China particularly, and many others tried to downplay it. But the cat was out of the bag, so to speak, and there were protests and riots, and the footage was all over the internet anyway.' She paused. 'Plus, some insider leaked your aerial photos. Eventually, the UN put out a press release on behalf of all the space agencies confirming what you lot had said. Scary couple of months, that.'

'Wow, glad we weren't around for that. So presumably you know—'

'That you were exploring the alien spaceship when you had an accident that knocked you into a coma? Yeah, I know,' Angela replied. 'The ESA rang me up to tell me that some area you were in had collapsed and you were injured.' Her eyes began to water again as she continued, 'For seven months I was worried sick, constantly questioning whether you'd died on that ship, until finally they told me you'd returned and been brought here. I came to visit you every day. Eventually, the doctors told me there was little to no chance of you recovering.'

James slammed his fist into the mattress and raised his voice as he said, 'Damn it, that's not what happened out there! This is the second time I've been told I was in a cave-in. The doctor told me that's what they reported on the news?'

Angela raised her eyebrows and her posture stiffened. 'What?' she stammered. 'Yes, the ESA's administrator told me that himself. And it's been all over the news since you came back to Earth.'

'Well, it's a damn lie.'

'So… what *did* happen then?'

James sighed and rubbed his eyes. 'I'm sorry, love. Didn't mean to lose my temper,' he said. 'We found the spaceship and managed to get inside. It was great at first, really amazing stuff, but then…' He trailed off, gathering his thoughts. His face fell and his voice became sorrowful as he continued, 'There were survivors, Ange. Alien survivors. The ship knew we were there and sent one of them to hunt us down. Just as Yula and I were about to get out, it caught up with us.'

He stopped and steadied his breathing as Angela looked on in horror. He found it difficult to form the next words, as if speaking them aloud to her would make them real.

'They… he… *it killed her*, Ange. Right in front of me. It murdered Yula without a second thought. It threw me into some chamber, and the next thing I knew I woke up here missing a year of my life!'

The colour had drained from Angela's face and her mouth hung open. Her eyes darted between his as he clenched his jaw, trying to hold back the sudden onrush of emotion.

After a few seconds she stammered, 'I'm… I'm sorry, James. I don't know what to say.'

'The doctor seemed to think it was my mind playing tricks on me, a hallucination from the coma, but I know that's not true. It was absolutely real, Ange, and it's being covered up.'

* * *

James spent a further week in the hospital undergoing physical evaluations, and on the Friday he received notice that he was being discharged. Angela came by to collect him, and as they were packing his things into a duffel bag, the door to the ward opened.

'Ah, Commander. Ms Marie-Stewart,' said Dr Hales as he closed the door behind him. 'I heard the good news that you are to go home today.'

'Yep!' said Angela with a big smile. 'Thank you for all you've done to help him, Doctor.'

'Yeah, thanks, Doc,' James said, shoving the last of his clothes into the bag.

Dr Hales put his hand in his pocket and brought out a business card. He handed it to Angela and said, 'Here is my personal contact number. If there's any change in his condition, please call me directly.'

James looked up. 'What's your interest in my case anyway, Doc?'

Dr Hales smiled at him. 'It's quite simple. I enjoy taking on… exotic… cases, Commander. And none is more intriguing than yours. Remember: any change, call me. Farewell to you both.' And with that, he left the room.

James stared at the closed door with a look of confusion until Angela snapped him out of it by hoisting the bag into his hands.

'What's the matter?'

'"Exotic cases"? I'm not sure what he means by that,' James replied. 'And why is his private hospital willing to fund my treatment?'

'Oh, come on,' Angela groaned. 'He's only trying to help, and he's looked after you for a year already. The funding thing might be because, y'know, you're the bigshot hero astronaut.'

James sighed. 'You're probably right. But I don't feel very much like a hero right now.'

'He's just being a good doctor. Anyway, let's get you home.' She grabbed the other bag, lifted it onto her shoulder and opened the door.

Eventually, after absentmindedly going in the wrong direction around the hospital a couple of times, they arrived in the hospital car park, and at Angela's car. It was an old ice-blue Renault Clio that looked one kick away from failing its MOT. James lifted his holdall into the boot, shut the lid a little too hard and sat in the front passenger seat.

After an hour of driving and fighting through the rush-hour traffic—an experience of life back on Earth that made James sorely miss the *Magnum Opus*—they finally arrived at their home, a small semi-detached house near Chigwell in Essex. James remembered how they had chosen the area based on Angela's familiarity with it. James had visited Angela at her parents' house just around the corner over many years after they left university. It was a quiet neighbourhood, a side street off a side street filled with terraced and semi-detached two-storey homes, many of which had been built in the 1960s. Though they looked similar from the outside, they varied in size on the inside due to how they had been divided up over the years; some remained as houses, while others had been converted into maisonettes and apartments.

Their home was one of the newer builds, smaller than the rest and built on the end of a semi-detached row. Over the years, it had received the usual modifications: a few dividing walls knocked down here and there, and an extension built. The house was set back from the pavement by a diminutive driveway barely big enough for one car, but it was the type of area that had been mercifully forgotten by the borough council's traffic department and so there was plenty of on-street parking.

They pulled up on the drive in front of the bay window to the left of the dark-red front door, which was recessed in an archway with a single step leading up to it.

'Still haven't changed those windows from the last owner then?' remarked James, pointing to the gaudy stained-glass flowers embedded in the segments along the top of the bay window. James remembered back to when they had first bought the place four years ago: one of the first things Angela wanted to do, after removing the partition wall between the two lounge areas to create a larger open-plan living room, was replace those top panes with something plain so it at least didn't look like an eighty year old still lived there. As is usual for these things, they had got the rest of the house in a comfortable condition and Angela had forgotten all about the windows.

'You know what? I thought I'd keep them,' said Angela.

James was speechless and just gawked at her.

'What?' she cried, noticing James's exaggerated look of astonishment. 'They've kinda grown on me.'

After getting out of the car and retrieving James's things, they went inside the house and into the hallway. James stopped and looked at the familiar narrow entrance hall with its cool-grey carpet which ran up the stairs along the right-hand wall. As he moved further in, he removed his shoes and placed them on the old wooden shoe-rack he had bought from a boot sale for his previous home nearly seven years ago. He cast his gaze over the white walls and framed art prints and hand-lettered quotes from famous poets that Angela had acquired from boot sales and craft fairs over the years. He noticed a couple of new ones and wondered whether she had paid over the odds for them like the last few.

As he moved through the doorway to his left, he ran his hand over the smooth doorframe and felt for the little patch of roughness under his fingertips that he had never got around to painting another coat over.

In the living room, much was the same as he remembered it: his games console and HOTAS controller sat on the TV stand, and photos of himself and Angela from their various date nights were arranged on the mantelpiece. He chucked the holdall onto one of the leather sofas, and Angela squeezed past him, as he had remained almost blocking the doorway.

'I'll be right back. Make yourself at home,' she said and walked to the far end of the room and into the extension, disappearing out of sight.

James looked around the room again. His eyes shot to the seam running across the middle of the ceiling where the dividing wall had been, and then over to the utter mess he had made of the coving. He then noticed, over to his left, a short oak sideboard next to the other two-seater sofa.

That wasn't there before… looks nice.

On it, there was an oak photo frame to match with a picture of the two of them inside. James leaned over, picked it up and reminisced. It was a picture from the campus nightclub they'd gone to on the day they first started dating back at university.

At the time, James had been in the second year of his undergraduate degree in physics. He had always, from a very young age, aspired to become an astronaut and go into space, and was interested in the sciences. No one truly believed he would ever stick to it; after all, most kids like to dream big. No one believed, that is, until he started choosing courses. So all his course choices from college onwards had been working towards that goal. In order to continue on this path, he'd chosen the combined four-year master's course that the university was offering.

About halfway through the second year, one of his housemates—his best friend at the time—became heavily interested in table-top role-playing games and joined the campus TRPG society. After much protesting from James, his friend had managed to drag him along to a game, and that was when he first met Angela, who was in the third year of her English literature degree course. She was sitting across the table, in full costume as her character, wearing black robes and black horns on her head that stood out against her striking flame-red hair. James laughed as he remembered how ridiculous he'd thought she looked at the time. But after a few games, he found himself getting into it too, and it certainly helped that he and Angela got on like a house on fire. After a few months of hanging out together and getting to know one another, they decided to start dating; well, she told him that they were going to go out that evening to the campus nightclub as their first date, and he didn't disagree as he had already fallen madly in love with her.

James smiled and put the photo back down on the sideboard, and he heard a rustling from the other end of the room as Angela came around the corner, followed by an excitable little lemon-and-white beagle puppy. The dog came bounding up to James and starting bouncing up and down at his knees, wagging his tail furiously. At first James recoiled in surprise, but then he bent down to stroke the puppy and let him lick his face.

'Aw, Ange! Where'd this widdle guy come from?' asked James, completely enamoured.

Angela laughed. 'His name is Sputnik. I got him about six months ago while you were in the hospital. I was getting pretty lonely, y'know? And I thought, since we both love dogs… and he's *wonderful*! He's really been helping to take my mind off things. I think he'll be a big help to you too.'

'I can imagine. He looks like he's a bit of a handful— *aren't you, Sputnik? Yes, you are, good boy.*'

CHAPTER TWELVE
CONSEQUENCES
Friday 9th October 2026

SPUTNIK WATCHED ON HOPEFULLY from the sidelines as James and Angela tucked into their evening meal while relaxing on the sofa with the television on. The rest of the day had gone by in relative silence, with James making a fuss of the puppy for the most part while Angela caught up on some work emails. She had taken some time off during the week just in case James needed to be brought home from the hospital early, but she was still expected to keep an eye on what was going on at her office.

For James, the peace and quiet of a familiar setting put his mind at ease, and the time spent playing with Sputnik gave him space to process the ordeal. By the time Angela had finished dealing with her work business, it was dinnertime, and so the two of them cooked together, just as they used to before James left on the Mars mission.

As they sat on the sofa eating their food, the news came on the TV, moving into a segment with various religious leaders giving their thoughts on the impact of the Martian discovery.

'I can turn it off, if you like?' said Angela, looking over at James with a worried expression.

'No,' said James through a mouthful of food, shaking his head. He swallowed and glanced at Angela. 'No, I need to know what's been going on here the last couple of years. I've missed so much.'

'You of all people are interested in what the Church has to say about it all?'

James scoffed, 'We discovered *aliens*, Ange. Definitive proof we're not alone in the universe. It raises profound philosophical questions.' He took another mouthful and continued, 'And besides, I know it's been a while since I've been to church, but... y'know.'

'Deep down, part of you still believes...' said Angela, nodding as she cut a bit off her meat.

The Roman Catholic priest on the television leaned forwards and smiled, looking at the newscaster. He was bald and clean-shaven, and was wearing a white clerical collar and black shirt. An older diocesan bishop, he appeared to carry himself with solemnity, but when he spoke his voice was kindly.

'Well, the Catholic Church and I are in agreement with our Anglican counterparts,' he said, nodding towards the Anglican bishop of London. 'While the revelations of the last couple of years are certainly incredible and give us much to think about, the central tenets and doctrines of our common faith are not upended by them.

'We recognise that we have a solemn pastoral duty to work through these things with our congregations, some of whom may feel a challenge to their personal convictions in all this. But as a policy, the Vatican has considered the possibility of a First Contact situation for quite some time, and we feel we are well prepared.'

Wow, they're taking it a lot better than I expected.

'And how do you feel about the protests in America?' asked the host. 'We have heard just today that many of the more fundamentalist congregations in the Bible Belt have been continuing to turn out in force to oppose the next Mars mission.'

'I understand their fears but do not share in them, "For God hath not given us the spirit of fear: but of power, and of love, and of sobriety." And the Catholic Church in general supports the efforts for the return mission. It is important to do more research into these beings so we may further our understanding of our place in creation.'

'Thank you, Bishop Thomas,' said the host. 'Bishop Peter, have you any more to say on the subject?'

The Anglican bishop looked thoughtful for a few moments and then half-laughed and said, 'If these extraterrestrials came here to Earth, I'm sure many of the churches in our diocese would rush to invite them to bring-and-share lunches. It's a shame they're all the way over on Mars, really.'

James stifled a laugh, nearly spitting out his mouthful of food. He swallowed and regained his composure, and said, 'I can't imagine one of those *things* taking up the offer.'

Angela put her cutlery down and looked at James. 'What were they like?' she asked cautiously.

James sighed. 'Big. Scary. Nightmare fuel. They wear these huge nanotech suits of armour that have retractable swords…' His voice trailed off and he went silent, staring into the middle distance, his eyes starting to water. 'That's how they got her. That's… how she died. In abject terror. I couldn't save her.'

Angela picked up her tray and placed it on the floor, then scooted over and held James in her arms.

'I'm okay,' he said after a few seconds. 'It still feels raw, y'know. Like I'm still there sometimes.'

'I understand,' said Angela, sitting back on her side of the sofa and looking down at her dinner, which was being eaten by Sputnik. 'Oh, you naughty dog! No! Get away.' She batted the puppy away from the plate, then picked him up and took him out into the back room.

A few moments later she returned to the sofa, having closed the back room door behind her, and looked at James. 'We don't have to talk about it if you don't want to.'

James smiled. 'Thanks, love, but no. I think I need this. You've already given me some of the broad strokes, but what's it *really* been like since the broadcast?'

Angela nodded and said, 'Okay then, if you're sure... Well, it's been difficult to get to work, for one thing. People are so scared. They said on the TV about the protests in America, but we've had them here too. Almost daily outside Parliament. Guy Furious is riling people up all over the world. Hundreds of thousands of people lining the streets and blocking roads. There were a few riots too, one of which I had to walk past just to get to the next Tube station.

'Then, a couple of weeks ago, some nutter in one of those sandwich boards actually grabbed me and started yelling in my face about the world ending or some shit. Thankfully, some of my train buddies were nearby. They saw what was happening and dragged him off me. Turned around and came straight home after that.'

James's eyes widened and he rubbed his face. 'I am so sorry, Ange, I had no idea. Were you okay?'

'A bit shaken, but fine. I've not seen him again, but I

was wary for the first few days afterwards.' Angela sighed. 'It just seems that for every few of us who are trying to be level-headed about the whole thing, there's someone flying into a panic. It doesn't help that there's been something in the news about it daily over the last two years.'

'What about your family, how are they doing? And my mum, have you seen her at all?'

'Our families are *fine*. My dad doesn't believe it at all and none of the rest of them are interested. I went to see your mum the other day, actually, after I visited you in the hospital. She knows you're awake and she's relieved. Said we could go see her next weekend, if that's alright with you?'

James nodded. 'Yeah, that sounds like a great idea. Hey, have the ESA been in contact with you at all?'

'No, not since before, when I was told their stupid cave-in story. They're probably just swamped with the prep for the next mission on the *Magnum Opus*.'

'They want to go *again*?' said James. 'After what happened to us over there, I'd have thought they'd be decommissioning the *Magnum*! Those aliens we saw? There were hundreds of them, all in stasis. I saw what just one of them could do. But a whole army? No way.'

'It's true! Your discoveries have prompted a proper space race. All the agencies are vying to go back and set up something permanent over there. Even Japan and India are getting involved, and that's not even counting the commercial organisations.'

James tensed up and frowned. 'I bet some of them just want the weapons. Bloody great particle cannons on that ship. Will do a lot of damage if the wrong people get hold of them.'

'Yeah, I've seen the pictures. They absolutely blew up

the socials; it was like back when we saw the pictures of Pluto for the first time.'

'Except,' said James, 'no one was supposed to see *these* pictures. I'm guessing it was Guy Furious again?'

Angela laughed and shook her head. 'Well, he shared them around a lot, but he didn't leak them. It was some smaller conspiracy channel in… Ah, damn, I can't remember where he was from now. Never mind… Anyway, he got hold of them first.' Her voice dropped and became sullen. 'Poor idiot turned up dead a week later. Supposedly had a car accident.'

James grimaced and looked back at the TV. The news had changed and was displaying aerial views of crowds of fundamentalists in the US carrying placards equating the aliens with demonic forces.

Demons? They're not far off.

He cleared his throat and tapped Angela on the arm. 'Well, what about you? How have you been coping with the news?'

She looked down at her lap and played with her hands for a short while, then shifted in her seat to face James. 'I…' she started. 'I'm not scared. I mean, I was at first. It was a big shock, finding out we're not alone and there are actual space-travelling civilisations out there. It kinda made me feel really small.'

James nodded. 'A few of us went through something similar on the *Magnum* when we saw the ship.'

'But after I thought about it for a bit, it seemed more exciting, if that makes sense? The possibilities! The things we could learn from them and… Then I heard you were injured, and it was like my world suddenly crumbled around me.'

'I'm sorry, Ange,' said James.

She shook her head. 'Never mind that. It's not your fault.

But I was very grateful for Jenny, Harriet and Mum. They were really supportive. I think I must have slept in their beds more than I did my own!' She paused, staring at the television, and her eyes lit up. 'Oh! I also got back into writing poetry.'

'Wow, you haven't done that in a while,' James said. 'That's great. Did it help?'

'Immensely. Really helped take my mind off things. I even got some of them published. I must have submitted to hundreds of anthologies, but five got accepted!'

'Oh, that's amazing,' James cried, a huge smile spreading across his face.

'Well, I didn't set out to publish them at first—you know how I got the last time I was writing. But yeah, I'm well chuffed.'

'And I'm happy for you,' said James, reaching out and squeezing her hand.

'Anyway,' said Angela, her tone softening. 'Now that you're awake and home, I'm starting to wonder about these aliens again. Who were they? Why were they even here? What was the other object that flew away?'

'To tell you the truth, Ange, we didn't really find out anything to answer those questions. The answers are probably in the logs on the ship, but we were more concerned with finding a way out at the time. I have to wonder if anything came back with us at all...'

CHAPTER THIRTEEN
ADJUSTMENT

THAT NIGHT, JAMES'S SLEEP WAS RESTLESS as he continued to relive the events of the Mars mission, but
now his brain kept putting a different spin on it,
giving him options that were never truly there and making
him feel even worse for not having taken them. In one
twisted scenario, there was more time before the chamber
doors closed, so if he had just been faster, he could have
dived for his weapon. In another, the alien's arm swung in
slow motion, and if he had been paying attention, he surely
could have dodged it. In a third, there was a small gap in
the chamber doors and he could have prised them open with
one of his belt tools, if only he had noticed it. But in all, the
outcome was the same: Yula still died.

All the tossing and turning, grunting and sleep-talking
woke Angela several times during the night. And though
she said she understood, through James's bleary apologies,
he knew she was very grateful it was a Friday night and she

didn't have to get up for work in the morning.

James woke at six a.m. sharp and went downstairs to the kitchen to grab breakfast, allowing Angela to have a more restful lie-in. He sat at the oak dining table in the kitchen holding his pounding head and eating a simple bowl of honey granola and cold milk. It felt good to finally be able to wake up in his own house and eat some real food, and not the freeze-dried rations or energy bars from the mission.

Oh God, then there's the hospital food...

The bland, lukewarm food he'd been served in the hospital was just as bad as the rations. He'd enjoyed cooking with Angela last night but his stomach hadn't truly felt like it was at home until now.

There was the pitter-patter of tiny paws on the kitchen tiles behind James, and he turned just as Sputnik jumped up at his chair, whimpering and whining.

'You hungry, boy?' James grunted. He stroked the dog, got up from his chair and went rummaging through the numerous kitchen cupboards to find the dog food.

'Second cupboard to the right,' came a bleary voice behind James. He closed the under-sink cupboard, shuffled two to the right and located a big bag of dry dog food.

'Cheers, love.'

He looked over at Angela shuffling through the kitchen doorway. Her normally wavy hair was all over the place like she had been dragged through a hedge backwards, and she was still wearing the long white t-shirt sporting a line drawing of a twelve-sided dice that she had slept in. James stopped and admired her as she raised her arms and arched her back, leaning against the doorframe. She yawned and stretched, and the hem of the t-shirt rose up her bare thighs. She was radiant.

170

James then picked up the bag of dog food and tipped some into Sputnik's bowl. The excitable puppy gobbled it impatiently.

Angela scratched her head, blinked and said, 'I've got some errands to run today. You alright looking after Sputnik?'

'Would be my pleasure,' he replied, scooping up his breakfast bowl and taking it over to the sink. 'Anything I can help with?'

'Nah, just a bit of shopping really. Hey, I've got the guys coming over for our weekly game night this evening, and I was just gonna go pick up a new game to try out. You want to join us?' she asked.

'Hmmm, it's been a while… maybe. I do love a good campaign. Who's coming?'

'Ah, the usual suspects,' she said and began to count out on her fingers. 'Let's see. There's Jenny, Max, Adrian, Spider and… oh, Winston.'

'Good old Officer Winston. Wait…' He paused. 'Who on earth is "Spider"? New person?'

Angela laughed. 'No, no, no, that's Harriet's new nickname. Her other mates started calling her it about a year ago because she went shopping with them for an outfit for a weekend away but bought nothing except four pairs of jeans. We thought it was completely ridiculous, so naturally we started calling her it as well. Anyway, I'm going for a shower and heading out. Love you.'

'You too, Ange.'

She walked over, pecked James on the cheek as he was washing up his bowl and departed for the stairs.

Later that evening, after Angela had set up the table at the far end of the living room with plenty of chairs, there was a knock at the door. She motioned for James to answer it and he obliged. A petite woman with short, light-brown curly hair and thick-rimmed glasses stood on the step. When she saw who had answered the door, her striking hazel eyes lit up, her expression loosened and her mouth opened in a wide, surprised grin.

'James!' she screeched, throwing her arms up and rushing in for a hug. 'I had no idea you were out of the hospital already!' She pulled away and patted his arms. 'It's so good to see you back on your feet and on good ol' terra firma.'

He laughed, taken aback by the sudden burst of affection. 'Hi, Harriet. Or... should I say "Spider" now?' he said as she stepped over the threshold.

Spider went silent and looked past him, glaring daggers at Angela, who had come to see what all the noise was about.

'I can't believe you told him that already!' Spider pointed her finger at Angela and waggled it around. 'Bad Angie. Urgh, I am *never* going to live that down!'

She took off her leather jacket and handed it to James. Moments after she had walked through into the living room and been offered a drink by Angela, there was another knock at the door. Amused by the exchange that had just happened, and still holding Spider's jacket, James turned back to welcome the next guest at the door. As he opened it once again, he was greeted by another familiar sight. A tall man in an airman's jacket stood before him, sporting fashionable stubble on his square jaw. He saw James and, just like Spider, his face erupted into a huge smile.

'Lieutenant Fowler... or is it Commander? I'm losing track. You are a sight for sore eyes. Do I need to call you "sir" now?'

James shook his hand and replied with a playful smile,

'You've always had to call me "sir", *Officer* Winston.'

'Hey, hey, hey, you are looking at *Squadron Leader* Archibald Winston, thank you very much… sir.'

James laughed. 'Some senile old git finally promoted you then, eh?'

'Yeah, and *twice* no less!' Winston announced, puffing his chest out with pride.

'Well, come on in, Squadron Leader Winston. Here, I'll hang your coat up,' said James, welcoming in his old friend past the threshold.

It wasn't long before Jenny, Max and Adrian arrived. James didn't know them quite as well. He knew Jenny and Adrian were old friends of Angela's from university and he had met them on a number of occasions, but he'd never really got to know them. As for Max, James had never even heard of him. Angela had told him that he was one of the conveyancing solicitors in the large firm she worked in as a receptionist. He was fairly stumpy and balding, somewhat reminiscent of Danny DeVito.

He also seemed, to James, to not be the full ticket, as, star-struck, he proclaimed to Angela, 'I didn't realise your boyfriend was *the* James Fowler! Wow, I'm actually meeting a real astronaut.' And then, turning to James, he said, 'Can I have your autograph? You're a hero.'

James obliged, signing a small book Max pulled from his jacket pocket, but he didn't feel very heroic. A moment later, Angela dragged him aside into the kitchen.

'You wouldn't believe how many times I've told him who you are and he's *never* believed me. He's a few pints short of a round, to be honest. I wouldn't have kept inviting him to play, but he happens to be an excellent dungeon master,' she explained.

173

'Some stroke of luck,' James commiserated. 'Is he doing it tonight?'

'Hell no. That's me.'

'Hey, what're we playing anyway?'

'Oh, did I not say? It's a game I thought you'd like. It's a sci-fi RPG about being a spaceship commander in a cut-throat galaxy, doing trading, bounty hunting and all kinds of other things.'

'Hmm, sounds good; like a game I used to play with my dad on his old Spectrum.'

It was around half past nine, they were more than halfway through the game and everyone was having a great time. All of them had really got into their characters and Angela seemed to be thoroughly enjoying her session as games master. Some, like Spider and Adrian, had been a little too heavy-handed with their drinks and were feeling the effects, which had made the game take a humorous turn.

Ange was right, this game is great; and it feels so good to be able to relax with friends.

James leaned back in his chair. It was getting very late, but he didn't want the evening's entertainment to end. However, any semblance of staying in character had long since ended.

Winston was busy trying to tell anyone who'd listen about the time that James nearly crashed his aircraft while on manoeuvres as a pilot in the RAF. It was a story he had told many times already, but in some kind of celebration for James's return, he thought it was worth sharing once again, much to everyone's chagrin.

'... And then there's the tower control yelling down the mic for him to pull up. Commodore's gone red in the face, spitting all over the desk, vowing that if ol' Jimmy lives, he's gonna kill him!'

'We *know*, Winnie,' cried Spider, sloshing her drink around, spilling some on the tablecloth.

Max was sitting quietly, flicking through one of the hefty rulebooks, admiring the artwork, lore and details. He stopped, cleared his throat and spoke up in a raised voice: 'Hey! It says there's aliens in this game too. That's so cool!'

Angela grabbed the rulebook from him and put it back with the rest of the stack near her. 'No meta-gaming, please,' she said, chastising Max. 'Stay in character, everyone!' she called.

'I'm just saying, if we get to meet some aliens, I'll be glad we've got Commander Fowler here,' Max said, holding up his hands.

James's eyes shot up from his character sheet and glared at Max. 'What exactly do you mean by that?' he growled.

'Well, you know…' Max replied, laughing.

'No. I don't. Enlighten me.'

Max's smile faded as he saw James's livid expression. The room fell silent as the others stopped talking, and their eyes flitted between the two men.

'Well, umm…' Max started. He looked, dumbstruck, at James for a few moments, before his expression morphed into an ugly smirk and he said, with a scoff, 'You were on that alien spaceship. Bet there were loads of 'em in there. So you'd be able to save us all if we got attacked.'

The memory of the attack flashed into James's mind, and he could feel intense anger rising from the pit of his stomach.

You little prick. You have no idea. Maybe I should show you what really happ—

James suddenly caught himself, and rage was replaced by shame. He knew he had overreacted; Max really did have no idea. He, along with the rest of the world, thought

175

James had been in an accident. He placed his drink down, cleared his throat and stood up to address the group around the table.

'Sorry, everyone, it's been a fun evening, but I really need to get to bed. Please excuse me,' he said.

Angela looked at him with a concerned expression and mouthed, 'Are you okay?'

James simply nodded in response and motioned for her to continue with the game. Perplexed, everyone watched him in silence as he left the room and closed the door behind him. He started making his way up the stairs, but then stopped a few steps up and heard Max ask whether he had said something wrong.

Angela dismissed the concerns and told them that James was still feeling the aftereffects of the coma. He appreciated her diffusing the situation and trying to get everyone back into the game. After all, the last thing he wanted was to put a downer on their evening. It wasn't long before the group returned to their raucous laughter and merriment, and James nodded to himself, satisfied that they probably wouldn't remember his near-meltdown in the morning. He sighed, shook his head and continued ascending the stairs.

Maybe counselling isn't such a bad idea after all.

James woke with a start and rolled over, stretching his arm out and grabbing his phone from the bedside table. He fumbled it in his hands and recoiled as the dazzling light of the screen shone into his eyes—brighter, he thought, than a thousand suns. Once his eyes had recovered from their momentary blindness and adjusted to the light level (or was that just the phone's auto-brightness sensor picking up the ambient light of the room and kicking in?), he saw that it was eight in the morning. He frowned; it was still pitch black in the room. Putting the phone back down, he shuffled up on the bed and turned around to open the curtains behind him. Thick, dark clouds covered the sky, enveloping the street in deep shadow. He saw the light spattering of raindrops on the window and heard a low rumble off in the distance.

Great, thunderstorm's starting. They said it would be sunny today.

James looked down at the pillow beside his. The outside light, now filtering into the room through the break in the curtains, was enough for him to see that Angela's side of the bed was vacant. He wondered where she had got to for a moment, but his residual tiredness from yet another night of restless sleep overwhelmed him and he snuggled back down under the covers and snoozed.

A few minutes later, he heard the bedroom door open, and the darkness of his eyelids lit up with the light spillage from the landing. He opened one bleary eye and saw Angela walk into the room, stark naked and drying her hair with a towel. He smiled and weighed up whether he should muster the energy to say good morning or simply go back to snoozing.

Just as he had decided on the latter and closed his eye, Angela put the towel down on the bed, put her hands on her hips and said, 'I know you're awake. Talk to me about last night. What happened?'

James grumbled and rubbed the sleep from his eyes. He looked up at her; despite the nudity, her interrogatory stance was powerful and intimidating.

'I don't know what happened. Something Max said made me really angry. I nearly launched across the table at him.'

'Yeah, I saw you tense up. Do we need to speak to the doctor again?' she replied as she reached down and pulled some underwear from the under-bed drawer.

'No. But he gave me a card for a counsellor and I was thinking of giving him a ring today.'

'On a Sunday?' Angela laughed as she continued to get dressed. 'Good luck with that.'

James shrugged. 'Back of the card says he's available all week.'

'Better phone him soon as then,' she said as she looked between two of her t-shirts. She turned to James with them both held up and said, 'I'm meeting Spider for lunch this afternoon. Which one should I wear? Custom D&D guild or Byron quote?'

A couple of hours later, after James had got dressed, eaten breakfast and taken Sputnik for a walk around the block, he stood in the kitchen holding the flimsy card, turning it over in his fingers. In his other hand, he held his phone, with the dialler app open and his thumb poised over the first number. He was looking towards the screen but not at it; instead, his eyes were unfocused as he considered what he had to do.

Am I overreacting? Sure, I've had some nightmares and I'm not sleeping well, but… can I get a handle on this by myself? But what if I get angry again and don't catch it… what if I snap at Angela?

The final thought strengthened his resolve and he focused on the phone screen, tapping in the number and pressing the call button. He lifted the phone to his ear and waited.

'Good morning, Dr Volpe's office, how may I help you?' came a youthful male voice.

'Hello. I would like to book a counselling session, please?'

'Do you have a referral?'

'No… I don't. But Dr Joshua Hales gave me this number.

My name is—'

'Ah, Commander James Fowler?'

'Y-yes…'

'Excellent, yes, I have your referral right here on our system. It seems the doctor submitted it on Friday. Dr Volpe has a slot available today if you would like it?'

'Great! What time?'

'This afternoon, half past two.'

'Wow. Thank you. Truth be told I wasn't expecting to get an appointment so soon.'

'That's no problem, Commander. You have a great day and we'll see you later. My name is Stephen and I'm the receptionist here. When you arrive, come straight through to the desk on the right and I'll let Dr Volpe know you're here.'

And with that, before James could say goodbye, the call ended. He took the phone away from his ear and looked at it as the screen went dark, then put it back in his pocket.

Lucky.

James arrived at the address on Dr Volpe's business card around ten minutes early for his appointment. From the outside, it looked as though it used to be a GP's surgery or dental practice. It was a small white building, all on a single level, with a window to the waiting room to the left and blinds drawn on the window to the right—probably the admin office, James reasoned.

He walked through the main entrance and stopped in a short corridor. It extended a little way ahead, with a number of closed doors between him and the corner. Before the bend was the entrance to the waiting room and he could just see the edge of a plastic chair through the opening. Everything smelled clinical and that, coupled with the slight greenish tint of the fluorescent lighting, reminded James of his old family GP's practice back in the East End that his parents had brought him to as a child.

He walked over to the closed-in reception desk, which was behind toughened glass, and tapped the bell on the countertop. He peered into the office area as best he could, squishing his face up against the glass, and could just about see a man rise from a desk. Moments later, he appeared through a narrow doorway and sat down at the reception desk. He was tall and dressed smartly in a blue collared shirt, and he had a thin face and shaved brown hair. The man looked to be in his early twenties and he had the scars from teenage acne on his cheeks.

'How may I help you?' he said.

As he spoke, James recognised his voice from the phone call and he replied, 'Are you Stephen? We spoke this morning. I'm Commander Fowler.'

Stephen's face lit up in recognition. 'Ah, yes. I'll go get Dr Volpe. Please bear with me one moment,' he said, backing up from his chair. He then exited the reception desk area into the corridor and disappeared around the corner.

Not more than a couple of minutes later, Stephen returned, leading a sweaty, portly gentleman with a light-brown neckbeard and walrus moustache. He wore white thick-rimmed glasses, the arms of which sat awkwardly on his scruffy tawny and blonde-highlighted hair. His shirt, light-blue plaid flannel, had a variety of coloured ink stains underneath the breast pocket.

The moment he saw James, he came towards him, beaming and with his hand outstretched. 'Ah! The great Commander Fowler. I watched all of the mission broadcasts on the television, although I thought you would be taller, yes?' he said with the remnants of an Italian accent. 'I am Dr Volpe, but *you* may call me "Tony".' He gripped James's hand with both of his sweaty palms and shook his arm so hard it felt like he was going to rip it off.

James looked around and saw that Stephen had retreated without another word back into the reception area, leaving him alone with Tony. 'Err, it's nice to meet you... Tony.'

'Yes, yes. Come. We shall just be having an introductory session today, eh? Please, through here,' Tony said, gesturing to a door in the corner of the corridor, just past the reception desk. He walked over, opened the door and stood aside to allow James to go through first. Once James had stepped through, Tony closed it behind him and lowered himself with effort into his office chair. He motioned for James to sit on a comfortable armchair in the middle of the room, and he obliged.

While Tony searched through some documents on his desk, James took a moment to look around him. The room was small but bright, and the style of furniture as well as the small houseplants dotted around made it feel quite homely. Like he had stepped from a doctor's surgery into a living room. He relaxed into the softness of the armchair and put his hands together, interlinking his fingers.

After a few moments, Tony whipped around in his chair and deposited a full manila folder onto the small coffee table between them. He then sat back and interlinked his own fingers under his moustache, resting his elbows on the arms of the chair.

He examined James for a couple of seconds and then said, 'So, Commander Fowler, what brings you here today?'

'Umm... hold on. What are those?' asked James in return, pointing at the papers on the table.

'Those? Oh, just your medical records. Dr Hales forwarded

them to me. He felt it pertinent information, as the history of your case is… unusual.'

'Right…' said James, leaning forwards and staring at the table.

A few seconds passed in silence before Tony cleared his throat and asked James again what had brought him to his practice.

James sighed and launched into explaining about his trouble sleeping, the nightmares and his concerns about his temper since waking from the coma. He was unsure how much to share about his memories of the incident, unsure whether Dr Volpe would dismiss his account of it as a hallucination like Hales had, so he decided to withhold that for a later session, once he had a better feel for Tony.

The therapist looked at James intently, listening and making the occasional note on a pad of paper. He asked a couple of questions to clarify James's symptoms and asked generally how the nightmares made him feel. However, he didn't press any issue that James felt uncomfortable with, and only touched on the topic of his relationship with his parents.

After James had finished talking, Tony made his best attempt to summarise what he had said, and explained that due to the nature of his trauma—at this point, still referring to the event as a cave-in, with no push-back from James— he felt it best to proceed with treatment using a long-term psychodynamic approach.

'Do you have any specific goals in mind?' Tony asked after he had finished explaining his methodology.

'Well, I guess I'd like to stop having the nightmares and flashes. That'd be nice. And to have a decent night's sleep. I mean, I know I had a year and a half of sleep, but somehow that wasn't enough,' James joked.

Tony gave a small laugh. 'I understand. Well, I am confident that this approach will help immensely with that. I believe that brings us to the end of our session today. If you are happy to continue, I can schedule you in for the same time on a weekly basis?'

'Yes, thank you. Are... there any forms for me to fill out?'

'No, no, that has all been taken care of already.' James looked at Tony inquisitively and he continued, 'It's quite alright, Commander. Nothing out of the ordinary. I will see you next week.' And he gestured to the door.

James thanked him once again and left the practice, heading for home.

CHAPTER FOURTEEN
THE VISIT

Sunday 6th December 2026

A COUPLE OF MONTHS HAD PASSED since James had started attending counselling following the incident on that games evening. He had refrained from attending another games night with the group, much to Spider and Winston's dismay, and since that evening the group's taste for that particular RPG had waned and they'd returned to D&D.

James's sessions with Tony were proving fruitful, although he found the trips back and forth on public transport a chore. Both he and the counsellor felt his progress was good, and he was beginning to come to terms with the incident. Having adopted some coping strategies, he found he was also starting to have fewer nightmares and was feeling much more in control of his emotional state. James had always been a keenly self-aware individual, but even he was surprised at how okay he was feeling. Maybe it was the unthreatening and serene atmosphere of the counselling room which allowed him to open up about his experiences more easily—not that being open had ever really been a problem for him; or maybe it was because Tony hadn't immediately invalidated James's memories when he felt comfortable enough to bring them up. Either way, he was beginning to feel a semblance of normality return to his life.

As he sat on the cramped, loud bus on the way back from that day's session, his mind was weighed down by a curiosity. In the months since his awakening, he had not heard from anyone at the ESA about his job, save for confirming his long-term sick leave; they hadn't checked to see how he was, or even debrief him. At first he felt perhaps they were giving him space to recover, or—after a few weeks—that maybe there were other priorities. But it had now been a lot longer than James felt was reasonable, after all, they were still paying him, and he made up his mind to get in contact with their HR department as soon as he got home.

Only two more stops, he consoled himself as the bus jolted and he was jostled by the person sitting next to him. He looked out of the scratched, fogged window and tried to ignore the stale smell emanating from his portly neighbour's tattered jacket. It was bitterly cold outside, but all the people packed onto the bus created an unpleasant, warm miasma that made it difficult to breathe in spite of the occasional blast of ice-cold air when the bus doors opened.

It wasn't too long before it was time for him to ring the bell for his stop, and as the bus pulled up and once again jostled everyone inside, James squeezed his way past his odorous bus buddy and negotiated his way through the crowd to the open double doors, muttering the occasional 'Excuse me' and 'Sorry' in the proper British manner. He got off the bus and received a face full of the biting December wind. Shivering, he pulled his black, puffy down coat tighter around his neck and wished he had had the good sense to take it off on the bus as his mother's words from his childhood echoed through his mind: *You won't feel the benefit.*

After arriving home and getting safely inside, he had barely put his things down and hung up his coat on the hook in the entrance hall when there was a loud knock at the door behind him, making him jump out of his skin.

A visitor? Can't be for Ange. She's at work.

He reached out and opened the door.

'James! You sonuvabitch!' cried Captain Austin Queen in his characteristic southern drawl. He threw his arms wide open, launched forwards and grabbed James in a rib-crushing hug. James groaned as all the air was forced out of his chest. Austin slapped him on the back, pulled away and looked him over.

'You are some tough-as-nails, cast-iron, rock-hard bastard, you know that?' he said with a massive grin on his face. He stepped through the doorway, almost pushing James aside, walked through into the living room and slumped down onto one of the sofas, putting his satchel next to the chair. 'So this is where you're livin', huh?' he asked as he looked around the room.

'Captain,' replied James, catching his breath. 'It's good to see you. To what do I owe this visit?'

'Ah, I've been meaning to come by for a while now,' replied Austin with a hint of regret in his voice. 'Ever since I found out you woke up from your coma. But work hasn't really let up at all since we got back from the *Magnum*.'

James sat on the arm of the adjacent sofa. 'You are a sight for sore eyes, my friend. I'm sorry I didn't get in touch sooner. I've been so busy getting re-adjusted that I didn't think to, and I've not had any contact from anyone about

187

the mission since I left the hospital.'

'Well, you must have plenty of questions then. I'm happy to catch you up on what's been going down this past couple of years.'

'Fancy a drink? I've got beers.'

Austin nodded and James got up to get them both a couple of bottles from the fridge. He grabbed the bottle-opener magnet from the fridge door and opened the caps, which popped off with a hiss. He went back into the living room and handed one to the captain before sitting down, this time on the cushion of the adjacent sofa. Austin took a swig from his bottle, leaning forwards, his elbows resting on his knees.

'So, this yours and Angie's place then?' he asked, taking another swig.

'Yeah, it is. How did you find our address?'

'I got my sources…' He saw James's concerned look and laughed. 'Just kidding. I asked around, said I wanted to pay you a visit, and the ESA happily provided details of where you were staying.'

'Ah, so they haven't totally forgotten about me then,' James said bitterly and took a swig from his own drink.

'Feels that way, huh?' Austin nodded.

There were a few seconds of awkward silence between them as they drank some more and stared into the middle distance.

James broke the silence with a question. 'So… what happened? Y'know, *after*? First thing I was told when I woke up was that I was in a cave-in, but I know that's not true. I remember everything.'

Austin juggled his bottle from one hand to the other for a bit, thinking, then set the bottle down on the sideboard to his left.

He looked directly at James, sighed and said, 'Alright…

Well, a cave-in is the official line. But you and I know better. As for what happened, Grant and I arrived on your deck and found the armoury. We grabbed some weapons and rushed through as quickly as we could to the medical bay. When we got there, we saw Yula on the floor and you floating unconscious in the chamber. The alien was just casually leaning up against a bed, treating its shoulder wound.'

'That was Yula's doing,'

Austin snorted, 'Well, we didn't even think about it. Just opened fire with everything we had. Laid it all into the bastard. Practically blew it to pieces.' He picked his drink back up again and took a swig, then stared at the bottle.

'And... Yula?' James asked, his eyes becoming red and watery.

'Yeah, she was gone, man,' Austin replied without looking up from the bottle. 'You, on the other hand... At first we thought you were dead too, but we quickly realised the chamber was keeping you alive. Eventually, we found a way to empty out the liquid, open it up and pull all the needles out of you, but—'

'I was comatose,' interjected James.

Austin just nodded a little before leaning all the way back and resting his head on the back of the sofa, letting out a groan. The clouds outside had broken and winter sunlight streamed through the bay window behind the sofa, falling on Austin's face and lighting up the thousands of tiny dust particles floating in the air. He sat back up and looked at James with sadness in his eyes.

'Anyway, that's when I scrubbed the mission, and when Grant snapped.'

'What do you mean?'

'Man, he went crazy. Seeing Yula totally broke him; did

you know he had a thing for her? Anyway, we were just about to take you both back to the habitat when he ran out of the medical bay. I tried to raise him on comms, but he just ignored me. So I had to leave you on the floor and run after him.

'By the time I found him in one of the other labs, he was sitting at a console laughing like a maniac. By this point he knew enough about the ship's systems to do whatever he wanted, so he shut off the power to all the stasis pods. Killed them all.

'He was… well, I don't know what he was. But after a while, I got him to come back to the medical bay and help. We carried you both out of the ship and took you back to the habitat. We had to wait a while for the *Magnum* to be back in communications range, but we eventually got you back up there.'

'So the mission was a failure?' asked James. The success of the mission was the least of his concerns, but all the same, to imagine that it had all been in vain, that nothing good would come out of Yula's sacrifice, would have been too much to bear. And Grant, well, he couldn't think less of him for taking vengeance; James recalled the raging fury he'd felt when he saw Yula die and thought that he would probably have done something equally as vindictive had he not gone under.

'Nah, not completely. Grant and I still managed to procure plenty of data, digital schematics and technology samples to bring back with us—including the rifles. But…'

'It wasn't worth the cost,' said James, finishing Austin's thought.

'*Nothing* makes what happened worthwhile. I don't care what anybody says.' Austin downed the rest of his beer and set the bottle back down on the sideboard. 'What about you,

James? How're you holding up?' he asked, hoping to have a more positive conversation.

James replied, 'Yeah, not too bad, I guess.'

Austin frowned and his tone became interrogatory. 'Don't you be glib with me now; this ain't a damn tea party. Let's have some real talk.'

Taken aback by Austin's directness, James stared for a few moments, processing what his friend had said. He decided that there was no point being insincere with Austin; there was no way to avoid talking about his experience.

'Better,' he replied, nodding and exhaling. 'Waking up in the hospital was a shock to be honest. Last thing I remember is that alien bastard turning the chamber on after it killed Yula. I've been glad of the counselling. I'd been having nightmares and anxiety attacks almost every evening before I started going. It's helped a lot; in fact, I'd only just got in from a session when you knocked.'

Austin listened quietly as James continued, 'I'm still struggling with the guilt, though. I feel so responsible, y'know? I made a promise to Yula that we'd both get out alive. Counsellor calls it "survivor's guilt", but putting a name to it hasn't really helped any.'

The captain interjected with an incredulous laugh. 'It's *far* from your fault, bro. Doesn't do you any good to hold on to that stuff. And you know full well Yula was a stone-cold badass; she didn't need you, or any of us, to keep her safe.'

That's true. She tried to rescue me.

'I just can't help feeling if I hadn't been so hopeless, she'd still be alive. She only died because she was trying to lure that monster away from me while I was trapped in that stupid tube.'

'You can't afford to think like that. She did what any one of

191

us would have done without hesitation. And you know what?' said Austin with a kind of smug poignancy. 'You're not doing her act of heroism justice by trying to take responsibility.' He reached across and patted James roughly on the shoulder. 'But I'm glad you're doing better, my man.'

'You've rehearsed this, haven't you?' James said with a small laugh.

Austin nodded solemnly. 'Every day for two years,' he admitted, his uneasy tone betraying a lingering guilt.

James finished his drink and got up from the sofa. Austin picked up his empty bottle and followed James into the kitchen.

'Okay, so what about Zhu and Grant? What are they up to these days?' asked James as he took the bottle from Austin and placed it along with his inside a squat plastic bucket underneath the kitchen worktop.

'These days?' Austin laughed bitterly. 'I guess you haven't seen the news then… Probably best you hear it from me first. That's actually why I'm here now. Pretty much straight after we got back, Grant quit.'

'He quit?' echoed James, his eyes widening.

'Yeah, straight up flew back to Cologne with barely a goodbye and handed in his resignation. Before he went, he said something vague about changing careers and going to see his dad. Turns out he went to Montpellier to work in his dad's bakery after all.'

James cocked his head. 'What do you mean by "news"? What's better for me to hear from you?'

Without saying a word, Austin walked back into the living room. James heard a brief rustling sound, and then the captain returned to the kitchen holding a newspaper in his hand. Even in its rolled-up state, James could see that it wasn't a

UK paper but an American one. He considered for a moment how odd it was for Austin to have bought a paper in the US and brought it all the way here, but at the same time that very fact solidified its importance and James was intrigued.

Austin unfurled it and riffled through a few pages before folding the paper back on itself and handing it to James. On the page was an official portrait of Grant in his spacesuit holding a mock helmet—one of the photographs taken just before their launch to rendezvous with the *Magnum*—and the headline next to it read 'Former ESA Astronaut Takes Own Life'.

James's eyes widened as he stared at the page, dated that day, the 6th of December. He shook his head and mouthed the word 'No' over and over before looking up at Austin, who stood silently with his arms crossed.

'What happened?' James demanded quietly.

'I knew something was up a few months back when the ESA called me to ask if I had any contact details for Grant as they hadn't been able to get in touch following his resignation. They were concerned about his mental health. I directed them to try his pop's place, but I gather he ignored their calls.'

'But… His dad—'

'Passed last year. Article says he left the bakery to Grant, but it proved too much and he started drinking heavily. Says he died on November 29th, so two weeks ago.'

'Damn it.' James sighed, handing the newspaper back to Austin, who rolled it back up again.

For a couple of minutes, James contemplated the news of Grant's death. He had always attributed Grant's feelings for Yula to mere infatuation, more a form of creepy lust than anything genuine. So it came as a surprise that the whole ordeal had affected him so profoundly. Though James knew the trip itself had made Grant uncomfortable, thrown his expectations out of the window, and his smug worldview had crumbled to dust, reducing him to a gibbering mess throughout the excursion. So that, more than anything, may have contributed to his self-destructive spiral. James pitied the man and was saddened by his passing, but expended no mental energy mourning him.

He focused his eyes on the captain, who was staring into space with a thoughtful and sombre expression, and asked, 'Okay, so what about Zhu?' He leaned back on the counter-top with both hands either side.

Austin waved his hand and replied, 'Ah, you know her. She went back to China, and last I heard, she was deployed to the ISS pretty soon after.'

'Mmm, yeah, she *was* looking forward to that. Good for her. Must've been a shock when you and Grant came back to the *Magnum* with us in the state we were in.'

'Absolutely, but y'know, you gotta give Zhu more credit. She did more to look after you on the return journey than you realise. I had no idea she was medically trained; I'd wager she's the reason you made it back in one piece.'

'I wish we still had our beers; I'd toast to her right now,' replied James, half-sarcastically, half-looking for a reason to open another bottle.

'Heh, you got any more then? I'll drink to that!'

James smiled and moved past Austin, opening the fridge and pulling out another couple of ice-cold beers. He handed one to Austin, then raised his into the air.

'To Major Zhu O-Huang. Excellent pilot, and the very best off-world medic.'

Austin raised his glass and touched it to James's, repeating,

'To Major Zhu.'

The companions shared a few moments of silence as they sipped their drinks and leant against the dining room furniture.

'I suppose I missed Yula's funeral then?' said James as he examined the label of his bottle, turning it around in his hands.

'Funny you should say that…' replied Austin, holding his bottle up and allowing the soft natural light from the window to refract through it. 'We never did have a funeral for her. Russian government came and retrieved her body, and that was it. Official line is that she was killed in the "accident" that injured you, but otherwise nothing happened to memorialise her; at least, nothing we were invited to. We would've had our own private service, but Grant left so abruptly and Zhu got called away by the CNSA, so it never happened.'

'That's out of order. Just plain wrong,' snarled James. 'They should've done something for her. She deserves better. What, are they just expecting us to keep quiet about the real story?'

Austin looked at James for a second with a furrowed brow and puzzled expression before realising what James was getting at.

He took another sip of his drink and replied, 'Ah. I take it no one's told you where the ground lies then?'

James shook his head.

Austin set his bottle down on the dining table behind him and explained, 'Well, everyone knows about the ship and that you were injured, right? But officially, any talk of there being living aliens over there is off limits. The cave-in story is the only one that they'll allow, and they're damn sure to do all they can to discredit you if you don't play ball. In fact, it's the only thing that's allowing them to prep for a second mission.'

James was flabbergasted and appalled at this news. He

could feel himself becoming angry and he spat out, 'Well, I damn well hope they liked the stuff you brought them, and I hope they remember it was paid for in blood.'

'Man, you wouldn't believe what it was that we found,' replied Austin. 'We've managed to translate some of the language already. It's all ongoing, but we've got a good idea of what we got. Detailed descriptions and instructions for their engine technology, schematics that show how they cracked faster-than-light travel, energy shielding, weapons systems—you name it, we found data on it. Must have been a reference guide for their maintenance dudes. We were told we really hit the jackpot.'

'All that, and they—who? NASA, the ESA, the UN?— won't even show the proper respect for someone who gave their life to change the course of human history? Disgusting.' James turned and slammed the base of his bottle on the table and leant forwards over the tucked-in dining chair he had been leaning against.

'I'm with you all the way there, my man.'

All of a sudden, the room was filled with the sound of electro-pop music with a heavy synthesised beat. Austin let out a surprised shout and his hand shot to his leg, searching for the pocket of his dark-blue jeans. He lifted the hem of his patterned white button-down shirt, revealing a huge brass belt buckle, and his hand finally found the pocket and pulled out—with difficulty—a narrow black bar, the latest in foldable smartphone technology. The music had become even louder now that the phone was out and waving around. Without silencing it first, he took a pair of rimless glasses out of his breast pocket, put them on and examined the front of the phone with a pained expression. Realising it was a video call, he unfolded it, pressed the accept button and held it out in front of his face almost at arm's length.

'Hey, what's the big deal? I'm visiting a friend. I told you guys I'd be out of the country for a few days, so I don't expect to be harassed like this,' he yelled into the phone.

James leaned in and tried to get a peek at whoever was on the other end of the video call, but Austin twisted the handset around ever so slightly so it remained out of his view.

'But Capt—' came a flustered reply, cut off by Austin continuing his rant.

'No buts! If the director wants me back, she's gonna have to wait until I'm done. Do you know how many leave days I've accumulated?'

'Uh, no, sir, uh, I—'

'Of course you don't! You people and your newfangled quantum network. *Still* can't see when I've taken time off. Time, I might add, that I have *never* taken before!'

'Sir! This is urg—'

'And another thing! I have barely left the compound (honestly, that place is starting to feel like a prison) to go see my poor widdle poochie in months. So I don't give a *damn* how urgent it is, you can tell Barnes to shove that urgency right up—'

'*Captain*! *Look*!'

A few moments of silence passed as Austin stared at something on the screen. His eyes widened and he mumbled an apology. He wiped his hand over his face, muttered something about making his way back early and ended the call.

'*Goddammit*,' he sighed.

He turned to James, who was fighting to keep a straight face, covering his mouth and almost biting his finger.

'Heh, I get pretty territorial about my leave time,' said Austin, folding his phone smaller and stuffing it back into his jeans pocket. 'But y'know, when they want you in, they want you in.'

'I get you,' replied James, thoroughly amused by the exchange and imagining the reaction of the poor schmuck who'd pulled the short straw to make that call.

Austin grunted and grumbled something about James's 'cushy paid rehab'. He picked his drink up again from the table and finished what was left in the bottle—about half—and let loose a loud, satisfied sigh.

He looked at James and smiled. 'Well, buddy, it's been great to see you again, but I'm gonna have to go. Got a lot to unpack with that call...'

'Anything bad?' asked James.

'Nah, nah....' Austin looked around, then leaned in close and said in a half-whisper, 'Hey, you can't tell *anyone* this—not even Angie—but our focus at the moment is on the aliens' FTL drive tech. I left my team running some simulations while I came here and, well, it sounds like they worked. That's what the call was about.'

'You're working on a warp drive?' cried James a little too loudly. 'That's incredible! Tell me more—how long until there's a working prototype? And...' He paused and lowered his voice again. 'Don't worry, mate, this'll stay between you, me and the gatepost, I swear.'

'A working prototype? You mean, like, an engine?' Austin scoffed, 'Dude, we're still talking fifteen, maybe twenty years! But now we know the Alcubierre-White metric is viable and how to generate what we need to make it happen.'

'At least there's something good coming out of all this,' James stressed.

'Absolutely. I'm sure Yula would be thrilled. Anyway, man, I gotta go—and remember, keep that to yourself,' said

Austin as he hurried out of the kitchen and towards the front door with James in tow to see him out.

'Thanks for coming, Captain. Honestly, you dropping by feels like it's helped me a lot more than the last few months of counselling—y'know, closure an' all,' James said as his friend and former commanding officer swung the front door wide and stepped out of the house. When he was halfway down the driveway, James called out one final time: 'Oh, hey. Remember me if you ever need a pilot, mate!'

Austin simply threw a thumb high into the air as he stepped onto the pavement and disappeared down the road.

CHAPTER FIFTEEN
TRANSLATION

AUSTIN BURST THROUGH THE DOUBLE DOORS of his department at the facility. He had taken the first available flight back to the US after leaving James's house and travelled straight to the test centre from the airport without stopping to rest.

Out in the New Mexican desert, on the western slopes of the San Andres Mountains, the White Sands Test Facility—a component of NASA's Johnson Space Center—stretched across nearly thirty square miles, its buildings and laboratories spread sparsely throughout the area in small clusters. Austin's department lay in the largest cluster of buildings, along with the main entrance and staff car park. White Sands was notable for its work on hazardous experimental technologies related to spaceflight and so was the perfect candidate for Austin's project.

As he marched through the facility, a lab technician rushed up to him with a stack of paperwork in his arms.

'Captain Queen, sir. They told me you were back. Sorry to cut your leave short,' the technician started as Austin took the stack of papers from him and the two walked together.

Austin grunted in acknowledgment and said, 'Enough of that crap, Kolton. Tell me about the simulation.'

'Well, we followed the equations in the alien database as you instructed and plugged them into the software.'

'And?'

Kolton pointed to the paperwork in Austin's hands. 'See for yourself, sir.'

Austin stopped in the corridor with a disgruntled expression on his face and opened the first report. He looked down at the papers and his eyes widened. His gaze darted back and forth across the page, taking in the complex mathematics and data from the simulation.

'As you can see, sir, it's far more doable than we anticipated,' said the technician, bouncing on the balls of his feet.

'God damn…' Austin muttered. 'This is great work. When you called and told me we'd cracked it, I didn't expect that we'd actually be able to do this *now*, with our current technology.'

'I know, right?' Kolton said. 'These initial power requirements for the device are astonishingly low.'

Austin handed the paperwork back to the technician and continued walking along the corridor. 'Yeah, but that's a shit ton of negative energy. Are you sure we can generate that?'

Kolton skipped along to keep up with Austin as he marched further into the facility. 'Yes, sir. We still have a lot of translations to go from the alien database, but we're confident we'll get the precise measurements we need out of it.'

'Well, let's get to it then. The sooner we have a working generator, the sooner we can run an interferometer,' said Austin.

The two of them turned a corner and walked through

another set of double doors, coming into a large, dimly lit room. The walls were lined with computers, with another bay in the middle of the floor space. Beyond the computers, at the back of the room, was a strange device in a glass container. It looked broken in places, as if it had been ripped from somewhere, with wires sticking out of the back end. Cables trailed from the plinth below it towards an array of servers over in the far corner.

The device had been difficult to remove from the ship. It hadn't been out in the open; Austin and Grant had had to dig for it amongst other strange computer components tucked away behind a wall panel. It was a data core of some kind, but like nothing they had ever seen before. It was only through accessing the terminal in the room on the ship that they'd realised it was worth retrieving. Extracting the device was part of the reason Grant and Austin had lost the alien they were following. Whether taking the device had been right or not, Austin considered it part of the reason Yula had died. If they hadn't spent so much time on it, they may have arrived in the medical bay before James and Yula's confrontation with the alien. Then, with all four of them together for the fight, it may have gone much more in their favour.

A large number of lab technicians and translation specialists were moving between the computer terminals, sharing notes, tapping away at keyboards and scrolling through data—different teams working fervently on different parts of the alien database.

All activity stopped and the staff looked at the doorway when Austin and his companion stepped through. After a moment, and without a word, Austin nodded to them and they resumed their duties. He walked over to a free terminal and sat down, with Kolton hovering close behind.

Gripping the mouse and leaning close to the screen, Austin woke the monitor and scrolled through the newest set of translation data.

After a short while, Kolton cleared his throat and said, 'Uh, Captain?'

'You still here?' said Austin without turning around. 'Go report in to your team already. I already said we need to prioritise the generator; I wanna get a test build of the machine up and running by end of day.'

'Yes, sir,' Kolton said. He hesitated as he began to move away. 'What are you gonna do, sir?'

'Familiarise myself with this new info first, then I'll be over to check your team's progress.'

Kolton nodded and walked away and joined a group of colleagues clustered around another bank of terminals.

Austin sighed.

These new kids keep on talkin' back. Weren't like this back in the air force...

He stopped himself. This wasn't the military and he couldn't very well expect that kind of discipline from a bunch of scientists. At any rate, that culture was part of the reason he'd transferred over to the space programme in the first place.

The captain continued scrolling through the new translations line by line. There were over eighty distinct characters in the alien language, with very little in the way of punctuation, and context was given in the form of colour-coding. Its complexity meant that in the last couple of years Austin's team hadn't got very far. It was the technical nature of the archive, with its abundance of context clues, that had allowed them to progress as far as they had.

Something caught Austin's eye and he stopped. 'What in

the hell is this? Modification?' he muttered. Scrolling back up a line, he began to read under his breath: 'Superior performance in infantry units is achieved through modification of the genome and "Elysian enzyme" insertion... *Jesus.* Gene therapy? Super-soldiers? Who the fuck *were* these guys?'

Austin continued scrolling through, and the detailed explanations gave way to complex equations and dosages, as well as anatomical diagrams and machine schematics, some of which Austin recognised from his time on board the wreck.

After a few minutes, he leaned back in his chair and called out to one of the teams at the side wall, 'Hey, D'Amico, have we got any history on the aliens outta this thing yet?'

'Uh, the other day we got done with their wall carvings, sir,' one of the translators called back. 'Look to be religious texts of some kind. Could look there for clues?'

'I mean anything specific on *where* they came from or *who* they are as a civilisation?'

Another technician piped up from the other side of the room, 'Nothing detailed, but in our segment we've seen several references to a name.'

'And what's that?'

'Achelon, sir.'

Austin rose from his seat and walked across to the other terminal. Leaning on the back of the techie's chair, he peered at the screen.

'There, sir,' said the technician, pointing at a portion of the translation.

Austin looked it over for a few moments and said, 'This could be anything. Their planet, their star, their goddamn favourite pizza topping for all we know.'

'No, sir, we're pretty sure it's what they call themselves. This section down here talks of an ongoing battle with another faction or something; could even be a different species.'

'You think that could've been the other ship?' asked Austin.

'Impossible to tell, sir. But in the context, we're confident our Mars aliens are the Achelon. Doesn't seem to be anything on where they're from or why they came here, though.'

'Right… And what about the "Achelon" ship itself? On the *Magnum*, we speculated that it was a warship. Too heavily armed to be anything else as far as we were concerned. Does the database give any indication of what the ship was for?'

The technician tapped away at his keyboard for a moment, then replied, 'I'm not seeing anything to contradict that hypothesis, sir. It was certainly in a battle, it's heavily armed and clearly full of soldiers—'

'*Augmented* super-soldiers apparently,' Austin interjected.

'Yes, but we do have some further data on the ship's technical specifications. Apparently, it's something called an "Encounter Class" vessel, which could suggest it's meant for first-contact scenarios. But equally it could be a vanguard or scout ship.'

'Sounds like the latter to me.'

Just then, Kolton called out from across the room, 'Captain Queen, sir! We've got what we need for the generator!'

Hours later, a group of engineers stood around the small device on the table in the testing room. One of the engineers was bent low, making some final adjustments to the completed machine. They had built the box to the captain's exact specifications and now all that was left was to switch it on.

Austin and his team were standing back behind a plastic shield several metres away, watching while the last engineer finished up and stood back.

'Ready when you are, boss,' said one of the engineers.

'Alright,' Austin said, leaning on the shielding. 'Best you boys and girls get back here.'

The engineers nodded and moved to join the rest of the team while Austin picked up a yellow-and-black box with a red switch on it. He held the box with both hands and waited for the last engineer to come behind the screen, his thumb hovering over the switch.

'Alright, brace yourselves, kiddos,' said Austin. 'This is gonna be the largest field of negative energy ever produced on Earth. Fairly sure it's not gonna explode… but all the same, there's no telling *exactly* what could happen here.'

He rocked the controller back and forth in his hands for a few moments and then continued for the recording, 'Project *Aurora*, Achelon Macroscopic Exotic Mass-Energy Field Generator Test One. Wednesday, December 9th, 2026. Commencing in three, two, one…'

Austin pushed his thumb down hard on the switch, which depressed with a clack. The machine started up with a loud buzz, followed by the growing whir of fans, gyros and other complex moving parts as they slowly spun up to speed.

It's working! I can't believe it.

The lights in the testing room began to flicker and the whirring sound grew in pitch and volume to an uncomfortable whine, amplified by the high ceiling of the old hangar.

With a pained expression and covering his ears, Austin looked over at one of the lab technicians. 'We getting anything yet, Cass?' he shouted.

'Not yet, sir,' she called back, struggling to be heard over the noise.

'Tell me as soon as we get— Wait, that's not right!' cried Austin.

The machine on the table was vibrating violently, clattering on the surface, threatening to throw itself off. Still the whine continued, rising further in pitch.

'Aborting test,' Austin said, and he pressed the switch again.

Oh, shit...

He looked down at the box in his hands, dumbfounded, and pressed the switch a few more times. The machine had not stopped; it was as if it had a mind of its own and had broken free of his control.

'Get down!' he cried, throwing himself onto the floor as the whir of the machine reached its peak.

There was a deafening bang which shook the room, and a loud crack. In the same moment the team were plunged into total darkness and an acrid smell filled the room.

After a long minute, Austin and the team slowly lifted their heads. One of the engineers switched on a torch, rushed out to the circuit breaker and reset the fuses. One by one the lights came on, bathing the hangar in their sickly fluorescent glow once more.

Austin looked over at the table.

'Woah,' he said, ducking his head sideways as he narrowly avoided a jagged metal shard that had penetrated the plastic shield by a good six inches at his head height. The plastic was cracked and bent around it.

Goddamn, Austin, you lucky duck...

He breathed a sigh of relief and peered around the shard at the table. The engineers had already gone forwards to inspect the device. Where before there had been a machine, there was now a burnt husk of twisted metal. Smoke poured from one of the openings and parts glowed with residual heat. A moment later, the device disappeared in a cloud of gas as an engineer sprayed it with a fire extinguisher.

One of the technicians walked up and patted Austin on the back. 'Sure it's not gonna explode, huh, sir?' he said.

Austin frowned and rolled his eyes at him. 'Ha-ha, very funny, Owen. Now, go make yourself useful.'

Owen scoffed, then shook his head as he skulked away, out of the testing room.

What a mess. I don't get it; we followed the instructions to the letter. What went wrong?

Austin rubbed his eyes and turned to Cass, who was still sitting at the monitoring station. 'Please tell me we got something useful before it blew?' he said.

'Sorry, sir, I'm not seeing anything useful right now. We did register a couple of small spikes just before it went poof, but it's gonna take a while to go through the data to confirm,' she replied.

'A small spike? Better than nothin'; I'll take it,' said Austin with a shrug. 'Any indications of what went wrong?'

'A loose screw is my best guess,' said one of the engineers as he walked over. He leaned on the edge of the plastic shielding and put a hand on his hip. 'Could've caused a vibration that pushed the plates out of alignment.'

Austin groaned. 'Thousands of dollars on this project, and it all comes down to not being tightened properly? Christ.'

'It's a promising sign, sir,' said Cass, turning around in her seat.

'How so?'

'Well, we're trying to scale up quantum effects to levels they don't normally work at,' she said. 'An explosion like that should have been impossible in a quantum system, and if the small spikes turn out to indicate a negative energy density, then that's something.'

'Hmm, it's a bit of a stretch,' said Austin. He thought for

a few moments, then sighed. He looked up at the technician with a smile and continued, 'But it might be enough for me to take to the director and convince her to let us run another test.' He paused and looked at the engineers carrying the burnt chunk of metal away, then said, 'Y'know what, it's been a long day. We'll get all this cleared away, then I'm calling time. Start fresh in the morning.'

Early the next morning, Austin drove along the highway towards the facility. The weather and roads were clear, and the winter sun had not yet risen above the mountains, giving the surrounding desert an eerie twilight ambiance. As he pulled in through the front gates and travelled up the drive-way, there appeared to be a large congregation of people clustered around the front entrance.

Austin frowned and squinted, muttering to himself, 'What in the ever-lovin' hell is that? Bit early for a tour…'

From this distance and in the pre-dawn light, it was difficult to see what was going on. Soon, the group slipped out of sight behind some large desert shrubs and planters as Austin continued around to the staff car park.

Ah well, I got more important things to worry about, like convincing the boss to let us build another generator. We really fucked up yesterday.

He pulled the car into his designated bay and shivered as he stepped out into the chill December air, the fog of his breath rising in front of his face. He walked around to the boot and retrieved his jacket, pulling it on as quickly as he could, then started for the main entrance.

It wasn't long before he came close enough to see what all the hubbub was about. A large group of angry protesters surrounded the doorway, shouting, chanting and waving placards around. The placards varied in their messaging, ranging from fearful misunderstandings of the work of the facility to religious slogans equating their research with satanic worship. At the centre of them all, standing on one of the facility's planters and carrying a megaphone, was a figure who made Austin stop in his tracks.

Jesus, what's he doing here? Guess that explains the turnout...

'You're lying to these people!' cried Guy Furious, his amplified voice echoing through the still morning air. 'You've got the aliens in there, I know it! Your inhuman experiments will bring their wrath down upon us. We're here to tell you, stop the research. If you don't comply, you'll doom us all.'

Nah, I ain't dealing with this BS today. Back entrance it is...

Austin backed away slowly and made to go in the other direction. Guy lowered the megaphone for a moment and peered through the gloom.

After a second, he raised the device to his lips and called, 'Captain Queen! You can't get away from us that easy.'

Fuck. I've been made. Can't sneak away now.

It was too much for Austin to hope to slip by unrecognised. Though he'd eschewed most public appearances since his return from the *Magnum*, his face was well known, having been featured prominently in the mission's publicity.

Steeling his nerves, Austin muttered, 'Come on now, Austin. You can do this. Just get through to the entrance.' And he began to walk towards the group of protesters.

Many of the group had raised their phones, taking footage of his approach. Austin tried to keep his head down and not look at any of them. As he drew closer, they began to crowd around him, the din of their angry wailing ringing in his ears.

I can't believe it's been like this since we got back.

Various NASA facilities around the US had faced regular protests over the last two years, but White Sands had been relatively quiet until recently, with only the odd small group quietly standing to one side. It was understandable: the facility was a way out from the nearest town and in the middle of a desert. But a few months back, Guy Furious and his new anti-alien group had announced a 'tour' of sorts, pledging to lead large demonstrations at every facility in the country, and it seemed today was White Sands' turn. Guy's presence always drew huge crowds, ever since he had managed to convince his followers that he had been right about the alien wreck. Local news vans were also present, on the outskirts of the congregation, reporting on the appearance.

Austin continued to push through the growing crowd, making his way towards the entrance, and closer to Guy Furious.

'Hey, Captain, you can't ignore us forever. How do you sleep at night knowing you're contributing to the downfall of mankind?' Guy called through the megaphone, drawing cheers of approval from the crowd.

Pay him no attention. Focus on the entrance.

Guy jumped down from the planter and stepped right up in front of Austin. He was not a particularly tall man, but he towered over the captain. Guy wore what had—following that fateful talk show seven years ago—become his signature outfit: a claret velour blazer and matching pants with an open-necked shirt and colourful tie. Over the years, his slicked-back hairstyle had morphed into a kind of ragged afro, and his paintbrush beard had become scragglier, giving him the appearance of an endearing and instantly recognisable force of utter chaos. He smiled as he blocked Austin's path, and

Austin was forced to look up, glaring as he made eye contact.

'Move aside, Guy. I gotta get to work,' said Austin.

'Captain Queen, or should I call you'—Guy raised his voice—'Captain "Prince of *Lies*"? Care to comment on the mounting evidence that you're working on top-secret spaceship technology?'

Austin scoffed, 'This is a NASA facility, you idiot. Of course we're working on spacecraft. Now if you're done making a spectacle of yourself, kindly get *the fuck* outta my way.'

Austin moved to push past Guy, but the man stepped sideways to block his path again.

'Ooh, feisty, Captain. Be careful, the cameras are rolling,' said Guy with a big grin on his face.

Leaning close to Guy and lowering his voice, Austin said, 'Look, dude. I don't believe your whole "crazy man" shtick for a second. You're just a shrewd businessman like every other con artist in this country. You may think you're the new hotness right now, but I ain't impressed. Just step aside and let me through. You ain't getting nothin' from me.'

'Alright,' said Guy, standing to one side.

After a few seconds glaring at him, Austin began to move past.

'But how about this, Captain?' said Guy as Austin walked away. 'What about the Russian? Care to comment on *her*?'

His words made Austin stop in his tracks.

Guy raised the megaphone to his lips once more and belted out, 'How does it feel, knowing you're the reason she's dead?'

What?

Austin's face scrunched up in anger and he was rooted to the spot. He clenched his fists and began to shake as he recalled finding Yula on the floor of the ship's medical bay.

He has no idea what we went through on that ship. How dare he? No idea what I've been through the last two years!

Austin had long blamed himself for what had happened on Mars. As the mission commander, it had been his responsibility to safeguard the lives of his crew. The guilt had driven him to a dark place, and it had taken most of the last two years to bring himself out of it and come to terms with the incident.

Guy continued, 'Yeah, you know! Don't you? You G-men are all alike. She probably figured out too much, so you sent her to her death. Her blood is on your hands, Queen—'

Austin blacked out. When he came to seconds later, he found himself standing over Guy, who was flat on his back and holding his face with both hands. The crowd were screaming obscenities at Austin and brandishing their fists and placards. Some were holding their phones up and had clearly been recording the whole thing. Austin panted, his eyes wide with shock. He looked at his hand, still raised and balled into a fist; it was spattered with Guy's blood.

'You broke my nose!' cried Guy, trying to stem the flow of his nosebleed. His cheek and eye were already bruising. 'You all saw it!'

A few of Guy's supporters rushed forwards, helped him to his feet and pulled him back, away from Austin.

'I'm… I'm sorry,' Austin muttered, staring, wide-eyed, back and forth from his fist to Guy's bloodied face. He started to back away towards the entrance of the facility, stumbling a little as he stepped.

As Guy was dragged away by his supporters, he screamed, 'I'm gonna sue your ass, Queen! Mark my words, you're done, G-man!'

Moments later, Austin was through the front doors and into the atrium. Still in shock, he leaned on one side of the doorframe and took deep breaths.

Fuck, this is bad. I didn't even feel myself move. Just blacked right out. I thought I was over this. I played right into that asshole's hands.

Taking another deep breath and with his eyes beginning to water, he gave a shout. He roared so loudly in frustration that several staff members, including the receptionist, looked up and came running over. As they approached, he dropped to his knees and tears streaked down his face and wet the floor.

I'm done. I've messed it all up. I'm gonna lose my job for sure. Poochie's gonna have to go to a new home! I can't bear it.

The staff helped him up off the floor and asked if he was okay, but their voices blurred into an unintelligible noise as Austin replayed his loss of control over in his mind.

Austin was assisted into a chair, and the medics were called to have a look at his hand while he stared into space. His hand had been cut in the initial impact with Guy's glasses and his knuckles were bruised from the subsequent blows. As he was being bandaged up, his trance was broken by the appearance of the assistant director, his shined shoes clomping on the polished floor of the atrium.

He stood before Austin, looking down on him with a scowl on his face. His words were simple and curt: 'Queen. The director wants to see you. Now.'

Silently and looking glum, Austin rose from his seat. He glanced at his newly bandaged hand, turning it over and flexing his fingers. He then gave a nod to the medics, hung his head and plodded after the assistant director.

The director's office wasn't far, but each of Austin's

steps was slow and heavy, and the journey felt long and drawn-out.

We were so close. So damn close to figuring this out. Now I can kiss goodbye to getting clearance for another machine. But that's the least of my worries. They're probably gonna shut down the project altogether. And it's all my own damn fault.

The two of them turned a corner and came to a door at the end of a short stretch of corridor. The door was of dark wood, with a large frosted pane in the upper half and the name 'Dr Leotie Barnes, Center Director' printed on the glass.

The assistant director knocked twice, then pushed the door open with an extended creak and strode through. Austin brought up the rear and closed it behind him.

Dr Barnes looked up at Austin from writing at her desk and motioned to the chair in front of her. 'Sit.'

Austin grunted in acknowledgement, shuffled forwards and lowered himself into the seat.

The director took off her gold, thin-rimmed glasses and stared at Austin. Her eyes were dark brown, like her hair, which was short and curly, and she had stern features.

'Captain, I want you to explain to me why I have just received a call from Mr Furious's lawyers threatening this facility with legal action,' she said through pursed lips.

'The facility? That'll never stick,' Austin laughed.

Dr Barnes remained stern. 'Don't you think I know that?' she spat. 'But an incident like this is going to do untold damage to our public perception. Guy Furious knows how to kick up a stink, and you know that as well as I do.'

Austin looked down at his hands and muttered, 'Y-yes—'

'Then why, on God's green earth, did you have to break his damn nose!' Dr Barnes screeched, jumping up from her chair and slamming her hands down onto the desk. She leaned over it, towering over Austin, and snarled, 'Give me one good goddamn reason why I shouldn't throw you under the bus?'

Austin sighed and looked up at the director. 'We're making good progress—' he started, but was cut off by a huff from Dr Barnes.

'Good progress?' she scoffed. '*Good progress*? Don't bullshit me, Austin. I already know you nearly blew up the testing lab! What kind of progress is that?'

Austin opened his mouth to speak, but was cut off once more.

'No. You know what? I don't want to know,' said Dr Barnes. She tutted and lowered herself back into the seat. She pointed at Austin and continued, 'You are on thin ice. If I didn't need your experience, I'd throw you out on your ass just for that little "accident". I expected better of you, Austin.'

He frowned and sat up straight. 'Now wait just one second. Yeah sure, I made a mistake. I let him goad me. He was being an asshole and I lost control—'

'Guy Furious is *always* an asshole! And anyway, I'm talking about nearly killing your entire team.' Barnes scowled at Austin for a moment, then said, 'You have one more chance. Make this... *thing*... with Guy Furious go away, or you're through. Now, get out of my sight.'

Moments later, Austin was outside the office. He gave a heavy sigh and leaned his head back against the wall.

That went better than I expected. Not sure what she means by 'make it go away', though... How the hell am I gonna convince the biggest mouth in America to just clam up?

CHAPTER SIXTEEN
ATHANASIA

TWO WEEKS HAD PASSED SINCE Austin's surprise visit at the start of December, and James now walked with a spring in his step, as though a heavy load he didn't realise he'd been carrying was suddenly gone. Thinking back to his conversation with the captain brought an unexpected sense of relief and solidarity. The doctor's off-hand comments about coma-induced hallucinations had affected James more than he realised.

Emboldened by Austin's confirmation that the Mars incident had indeed been as he remembered it, James had finally opened up to Tony about his experiences during his weekly sessions. Tony had listened as James recounted the mission in detail and even described the nightmares, in which his mind had played tricks on him. However, far from feeling better for it, James was concerned. He'd noticed the counsellor shuffle slightly a number of a times during the story; Tony kept his professional air and friendly nature, but his body language betrayed a discomfort that James found it impossible to dismiss. When challenged on it, the portly therapist simply waved his hand and blamed it on some painful constipation—far too much information, James thought, and he didn't fully believe it. Tony pledged to help James come to terms with whatever his memory told him, but the counsellor continued to display visible discomfort when James raised the topic of the aliens, and that weighed heavily on James's mind, causing him to become distracted and guarded.

As the weeks progressed, the nightmares had returned in dribs and drabs, and though James could suppress them most of the time using his coping strategies, he had occasions even during the day when his mind would flash to some aspect of the mission and he'd become disoriented with vertigo. He had hidden this from Angela, as he couldn't bear for her to think he was getting worse.

Christmas was just around the corner, but as they were still piecing their lives back together and James was getting used to the new-old-normal, neither he nor Angela had paid much attention. However, that weekend Angela was filled with festive excitement and so set them both to the task of decorating the house. James suspected she was convinced that if she turned his mind towards the joyous occasion of their first Christmas together since their reunion then he would find it that much easier to cope. He didn't dare tell her that it didn't work like that, or disclose his sudden lack of trust in Dr Volpe.

So, on that blustery, frigid Saturday of the 19th of December, James and Angela began the task of putting up the Christmas decorations. Angela had called around the guys that morning and cancelled their games night for the occasion. After lunch, they dug out numerous heavy, dusty boxes from the loft, including one long box covered in strips of peeling gaffer tape of various brands and colours, which indicated its age like rings in a tree trunk. They—James, mainly—dragged the boxes down the stairs and set about opening them in the middle of the living room floor, pulling out festive ornaments, wreaths and a gaudy knitted advent calendar that Angela's grandmother had made for them when they first moved in together.

Sputnik seemed overjoyed at the chaos, bounding and leaping between boxes, knocking down statuettes of penguins and Santas, scattering baubles and running off with lengths of tinsel. It was a rather good distraction, James conceded, and Sputnik's endless energy and cheek left them both howling with laughter.

After clearing the ornaments from the floor and placing them around the room, James pulled open the aged box, peeling off the tired and worn strips of tape, assembled the imitation Christmas tree and placed it in the far corner of the room. Meanwhile, Angela got herself tangled up in knots of string lights, trying to make sure all the bulbs worked.

A couple of hours later, following some light bickering over the layout of the baubles on the tree, and while Angela took selfies in front of it to send to her friends, James picked up some of the exterior decorations and made his way outside. He planned to put a plastic Father Christmas on the roof this year, one that looked like it was falling into the chimney. He had put it up for the first time many years before and received many positive comments from the neighbours, and he felt its return would complement his own in some fashion.

He grabbed the telescopic ladder out of the shed and extended it up the front of the house to the roof. Angela joined him and held the ladder steady as he ascended with a rope attached to him to pull the Santa up with. He got to the top and climbed up onto the roof on all fours, and then hoisted the ornament up using the rope. Angela popped inside to bring out some lights to hang on the guttering.

'Urgh, they're all tangled,' she cried out of the front door.

James leaned over the guttering, looking back down, and said, 'Alright, I'll get on with this while you sort them out.'

As she ducked back inside, he moved along the rooftop towards the chimney with the Father Christmas under his arm. He found that the fittings were caked with a foul-smelling grime, and so he spent a few minutes cleaning them with his gloves. As he lifted the Santa into place, movement in the tiles made him wobble and he grabbed the apex to steady himself. He searched in his pockets for the bolts and spanner, and set about fixing the ornament in place. As he tightened the final bolt, a vision flashed into his mind, freezing him in place.

He was back on the alien craft; it was dark, and inexplicably cold.

Yula's voice came from behind him; she was sitting on the upturned cabinet. 'You are going to propose to Angela as soon as we are home, are you not?'

'Well, yes. When I find a way—'

'No! You are to do it immediately. Waste no time, or I swear I will beat sense into you.'

Great, yet another promise to Yula I failed to keep…

The vision ended and reality rushed back into focus. James tried to look around, for a moment wondering where he was, but dizziness hit. He shifted his weight and a couple of loose tiles slid out from under him, causing him to stumble.

'Shit!' he exclaimed under his breath, the movement jolting him back to his senses. Instinctively, he reached out to grab the apex. This time, the ridge tile broke away with the force of his grip. More tiles under his body slipped from the jolt, sending him careening down towards the edge of the roof.

'No, no, no!' he shouted as he hurtled down the slope, still scrambling for some purchase.

The sliding tiles sent him flying off the roof of the house. As if in slow motion, he reached out with his trailing arm and tried to grab the guttering as he fell, but he missed and tumbled down past the windows. He closed his eyes as the ground approached.

There was a deafening thud and a smattering of ceramic crashes as James and the tiles hit the ground. His head hit the concrete and all went black.

He opened his eyes slowly. Everything was blurry and swimming. He blinked to clear his vision and saw Angela kneeling beside him with her phone to her ear. She had tears streaming down her face and her expression was one of abject terror. He couldn't hear what she was saying at first due to an awful ringing in his ears. However, it soon cleared and he could just make out through her nervous stammering that she was speaking to the emergency services.

He groaned and moved, raising himself onto all fours with surprising ease. When Angela saw this, she stopped speaking and watched as he turned towards her and sat on the driveway, resting on his hip and one hand. He used his free hand to rub his face and then looked up to the roof.

'Oh, for goodness' sake,' he grunted and started to move again, but then he stopped dead and frowned. He realised from the croakiness of his voice that he had been winded, and he remembered falling from the roof, hitting his head and blacking out. But there was something wrong.

Nothing hurts apart from my head... What's going on?

I should be in agony. Am I dead? No, Ange saw me sit up, reacted to me. I'm alive and I'm... fine. But why?

He lowered his gaze from the roof and saw Angela's worried expression. She had continued her conversation with the emergency services, updating them on his status, but was staring at him like he had just risen from the grave.

'Ange?' he croaked. 'Hey, I'm... I'm fine, really.' He then lifted himself up from the ground and stood upright, looking down at Angela's wide, confused eyes. 'See?'

She hung up the call and her arms dropped to her sides. Amazed and frozen in place, she stared up at him, still kneeling on the floor among the broken tiles.

From his vantage point, James could see that Angela's bare feet, which were tucked back underneath her as she kneeled, had been cut badly by the broken shards when she ran out to get to him and were bleeding. He barely had a chance to tell her so before an ambulance screeched to a halt outside their driveway, its lights flashing. James turned and saw the paramedics grab their gear and rush towards him.

They checked both of them over, but aside from the cuts on Angela's feet and minor bruising on James's head, there were no injuries. The paramedics cleaned and dressed Angela's cuts and recommended that James get himself to the hospital and watch out for signs of concussion in the meantime. Despite Angela's objections, James insisted he didn't need to go and that he felt fine. He was more concerned with Angela's injuries than anything else.

The time the paramedics spent with them seemed to slip by with James barely speaking a word. He replayed the fall from the roof over and over in his mind and questions flew in and out of his thoughts. How had he survived a blow to the head like that? Why did he feel fine? Was it in the way he'd landed? No, it couldn't have been; he'd landed flat on his front with no support for his head at all. What's more, it was solid concrete. At the very least he should have broken a bone, surely?

He felt a deep pit in his stomach as he recalled the vision of Yula.

How could I have been so stupid? So weak…

The shame of losing control and the thought that all this had been caused by some lack of mental fortitude enveloped him. It wasn't until the paramedics announced their departure that reality came back into focus.

Soon after the paramedics left, James took Angela indoors to rest. Her feet were sore, and James went to get her an ice pack to help with the bruising.

Angela stared at James, frowning and clearly confused about all that had happened. She said to him in a stern tone, 'What the hell was that, Jim? I thought you were dead! How can you fall two storeys and walk away like you just tripped over your own feet?'

'I… I have no idea, love. I thought I was going to die too,' he replied, just as confused as she was. Then he remembered the business card Dr Hales had given him when he was discharged from the hospital and how enthusiastic he'd been about working on James's case. He rose from his seat and walked upstairs with a worried Angela limping behind him.

'What on earth are you doing? You should be resting too! What's going on, James?' she protested, but he ignored her.

He went into the upstairs office and unpinned the business card from the corkboard on the wall. He showed it to Angela.

'I don't know, love,' he said. 'But I know someone who might help us find out…'

The very next morning, after an unsuccessful evening of trying to call Dr Hales and broken sleep due to Angela waking him throughout the night to check on him, a bleary-eyed James finally got through on the phone not long after having devoured a hearty breakfast.

The distinctive growl of Dr Hales's voice came through the phone's speaker, his terse introduction interspersed with the sound of chewing, for which he made no apology.

'So, Commander, I take that you are calling me because there has been a change in your condition?'

James stammered a response; he hadn't expected the doctor to remember him so readily, especially after so long. He took a moment to gather his thoughts and then launched into a full explanation of what had happened. Dr Hales remained silent throughout James's regurgitation, offering only the occasional grunt of acknowledgement.

The doctor cleared his throat as James's report came to an end. 'To be completely honest with you, Commander, I have been expecting this. I have had my suspicions about you since you were admitted into my care.' He gave a short laugh. 'I was starting to think I was wrong.'

James was lost for words; the hairs on the back of his neck stood on end.

Expecting it? What is he talking about?

Dr Hales continued, 'I would like you to meet me at the Royal London today. Even for one such as yourself, we need to be cautious about head injuries. When you get here, ask for me at the reception. One of my colleagues will escort you to my office. It seems we have much to discuss.'

One such as myself? James thought, pulling the phone away from his ear and looking at the receiver with a puzzled expression. He put the phone back to his ear and replied cautiously, 'I agree. It seems we do have a lot to talk about. I'll be right over.'

'Excellent. I shall see you soon.'

Dr Hales hung up and James set the handset down in its dock, staring into space, processing what the doctor had said.

'So, what did he say?' asked Angela, appearing behind him and making him jump.

'He wants me to go to the hospital to see him…' James trailed off.

Angela noticed and said in a concerned tone, 'What else? What's wrong?'

'I don't know,' he replied. 'But I have to find out what's going on.'

'Well, what are we waiting for? Let's go!' exclaimed Angela, grabbing James's hand and dragging him to the door. She saw him looking at her, bewildered, and said, 'What? We've got nothing else to do today, and you'd better believe I'm coming with you.'

It took them around an hour to get to the Royal London Hospital, and once there they drove up and down the new multi-storey car park for a further ten minutes looking for a space, crawling at a snail's pace at the back of a very long queue. Eventually, James managed to park up and they went in through the hospital's main entrance.

The reception area was directly in front of them, inset underneath a fascia of blue glass, in a bright atrium filled with waiting room chairs. James and Angela walked up to the receptionist and announced themselves. The waiting room was packed with people and the smooth surfaces reflected and amplified the sound of talking, creating an unintelligible din. This was, perhaps, why neither James nor Angela noticed the sound of shuffling footsteps coming up behind them.

'Commander. Ms Marie-Stewart,' a male voice said sharply from between the pair, startling them.

James and Angela whipped around on the spot. They were surprised to see a diminutive young doctor standing before them. He smiled at them and gave a slight bow. He wore a long white lab coat, left open, with a light-blue shirt underneath, black trousers and smart shoes so shiny they would do a drill sergeant proud. His short black hair was cut military-style, but his smooth skin made him seem altogether too young, as though he had yet to finish school. He adjusted his glasses as the couple stared; they were large and round and didn't suit him at all.

'We've been expecting you. Please, follow me, if you will,' said the doctor, gesturing to the left.

James and Angela did as they were instructed and followed him through the winding hospital corridors.

'So, what's your name?' asked Angela, skipping ahead to walk next to their new companion.

'Dr Makewell.'

'Wow, talk about nominative determinism…'

'Quite,' replied Dr Makewell with a straight face. 'Rest assured, I've heard all the jokes. Ah! Here we are.'

He stopped in front of an ordinary-looking door and pressed the green buzzer to be let in. He held the door open for James and Angela and they filed through into a corridor, much like the ones in the rest of the hospital but minus the wall art. It was an administrative wing, with offices replacing wards and consultation rooms.

'Dr Hales's office is the second on the right,' said the young doctor, and he vanished just as quickly and silently as he had appeared.

James looked at Angela and they both shrugged at one another. He moved to knock on the door of the office. It was made of plain wood and, like all the others in the hallway, bore a plaque. It read, 'Dr Hales, Neurology Consultant'.

Well, he did say he had his own private practice elsewhere…

'Come in,' called a voice from inside mere fractions of a second after James knocked on the door.

They entered the room and saw Dr Hales sitting behind a large mahogany desk with a computer monitor to one side and a telephone to the other. Otherwise, the desk was clear. The doctor was leaning back in his chair flicking through a file of paperwork and he looked up at them as they entered.

'Ah, Commander Fowler, welcome!' he exclaimed with a smile. 'And Ms Marie-Stewart.'

Angela waved awkwardly and she and James advanced into the room and took the two seats in front of the doctor's desk. Dr Hales leaned over and extended his hand; James and Angela ignored it.

'Let's cut to the chase—what's this all about, Doctor?' James said, leaning forwards on the edge of the chair.

Closing his outstretched hand and giving a meagre smile, Dr Hales sat back down and clasped his hands together on the desktop.

'Very well,' he said. 'Do you remember what I told you when you awoke from your coma, Commander? Particularly about the results of our testing.'

'Yes, I do. You mentioned something about some changes to my genome—'

'Well, what the hell is happening with him, Doc?' interjected Angela. 'He just fell more than twenty feet yesterday and walked away with one bruise! How does that happen?

And how did you know to expect his call?' She pointed at him and squinted.

'Ms Marie-Stewart,' replied Dr Hales, sighing and leaning forwards, his chair creaking as he did so, 'falls from that height, while potentially dangerous, do carry a high rate of survivability. As to the severity of the commander's injuries—or lack thereof—I believe that may have something to do with his genetic abnormalities. It's either that, or he got extremely lucky.'

'Which were caused by the incident on Mars?' asked James.

'I believe so. And that is also the reason I expected your call: simple deduction based on the initial genome test results, coupled with your version of the events of the mission. Have you experienced any other unusual symptoms at all? Manifestations of strange abilities?'

'No, I don't believe—' James cut himself short. The memory of an incident flashed in his mind, one that he had disregarded before as a freak accident. 'I… I broke a glass…'

'What? What's so unusual about breaking a glass?' asked Angela.

James looked at her. 'Sorry, Ange. I picked it up off the kitchen counter and it just smashed in my hand. I thought it was already cracked.'

'Anything else?' asked Dr Hales, intrigued.

'Now that I think about it, I've been able to run for longer without getting tired and pick up things that looked heavy without much effort. I haven't really done anything much in the way of physical training since I've been back on Earth, what with the ESA shutting me out.'

Angela sat there with eyebrows raised in surprise at James's revelations. The changes had been so slight that he had never really noticed them until now, so had felt no need to say anything.

'So what are you now, a superhero?' she gibed.

James shrugged as Dr Hales said, 'I would like to run some more tests. Compare your genetic makeup now with our results from last time. And, of course, I would like to quickly check for signs of concussion.'

James nodded in agreement, and Dr Hales called for some nurses to help with the blood test while he checked James's head and pupillary reaction. The nurses entered the room and took a few samples of blood and tissue.

'Hmm,' said Dr Hales. 'No signs of concussion at all. Remarkable. Signs can take a few days to come out, so if you experience any of the symptoms, come into the A&E here and contact me, as I will be following your condition closely.'

After the nurses left, Angela asked, 'How long can we expect to wait for the results?'

'A week or so. I will contact Commander Fowler when I have them. But for now you are free to go home and rest. Thank you both very much for coming in.' And Dr Hales gestured to the door.

A couple of weeks passed. Christmas came and went and the New Year was marked with nervous introspection. It was now the 8th of January; James was growing anxious for news of the results from Dr Hales, and he knew that Angela was too.

In the intervening time, James had begun privately testing his physical limits. The suggestion from Dr Hales that he might have some superhuman abilities both terrified and excited him. Angela was sceptical, but at the same time worried; she had expressed her concerns to James during many a late-night conversation as they lay in bed. Mainly, she worried that what had happened to James was malignant and that his mild physical enhancements were just the beginning of some new form of cancer. She told him in no uncertain terms that he was not to exert himself, fearing it would accelerate his deterioration.

However, while she was out at work, James spent his time either running around the block or at the local sports centre. He found that no matter how long he ran for, he couldn't get out of breath, and he could lift a little more than he could before. As an astronaut, he was in a good physical condition and had worked out often as part of his training, keeping his muscles fit and working, ready for the challenges posed by extended stints in a microgravity environment. Since his return, however, he had done next to nothing. So it came as a surprise that despite having done no exercise for the last two years, his body acted as though no time had passed at all. He was still in the same peak physical condition he had been in when he set foot on Mars.

One day, in the early afternoon, James returned home from a session at the sports centre. He had decided that morning to try swimming underwater, to see how long he could hold his breath. His investigation had ended in an emergency. After he'd spent more than ten minutes swimming back and forth along the bottom of the pool without surfacing, concerned lifeguards had jumped into the water to drag him out. Perplexed that he hadn't drowned and that there was no need for an ambulance, they'd sent him home.

No sooner had he stepped through the door than his phone rang. He threw down his swimming bag at the base of the stairs and fished the phone out of his pocket and unfolded it. He saw on the screen that it was Dr Hales calling, and so he jabbed the answer button before shooting the handset to his ear.

'Commander, apologies for the delay in getting back to you,' said the doctor. 'I have your test results back, and I strongly advise you to be seated as I tell you this.'

James kicked off his shoes and marched through into the living room. He lowered himself onto the sofa and replied, 'Alright, I'm sitting down. What you got for me then?'

Dr Hales breathed a heavy sigh in a vain attempt to control the clear excitement in his voice, and after a short pause he said, 'I must say this is truly remarkable. The results show your cells are expressing a very unusual type of enzyme, which is both regenerating your chromosomes and repairing your DNA.'

'That doesn't sound unusual.'

'Well, the unusual part is that it is a single enzyme doing both of these tasks. You see, there is a series of enzymes found throughout the animal kingdom which might perform one of these tasks or another, but not in adult humans. At least, not to the extent and efficiency of this single, *alien* enzyme.'

'Alien?' replied James. He had known this was coming, and he recalled what Austin had told him about the subject of aliens being off limits, so he continued, 'I'm afraid I have no idea what you're talking about, Doctor.'

'Come now, Commander,' Dr Hales scoffed. 'We both know that's not true. How else would you have had your genome modified in this manner unless you came into contact with alien medical technology when you were aboard their starship?'

James fidgeted in his seat; he had never been a very good liar. 'The ESA's public records from the Mars mission clearly show that I have never been exposed to any alien medical technology and state quite categorically that I sustained my injuries during a cave-in. You said so yourself.'

'Yes, yes. That is indeed what they say.' The doctor laughed. 'Very well, Commander. Irrespective of the manner in which a cave-in could have altered your fundamental genetic structure, the fact of the matter is that your chromosomes are now regenerating with every division.'

'Look, Doctor, I'm a physicist, not a biologist. What does that actually mean?'

'Dear boy, it means your cells are no longer aging!' Without waiting for James's reaction, he explained, 'Normally, this kind of thing carries a massively increased risk of cancer and other cellular defects due to imperfect repairs, but this enzyme... it is *perfect*. In fact, as long as you don't catch some horrible disease or become gravely injured, you could very well be biologically immortal.'

James almost dropped the phone. After a few seconds staring, dumbfounded, he snorted, 'Immortal? As in, the "live forever" kind?'

'Precisely.'

'You must be having a giggle, right? Tell me you're pulling my leg.' He burst into full laughter. 'What next? Is some hench fella with a big sword coming to cut my head off?'

'Commander Fowler!' Dr Hales said. 'This is no joke.'

James stopped laughing and replied, 'Oh... you're serious?'

'Yes, I am, and I'll thank you not to waste my time with your puerile pop-culture references.'

'Err... sorry,' James muttered, turning red.

Dr Hales cleared his throat. 'If you would allow me to continue. In addition to your newly acquired agelessness, your enhanced cellular repair mechanisms should also make you much more *durable*, which explains how you were barely injured when you fell from the roof.'

Once again taking things seriously, James explained

to the doctor about his light experimentation over the last couple of weeks.

'Incredible,' remarked the doctor. 'It is possible that there is more than just the genetic aspect of your augmentation. I would like you to take part in some further experiments to determine the extent of your extraordinary abilities. Meet me back at the hospital on Monday. Goodbye, Commander.'

'Just a second, there's one thing I don't understand,' said James. '*Why* are you so interested in all this?'

There was a long pause before Dr Hales replied simply, 'In time,' and disconnected the call.

CHAPTER SEVENTEEN
Austinium

AUSTIN FORCED HIS WAY FORWARDS amid the gathering outside the Las Cruces City Hall on Saturday the 19th of December. Icy rain bounced off his hood as he pushed through the boisterous crowd of Guy Furious's fanatical supporters. He had already made his way into the thickest part of the congregation, between the line of railings and planters on the path that led to the building's front entrance. It was warmer in the crowd, a fact for which he was thankful, but despite the earthen smell of the rain, the body odour of the protesters came through strongly and it was clear some of them paid no heed to basic hygiene.

This is my only chance to get to the bastard before Christmas. Make my way to the front and wait until he steps off the stage...

The crowd were waving placards and holding signs signalling their discontent with phrases such as 'No More Giant Leaps', 'Aliens Not Welcome' and 'Humans Above All'.

Some of the words had been reduced to barely legible streaks of coloured pigments by the rain, which ran off the placards and stained the wrists and coat sleeves of the protesters.

The rally had been organised well in advance as part of Guy's Stateside Tour. Despite the uncharacteristic weather, the event had attracted so many people that they filled the car park and spilled out onto Main Street, almost blocking traffic. There were even people gathered on the nearby roundabout, chanting and yelling and waving their signs in the downpour.

Guy stood on a portable stage which had been placed in front of the entrance to the building, making access difficult. His trademark velour suit was sodden and dark, which made him look even more dishevelled than usual. He was leaning over a lectern and shouting his speech into his megaphone with one hand, while the other gripped the side of the lectern like a vice.

'… and I'm told these people, your governors, don't even know? What a load of trash—of course they know! They're in on it too!' Guy cried, gesticulating wildly. 'The dangers of space are plain to see. If we carry on pushing out there, who knows what sleeping bears we might be prodding? And going back to Mars? We're like Atlas stealing the fire from Mount Etna!'

The crowd around Austin gave shouts of approval, jostling him in the process. Austin snorted and shook his head under his hood, and he pressed onwards, squeezing through the tight-knit group ahead of him.

What a moron. And people are just lapping up all this horseshit? The guy can't even get his metaphors straight.

'You all understand the truth!' Guy continued, nodding and pointing into the crowd. 'We're stealing from the grave of the gods themselves. Beings so far beyond our understanding that we are insignificant in comparison. They won't take too kindly to that, and if they find out, instead of ridding us of our lizard overlords like they were supposed to, they'll come back to wipe us all out.

'Humans belong on this big, beautiful, flat disk, not out there beyond the dome. And only *we* can stop this foolishness. Say no to ET!'

The protesters thrust their fists into the air and chanted, 'No to ET! No to ET! No to ET!'

Almost there, just a little further… Is this even the right thing to do?

Dr Barnes had been far too vague for Austin's liking. He had no idea what she meant by 'make it go away'.

I hope this is it; otherwise I'll just be making things worse.

The chanting and fist pumping died down and Guy continued, standing up straight at the lectern and swapping the megaphone to his other hand. 'And y'know what? The G-men know *we* hold the power to make the change. They're trying to silence me, and they'll try to silence you too. I've been uncovering the great secrets of the Illuminati's New World Order for years, and I have never felt so much pushback as I feel now. It means we're getting close, and growing to such numbers that it's making Them uncomfortable.

'Many of you were there at White Sands when an agent of the NWO assaulted me, and thanks to all your uploads, the rest of the world can see it too.' He paused and lowered the megaphone for a second. He lifted the megaphone back to his lips and sighed, placing a hand on his chest. 'I owe you all a debt. You saved my life that day. If I had been there alone, I know for certain I'd be dead, or dumped in some secret government black site. And for that, I thank you from the bottom of my heart.'

'We love you, Guy!' a protester shouted. It came from somewhere towards the back, impossible for Austin to tell where, and it was accompanied by cries of solidarity.

Austin was close to the front, a few rows back from where Guy was standing, keeping himself low.

Damn it, Austin, this is no time to be second-guessing yourself. Just wait for him to finish, then pounce.

'Now, you all keep fighting the good fight,' said Guy. 'That's all I've got for you today. I'll be taking a break over the holidays, but our next meet, which will be the last in this state'—there were audible groans from the crowd—'will be January ninth. Same time. Same place. You take care, stay alert, stay vigilant.'

Guy waved at the crowd, which erupted into cheering and applause, and he began to step down from the lectern.

The jostling of the people around Austin nearly knocked him off his feet. He put out his arms and steadied himself on the people either side. Just then, an errant arm flew up towards him and knocked the side of his head. Austin recoiled with a shout and his hood fell backwards.

The protester who'd knocked him turned around to look. 'Hey, man, I'm really sorry abou—' The protester stopped in his tracks and his eyes widened. 'You!' he cried. 'You're that dude who punched Guy!'

Shit, I've been made again.

Austin stood straight and looked around with a grimace. Several members of the crowd had heard the man shout and were now staring in Austin's direction and moving to surround him. He continued looking all around, turning this way and that, as the circle of angry protesters closed.

Another of them stepped forwards and spat on the ground at Austin's feet. 'You're not welcome here, G-man,' she said, glaring at him. 'You'd best leave before this turns ugly.'

Austin raised his hands, showing his palms and still turning. 'Hey, look. I'm… I'm just here to talk to Guy. I don't want no trouble.'

'Lies!' cried another. 'You're here to finish the job.' The protester turned and screamed into the crowd, 'State-sanctioned murder!'

Great, they think I'm here to assassinate him? I'd better go before Guy notices I'm here.

The hubbub drew Guy's attention, and he peered over the lectern into the rain-soaked crowd. His mouth fell open as he spotted Austin and he grabbed the megaphone once more.

'You see! The G-men have sent Captain Queen to take me out,' said Guy. 'But once again their attempt to silence the truth has failed. Get him outta here.'

The group of protesters surrounding Austin stepped forwards and grabbed him by the arms. He tried to shake them off, but they gripped even harder.

'Wait!' Austin called, looking up at Guy. 'I just want to talk! Maybe we can work this out?'

Guy gave a short laugh and said into the megaphone, 'Talk to my lawyers, Captain.' Then he dropped the megaphone to the ground and strode off, disappearing around the back of the building.

Damn it. Last chance to get him.

Austin launched himself forwards, trying to break free of the hold the protesters had on him and pursue Guy, but the protesters gripped tighter and shoved him backwards, causing him to stumble. He hit the sodden ground with a wet thump, landing on his elbow. With a pained grunt, and covered in grit and mud, he stood back up and stepped away, shaking his jacket back onto his shoulders. He watched the protesters glaring at him as he backed off and only turned around when he was sure they weren't going to follow him. With a grumble to himself, he set off down Main Street towards the town centre.

Gonna have to wait until after Christmas now… And I'll need a different approach. No more room for failure. I need to speak to the director and pray to God she understands.

'Fine,' the director said the next day, looking back down at the forms on her desk as the winter sun streaked in through the window behind her. 'We haven't heard anything else from Mr Furious's lawyers as yet, so you've got time. But the footage is still all over the internet. It's too late to stop it now and our reputation will tank over the holidays. You'll need to catch Mr Furious at the next rally and convince him to issue a retraction.'

Austin's mouth hung open and he stared at the director. After a moment he recovered himself and stammered, 'Wait, you're… really giving me the time on this?'

He hadn't expected to be given such leniency and had instead predicted a thorough telling-off before a swift removal by security.

Dr Barnes sighed and looked up from her forms, rolling her eyes at the same time. 'Austin. You're a huge pain in the ass, but God help me, I like you. Besides that, you're brilliant and we need you on the *Aurora* project. But if you can't get a handle on this, there'll be questions coming down from on high.'

'What kinda questions?'

'Questions about why I haven't fired you yet, for starters. Questions about *my* competence. Questions that'll end in the top brass throwing you out anyway. The project can't afford that, and I don't wanna do that to you either.'

'I understand, Director. Thank you,' said Austin, rising from his chair.

Dr Barnes nodded and continued writing in swift, scratchy movements.

He made his way to the door and reached out for the handle but hesitated. Steeling himself and taking his hand away, Austin turned back to face the director.

'Was there something else?' asked Dr Barnes without looking up.

'Err… yeah. There is actually,' said Austin, taking a step forwards and rubbing the back of his neck. 'We, uhh… we need approval to build a new generator from the Achelon specs.'

Dr Barnes stopped writing abruptly, leaving a long scratch across the page. She put the pen down on the desk with a snap and glared at Austin.

'I—I know we nearly blew up the lab,' he said, holding his hands up and taking another small step towards the desk. 'And I'm sorry for that. But we found the cause, and we think the device worked, if only for a fraction of a second. We need to build another one; otherwise this whole project is out.'

'The device worked?'

Placing one hand on his hip and rubbing his stubbly chin with the other, Austin said, 'Yeah. We think so. The instruments registered a couple of small spikes that correspond with the type of exotic matter we're trying to generate. The theory is that one of the plates slipped out of alignment, causing an instability in the system that released a huge burst of energy.'

The director's eyebrows rose and she stared at him for a short moment. Sighing heavily, she placed her head in her hands and said, 'If I approve this, just… promise me it's not going to explode again.'

'Like I said, we think we know the cause of the explosion. It's an easy fix. We just need to ensure the plates won't slip this time.'

'Okay. But I'm gonna hold you to that,' said Dr Barnes, looking up and pointing at him. 'Get one of your team to submit the paperwork and I'll file the approval. But... do it *after* the holidays for goodness' sake. I don't need this stress right before Christmas. Take your vacation time, and tell your team to do the same.'

Fighting back a grin, Austin replied, 'Thank you, Director,' then turned and left the room.

Following a welcome break for Christmas and New Year, Austin and his team returned to the Alien Research Department at White Sands.

'Morning, everyone,' cried Austin, peeking his head around the doors to the various labs on the way to his office at the end of the corridor.

Flinging the door open, he stepped through into the room. It was small and cramped, having formerly served as a storage closet, as was evident from the lingering musty smell of mould and dust. Austin's desk was in the centre of the room, situated just in front of the window, which looked as though it had been installed in a hurry. On the desk, to one side of the computer, Austin kept the photograph of Poochie he had taken on the *Magnum Opus*, and there was a variety of pens strewn across the worktop.

As Austin moved further into the diminutive space, he looked at the desk and raised an eyebrow; on top of his writing mat was a stack of papers, neatly stapled down one side.

That's the paperwork Cass gave to the director...

He leaned over the desk and picked up the document and

flicked through until he got to a few pages from the back.

'Hah!' he laughed as he looked at the page. Quickly closing the document and rolling it up in his hands, he shot back out into the corridor.

Moments later, and following a frantic run around the labs, Austin stood in the spacious testing room with his team of technicians and engineers gathered around, explaining that the director had approved their request to build the new machine.

'We've already made the necessary adjustments on the blueprints, sir. Shouldn't take us beyond the end of the week to actually build the thing,' said Anders, the lead engineer, amid a smattering of affirmative murmurs from his subordinates.

'And I've recalibrated the sensors to focus in better on the bands we found the spikes in last time,' Cass offered. 'They'll be more sensitive and give us a more accurate measure of the amounts and types of energy we're generating.'

Cracking a smile, Austin gave a small laugh and put his hands on his hips. 'That's great news, guys,' he said, 'well done, everyone. Let's get down to it.' He glanced at Anders. 'I'll need to review those blueprints first. I don't wanna take any chances this time.'

'Yes, sir,' Anders replied. 'I'll have them sent to your office immediately.'

Austin nodded and told the group to disperse to their various tasks, building, calibrating, checking and supervising the construction of the Macroscopic Exotic Mass-Energy Field Generator, Mark II.

And so it was, on Friday the 8th of January, the team gathered once again in the testing room. The engineers heaved the large box onto a small plinth in the centre of the floor space. Once the device was placed and plugged in, the team retreated to join Austin and Cass behind the new protective screen.

'Second time's a charm,' Austin muttered, holding the controller. His hands shook and sweat accumulated on his brow as he stared at the generator. The testing room was cold; its high ceiling and thin walls offered little protection from the winter air. It had been converted from an old aircraft hangar especially for the *Aurora* project. Just like everything else to do with the project, it had been converted in a hurry. Since he had returned to Earth from the *Magnum*, Austin had lamented the fact that his superiors hadn't bothered getting things ready while he and his crew were on the way back from Mars—despite Austin having informed them of what he was bringing back. And so, three years down the line, his team still had to make do with a draughty hangar and a couple of glorified broom closets. At least the laboratories were suitable, and they had been able to make good progress.

If they were so concerned about this new space race against the Russians and the Chinese, they could've given us better facilities…

A hand appeared on Austin's shoulder, breaking his stare. He glanced around to see Anders smiling at him.

'It'll be fine, sir,' he said. 'Everything is secured in place. God himself couldn't move those plates.'

Austin scoffed. 'Don't get cocky,' he said, turning back to look at the generator.

Nineteen hundred pounds of mass. If this thing explodes…

His thumb hovered over the button as before. The metal control unit was cold, chilling his fingers to the bone, and it was covered in raised flecks of peeling paint which crackled as he flexed his hand.

Images of Poochie rushed into his mind, followed by

Alex, Emily and the boys; then his mind wandered on to James and Zhu.

Is this gonna be it? Will I ever see them again? Stop it; it'll be fine. The new design is sound, and we've checked and double-checked for any irregularities. Trust the science. But...

'Ah, screw it,' he muttered, shaking his head. Standing straight, rolling back his shoulders and raising his voice, he said, 'Project *Aurora*, Achelon Macroscopic Exotic Mass-Energy Field Generator Test Two. Friday, January eighth, 2027. Commencing in three... two... one...'

Here goes nothin'...

There was a loud clack from the controller as he forced the switch down, and the machine whirred to life. All was calm for the first couple of minutes, the only sound in the room the rising hum as the gathered scientists looked on.

Lights began to flicker and the team exchanged worried glances, but still the machine continued whirring.

Nothing unusual yet... No funny smells. Gotta watch for vibrations.

Tearing his gaze away from the machine, Austin looked over at Cass at the monitoring station. 'Any readings yet?' he called.

'Yes, sir!' she replied, shouting above the din. 'We're getting the same small spikes as before, and they're growing. It looks like the new design is holding.'

'Don't count your chickens,' called Austin, turning his attention back to the generator. 'No matter how the machine holds, if we can't get enough energy, the project's a wash-out. No way we'll generate a warp field without it.'

'Well, isn't someone being a Negative Nancy lately!'

Without taking his eyes off the box, he said, 'Yeah, well, I got a lot on my plate right now. Can't always be Mr Positive. Just keep your eyes on those sensors!'

There was a loud bang and a shower of sparks, and Austin and the team threw themselves to the ground.

Wait... the machine's still going? It didn't explode. Thank God.

Austin looked up and saw that the box was still intact. 'False alarm, people,' he called, standing up and dusting himself off. 'Just one of the light fittings. At least it stopped 'em flickering!'

Cass pulled herself off the floor and back into her chair. 'Captain! Come take a look.'

Austin rushed over and leaned towards the monitor, the back of Cass's chair creaking as he pushed his hand down onto it.

'Alright, Cass, what am I lookin' at here?' he asked.

Cass pointed at the screen and explained, 'This graph shows the ranges in which we expect to see a generation of negative energy. You can see there's a huge ongoing spike here. It rose rapidly but has levelled off and is holding steady.'

'Looks great! But is it enough?'

'That's what's remarkable, sir,' said Cass, giving him a sidelong glance. 'There's a negative energy density inside that generator that corresponds to the *exact* amount the Achelon specs indicated.'

Austin's mouth fell open. 'It... It's working? It's *really* working?'

'Yes, sir. We have officially generated Austinium.'

Austin gave her a confused look and said, 'Austinium? What the hell is that?'

Cass shrugged. 'It needs a name, right? And you're the team leader. All those exotic particles doing their quantum

thing and exerting a negative energy field inside that box…'
She looked around at Austin and smiled. 'Besides, I think
it's catchy.'

Austin's cheeks warmed. 'We are *not* calling it that,' he
said, half-laughing and rubbing the back of his neck.

'I dunno, sir,' said Anders from across the way. 'It's a
good name.'

Austin grumbled, 'I don't want anything named after me.'

'Well, if it's good enough for Casimir…' Anders snorted.

The captain frowned and grumbled. After a moment he
cleared his throat and turned back to Cass, saying, 'I think
that's enough for test number two. Would you like to do the
honours of powering it down?'

He handed Cass the control unit, and she took it with a
firm grip. She held her thumb on the switch and pushed down
as hard as she could. With a glance and a smirk at Austin, she
raised her voice and said, 'Test two successful. Austinium
Generator powering down.'

CHAPTER EIGHTEEN
TELOMER LABS

I*MMORTAL? HOW THE HELL AM I supposed to tell Angela some crazy bullshit like that?*

James sat with his eyes closed and his head in his hands, the conversation with Dr Hales playing on repeat in his mind. He revisited every one of the doctor's words over and over in careful detail. Perhaps he had misinterpreted something. Perhaps there was a crackle on the phone and it only sounded like the doctor had said that. Maybe he had imagined the whole thing?

James looked down at the phone, still in his hand, and unlocked it. The screen opened up to his call history, which displayed the details, clear as day:

Incoming Call: Dr Hales – Friday 8 January 2027 – 3 minutes, 24 seconds.

He had checked to make sure the call had really happened

three times already. With a grumble, he locked the phone again and stuffed it into his pocket, then went back to holding his face in his hands. He pressed his eyes with his palms and watched the colourful fireworks and morphing shapes behind his eyelids for a few moments, before pulling his hands away with a groan. He slumped back into the sofa.

It's real. Angela's been as desperate for these test results as I have. What do I say? Maybe I could say they were inconclusive and wait until after I've been to the hospital on Monday.

The thought of lying to Angela instantly made him feel guilty for even considering it.

No. I'd rather say nothing than an outright lie. Oh, God. What does all this mean for our relationship? I haven't even had a chance to propose yet. Maybe she won't want to…

James got up and wandered up and down the length of the living room, feeling melancholic. Sputnik looked up wearily from his bed in the back room, then laid his head back down again and closed his eyes. James's thoughts dwelled on a grim future. If it were true that he could not age and die, then even if Angela still agreed to be with him, he would have to watch as she withered away while he remained unchanging. Then he would remain long after she was gone, frozen in time.

When we get older, I'll look young enough to be her son. How would we explain that? I'd be prepared to do it, if she wanted to. But she'd be better off without me now. Better for her to find a mortal she can grow old and share the experiences of life with. Someone who could relate to her. I can't do that now. They took that from me.

He stopped and stood in front of the sofa, where Austin had sat months before, filling in the gaps in the story for

James. He stared out of the window, through the bright-white net curtains, at the calm neighbourhood outside, the residents completely unaware they now had a mythological being living among them. James exhaled lightly in amusement and considered that he now felt he had more in common with the trees planted along the roadside than his neighbours.

Sputnik padded up to him and sniffed at his dangling hand, whimpering a little, seemingly feeling James's internal strife. James bent down without taking his unfocused eyes off the view outside and stroked him. It lightened his mood; the little puppy had a knack for cheering him up.

No wonder the captain loves his dog so much…

He sighed and resolved to say nothing to Angela about the call unless she asked. He would wait until after his meeting with Dr Hales on Monday, when he hoped he would have more information.

But one thing nagged at him throughout the rest of the day: what had the doctor meant by 'in time' when James had asked what his interest was? What were Dr Hales's true intentions with his case? It seemed to James a little farfetched at this stage that it was simply the allure of the exotic, and so he resolved to do some digging.

The weekend went by without incident, and James's initial forays into researching Dr Hales turned up nothing out of the ordinary for a private neurology consultant. If there was anything to be found, he would have to go deeper. But he made the decision to do this another time. Angela had been so exhausted when she got in from work on that Friday night that she'd skipped dinner and gone straight to bed. When she failed to ask about any news of the results the next day, it seemed to James that she had simply assumed there would be no calls on a Saturday or Sunday.

So, on the Monday morning, just after Angela left for work, James said goodbye to Sputnik and set off for the hospital. Despite his having to take public transport this time around, the journey didn't take much longer than it had by car. When he arrived at the hospital, he found Dr Makewell sitting in one of the reception area chairs, looking down at his phone.

James chuckled to himself as he approached the doctor, who was facing away from him. The thought of Dr Makewell having to wait there all day for James to turn up was amusing. Without a word, James walked around and sat next to the man. He waited a few moments before clearing his throat.

Dr Makewell looked around, startled. He apologised for his absentmindedness and then led James through the corridors once more to Dr Hales's office. Leaving James at the door, he did his disappearing act again.

James knocked on the door and entered after hearing Dr Hales's response. The doctor was once again seated behind his desk examining a thick file filled with papers. He greeted James in his usual fashion—though this time not attempting to shake his hand—then picked up the file and slotted it into the drawer of a short cabinet next to his desk.

'I am so glad you could make it, Commander,' he said, walking around the desk and patting James on the arm. 'Please, come with me.' He then opened the door and motioned for James to walk through.

'Where are we going, Doc?' asked James as Dr Hales shut and locked the office door behind him.

'You'll see,' he grinned.

He led James in the opposite direction to the one he had come from, through unfamiliar, quiet, winding corridors, through back doors and access stairwells which echoed and clanged with their footsteps. The clinical white of the hospital gave way to industrial grey as they headed away from the public-facing areas. After several minutes, the passageways ended in a set of double doors, which in turn led out into a small, gloomy car park at the rear of the hospital. In it sat a solitary vehicle, a black Range Rover with tinted windows, situated in a bay in the darkest corner.

James felt a measure of concern and slowed his pace behind the doctor, saying, 'Hold on. Where are we going?'

'Hmm?' Dr Hales grunted in reply, stopping abruptly and turning to face James. The doctor turned towards the car, then looked back at James with a confused expression. He raised his eyebrows as if he'd had an epiphany, then his wrinkled face relaxed into a smile. He let out a short laugh and said, 'Oh, no need to worry, dear boy. You're not in any danger. Please, step inside the vehicle.'

But James stood his ground as the doctor unlocked the car remotely. 'I am not getting into that car until you tell me where we're going. I thought we were doing some experiments in a hospital lab?'

Dr Hales sighed and said, with an air of excited impatience, 'We are simply going to a facility that is better equipped to deal with your specific needs. Please, trust me. You're going to like this.'

James grumbled and then relented, reluctantly opening the passenger door of the Range Rover and climbing inside. He buckled himself in as Dr Hales jumped into the driver's seat, started the car and drove away, out of the dingy parking area.

During the drive, James stared vacantly out of the darkened side window. The car was quiet, and all he could hear was the muffled noises of the outside world: the sound of wheels on wet tarmac reverberating up into the cab, the whoosh of passing cars and the bleeping of the odd pedestrian crossing. He allowed his mind to empty, trying not to think too much about the uncertainty of the situation. Nevertheless, questions bounced around in the background of his mind. Could Dr Hales be trusted? He seemed legit, based on James's earlier research, but all this seemed rather strange. The doctor had said 'facility', which meant they weren't going to his private hospital but somewhere else. And what kind of facility would be better equipped for diagnostic tests than a hospital? But Dr Hales had offered to help him, and he was the only one with even the first clue as to what was happening to him, so James concluded that if he wanted to learn more, he had no choice but to trust him.

James had barely felt the time of their short and silent journey pass, but his eyes pulled back into focus as the car turned and rolled through the gateway to a large grey-blue industrial warehouse. He looked around through the windscreen, and then craned his neck a little to see around the doctor, through the driver's side window. He needn't have bothered, as moments later the car stopped and both James and the doctor got out of the vehicle.

The warehouse looked as though it had seen better days, with large patches of rust visible through chipped paint on the walls. James surveyed his surroundings to get his bearings and to assess the area.

No other cars here. High fences, a perimeter of thick bushes, barbed wire… At least I can see the Thames over the back there. Otherwise, pretty isolated. Only escape route is through the big gate. I'd be buggered if that gets closed.

Dr Hales had rushed over to a small door in the side of the warehouse. His keys jangled as he took them out of his pocket and fumbled for the keyhole.

What's his rush?

The doctor opened the door and beckoned to James, who began his cautious approach, wondering how easily he'd be able to grab the keys and get to the car if things went south.

I've seen this movie. Things always go south.

Dr Hales held the door open as James went through. He pushed aside the net of cloudy plastic curtains that dangled just in the entranceway. As they clattered behind him, he stopped and stared with wide eyes and mouth agape, taken aback by the sight before him.

What had appeared to be a dilapidated warehouse from the outside gave way to a high-tech clinical environment on the inside, bathed in the almost blinding white of the lights on the metal rafters high above. Transparent walls showed the space to be subdivided into rooms full of advanced electronic equipment and computers, and server rooms. There were people dressed in white lab coats milling about, while others occupied chairs in the various labs. James could hear the sound of fans, and through the transparent walls he could just about see gym equipment and other, larger opaque objects at the far end of the warehouse.

He felt a slap on his back as Dr Hales stopped next to him.

'Magnificent, isn't it?' said the doctor, continuing to clank down the metal gangway towards the first of the laboratories. 'Welcome, Commander, to TELOMER Labs,' he cried, stopping and turning to face James.

'Telomere?' said James, confused. 'Like in chromosomes?'

'It's a good pun, isn't it?' Dr Hales replied with glee. 'T.E.L.O.M.E.R. Short for the Thames Estuary Laboratory of MEtagenic Research. I realise it's a little wordy, but we didn't have a lot of time.'

James followed Dr Hales down the gangway, looking

around in astonishment.

What the hell is all this...? 'Metagenic research', 'didn't have the time'—it almost sounds like he set this up in a hurry. How much money does his hospital have?

He continued to follow the doctor into the first laboratory. Dr Hales sat down at a computer terminal and started tapping away at the keyboard, filling out some form on the screen.

'This is incredible, Doc. I wasn't expecting anything like this. What kind of experiments are we doing? How long is it going to take?' asked James, looking around in wonder, his prior misgivings eroded.

There was a sharp, rhythmic buzzing sound behind him and the clatter of plastic. He turned and saw a small printer on the desk along the far wall.

'Oh, get that, would you?' said Dr Hales, motioning with his hand without looking up from the screen.

James wandered over to the printer and picked up the small plastic object that had finished printing. He turned it over and saw that it was an ID card, with a photograph of him and his details printed on one side. In the top corner was the TELOMER Labs logo in a stylish blue.

'That is yours, Commander.' The suddenness of Dr Hales's voice almost made James jump as he stared at the card. The doctor continued, 'You'll need it to come and go from this facility in the future. When we've installed the reader, that is. Now, come with me, please, and we will get started.'

The next ten minutes had James following Dr Hales through the facility, greeting the other staff members. They all seemed to stare at James with some kind of reverence, which unnerved him. He couldn't be sure whether it was because he was an astronaut and the first man on Mars— fame he could handle—or because they all knew about his supposed immortality. At last, after many handshakes on James's part, the two came to the testing area with treadmills and other gym equipment.

There was a—thankfully opaque—changing area to his left, and Dr Hales told him to enter and change into the clothes he found in there.

James walked through and found neatly folded grey shorts and a tank top sitting on a wooden bench in the middle of the room which was surrounded by bays of swimming-pool lockers. He stuffed his clothes into one and changed into the outfit. There was another door at the opposite end of the changing room from where he had entered, and so once he was dressed, he walked through it.

Immediately, he was greeted by a woman with short brown hair wearing the same pristine white lab coat as the rest of her colleagues. She led him to the treadmill in the centre of the testing room, which was overlooked by Dr Hales in one of the laboratories. Just before James stepped on, she picked up a set of wires with sticky pads on and, without a word, set about attaching them all over James's body.

Dr Hales's voice came over an intercom: 'Now, we'll begin with something easy. Get on the treadmill, Commander. Start with a light jog and work slowly up to a sprint. I will be monitoring your vitals from here and I'll let you know when to stop.'

Later that afternoon, James stood on a crowded Tube train, holding on to the overhead rail to keep himself from jostling the other squashed passengers as the carriage rocked and bumped. He was travelling home from the hospital on the same route he had taken to get there—a journey which seemed to be taking three times as long, and he definitely felt like he could have done without making it during the rush hour. Still, he was glad that his wary assessment of the facility had proven unnecessary, as things had not gone south as he'd feared.

At the end of their session at the warehouse, Dr Hales had dropped him back off at the same dingy car park and instructed him to meet him in the office the following Monday for their next session. It was only temporary, the doctor assured him, and hopefully in the next few weeks James would be able to use the ID card to come and go directly from the warehouse.

Physically, he felt fine, but mentally he was drained, exhausted from the supposed 'light' experiments that Dr Hales had insisted upon after the treadmill. James had ended up running for well over two hours before the doctor was satisfied. As expected from his own testing, James felt fine, but it was still strange to know he had run at full pelt for that long and not even broken a sweat. After that, he had been given a break to have lunch while Dr Hales went off to another laboratory to analyse the findings. Then, upon his return, more blood and tissue samples had been taken and they'd moved on to other experiments, similar in nature to the things James had tried—like underwater tests and weight training—but more scientifically rigorous.

At the end of the session, Dr Hales had shared some provisional results from the experiments and explained that these showed James's respiratory system had become vastly more efficient than any human's—something which James felt went without saying. It was the effect of the augmentation on his muscular system that surprised him the most, however. His muscles now prevented the exhausting build-up of lactic acid and allowed the fibres to contract with greater force. Dr Hales had also showed James the detailed results of his last genome test compared with the one he'd had during his coma. The doctor explained the numbers and figures, and how they showed that James was indeed immortal.

Maybe I am becoming a superhero…

It wasn't long before the train came to James's stop and he alighted. The moment he exited the station, squinting in the bright afternoon sun and breathing the chill wintry air, he felt a series of buzzes in his pocket. He pulled his phone out and watched as various messages and notifications populated the screen, all from Angela. He looked at one of the earliest and saw that she had come home from work early and wondered where he was. Her inability to contact him for the last couple of hours had led to her sending more messages and attempting to call him:

> *Love of my Life: Jst got bk early. Ur not homw???*
> *Love of my Life: home***
> *Love of my Life: Where r u????*
> *Love of my Life: Im worried*

As he cycled through the worried texts, he began to feel guilty. He hadn't wanted her to find out like this. He'd wanted to bring the subject up in the calm of a restful evening together; he hadn't banked on her coming home early, and worried what she would think about his disappearance.

Damn. Think I'm in the shit now…

He made his way over to the nearest bus stop and didn't have to wait long for the next to come along. It was crowded, and he stood in the middle in front of some buggies, staring down at his phone and wondering whether to text back or just wait until he was home.

Eventually, about halfway through the bus journey, he sent a single message:

James: Omw <3

'You are WHAT?' cried Angela, leaning forwards on the sofa and setting her mouth agape.

Her eyes were red and damp and her legs were crossed with her feet tucked under as she cuddled a cushion. She had flung herself at him, embracing him tightly as soon as he had walked through the door. Then she'd cried into his chest, explaining that she had imagined an entire scenario where he had broken down and gone off wandering, never to be heard from again. Her relief, however, had quickly turned to frustration at what she perceived as his carelessness.

James had sat her down on the sofa in the living room and gone to make them both a hot chocolate, promising a full explanation while she calmed her nerves. When he'd returned he'd sat on the adjacent sofa and told her of the Friday call from Dr Hales. But he'd only got as far as the results when she cried out in shock.

'Yeah, I didn't believe it at first either,' he said, taking a sip of his cocoa. The liquid was still far too hot and burned his tongue a little. He had done it more for a natural pause to gather his thoughts than because he was thirsty.

Coming to her senses and shaking her head, Angela spat, 'We can talk about that later. Where the hell did you go? Is there… another woman?'

'What?' James nearly spat his drink out. 'No! Of course not. Dr Hales asked me to go to some facility to run some experiments.'

'And you didn't think to tell me?' she said, looking hurt

and scowling.

'Ange… I'm sorry to have made you worry. In fact, I did it this way *because* I didn't want to worry you. I thought I'd, you know, find out a bit more about those results first before telling you. It's a pretty big thing to get your head around.'

Her scowl softened and she huffed, 'I suppose so.'

'Another woman indeed!' James scoffed.

Angela sniffed and cracked a sad smile, letting out a short laugh. She extended her arms outwards, the over-long sleeves of her cardigan drooping over her hands. James got up and sat next to her, and the two relaxed into each other's arms.

'Tell me about it then,' she said softly after a few minutes.

James explained all that had happened at TELOMER Labs and went into depth about the preliminary findings on his abilities. Angela remained quiet throughout and just hugged James all the more.

She pulled away and looked up at him. 'So they're serious then. You really *are* immortal. Oh, James! There has to be a way to reverse this, surely?' she said with growing urgency.

'You mean a cure?' James looked down at her as she rested her head back on his shoulder. 'Sorry, love, I… didn't think to ask.'

Angela sat up and glared at him. 'You didn't think to ask?'

'Next week's session. I promise,' he replied, holding up his hands.

'How could you not think to ask? Have you even thought about what this could mean for us?'

James backed up on the sofa and turned to face Angela. His tone became defensive as he said, 'Of course I have! What, do you think I want this?'

Angela raised her voice: 'Sure seems like it to me. Living forever, never aging, immunity to cancer *and* super strength, speed and stamina? Sounds like you're enjoying it!'

'I do *not* have super strength, or super speed,' James retorted. 'And how dare you accuse me of enjoying this! I just want to be normal, Ange. To get back to a normal life and spend it with you.'

Angela slammed her fists impotently into the sofa cushions and shouted, 'But it's never going to be normal, is it? Everything's changed. You're going to leave me behind to wither and rot. Then in a thousand fucking years you'll have forgotten me.'

'I will *never* forget you!' James roared.

'Don't be stupid, you won't have a choice,' she yelled, her voice cracking. 'Our minds aren't meant to go on forever. Your memories of this time and place—of me—will fade away whether you like it or not.'

Tears streamed down Angela's reddened cheeks. Her face crumpled. She grabbed a cushion and buried her face in it with only messy tufts of hair visible around the edges, and sobbed.

James sat and watched, speechless, helpless, as Angela broke down in front of him. His cheeks were flushed and hot, and his heart ached. He wiped his face with his hands and leant forwards. He'd known this would happen, that she wouldn't take it well, and he hated being right. He loved her more than anything and she was right: if there was no cure, they would have no future; it would be the end. But he wasn't ready to give up just yet.

'Ange,' he said softly after her convulsions had subsided. 'It's all been so much to take in. I just wanted to find out more, to confirm it wasn't just some cruel joke. Believe me, I don't want this. Finding out about a cure is my top priority. But… if there is no cure—'

'Then we're finished,' Angela growled, looking up from her cushion.

It was like a knife to James's heart. He stared at her, dumbstruck at her anger. After a few moments, her expression changed to one of surprise and sorrow, and she seemed to realise what she had said.

'Did you... really mean that?' he asked.

She looked down and tightened her grip on the cushion, letting out a heavy sigh. 'No...' she whispered.

James breathed a sigh of relief and said, 'Look, I don't care what people might say about us in the future. Even if my condition can't be reversed, I'm still willing to make a go of it. Unless you don't want to...'

Angela sighed heavily and wiped her eyes, looking around the room and straightening her messy hair. 'Of course I want to,' she said with a sniff. 'I'm sorry.'

'Let's just take this one day at a time, eh, love?' said James, mustering a weak smile.

Nodding silently, Angela smiled, then leaned forwards and kissed him. He placed his hands on her lower back and she moaned quietly. She pulled back a little and looked into his eyes, before getting up from the sofa and grabbing his hand.

'Come on,' she said with a wry smile, tugging on his arm to pull him to his feet. 'I need to feel better. Show me some of that extra stamina.'

James blushed and laughed, gladly following her lead up the stairs.

CHAPTER NINETEEN
CONSPIRACY

DING! The hotel receptionist turned at the sound of the bell and walked over to the counter with a tut, folding her phone closed and dropping it into her pocket. This was the third time in the last half hour that she had been interrupted from her very important work watching cat videos in 8K on her phone, and at this point in her over-long shift, she was having none of it.

A stout, muscular man in a grey hooded sweatshirt stood before her at the counter. From what she could see of his face, he had longish stubble covering his square jaw, as though he hadn't bothered to shave in over a week. His eyes were in the shadow of his hood, but he soon raised both hands and pulled it back, revealing short, greying crew-cut hair and dark eyes. He seemed vaguely familiar to her, but she couldn't place where she recognised him from, and in any case she was so far done with work that she no longer cared to wonder.

'What do you want?' she snapped, leaning on the counter with her head in her hand.

The man began to speak, but she cut him off.

'Let me guess,' she said. 'You're one of his lunatic followers and you're hoping I'll let you past to go see him. Well, I'm afraid the rally finished hours ago and I can't let you through unless you've got a reservation, or express permission, which I doubt you've got. So, scram.'

It was Saturday the 9th of January and Guy's last rally in New Mexico had brought waves of rowdy visitors through the hotel, even after it ended. They all wanted to go see the man himself, and the receptionist had had quite enough of it.

The man smiled and gave a small laugh at her words. It wasn't derisive or cocky, and that caught her off guard.

As she frowned, the man spoke in a soft, understanding tone. 'Naw, I ain't no follower of Guy Furious, but I guess you've been getting 'em coming through that door like clockwork, right?'

The receptionist nodded and said, 'They're infuriating, and freakin' rude!'

'They sure are! But you're right, I am hoping to see him,' said the man, continuing to smile. 'The name's Austin, by the way. Captain Austin Queen. I work for NASA out of White Sands, and I have urgent business with Guy.'

Austin Queen? The astronaut! Wait… didn't he assault Guy recently?

'Wait… didn't you assault Guy recently?' she blurted.

Shit, I said the quiet part out loud!

Her cheeks turned a deep shade of red and her hands shot to her mouth as she stumbled an apology. 'Oh, God! I am so sorry. I meant…'

Austin laughed, holding up his hands, and said, 'Don't

worry about it. You're absolutely right, I did. Made a damn fool of myself, and I'm here to put things straight. Don't worry, I don't mean Guy any harm, but I gotta make my apologies before he leaves the state. So can you help me out here?'

The receptionist shook her head. 'I can't. Like I said, no one can get through without a reservation or express permission.'

Austin nodded, still maintaining his smile. 'I understand. Listen, I'm sorry to trouble you like this, but could I have the phone extension for the room perhaps?'

'Normally, I'd say no,' said the receptionist. She saw Austin's face fall slightly. 'But y'know what? You're the only person who's been even halfway nice to me today, so… sure, whatever.'

She grabbed a pen and a piece of scrap paper from under the desk, scribbled a number on it and handed it to Austin. He thanked her and retreated to the corner of the foyer, pulling out his phone.

The receptionist watched as he unfolded the phone, dialled the number and placed the device to his ear. She shook her head.

Nice guy, but as if Guy's gonna agree to meet him. Paranoid weirdo.

* * *

The phone rang in his ear for a long time, and Austin wondered whether the receptionist had purposely given him the wrong number. He couldn't blame her; after all, she wasn't obligated to help him, and for all he knew she could be putting her job on the line by giving him the number. He glanced over to the desk and saw that she had gone back to staring at her phone.

269

As he did so, he heard a click on the line, which made him turn back towards the corner.

An irate voice came over the line. 'Hey! I thought I told you not to let anybody up here already. That means no one. *Nada*. Zilch. Capiche? I'm tryna reach my Zen here!'

'What the hell does that even mean, Guy?' said Austin.

There was a moment of silence. It seemed to Austin as though he could hear the slow turning of cogs inside Guy's mind.

'What—Captain Queen? How'd you get this number? I'm gonna call the cops!' shouted Guy.

'No, no, don't hang up,' said Austin. 'Now, hold on just a minute. I need to speak with you. Face to face.'

Guy laughed. 'Why on the flat Earth would I wanna do that?'

'Because,' Austin replied. He glanced around and then lowered his voice further, covering his mouth with his hand, as he said, 'You'll get something out of it. Something you want. So if you just let me speak with you face to face, it'll be worth your while, I promise.'

'And how do I know this ain't just some government trick?'

My God, he really does believe all this nonsense.

'No tricks,' said Austin. 'Now, I'm gonna hang up. You call down to reception and tell the nice lady that you're giving me permission to come up, alright?'

'Fine,' said Guy after another moment of silence, before he disconnected the call.

Austin folded the phone away in his pocket and waited. He looked around the foyer. It was dimly lit despite the darkness of the evening outside, but the light was warm and comforting. Both the corner he was standing in and the one at the opposite end had seating areas with sofas in brown leather and low tables adorned with a single flower in a vase.

The reception desk was long and had a fascia of marble. It took up most of the space in the middle of the foyer, and a short red carpet led from it to the revolving doors. The hotel itself was newly built and situated on the outskirts of Las Cruces, but it seemed busy enough—especially good for the small number of protesters wanting easy access to White Sands—though Austin mused that Guy's tour had been like a double-edged sword for the hotel—more footfall, but trouble to go along with it.

It was only about a minute's wait until the ringing of the reception desk's phone echoed in the foyer. Austin smiled as he watched the receptionist answer it. It looked from her expression that she was probably talking to Guy, but Austin didn't need to wonder for long, as she called him over the moment she put the phone down.

'Well, colour me surprised,' she said as Austin trundled over. 'I don't know what you said to the man, but he's happy for you to go up. He's in room one-seventeen. Go through that way,' she said, pointing to a door to Austin's right. 'One floor up, halfway along.'

'Thank you kindly,' he said with a smile and a nod of the head.

In no time at all, Austin had made his way up to Guy's floor and, finding room 117, he knocked once.

A few seconds later, the door opened a crack and half of Guy's face appeared in the opening.

'Speak your piece and go,' said Guy. There was an uncharacteristic tremble in his voice and his only visible eye was wide and darted frantically.

Staring back at him with a deadpan expression, Austin said, barely above a whisper, 'What I gotta say can't be said in the corridor. Now let me in.'

Guy's face disappeared from the opening in the doorway. Scuffling and scrambling could be heard beyond, until finally Guy called from somewhere further back in the room, 'Enter!'

Austin pushed the door, easing it open with a creak, then stepped through. The entranceway was narrow, with a bathroom to one side and a built-in wardrobe to the other, but beyond, the room opened out to a luxurious size. It was stylishly furnished and comfortably lit, with a king-size bed on one wall, and there was ample floor space between it and the desk, upon which sat a large ultra-flat television along with other modern accoutrements. Austin allowed his gaze to wander around the room until it settled on a curiosity: a small table lying on its side between the bed and the desk, in front of the balcony doors.

Stifling a laugh, Austin made his way further into the room. The top of Guy's head poked out above the table, his man-bun wobbling as he trembled.

Austin sauntered over to an armchair behind the wall of the entranceway and sat down. He threw one leg over the other and stared, amused, waiting for Guy to show himself.

Without relinquishing his cover, Guy said, 'Okay, you're in. Say what you gotta say and leave.'

'I ain't here to hurt you, if that's what's got you rattled,' said Austin. Guy remained silent and unmoving, so Austin continued, 'Y'know, this conversation'd go a lot easier if I weren't talkin' to a table.'

'Yeah? Well, it's the best you're gonna get, G-man,' Guy spat, rattling the table. 'I'm not giving you a shot!'

Austin's amusement at the situation began to wear thin and he exclaimed with a frown, 'Christ, man, how'd you *think* guns work? If I were to shoot you, the bullet would go right through that table. Now get your ass out from there—you're making yourself look even more of a fool!'

If that were possible.

Slowly, reluctantly, Guy lifted his head over the edge of the table. His eyes were wide, manic, and his face was pale. With raised hands he stood, his posture submissive.

'Take a seat,' said Austin, motioning to the bed.

Guy obeyed, perching awkwardly on the edge, his body sinking low.

'Thank you,' Austin said with a sigh. He leaned forwards in the chair, looking down at his hands, considering his next words. Clearing his throat, he looked up at Guy and said, 'Now, look… First off I wanna be straight with you and apologise for hittin' you. I let you rile me and I lost control, and for that I'm sorry. It's just, I've been dealing with a lot of stuff since I came back, and I thought I was making good progress. But the guilt and the weight of what happened out there are still sitting with me, and when you said those things about Yula, I…'

Austin's gaze suddenly became fierce, despite his eyes welling up, and he raised his voice as he continued, 'You don't know what it's like! You're sitting here in your hotel room goin' on about "conspiracy this, conspiracy that". I was the commanding officer and I lost two members of my team; damn near lost a third! So while I regret taking it out on you, don't you dare presume to know what happened out there.'

Guy maintained his wide-eyed stare, but his expression loosened, the slight change turning it from one of terror to visible confusion. After a few seconds, Guy broke into a grin. He laughed and slapped his knees.

'Is that *all*? Is that what the great Captain Queen came all the way up here for? Some sob story and a half-baked apology? If you're expecting me to just accept it, you're even more delusional than I am!'

Austin raised an eyebrow.

Was that… self-awareness?

'No, Guy,' said Austin, lowering his voice again with a sigh. 'I know you're not that kind of person. And no, it's not the only reason I'm here, but it is related… I have a request.'

Seeing weakness, and emboldened by the captain's contrition, Guy stood up from the bed and placed his hands on his hips, looking down on Austin. He regarded the man for a short while, then laughed harshly.

'A request! The great Captain Prince of Lies, the Devil of White Sands himself, assaults me in public, then comes to *me* asking a favour? The size of your brass balls! The ordnancy!'

'Audacity,' said Austin, keeping his cool stare on Guy.

'Audacity!' Guy cried, throwing his hands up, then he took a seat on the bed once more. 'What is it then? Oh, I can't wait to hear this.'

Unblinking, Austin replied, 'I want you to issue a public retraction of the bad press you've given White Sands and stop pursuing the lawsuit.'

Guy looked at Austin, his mouth agape. The stunned silence in the room was palpable, and the two stared at one another for what seemed like minutes as Guy processed the ridiculousness of what Austin had said.

'Why the hell would I do a thing like that?' Guy muttered, almost to himself. He shook his head and refocused his eyes on Austin, who had not moved or shown any sign that he was joking, and said, 'Let me guess, that thing you said would be worth my while… you're gonna try and buy me off? Typical of you G-men, all buy-offs, pay-offs and bribes, and if that don't work…' Guy drew his thumb across his neck, making a scraping sound with his mouth.

Austin laughed. 'I did consider the money angle for a while,' he said with a smile. 'But I figure you're a man not easily bought. So no, I'm not offering you money, and I'm not here to kill you either. I have something much more to your tastes: information.'

With a snort Guy got up to turn away, and with a dismissive wave he said, 'No, thanks. I don't want official NASA lies. I am a spokesperson for the outrageous truth. Your currency's bad, Captain.'

'NASA doesn't know.'

Guy stopped in his tracks and looked around at Austin, giving him a sidelong stare. 'What do you mean?'

'I mean,' said Austin, 'that I was simply told to make you go away. The director was vague on the details. They have no idea that I'm here and they've given me no approval to reveal anything to you.'

'Well, then... this changes a few things,' Guy replied, turning to face Austin and scratching his chin. 'Consider my interest piqued, Captain.'

'I'm glad to hear it. So, if you would agree to making a public retraction and dropping the lawsuit, the information I have is yours. All I ask as regards the information is that when you broadcast it, I would appreciate it if I remained anonymous.'

'Very well. I always treat my sources with the utmost confidentiality,' said Guy, standing straight, almost to attention. He placed one hand on his heart and he raised the other as if reciting the Pledge of Allegiance. In a dramatic voice, he said, 'I, Leopold Augustus Thompson the Third, do hereby swear that if your intel turns out good, I will issue a full public acceptance of your apology and drop my case against both yourself and the White Sands facility... Satisfied, Captain?'

'Leopold Augustus Thompson?' asked Austin with a

small chuckle.

'*The Third*,' Guy stressed, puffing out his chest.

Austin stammered, 'Uhh, yeah… yeah, that'll about do it. And… I have your *word* on this?'

Jeez, no wonder he goes by 'Guy Furious'.

Feigning offence, Guy said, 'My word is my bond, Captain. I may be a lot of things, but I ain't no liar!'

'Alright,' said Austin, motioning for Guy to sit down on the side of the bed in front of him as he scooted the chair forwards a little.

Guy did as requested; it seemed a sense of childlike wonder had overtaken him and he had forgotten both his prior trepidation and his scorn. As he sat, he lowered his head towards Austin, who spoke, his voice barely above a whisper.

'First of all, there's a few things you're wrong about,' said Austin. 'Back in 2019 you theorised that NASA had sent a secret government spacecraft out to battle aliens, and that the *Magnum Opus* project was an elaborate scheme to dispose of the evidence before any private company could lay claim to it.'

Guy nodded.

'Well, I'm afraid that's horseshit,' Austin continued. 'We didn't know anything about the aliens until we got there.'

Raising his eyebrows and scoffing, Guy said, 'Are you just trying to discredit my research here or giving me actual information?'

'Shut up; this is important,' Austin hissed. 'We're pretty sure *both* objects were alien spacecraft. They were engaged in a battle of some kind, and one was shot down on Mars. Now, we don't have any intel on the other aliens, but as far as we can tell, they're a different species altogether.'

'All's I'm hearing is small potatoes here, Queen.'

'It's important background,' Austin said, becoming impatient. 'You may not have been right about our reasons for going to Mars, but there *is* a cover-up going on.'

'Better…'

'When we got inside the spacecraft, the aliens weren't dead like you supposed, or like the space agencies are saying. There was no cave-in. I did not send Yula to her death, or put Commander Fowler into a coma. It was the aliens; they caused all of it.'

'So the cave-in story is bullshit?' Guy said with a big grin on his face. 'I knew it! Tell me more!'

Austin sighed. 'There's not much else to it really. We got inside and triggered some kind of security response, and the ship woke up one of their warriors from stasis to deal with us. It caught up with Yula and James in the med bay, killed her and threw James into a big vat of some kind. By the time we got to him, he was comatose.'

'Oh, this is juicy,' said Guy, rubbing his hands together, his eyes darting back and forth at the possibilities. 'Living aliens on Mars.'

'Well…' said Austin. 'Actually, all the aliens're dead now. Grant killed them all. Something about an unsafe shutdown of their stasis pods. Boy *really* wanted revenge.'

'That doesn't matter,' Guy shot back. 'It just proves my point! We're inviting destruction upon ourselves. What are the odds that the first alien species we officially make contact with is so… violent? This is great material.'

That's all this is? Material?

'I'm glad you find it useful,' Austin said through gritted teeth.

'So, uhh… what are you guys doing over at White Sands then?'

Austin laughed and relaxed back in the chair. 'Don't push

it. I can't tell you that. Not because it's something untoward or anything; we're just researching the stuff we found on Mars. There's no point getting the public all excited when we don't know if what we're doing will even work yet.'

Guy raised his hands. 'I'll ask no more. Listen, I'm… sorry about the Russian. It sounds like you did all you could out there. I was an ass to accuse you like that, Captain.'

'Hopefully, now you see the benefit of being in possession of all the facts before you run your mouth,' said Austin.

Guy laughed. 'You may be right… But I meant what I said about keeping things confidential. I'll even wait a few months before I release this info, just to make sure it doesn't come back on you.'

'I appreciate that,' said Austin, getting up from the chair and walking towards the door.

'Pleasure doing business with you, Captain,' Guy called out as Austin closed it behind him.

The captain took a moment to lean against the wall and let out a huge sigh.

Why do I feel like I've just made a deal with the devil?

* * *

'… And it seems to me, as my team and I make our final stop-off en route to Pasadena, that I may have judged White Sands a bit too harshly here on this channel,' said Guy, the upward view of his face waving around on the screen as he walked and failed to keep the phone still and level. The background was dark, and the half-broken sign of a dingy motel could be seen entering and exiting the frame every so often. 'Sure I was assaulted there, but Queen and I have since come to a bit of an understanding after he came

278

grovelling, and it seems he was acting alone.'

The screen lit up with a dazzling brightness as Guy pushed open the door to his motel room. After a few seconds, the exposure of his camera compensated for the new light level, and he continued, 'So, while White Sands deserves our continued scrutiny for their heinous work leading humanity where we have no business going, I have accepted Queen's apology, and I'll be dropping the lawsuit as soon as we get to Los Angeles…'

* * *

'What in the hell are you watching?' said Austin, walking around Cass's workstation with an amused expression.

Cass quickly paused the video, turning red, and Guy Furious's pixelated visage was left in a highly unflattering position. 'Just thought I'd watch Guy's latest video,' she stammered, shuffling around in her chair to face Austin, who had dropped the stack of papers he was carrying onto a desk a short way behind her.

Austin snorted and leaned against the desk, almost sitting. 'Why on earth would you give that idiot more views?'

'I like to keep up to date with the latest conspiracy theories, since most of them nowadays involve us anyway. But this video's actually about you, sir,' she said with a playful smile. 'I can't fathom what you said to get him to back down. Were you *really* grovelling? That doesn't sound like the Austin Queen I know…'

With a great, harsh laugh, Austin replied, 'And you'd be right; I did no such thing! We just had a… *heart to heart*, that's all. And we reached a… *mutual understanding.* He's not that bad in person actually.'

'No, I imagine he's much worse,' Cass said with a giggle.

It had been almost a week since Austin had struck his deal with Guy. The captain had informed Dr Barnes of his success the following morning, naturally leaving out the part where he'd leaked sensitive information to a notoriously indiscrete conspiracy theorist. But to Austin, there had been no other choice: the options open to him went from guaranteed to fail, to so unsavoury as to be out of the question. He had given careful consideration to which information he should leak, and after days of agonising had come to the conclusion that the truth about what happened on Mars would do the least damage. The space agencies of the world would take a hit, but it would be something they could recover from. It also happened that their decision to run the cave-in story was something Austin was vehemently against, and it gave him a certain satisfaction knowing that particular house of cards would soon come tumbling down. What remained to be seen was whether Guy would be as good as his word and keep Austin's involvement on the down-low.

So with the facility's reputation restored for the time being and his job secure once more, Austin was turning his full attention back to progressing the *Aurora* project.

'You ready, Cass?' Austin asked, tapping absentmindedly on the desk.

Cass stared at Austin, the palm of her hand resting on her chin as she leaned on the back of her chair. 'Why? Are you finally taking me out?'

Austin raised an eyebrow and said, 'I mean, it's the big day today. Rest of the team are in the testing room waiting.'

'Oh…' she replied, shifting back around to face the computer, her face turning a subtle shade of red. 'Almost. I'm just waiting on this calibration to complete. Should only be a few more minutes.' She turned back around to face him and said in a sharper tone, 'One of these days I'll get that date out of you.'

Austin sighed and rubbed his face. 'Look, Cass, we talked about this. I'm more than happy to go to dinner with you whenever you like. But as your *friend*. I'm not interested in anything more.'

'But—'

'Hey, maybe we could *all* go out and celebrate after we succeed in generating this warp field,' Austin said with a smile. 'Such a historic event merits a few drinks, right?'

'Yeah maybe…' said Cass, nodding, with a sullen smile. A small beep came from the computer, startling her, and she turned to face the screen once more. 'All done,' she said with a sigh. 'We can head over to the testing room whenever you're ready, sir.'

The interferometer sat inside its see-through box atop the Austinium Generator in the centre of the hangar. Unlike the generator, this new device was small and looked more like a school science-fair project than a serious piece of equipment. It was positioned on the generator so that the Austinium could flow upwards through the small hollow aluminium ring mounted between one of the device's mirrors and its helium-neon laser.

'So, this is the theory,' said Austin as his team, accompanied by Dr Barnes and the assistant director, gathered around for the test. 'We turn on the generator and let the… umm…'

'Austinium,' prompted Cass, who was standing next to him.

The captain frowned and cleared his throat. His cheeks flushed brightly as he continued, 'We let the *material* flow through the torus at the end. This should generate a bubble of warped spacetime in line with the Alcubierre-White metric.'

'And how are we detecting this bubble?' the director asked.

Cass stepped forwards and pointed to a metal tube at one end of the device. 'We fire this laser through the torus,' she said, tracing her finger along the path in the device. 'It will pass through the splitter in between. One beam will continue on through the torus, reflect off the mirror at the end and bounce into the detector. The other beam will be diverted to another mirror and bounce into the detector as well. We'll then measure the path length of each beam. If there's a significant difference, we've got our warp field.'

The director folded her arms and said, 'Why does this experiment seem really familiar to me?'

'It's based on the White-Juday experiment,' said Austin. 'They tried this over a decade ago.'

'But the results of that test were inconclusive. What makes you think it will work this time?' the director asked.

'They weren't using exotic matter for theirs,' Austin replied. 'The... *Austinium*,' he said through gritted teeth and with a glance at Cass, 'should make all the difference, because we know for sure this creates a negative energy density.'

'Alright, let's see it,' Dr Barnes said, nodding.

The team took their places back behind the familiar plastic shield. Cass sat at the monitoring workstation while Austin picked up the power switch for the generator. Dr Barnes and the assistant director stood together towards the back of the group, watching intently.

Austin turned around to face the team and said, raising his voice for the recording, 'Now, this time I ain't gonna say the device won't explode; that'd be tempting fate a bit too much for my liking. So I'll simply say that whichever way this first test goes will contribute massively to our understanding of this alien propulsion system. We *are* expecting a warp field in this test, but equally it could be that our numbers are too conservative. There's plenty of variables we can adjust if it doesn't go our way this time.'

'Understood, Captain,' said Dr Barnes. 'You may proceed.'

'Right,' said Austin, turning to face the device. 'Project *Aurora*, IXS-01, Warp Field Interferometer Test One. Friday, January 15th, 2027. Commencing in three… two… one… Engaging Austinium Generator.'

Austin pushed the switch on the controls and the generator began to hum as before.

After a few minutes of the generator charging, Cass looked up from her workstation and said, 'Austinium generation confirmed in expected quantities. Energy production is within tolerance. Ready to proceed to opening the torus aperture.'

Yelling over the noise, Austin said, 'Go ahead, open her up!'

The hum of the generator continued unabated as Cass tapped away at the keyboard. Under the noise, a gentle mechanical sound could be heard briefly from the device.

'Aperture open,' said Cass. 'Free flow of Austinium looks good. Maximum saturation in five seconds.'

'Alright, time to switch on the laser and get some readings off this thing,' said Austin. He paused and turned to Dr Barnes. 'Director, would you care to do the honours?'

Dr Barnes raised an eyebrow and made her way towards Austin, who picked up a small remote control from the desk next to him and handed it to the director. Without a word, Dr Barnes held it up, pointed it at the device and, with only the slightest hint of hesitation, pressed the button.

Almost immediately, the effect was noticeable, even from the other end of the room. The device emitted its laser, a shining beam of bright-red light. It passed through the beam splitter, and half was diverted as planned towards the control mirror, and the other half continued towards the Austinium-filled ring.

'Something's gone wrong, sir,' said Cass, looking up at Austin with a concerned expression.

'What is it?' he asked, striding over to her workstation and leaning on the back of the chair.

'The laser's on, so I should be getting readings from both beams streaming into the detector, but I'm only getting the control beam,' she replied. 'Something's misaligned.'

Austin glanced at the director with a look of confusion and said, 'We checked alignment earlier. It was on target for the centre of the mirror.'

'Could it have shifted in the move?' Dr Barnes asked with an exasperated sigh.

'No,' said Austin. 'Impossible. We built and tested the thing here. It hasn't mov— Wait a minute…'

With a curious frown, he looked over at the device, and after a moment's pause, he straightened up and walked out from the protection of the plastic shield amid protests from various team members.

Dr Barnes shot forwards and grabbed him by the arm, almost screeching, 'Are you crazy? You could get yourself killed. What if it explodes like last time?'

Austin shook her off and growled, 'I need a closer look.' He gave Cass a sidelong look and said, 'Is the Austinium flow stable?'

'Yes, sir,' Cass replied.

Refocusing his eyes on the director, Austin said, 'See? It's not gonna explode. I have a hunch. I need to see it while it's on, and drones weren't part of our budget.'

The two glared at one another for a long moment, and then Austin turned on his heel and marched over to the interferometer. But he didn't have to get that close. He stopped in his tracks a few yards from the device and his mouth fell open.

What the...? Well, I'll be damned!

'It works!' Austin shouted, turning to face the group huddled behind the screen. 'We've got a warp field!'

Dr Barnes shouted in reply, 'What are you talking about, Captain? How do you know?'

'The field spread further than we thought. That's why we're not getting any readings from it.'

Austin looked back at the primary beam. It was passing through the splitter on its way to the torus, but a few inches from it was being deflected by what seemed to be thin air. The laser light was curving around the ring, giving it a wide berth, and instead of hitting the mirror on the other side, it was hitting the wall next to it.

'The field's spread so far out from the torus, it's swallowing the mirror. It looks like the laser's hittin' the mounting plate a few inches to the left,' said Austin, half laughing.

He was joined a short minute later by Cass, the director and a number of the engineers, all of whom fell dead silent, transfixed by the impossible.

CHAPTER TWENTY
In Quest of New and Wonderful

'A cure? My dear boy, why on earth would you want that?' asked Dr Hales, half laughing.

Taken aback by his abrupt dismissal, James stared as the doctor turned to walk away. 'I—I just want a normal life, Doc,' he said, stammering.

It was Monday the 18th of January and the end of James's second session at TELOMER Labs. It had gone much the same way as the first, with the doctor this time interested in checking for variations in the measurements. So James had done the same sets of experiments again in the same order. Since he knew what to expect, he had allowed his mind to wander a little during the tests, wondering how he would broach the subject of a cure with the doctor. For the whole week since the first session he and Angela had engaged in lengthy, heated debates on the subject that had ended in tears on more than one occasion. He couldn't help but replay these in his mind as well.

Despite his introspection, the comings and goings of the laboratory had not escaped his attention. He'd observed, from his limited vantage point on the experimental apparatus, strange boxes and crates being delivered and unpacked. They appeared to contain various pieces of technological equipment far in advance of what James would expect of a hospital. Some of it he recognised from the particle physics lab at which he had interned straight out of finishing his master's.

Why would this place even need that stuff, and how much money does Dr Hales have access to anyway? That gear ain't cheap.

Dr Hales had noticed he had become distracted and enquired about his lack of focus, which at least answered James's question on how to bring up the subject of a cure. However, he hadn't expected the doctor to be quite so disparaging about it.

He stopped and turned, regarding James for a moment with a bemused expression. 'You're… being serious? Oh, well, in that case, it's difficult to say.'

'Then let me make it easy,' James spat, stopping the treadmill; he could feel himself becoming angry. 'Tell me, or I leave.'

The doctor sighed and said, 'Alright. We can run some more tests for that, but I find it unlikely you will get the answer you seek. Remember, we are dealing with vastly superior alien technology here.'

'How long?'

Dr Hales scoffed, 'Come now, I couldn't possibly know that. Anyway, I don't understand. Don't you *want* augmented strength and stamina? And immortality is a dream for many.'

'Well, I'm not them,' James replied defiantly.

'In any case,' said Dr Hales, suppressing a groan, 'it won't be next week. Now, I shall hear no more about this today. Let's take you back to the hospital.'

* * *

Weeks passed and the sessions continued. James's activities varied from week to week: sometimes he repeated experiments with slightly tweaked variables; other times he engaged in new ones. By the fourth week, James was able to get in and out of the warehouse with his ID, as the security card system had been installed. Dr Hales therefore insisted he meet James at the lab rather than waste time at the hospital.

It hadn't escaped James's attention that the doctor had now given up all pretence of believing the cave-in cover story and would speak confidently of James's condition in terms of alien medical technology. In the early days of their sessions, James had often lain awake in bed deep in thought. Dr Hales's dismissal of the cover story was no surprise considering the mounting physiological evidence to the contrary.

It's probably my fault. The first day I met Hales I blurted out the real events. Sure, he seemed ready to dismiss my ramblings as coma-induced nonsense, but it must have been really suspicious when I suddenly started pushing the cave-in story. And he's studying my physiology in depth… Perhaps I should come clean?

However, as the weeks wore on at the warehouse, James could have sworn the doctor caught himself a few times in the midst of an excited monologue, as if he'd almost said something he shouldn't have. The doctor's enthusiasm for his research was tangible, and contagious, which tracked with the idea that he loved working on 'exotic' cases. During their sessions, James found himself getting caught up in the excitement too. But the increasing minor inconsistencies and near slipups gave him pause, and he began to believe that Dr Hales knew more than he was letting on.

During his free time at home while Angela was at work, James resumed his background research on the enigmatic doctor, always accompanied by Sputnik curled up on his lap as he sat at the computer in the back room.

'This is so... argh!' he complained one quiet Tuesday afternoon in March, raising his voice suddenly and startling the sleepy puppy. 'Sorry, Sputnik. All these searches are just bringing up the same thing. Hales just seems to be an ordinary private neurology consultant at the Royal London, and apparently working out of his own practice in the West End. TELOMER Labs seems to be legit; it has a website detailing its experimental metagenic research. *Sans* me, of course. And the doctor is even listed as the guy in charge! It's all above board. So *why* do I feel like there's something really *off* about it?'

James sighed and stroked the dog, who then tried to roll over for a belly rub but toppled off James's lap onto the floor. He chuckled and picked the beagle puppy back up again, holding him close.

'But you don't care about any of this stuff, do you, boy? Oh, to be a dog...' he muttered, tickling Sputnik under the chin as the dog licked his face in turn. He then gave a bitter laugh and said, 'Oh, to be human...'

The computer screen became a blur as James's eyes defocused and he allowed his mind to wander. He recalled the boxes and crates that he had seen being brought in during his second session.

Wait a minute…

There had been a logo, one of several printed in the corner of a few of the boxes. Small and innocuous, barely noticeable, but decidedly out of place. Not a manufacturer's or removals logo like the others, but one for a business and technology integration company—one that James recognised. He closed his eyes with a frown, searching his mind for the name of the company.

Van de Velde Innovations! They took over management of the technology transfer network for… my God, the ESA!

He opened his eyes and quickly lowered Sputnik to the floor before scooting in closer to the computer. In seconds he'd brought up the ESA's website, and for the next half an hour he scoured the news and blog pages, not fully sure what he was looking for. He had a hunch, an inkling, perhaps a flash of madness, but he continued on regardless, driven by either epiphany or paranoia, he wasn't sure which.

Eventually, James came across one image that stood out. It was a wide shot of one of the ESA's facilities, a simple unrelated stock photo prettying up a drab news story from a few years ago about some acquisition or another. But there were people in the shot, facility staff milling around in the courtyard on a beautiful, sunny afternoon. Some were clearly in a hurry, carrying stacks of papers; others looked relaxed, talking within a group of colleagues. It was in one of these background groups that James saw the familiar figure and bearing of a man. There was no mistaking his features, which caught the sunlight clear as day: a younger Dr Joshua Hales.

James slumped back in his office chair, eyes wide and mouth agape. Here it was, staring him in the face: his eureka moment, confirmation of his shot-in-the-dark theory.

He works for the ESA! The bastard already knew the truth, and he lied right to my face. That's probably why the astronaut centre keeps fobbing me off every time I try to get in touch. They were keeping tabs on me all along! But why? Why go to such lengths to keep this from me?

Later that evening, when Angela came home from work, James sat her down before she could take off her coat and shoes and told her everything he had found. She sat and listened intently, her expression passing from shock to anger.

When James had finished, she was trembling with indignation. She growled, 'That utterly duplicitous piece of shit. I have half a mind to go there and shove a broken test tube up his arse!' She looked at James and cried, 'Is he even a real doctor?'

'I think so,' he said.

'And what about this lab of his? Is that some kind of front?'

'I don't know,' James replied, sitting down on the sofa next to her. 'It seems like a legitimate company.'

Angela sighed and buried her face in her hands. Her voice muffled, she said, 'You have to stop going.' She looked back up at him, her expression a mixture of fear and fury. 'I don't trust that he's got your wellbeing in mind. The other day I asked you about all these cuts and bruises you've been coming home with lately, and you said you'd noticed the experiments were, what was it? "Straddling an ethical grey area"? That Hales said he could "afford to push the boundaries" because of your abilities?'

James nodded. 'Yes, that's true, and I agree, Hales isn't to be trusted…'

'Why do I feel like there's a "but" coming?' Angela sighed.

Clasping her hands and holding them to his lips, James

said, 'I have to keep going. I don't like it, but I don't have a choice. *We* don't have a choice. It's the only way I'll understand my condition and come to terms with it. It's the only way I'll feel *whole* again, *human* again. And we need that cure.'

'Understanding yourself, I get,' said Angela, her voice softening, 'and I can't begin to relate to what you're going through. But you've only got his word that he's even working on a cure, and we know how much that's worth now!'

'I'm not going to say anything to Hales yet. I don't know what he'd do. The best way to get the answers I'm looking for is to go along with it and not let on that I know. I have to try.'

'I know,' she whispered. 'Just promise me you'll be careful.'

* * *

Weeks turned into months since James and Angela had found out the truth. James's forty-second birthday passed with little celebration, and by the end of June, all mention of a cure seemed to have been forgotten by Dr Hales. James continued to watch the doctor's movements, analysing everything he said and did—every irregularity—for more signs and clues. It had become exhausting, but the research itself was intriguing. Soon, the doctor had begun to increase the frequency of James's appointments. On a couple of occasions, he had asked James to come in a second time during the week, and eventually this had become a regular occurrence. Then there were extra sessions in between, featuring a reduced staff, and the two of them made great progress in understanding the limits of James's physical augmentation. All the while, James kept a weather eye on Hales, being careful to watch for any changes in his behaviour.

*The more we understand, the closer we get to a cure…
And then I can have a normal life with Angela.*

But the increased immersion did not come without a cost. Experiments overran, certainty became less, stresses rose and minor injuries became moderate, all putting a strain on James's relationship with Angela.

It was early afternoon on Saturday the 26th of June, and James had received an urgent message from Dr Hales. He got up from the sofa, rushed to the front door and called out to Angela, 'I'm just heading to the lab. I'll be back later.'

'What? You can't. Not today of all days,' she cried, her tone incredulous as she jogged from the back room to join him at the door.

'Sorry, love, the doc needs me,' James replied, pulling on his coat at the bottom of the stairs. 'Just got his text. We're *so* close to—'

'But *I* need you here,' Angela shot back, scooting around him and blocking the front door. 'It's our anniversary. The first date night we've had since this all started! I've already cancelled games night for it!'

James reached around her and grabbed the door handle. 'I'll only be a couple of hours. Be back before you know it, and we'll head to the restaurant.'

She stared into his eyes, her face a picture of desperation. 'Please, James. Not today,' she whispered, gripping the lapels of his jacket.

James leant forwards and kissed her gently on the forehead and sighed. 'Just a couple of hours. It'll be fine. I love you.'

He pressed the door handle down and pulled. Angela relented, moving aside as the door opened, and James left, closing it behind him.

The route by public transport was clear for a Saturday,

and he had made it to TELOMER Labs in what felt like no time at all. After he presented his card to the machine and greeted Dr Hales in the first laboratory, they got to work. They were continuing an experiment they had begun in their previous session but had been cut short by a ping on James's phone, a sharp message from Angela letting him know they had overrun again. The experiment involved using a large vacuum chamber to see whether there was a difference in the length of time James could remain without air in a zero-pressure environment compared to underwater. The previous test had determined that as long as James took a deep breath and kept his airways closed, he could stay underwater for several hours.

However, it seemed there was no such caveat in the vacuum; he didn't need to hold his breath, and he could even talk to a limited degree. After a few minutes, his ability to speak faded as his voice became croaky, his vocal cords having run out of air to vibrate against. But otherwise he was able to be in there, conscious, alert and unharmed, until Dr Hales decided to move on.

As he stepped out of the vacuum chamber after waiting some time for the gradual repressurisation process to complete, James picked up his phone, which he had placed alongside the rest of his personal effects on the nearest desk to the chamber. He looked down at the clock on the screen and gasped.

Shit, not again!

'Hey, sorry, Doc,' he croaked, his voice still not completely back to normal. 'I… I've gotta make a phone call.'

The doctor looked up and over at him from compiling results on the computer. 'Hmm? Oh, of course,' he said, giving a distracted wave in James's direction, and went back to staring at the screen.

James nodded in thanks and retreated a few steps before calling Angela and placing the phone to his ear. He braced himself for the worst.

'Do you have any idea what the time is?' Angela shouted down the line the moment the call connected.

James winced and the phone's tinny speaker crackled at the intensity of her voice. 'Err, yes… Sorry, love. Look, how about I just finish up here and meet you at the restaurant?'

Angela huffed and was silent for a long moment. 'Fine,' she said, and the call disconnected with an abrupt click.

James pulled the phone away from his ear and stared at the screen. His stomach churned with a mixture of hunger and guilt as he acknowledged that he had, yet again, allowed the time to run away. He and Angela had argued a few times recently about the increased frequency and irregular timings of his visits to the warehouse, and how it seemed like James was more interested in spending time with Dr Hales, despite his untrustworthiness, than with her. But this was probably the worst incident yet; he couldn't miss their anniversary meal.

If I miss this, my life will be forfeit.

Just then, James felt a pat on the shoulder, snapping him out of staring at the phone screen, which had long since switched off.

'These results are incredible, Commander,' said Dr Hales, waving a few stapled sheets of paper at him.

James took the papers and looked through the data. It was the usual medical jargon and acronyms he didn't know, followed by strings of meaningless numbers. He did recognise a graph showing his blood oxygen levels, but he couldn't figure out the relevance.

'We've talked about this, Doctor. I don't know what any

of this means,' he said with a laugh, handing the papers back to Dr Hales.

The doctor chuckled. 'It goes a significant way towards proving a hypothesis I have about your augmentation. You see…' He pointed at some of the numbers on the first page. 'When you are underwater, the newfound efficiency of your respiratory system allows it to keep you from needing to breathe for extended periods of time in that environment. However, something altogether different happens in the vacuum chamber. Here…' He turned the page and pointed at some numbers above the graph. 'In a zero-pressure environment, your cells seem to detect this and your respiratory response swaps over to a new method. I haven't got all the details worked out quite yet, but suffice it to say that your body's augmentation is much better suited to allowing you to survive in, say, the vacuum of space than to saving you from drowning.'

James thought for a moment. The injured aliens that had attacked them on the Martian wreck—the ones from the bridge and hydroponics lab—had survived for five years without helmets in a completely depressurised ship and yet still had the energy to make one final stand against him and Yula.

Perhaps this genetic augmentation is something they had too…

'It certainly would make sense from a military perspective,' Dr Hales continued. 'The ability to retrieve troops blown out of the ship during a battle.'

'Wh-what do you mean, Doctor?' James asked in surprise, as though the doctor had been reading his thoughts.

Dr Hales stared at James, bemused by his question. 'Well, of course I'm talking about the aliens on Mars.'

James groaned. 'We've talked about this, Doc. The ESA says I didn't meet any living aliens on Mars or get exposed to any alien medical technology.'

Dr Hales snorted and nodded sarcastically, walking back to his computer. He stopped at his chair and turned to face James. 'Oh, Commander, I would like to run just one more test this evening, if you please?'

'No way. It's our anniversary and I'm already late. I need to shoot off.'

'It won't take long. It's very important.'

'What is it?'

'While your body is still winding down from the effects of the vacuum chamber, I would like to run a few blood tests. I would be grateful if you would stay with me while they complete. I'll be able to give you the results as soon as they're done and they should finally tell us whether or not your condition can be reversed.'

James's eyes widened and considered this for a few moments. He looked down at his phone, knocking the power button to turn the screen on, displaying the time. He really didn't have long. He weighed up his options, but the prospect of getting his answer about a cure won out and he reluctantly gave Dr Hales the go-ahead.

He sat down and the doctor went to find the equipment he needed. After what James felt was far too long, Dr Hales returned and took several blood samples. Then he rushed off through the door of the lab into another room, and James—still holding a cotton pad to the needle mark—watched him deposit the samples into a few different machines and set them running. The silence in the lab was punctuated by the whirring, spinning and occasional clicking of the machines.

Dr Hales returned and, without a word, went back to

tapping away at the computer. After a few minutes, James began to get antsy. He looked over at the machines, still whirring, and back at Dr Hales, still tapping. As he fidgeted in his seat, the cotton pad slipped from his fingers to the floor. Looking down at his arm, he could see the puncture wound had stopped bleeding. He bent down to pick up the cotton pad and then got up; the chair legs scraped loudly as they scooted a few inches back, the sound cutting across the drone of spinning machinery and clackety keys. Walking a short way across the room, he put the pad in the bin, before nervously looking back over at the machines.

'How long is this going to take exactly?' he asked as he returned to his seat next to Dr Hales.

'Hmm?' the doctor grunted as he looked up. He looked down at his watch and then back at James. 'Oh, another… ten minutes I believe.'

'Cutting it close, Doc,' James replied.

You're doing this on purpose, aren't you…

Dr Hales shook his head and went back to working at the computer.

An hour and a half later, James sprinted out of the train station and down towards the high street. It was spitting with a fine rain, which made the street lights project a wider orange glow. The ground was slick, and James's shoes squeaked a little as he ran, the stamping of his feet louder thanks to the dampness. There were rows of lit-up restaurants and shops all along the winding road. He took the first left, still sprinting, and after a hundred metres the road curved to the right. There was a small alleyway on his side of the street just ahead of him.

James skidded to a halt—nearly losing his footing in the process—and bolted down the narrow passage, knocking his shoulder on the corner of the wall and stumbling a little. He recovered his footing, and a few seconds later he reached the end of the alley and came out into another part of the town centre. His head darted around as he looked to his left and right, trying to remember the way from here. He could see the sign of a fast-food place and a barber's pole in the distance to his left, and the front of a bathroom shop to the right as the road curved.

Has to be left.

He shot off again down the pavement, his feet now kicking up the thin layer of water on the ground. The fine rain had managed to soak James through; droplets fell from his hair, down his brow and into his eyes, and the smart shirt he had changed into was turning see-through.

After a short while he arrived at the restaurant, a small independent Italian place with a large bay window set in a dark-stained wood frame. The door was recessed into an open porch area and was made of the same colour wood as the rest of the frontage. James came close to the window, peering through the subdued, intimate lighting inside. Some of the patrons in the nearby seats stared back out at him with bewildered expressions. He couldn't blame them; he looked like a drowned rat and had been running hell for leather before coming to an abrupt and noisy stop right outside the window.

He cleared his throat and walked towards the door. A small bell chimed as it opened and he went through. He wiped his feet on a welcome mat and stepped up to a lectern, where a smartly dressed waiter stood looking at him with a smirk on his face.

'Have you a reservation, sir?' said the waiter.

'Yes, a table for two. Under "Fowler".'

'Fowler?' The waiter chuckled. 'Oh dear. You are a little

late, I'm afraid.'

'What the hell are you talking about?' James spat.

The waiter's grin was uncontained and his face eminently punchable. It was clear to James that he was enjoying the drama.

'Your lady friend, sir, left some time ago.'

Fuck.

'Shit.'

'She also left a note, which we were instructed to give you, should you ever arrive.' The waiter bent down and fished for a bit under the lectern, and eventually pulled out a folded napkin and handed it over to James.

He unfolded it and looked down from the waiter's expression of malicious glee to the paper, which contained a single word: 'Sofa.'

James hung his head and departed the restaurant to stand outside in the rain and call a taxi. It was only a short wait before the black cab pulled up in front of him and he got in. He instructed the driver to take him home and then sat staring out of the window in quiet contemplation as the vehicle moved, orange streetlamps flashing by rhythmically, lighting up his face. Normally, James enjoyed chatting to taxi drivers, particularly the ones who'd hung around the Cologne Bonn International Airport before the Mars mission. He would often tell them all about what he was doing at the European Astronaut Centre, which was just to the south side of the airport. Most of the drivers had been fascinated as they listened, as James was one of their more interesting regular fares. But this evening, he didn't much feel like engaging the driver in conversation.

As he thought about what he would say to Angela, he heard the driver turn up the radio. It was the news, reporting on widespread criticism from the European Parliament of the UK's proposal to rejoin the Union. The discovery of extraterrestrial life had sparked a renewed worldwide interest in pushing for closer international links, and had given rise to its own peculiar form of nationalism. Earth-centrism was the new zeitgeist. Talk of defending national borders and curbing immigration had morphed into rhetoric about jointly developing a planetary defence network to guard against the threat of the 'alien menace'.

World leaders—knowing that thanks to Grant's furious vengeance there was no real alien threat to stand up to— were all too happy to lean into this trend. The imaginary enemy was no longer at the borders but somewhere out in the depths of space.

James found himself distracted from his own thoughts by the volume, and he listened as the news changed to an excerpt of a speech by Guy Furious given at some kind of anti-alien rally in the States. Guy was criticising NASA and the other space agencies, as usual, for their plans for the second mission to Mars in the spring of 2028, over a year away. He was ranting and raving about the dangers of alien technology.

How on earth did he get so big?

James recalled the days before the mission, when Guy was just an internet personality with a moderate-sized following mostly made up of fellow conspiracy theorists. His following had been given a huge boost thanks to his appearance on that talk show in the days following the impact, but he had only ever been framed as a figure of derision.

The newsreaders and pundits on the radio briefly talked through the history of Guy's rise in influence. It seemed that Major Zhu's mistake in the pre-landing broadcast had had a significant influence in catapulting Guy to stardom. It didn't

302

take much for people to make the connection that he had been right about the alien spacecraft. In fact, it seemed that Guy was at the centre of the Earth-first movement and was now a key figure in calling for both a planetary defence network and the cancellation of all future exploratory space missions.

Fear of the aliens was the order of the day, and Guy's vehement disapproval of humanity's continued 'meddling in interplanetary affairs', as he called it, had influenced the growth of small political cells operating at the grassroots level all over the world, many of which took Guy as their figurehead.

'That Furious bloke's got a point, though, ain't he?' said the driver suddenly.

His outburst caused James to stammer, 'Err, what?'

'Yeah,' the driver continued without waiting for a reply, 'us humans need to stick together now. Can't be caught napping when them xenos come knocking, eh?'

'Well,' started James, 'I can understand why people are scared, but it's nonsense to use that as an excuse not to learn more about the universe. And the best way to do that is to keep pushing out.'

'Yeah, but if we end up pissing off a bunch of xenos and leading 'em back 'ere… If you ask me, we're better off keeping ourselves to ourselves and looking after our own.'

James grunted in a noncommittal way, and except for the radio, which had moved on to playing chart music, silence fell in the taxi again.

That kind of attitude does nothing to honour Yula's sacrifice. Or Grant's for that matter.

James chuckled to himself, wondering whether he should reveal his identity and savour the look on the driver's face or just leave it. After a long moment, he decided to leave it, and instead went back to looking out of the rain-soaked window.

Anyway, I've been a right arse. How am I going to make this up to Angela? And... how am I supposed to tell her what Dr Hales found?

Yet again, Yula's words echoed through his mind. 'You are going to propose to Angela as soon as we are home, are you not?'

She'll probably say no now. But I need to show her that I'm committed; it's been far too long.

Ten minutes later, the taxi pulled up outside James's house. He got out and paid the driver, then walked up the driveway to the front door. He pulled his keys out of his jacket pocket, and they jangled as he fumbled around in the darkness for the door key. He turned to his left and held them up in the light of the street lamps. Locating the correct one, he then turned back to unlock the door, and walked through into the hallway, closing and locking the door behind him.

He didn't bother to turn any lights on; though it was dark, he could see well enough to navigate due to the incandescent light from outside spilling through the windows of the front door. He sighed, took off his jacket and shoes, and stared wistfully up the stairs. Angela had already gone to bed, and he resigned himself to the idea of sleeping alone on the sofa; an unwelcome first for their relationship, but he knew he deserved it.

Quietly, he pushed open the door to the living room and went to creep to the sofa that would be his bed for the night.

'James.'

He jumped back with a yelp at the sharp voice that emanated suddenly from the darkness, stumbling and nearly hitting his head on the door frame behind him. As his heart raced and he caught his breath, he reached out with his right hand and flicked the wall switch, turning on the living room lights.

There, sitting on the sofa with her arms and legs crossed, and wearing nothing but a long t-shirt and a scowl, was Angela. Her face was twisted with anger, and James could have sworn that her eyes had turned the colour of her hair, such was the intensity of her gaze. He found it impossible to keep eye contact with her. He had seen her become angry many times before; the two of them had had their fair share of disagreements and arguments over the years. But this was different; not just irritation, frustration or even stubbornness, but disappointment, betrayal and even a hint of jealously.

'Explain,' she growled before James was able to make even the slightest utterance.

He stared, dumbfounded, at the figure of his girlfriend, and any explanations he had thought of on the way over in the taxi scarpered from his mind.

'Well?' she demanded, her voice becoming more high-pitched.

James sighed and slumped into the seat by the window. 'There is no good explanation,' he said, looking down at the floor. 'I'm sorry.'

Silence. A meek apology wasn't going to cut it.

'I tried to make it to the restaurant. I ran all the way th—'

'I waited. For thirty *goddamn minutes* at that table, James!' she shouted. 'I was already five minutes late for our booking and I had to endure all the other people in there staring at me: the pathetic jilted woman whose boyfriend had ghosted her on their anniversary!'

She uncrossed her arms and pointed at him. 'You said. *You* said that you wanted to give this a go regardless of a cure. *You* said you'd be careful and keep an eye on Hales. But I'm not seeing it, James. I'm not seeing your commitment here.

So you had better be about to tell me that the reason you stayed so long with that damned doctor is because you've found a cure.' She huffed and looked away from him.

'I… I can't tell you that,' replied James.

She huffed again and carried on staring at the fireplace.

'Dr Hales,' James continued, 'asked me to stay while he ran a blood test. It took a lot longer than I expected. I even told him that I needed to get away urgently, but he convinced me that it would be important and… it was.

'I thought he had forgotten all about searching for a cure. Then he said he wanted to do a couple more blood tests that would finally give us some answers. But there is no cure, Ange. I'm stuck like this. It's not going to wear off, and it's too deeply integrated into my genetics to be reversible.'

Angela looked around at him. The fire had gone from her eyes, the anger replaced by sorrow.

'I'm really sorry, Ange. I've been a prize prat. I've wronged you. I've let myself get too caught up in the work with that liar, and I've neglected our relationship. I will make it up to you, I promise… If you can find it in your heart to forgive me, that is.'

Angela scoffed, then sniffed and looked away from him. 'Of course I forgive you, you massive, massive arsehole,' she said, her voice barely audible.

She wiped her damp eyes and stood up, beginning to shuffle towards James. All of a sudden she stopped, her attention caught by something out the window. She frowned and crept towards where James was, staring out. She knelt up on the sofa and leaned towards the window, raising the net curtain up a little.

'What is it?' James asked, turning around on the chair to face her.

'There's a car outside…' she replied.

James shrugged. 'So?'

'I mean, the same car, still there. It's been there for days now, parked on the other side of the road. Always a couple of people in it, and I've never seen them leave.'

James got up and turned to kneel on the chair next to Angela. She raised up the net some more and pointed the car out to him. It was a black saloon car; it was impossible to tell the make and model in the darkness of the night.

'Neighbours acting strangely?' asked James.

Angela shook her head. 'I don't think so… You don't think the ESA would send someone to spy on us, do you?'

'Before all of this, I'd have said you were being paranoid, but now? I don't know; they might.'

'It's probably that bastard doctor's doing,' said Angela, her fists clenched. 'What *is* his angle? We figured out his connection to the ESA months ago, but there's been nothing since.'

James nodded, stroking his chin. 'I know, I can't figure it out. It's very odd. But he's grown distant lately, like hyper-focused on the experiments and less concerned about the procedures hurting me. Sometimes I think he forgets I'm an actual person.'

'Sounds like someone else I know,' Angela chided.

James sighed. 'Yeah, I'm sorry. It won't happen again.' He paused and looked back out to the car, saying, 'But Hales's change in behaviour is really concerning me. We'd best keep an eye on that car.'

CHAPTER TWENTY-ONE
PROJECT AUGMENT

ONTHS HAD PASSED SINCE THE FIRST successful warp-field interferometry test conducted by Austin and his team. The harshness of winter had given way to a comfortable spring, and in turn to the beginnings of a blazing southwestern summer. There had been three more experiments over the previous months, each an incremental step towards further control of the phenomenon, and the changing weather provided a good test of stability for the system. Analysis carried out by Cass, and supported by further Achelon translations provided by Kolton and his group, had allowed Anders's engineers to create a variable aperture, giving them fine control over the Austinium flow and, therefore, the geometry of the warp field.

On Monday the 28th of June, Captain Queen sat in his office, the single window behind him open as far as it could go—barely a crack. Sweat poured down his face as he fanned himself with some rogue paperwork and his cheeks were beet-red. Years he had worked out of this glorified storage closet and yet he'd been provided with no air conditioning. This was, perhaps, the reason he had spent little time here, preferring instead to be among the rest of his team in the labs.

But for all the discomfort of the New Mexican summer, he needed the privacy as he watched Guy Furious's latest video on his computer.

Damn it, I totally forgot about this... It's been a short six months! At least he's been true to his word and kept my anonymity so far.

'Thanks to an anonymous source, I have come into possession of most intriguing information regarding not just NASA but all the space agencies across the world,' said Guy, leaning forwards with his elbows on his desk, his manner sombre. The production values of his videos had skyrocketed over the last several years, in line with his growing fame. Guy had gone from making shaky cell-phone videos in his parents' bedroom to a full studio setup: a dark-blue defocused backdrop, professional lighting and camera equipment, and the services of a full-time video editor. His conspiracy news segments rivalled local news channels in quality, and all of this served to give his channel an air of legitimacy.

Here goes. I wonder how all this will play out? I might have to do some damage control...

Guy opened his mouth to continue speaking, and there was a loud rapping at the office door. Austin groaned internally and paused the video.

Of all the times to make his video a livestream... This is not good. He could be saying literally anything.

'Come in!' he said, a little more cantankerously than he'd intended. As the door swung open and Cass barged through, he minimised the webpage and brought up a random document. She was practically jumping up and down, and had a wide grin on her face.

'Sir, I've been looking at the field geometry and I think I may have a solution to—'

'Slow down, Cass,' said Austin, his voice quivering slightly. He wiped the sweat from his brow and his eyes darted to the computer and back to his colleague. 'Take it from the top, slow and steady now.'

Cass paused, closing her eyes and exhaling slowly. 'Okay,' she said. 'I think I've come up with a way to manipulate the field geometry further.' Stepping towards the desk, she handled a printout to Austin and continued, 'So far we've made good progress changing the intensity of the field, but in order to actually make use of this phenomenon on a spacecraft, we need to change its shape so it compresses spacetime in one direction and expands it in the other.'

'Otherwise the ship won't be able to move forwards,' said Austin, nodding his head as he examined the document, which was filled with line upon line of complex field equations. 'This looks like great work, and a pretty damn simple solution to boot. Get this over to the engineering team and see what they can whip up.'

'Yes, sir,' said Cass, taking the papers back from Austin. She headed out the door and closed it behind her.

Austin sighed and hit play on the video, once more turning his attention to the computer screen. No sooner had Guy begun talking, rambling through his introduction, than the phone on the desk rang. Austin let out an audible groan and slammed his finger on the spacebar, pausing the video once more. He was now several minutes behind on the stream, and his anxiety about its contents along with the constant interruptions were making him nervous and irritable.

He picked up the phone receiver and put it to his ear. 'What is it?' he said, his voice a low growl. A chill came over him as he received the icy reply from Dr Barnes:

'Queen. Conference room. Now.'

The call disconnected. Austin remained frozen in place, his eyes staring sightlessly, his grip on the receiver vice-like. He glanced at the time on the monitor and reasoned that the stream would have finished by now, as it was only supposed to be a short news update from Guy. He gingerly placed the handset back into its dock and lowered his head into his hands, leaning his closed eyes against his palms. Fireworks flashed and coloured sparks danced behind his eyelids, and he gave a great, shuddery sigh.

It's probably nothin'... right? She can't possibly have been watching Guy's stream, or deduced it was me so quickly. All this shit's got me rattled. I'll give away the secret if I don't pull myself together.

Austin left the office and navigated the stark grey corridors of the facility, deaf to the greetings of passing colleagues and subordinates. A twist to the right; a curve around a new, circular lab; a turn to the left. His footsteps seemed to thud and echo as he proceeded through the building, décor and friendly faces a barely perceived blur. Despite his earlier reasoning, his anxieties—which had come to the fore since his return from the *Magnum Opus*—flared, whispering to him in the recesses of his mind, telling him that they *knew*.

His mind flashed back to his school days and the times he had been sent to the principal's office for smoking on school grounds, for contradicting his know-nothing science teacher one too many times, or for beating up that punk kid who was always picking on his best friend. He hadn't always been as level-headed as he was now, in his middle age. This time

312

he knew his actions had been right, but even so, he dreaded the consequences. His mind raced, formulating reasons and responses, ways to make the director see how his actions were justified and ways to hopefully mitigate the fallout.

Without thinking, he pushed open the exit, depressing the bar and allowing the heavy fire door to swing out before him. The scorching brightness of the summer sun and a blast of desert heat assaulted him as he marched away from the building towards the one across the way, another building of a similar size.

Within minutes he was through the door to the other part of the facility and navigating its winding corridors. The lights at this end of the base were dim, not through design but through a lack of maintenance. There were bulbs clearly on their last legs, fighting to illuminate what little of the corridor they could. White Sands was not known for hosting visitors in the main conference room often, not since the pandemic of the early 2020s, and so its wing of the building on the staff side had fallen to a lower maintenance priority than the rest of the base.

Austin swerved around boxes and bits of old equipment that had been stored in this dingy staff corridor, until he arrived at the back entrance to the conference room, a large pair of fire doors. He stopped in front of the grotty burgundy doors and gathered his thoughts, steeling his nerves for what he now considered the inevitable. With a heavy exhale, he pushed the doors open and stepped through.

The room was brightly lit and expansive, with the woody, earthen smell that reminded Austin of academia. Its circular design was mirrored in the ring table at its centre. One of the walls was flat and held a large screen that encompassed most of its width and came halfway down to the floor. The screen was lit by a projector and the face of a man was displayed upon it. Austin recognised him as the administrator of the CNSA. High above, suspended from the ceiling, a ring of spotlights shone down on the table.

The people sitting around the table had been talking animatedly until Austin entered, but now they fell silent and looked at him as he advanced further into the room. Austin recognised many of the faces around the table, from the heads of the ESA and Roscosmos to NASA's own administrator, General Mahoney, as well as Dr Barnes and a number of her immediate directorial staff.

'Take a seat, Captain,' said Dr Barnes, motioning to one of the empty spaces opposite her and the other directors.

Without speaking, Austin nodded and settled into the seat at the table. There was a small camera embedded in the desk in one corner and a microphone on the other side. As he sat, he found the source of the smell that reminded him of a lecture hall: the table had been freshly polished, highlighting the natural wood scent.

'Ah, so glad you could join us, Captain Queen,' said the head of the CNSA on the screen, having seen Austin move into the view of his desk camera. 'I trust you are keeping well?'

'Well enough,' Austin replied with a measure of caution. 'But I would be interested to know how Major Zhu is gettin' on?'

The CNSA administrator smiled and said, 'She will be returning from the station on the next crew rotation. Perhaps we can arrange a call sometime.' He sat back in his chair, receding a little from the camera. 'Dr Barnes, please continue.'

The director cleared her throat and spoke, 'As I was saying, I don't think it needs stating, but this leak has the potential to cause a lot of harm to us and our projects,

314

especially with regards to our relationship with the public and the press.'

'Yes, it is problematic,' said the director-general of the ESA. 'The backlash is going to be immense if we don't get this situation handled *now*. I don't like to say it, but it could damage further international collaborations, including the upcoming Mars mission and Project Augment.'

Austin's ears pricked up and he looked at the ESA director. 'You mean Project *Aurora*, sir?'

The director considered Austin for a short time before replying, 'Quite.'

So that's a no then... What the hell is 'Project Augment'?

The Russian director leaned forwards with an intense stare and added, 'Russia is none too concerned. We are perfectly capable of getting to Mars without aid of *Magnum Opus*. After all, we supplied many of safety mechanisms for that ship.

'But... we are willing to wait while you Americans sort out your petty internal problems. We would rather not have to build our own ship when *Magnum* is already proven vessel.'

'How very gracious...' growled the general.

The head of Roscosmos shot him a stern look and continued, 'Make no mistake, General. This is no time for NASA to be lax. This needs to be resolved quickly. Wait too long, and crash site will be awash with commercial landers. We have already seen great strides being made by large private ventures. Even ISRO and JAXA threaten to take lead!'

'We may have got there first by working together,' said the CNSA administrator. 'But this space race is far from over, and the technology on that alien vessel must not fall into the hands of private militaries. We all agreed that it is better shared amongst us for the sake of mankind, so we cannot afford to jeopardise the mission.' He sighed and leaned closer to the camera. 'But I do not know for how long I can continue to convince my superiors that collaboration is the best way forward. If certain things like this are not kept secure…'

'That is why I have called Captain Queen here,' said Dr Barnes. She turned her attention to Austin and said, 'I take it you are aware of Guy Furious's latest leak of confidential information?'

Austin stared, dumbstruck; it was just as he feared. 'What do you mean?' he asked in return. 'I ain't seen that idiot's latest video—'

'Cut the crap, Austin,' Dr Barnes shot back, standing and leaning over the desk. 'We know it was you who gave him the information. Who else would it be?'

There was a murmur of agreement around the room before the ESA director added, 'Bloody obvious. It certainly couldn't have been Commander Fowler; we have been keeping a very close eye on him.'

'And there have been no unauthorised transmissions from the Space Station, so it cannot have been the major,' said the CNSA administrator.

Austin looked around at the stern faces staring at him, feeling their probing glares. He stammered a few noncommittal responses, but they were unconvinced.

'No excuses. Explain yourself, Captain,' said the general.

In the next moment Austin leaped from his chair, causing it to fall back and clatter on the floor. 'Well, what in the hell did y'all expect me to do?' he roared, his breathing rapid and his voice trembling. He pointed at Dr Barnes and continued, 'You told me to "make him go away"! What, did you *actually* expect me to kill the guy?'

'Don't be ridiculous! What were you thinking?' snapped Dr Barnes. 'I expected you to pay him off or some—'

Austin slammed his palms on the desk, crying in indignation, 'Pay off *Guy Furious*? Are you crazy? Christ almighty! Information is *all* he cares about. It was the only way to get him to back off.'

'Be that as it may,' said General Mahoney, 'but you have put the mission at risk. You knew that the cover story was what allowed us to put together a second mission in the first place. It was irresponsible to leak such sensitive information.'

'No, sir,' said Austin, lowering his voice and scowling at the general. 'Respectfully, you're wrong. It was irresponsible keeping the real events from the public, and'—he looked at the Russian director—'downright disrespectful to Yula's memory. I took the only right course of action available to me to get Guy Furious off our asses for a while!'

The agency heads stared at Austin in silence, many of them clasping their hands and leaning on them, for what seemed like an eternity, their eyes boring into him. But Austin endured, for his anger was righteous.

'He's not wrong,' said the ESA director after a long moment. 'But we do need to get this wrapped up fast. We're holding a funding auction for the alien fusion reactor blueprints this afternoon. We've already had speculative bids from ITER, Tokamak and MAST, and I don't want to risk losing them.'

General Mahoney cleared his throat and said, 'Alright. Here's what we do... Captain Queen agrees to step down and face public discreditation—for a significant pay-off, of course—and we get to keep our cover story. Queen must also agree to never speak of the Mars mission again and will be blacklisted from all public aerospace industries.'

Austin's face fell and he slumped back into his seat. Out

of the corner of his eye, he noticed Dr Barnes fidget in her seat, her eyes darting between him and the general.

The general looked directly at Austin and continued, 'We recognise and appreciate your contributions and your past heroism, which is why we're willing to ensure you're able to live very comfortably.'

All of a sudden, turning to the general, Dr Barnes raised her hand and said, 'S-sir?'

'What is it, Leotie?'

'We still need him on the *Aurora* project. He and his team have made rapid progress. There has to be another way.'

Austin's eyes widened. He stared at Dr Barnes for a few seconds, his heart lightening with hope, and he sat up, adding, 'That's right! We're on IXS-05 and designing for the sixth experiment as we speak. The technology is sound, General, but you need to let me continue my work.'

'Plus, Queen is rather famous,' offered the ESA director, playing with some of the papers in front of him. 'It might hurt our public perception if we were to crucify such a high-profile figure. We need someone else to take the fall.'

General Mahoney grumbled under his breath and then said, 'Fine, but who? The cover story was our idea.'

'I think our best course of action to save face with the public is to come clean,' said Austin. 'Tell them that Guy's intel is accurate.'

'Someone needs to take the hit, Austin,' said Dr Barnes. 'It's a huge deal. There will be calls for an investigation, and expectations of a resignation as well.'

'It was NASA's fault. So fall guy should be of NASA,' said the Russian director, taking off his hat and rubbing his short grey hair.

'Now wait just a minute!' the general started, moving

to get up and balling his hand into a fist, but Dr Barnes grabbed his arm lightly. He stopped and looked around at her, then sighed and sat back down. 'Fine,' he said. 'We'll pay off our PR manager to say the cover story was his idea and offer his resignation.'

'Is settled then,' said the head of Roscosmos with a smile, clapping his hands together and rising from his seat.

The other space agency heads and their support staff followed suit and each said brief farewells before hastily making their way out of the conference room. The Chinese administrator said goodbye and disappeared from the screen.

The room was empty but for Austin, General Mahoney and Dr Barnes. Silence hung thickly in the air as each of them stared into the middle distance for minutes, processing what had just taken place.

I can't believe I got away with that… I owe Barnes one, that's for damn sure; stickin' her neck out for me like that.

Austin rose from his seat, drawing the attention of the others. 'For what it's worth, Director… General,' he said, 'I apologise for all the trouble.'

Mahoney's face contorted with rage and turned red. He growled, 'You are on some goddamn thin ice, Queen. Now get the hell out.'

Austin made his way swiftly back to his department, but instead of going to his office, he made a beeline for the computer lab where Cass sat working at a terminal. This lab was much the same as the translation room, with row upon row of workstations, except without the strange alien artefact in the corner, and considerably brighter.

'Hey,' said Austin, sitting at the terminal next to her suddenly, giving her a scare.

'Sir! You made me jump,' she replied, turning to face him.

She saw him looking, confused, at the images on the screen. 'Oh, don't worry about all this. It's a little personal project I'm working on. I gave the documents to the engineering team and I thought I'd work on some research for my novel while I had some time.'

Austin nodded and leaned in closer to her, saying in a low voice barely above a whisper, 'You'll get no judgement from me. But I need your help on something. Can I trust you to be discreet?'

Cass's cheeks flushed and she smiled. Lowering her voice likewise, she said, 'Of course, sir. I'll help you out.'

For a moment, Austin looked at her, perplexed, and then realisation dawned and he hissed, 'Damn it, Cass, that's not what I'm talkin' about. Why would you even think— Y'know what? I don't wanna know. How good are you at, uhh… surreptitious digital infiltration?'

Cass sat back, her expression stony. 'Good enough,' she said. 'I haven't done it in years, though, not since I worked in cyber security. Why? What needs hacking?'

'Shh!' said Austin, checking around him to make sure nobody else had heard. Once he was satisfied they were the only two in the room, he breathed a sigh of relief and then leaned back in close to Cass. 'NASA,' he whispered.

Cass tensed at his words. 'No. No way. I am not hacking into NASA,' she whispered. 'I know I said I'd help, and I may have got the wrong idea at first, but no! I could lose my job. I could go to jail! Why do you even want me to do that?'

Austin sighed and said, 'I've just been in a meeting with the heads of all the other space agencies, and something the ESA director said concerned me greatly. It's something I'd never heard of, but no one else in the room batted an eyelid, even as he lied to me about it when I questioned it. That

320

tells me it's something beyond my clearance.'

'Respectfully, sir, it's not a stretch to imagine that some things might be out of your purview.'

'But this concerns our alien tech work, and I'm supposed to be in the loop on *everything* regarding the research. It's mighty suspicious, if you ask me.'

Cass stared at her screen for a long moment, then groaned. 'Alright,' she whispered, giving Austin a sidelong glance. 'What am I looking for?'

Austin's face broke into a wide grin and he placed his hand on her shoulder. 'Thank you, Cass. I really appreciate this. I'm looking for anything related to a Project Augment.'

Cass gave a short laugh and started typing into a command prompt. 'You know I'm only doing this because I like you. A lot. You owe me, Queen.'

Austin squeezed her shoulder lightly and said, 'I'm sorry I can't return your feelings, Cass. But I can at least take you out for dinner tonight—as friends—as a thank you.'

Cass gave a small smile and whispered, 'I'd like that a lot.'

Austin kept a lookout while Cass clicked her mouse and typed at the keyboard, staring intently at the screen. But for the tapping of keys, the silence of the proceeding minutes was punctuated only by Cass declaring that she had made it into the secure part of the system. Concerned that any direct search would alert someone to her covert presence, she spent time clicking meticulously through directories and files, and searching for loosely associated terms, anything that would get her closer to what they were looking for. There were plenty of files that would normally be of interest to a hacker, classified dossiers on secretive or abandoned propulsion technologies, spy planes and surveillance satellites. But Cass skimmed right through in her search for the elusive Project Augment.

After a further ten minutes, the clicking and tapping stopped and Cass's hand shot to her mouth. 'Sir!' she hissed. 'I've found it!'

Austin's mind was elsewhere, but Cass's voice brought him back into the room and he looked at her with raised eyebrows.

'Look here,' she said. 'This document had references to the Project Augment you mentioned, which then led me to this file...' She clicked open another file and Austin scooted closer.

His eyes darted back and forth as he read the particulars, his expression becoming more twisted with a mixture of confusion, shock and anger.

So that's what the bastard meant when he said he'd been keeping a close eye on Jimmy...

'What is it, sir?' asked Cass with a worried look.

'It's Jimmy... err, Commander Fowler,' Austin muttered. 'NASA and the ESA have been keeping tabs on him, surveilling him, ever since he woke from the coma. It says here the incident on Mars did something to his cells...' He trailed off as he continued reading.

'What do you mean, incident?'

Austin snorted and turned his head to her. 'Haven't you seen Guy Furious's video today? It turns out the cave-in story was a cover-up. Who knew, eh?'

Still looking confused, Cass replied, 'Well, you should! You were there...' Then it was as if a lightbulb had switched on in her mind as her eyes widened and she sat up, saying, 'Oh...'

'Yeah,' Austin replied, and then gave her a brief explanation of the true events of the Mars mission.

Once done, and with Cass still reeling from the revelation, he went back to reading, saying, 'Anyway, it looks like whatever that alien asshole did to the commander made him…' He paused, his face going as white as a sheet. A cold dread passed through him as though someone had poured ice water over his head. 'My *God*!' Austin exclaimed. 'He's *immortal*! Oh, Jimmy… the poor bastard.'

He finished reading the report and clicked through the file some more. It contained a folder of photographs of both Angela and James, files of medical notes, details of experimentations, psychological profiles and correspondence relating to the upcoming Mars mission.

Austin began to tremble with rage, a white-hot fury burning inside him, and his face flushed a deep red as his expression contorted.

They've been experimenting on him!

'Wait, sir,' said Cass, leaning across Austin's shaking form. 'What has all this got to do with the next mission?'

'They want to duplicate it,' Austin replied, his voice breaking as he tried to maintain his whisper. 'They're sending someone to be a test subject.' He laughed bitterly. 'The joke's on them, though. Grant and I had to utterly destroy the machine in order to get Jimmy out of it. I left that part out of my report; even Zhu doesn't know.'

Cass thought for a moment, then said, 'So if the machine's all busted…'

'There's no way for the landing party to replicate the incident,' Austin said, nodding. 'They're also gonna need the translation data to tell them how to do it. Better make sure that disappears.'

'Can you imagine, though, sir?' said Cass. 'If the military got their hands on this, they'd be able to create units of augmented soldiers.'

'Exactly what I fear they want to do,' Austin replied, rubbing his face with his hands. He leaned back in his seat and put his hands behind his head, staring at the ceiling.

So much for all that 'for the sake of mankind' horseshit.

'Are you done, sir?' asked Cass. 'I don't want to stay in the system for longer than we have to.'

Austin nodded and motioned for her to close down the connection.

'What are you going to do now?' she asked.

Closing his eyes and exhaling hard, Austin said, 'Honestly, I have no idea. I'm gonna have to speak with Jimmy as soon as I can do so without it seeming suspicious.'

'Well, I've covered my tracks,' said Cass, rising from her seat. 'I just hope it was enough.'

'I'll take responsibility if anything comes back to you,' said Austin, joining her in standing. 'Anyway… enough of this for today. I owe you dinner. Shall we go?'

'I'd be delighted, Captain,' said Cass with a smile, and she extended her hand towards him.

Austin smiled back and took it, giving it a supportive squeeze, and the two friends walked out of the lab.

III.

CHAPTER TWENTY-TWO
Unwitting Benefactors

James and Angela had kept an eye on the black car over the next few days, ensuring they remained out of sight so as not to arouse suspicion. There it stayed, in the same spot, with the same two occupants shrouded in the darkness of its tinted windows. As far as they could tell, there were no cameras or devices, no evidence at all that the car's occupants were watching them, and so they had no cause to raise the alarm. They decided, therefore, to bide their time and remain vigilant for any changes. Meanwhile, James continued going to TELOMER Labs as normal. Although following the disaster of the anniversary meal, he put his foot down to ensure sessions would no longer overrun.

It was on his way home from his session on Monday the 28th of June that James took a detour to a shopping centre nearby. Yula's words about the proposal had continued to go around in his mind, fuelled by his determination to make things right with Angela and by his guilt for not having honoured Yula's last wishes.

He'd realised that he no longer had the ring he'd showed the team on the *Magnum Opus*. He had searched all over the house before it became apparent to him that he had very likely lost it in the fight on Mars. Not to be discouraged, he made his way through the shopping centre on a straight course to the nearest jeweller's. After some lengthy perusing, as well as some back and forth with a clueless sales assistant, he finally located a ring that was almost identical to the one he had lost.

After this, he wandered aimlessly along the walkways of the expansive centre. He was on the second floor, and the walls were lined with a diverse variety of shops, including independent stores selling Mars- and alien-themed memorabilia, and pop-up stalls with overpriced models of the *Magnum Opus* and bad reconstructions of the crashed starship. The place, as always, was loud and crowded. There were many different groups of people about, either striding purposefully to somewhere in particular or strolling leisurely, enjoying the ambiance. The highly polished floors and smooth walls reflected the noise, creating an unintelligible din.

As James sauntered along, he thought about what else he could get for Angela. Her birthday was coming up soon and he had it in mind to propose then. But just the ring on its own wouldn't do. He needed something special, something specific to her.

Lost in thought and not paying attention, he suddenly found himself being knocked back by something on his shoulder, and he heard a clatter. He looked around and saw a girl glaring at him as she picked her phone up from the floor.

'Sorry,' he called as she swore under her breath and marched off.

He was about to continue wandering when he noticed a shopfront to his right that he hadn't seen in the centre before. It was a small, single-fronted premises with a wooden façade and a large window to the left of the doorway. James could see in the window display a variety of hand-carved wooden items: ornaments, boxes and candlesticks sitting atop real-wood coffee tables and other small items of furniture. The thing that caught James's attention, however, was almost hidden at the back of the display: an old, tattered, boxed copy of the original D&D starter set. An idea suddenly pinged into his mind.

He entered the store and had a look at the shelves along the narrow walls, which were full of bespoke carved ornaments. Behind the sizeable counter, which took up most of the space in the shop, was an older, balding gentleman with thin, round glasses and a full grey beard. He was polishing a small, elegant ornament ready for display.

'Hi there. I was wondering about that D&D set in your window—'

'About bloody time,' the man replied in a thick Yorkshire accent without looking at James.

James let out a small laugh. 'I noticed all these ornate carvings and wondered if you had any dice boxes for sale?'

'Aye, I do.' The man put down the ornament and looked over at him. 'What're yer looking for, lad?'

'My girlfriend's a big D&D player. She's had a campaign running for the last decade or so with our uni mates. She mains a Tiefling.'

The old man grunted. 'A Tiefling you say? Hmm, I've got just the thing.'

He shuffled over to a door in the wall at one end of the counter and disappeared through it into the back room.

When he returned, a few minutes later, he was holding a small, hexagonal wooden box that was carved with exquisite ornamentation on each side. On the lid was an impression of a Tiefling-themed twenty-sided die. The etching was intricate and detailed, with each of the die's triangular sides in the form of a horn and the numbers in the centre of a small circle. James took the box from the shopkeeper and examined it, turning it over in his hands. He opened the lid; the inside was lined with a deep-scarlet velvet and there were seven recesses for dice to fit in. He pulled the ring box out of its bag, removed the ring from the padded insert and popped it instead into the central recess of the dice box. It fitted perfectly.

'It's perfect. I'll take it,' he said, removing the ring and handing the box back to the shopkeeper, who proceeded to wrap it up. It was far more expensive than James was expecting, but he couldn't resist and paid the price anyway, then thanked the man as he left.

* * *

'Come on, damn it. Pick up already.'

Austin watched the three little dots on his monitor move back and forth underneath a blank avatar bearing the name 'CMDR James Fowler'. This was the second time this weekend that Austin had tried to get in contact with James. He knew the commander had this videoconferencing app, as it was the one they'd used for business before they departed for the *Magnum Opus*. Cass had kindly agreed to set up a secure protocol in case of surveillance, so he was confident the call would go unnoticed.

Austin leaned back in his chair and closed his eyes. It was

one thirty in the morning and a cool breeze wafted through the balcony doors. Stargazing had been a hobby of Austin's long before he joined NASA, and part of the reason he liked this apartment was that the balcony faced away from the lights of the city and into the desert, giving him a measure of shielding against the light pollution. He had been gifted the telescope by his brother-in-law, Alex, after his return to Earth and he'd wasted no time in setting it up outside. When it had reached what he considered to be a reasonable morning time in the UK, Austin had pulled himself away from the eyepiece and sat down at his cluttered desk, firing up the computer to make the call to James.

Austin heard a soft chime and opened his eyes, looking at the monitor. A familiar face stared back at him, tired-looking and somewhat pixelated. James was clearly seated on the sofa and holding his phone up to his face.

Austin sat forwards and exclaimed, 'Thank Christ, Jimmy. I was gettin' worried.'

'Hey, Captain, you're lucky you caught me,' said James. 'It's good to hear from you, mate.'

'Well, I wish it could be under better circumstances,' Austin replied, looking grim. 'I've got some urgent news to discuss with you.'

James raised an eyebrow. 'Is this to do with Guy Furious breaking the cover story?'

Laughing, Austin replied, 'No, but it is related. Do you know anything about something called Project Augment?'

James shook his head, looking confused.

'Alright,' said Austin. 'I guess I'd better start at the beginning…'

James remained silent as the captain spoke at length about their translations of the texts contained within the alien artefact. He told him of how the facilities on the Achelon warship were used to create super-soldiers, genetically modified with the elysian enzyme. And how the vessel's final encounter before being shot down was with another species as part of some religious war. The markings they'd seen on the walls of the ship were the Achelon scriptures, which spoke of war and conquest and birthright; of how they regarded their ancient home world as a spiritual paradise, lost to time. They made no mention of gods or demons but of how their civilisation had become a shadow of its former self and how they believed it was their sacred duty to cleanse the galaxy of inferior beings. They told of 'heroic' deeds by legendary vessels that had wiped out entire star systems, and the great 'evils' that stood against them, fighting for their freedom.

'… And what's more, this repository presents the processes for their gene editing down to the minutest detail. That's where Project Augment comes in.'

'Wow, this is a lot to take in,' said James, his face pale. 'We really dodged a bullet here. If that ship hadn't been shot down…'

Austin snorted, 'Yeah, we'd be up the shitter alright. But it gets worse.' James's face fell and went even paler, and Austin paused for a few seconds before continuing, 'The agencies know about your condition and they want to replicate it. I ain't gettin' into how I found out, but let's just say it wasn't strictly legal. They've been tailin' you, man. Says they were experimenting on you—some doctor called Hales?'

'I know,' said James with a frown. All of a sudden he looked surprised. 'Sorry, my screen went a bit funny for a second… Anyway, I've been working with the doctor out of a facility. Did some digging of my own and I found out he works for the ESA.'

'You know?' said Austin, shifting in his seat. 'Is this… TELOMER Labs?'

'Yeah, that's the one. I haven't told Dr Hales I know about his lies yet, because I need to understand my augmentation. I didn't know his angle in all this until now, but you're telling me they want to replicate it? As in, put it in other people?'

'Probably make their own super-soldiers,' said Austin. 'They're making provisions for a test subject to go to Mars on the *Magnum*. But the good news is the machine is busted. And they don't have the translation data: I've taken the precaution of removing it from the system. They can't do it without those details. I have the files stored here.'

'Good move,' said James. 'There's no telling how disastrous it would be if any military got their hands on this information.'

Austin paused, rubbing his chin. 'I know it's probably a terrible idea, but if it helps you, man, I can send you the files too.'

James nodded. 'I'd appreciate that.'

'I'm gonna do some more research at my end. I'll keep you apprised if I turn up anything new,' said Austin, moving the mouse to end the call. He paused once again and said, 'You be careful out there, alright?' before pressing the button.

Austin sighed and leaned back once more, idly spinning the chair and looking at the ceiling.

He already knew… Smart boy, but I hope his desperation doesn't blind him.

Groaning as he got up from his chair, Austin yawned and shuffled to close the balcony door. His phone rang, vibrating in his pocket. He fished it out and looked at the screen.

Who's calling me at this hour… Cass?

He answered the call, pressing the phone to his ear. 'Cass,

what the hell are you doing? It's the middle of the night. I was about to go to bed.'

'Good, sir, that means you're still up. I have news. I did some more digging through the Project Augment files—'

'Now wait just one damn minute,' Austin shot back, turning on his heel. 'I thought you didn't want to risk gettin' caught with all this hacking business?'

'What can I say?' said Cass in a wry tone. 'I didn't realise how much I missed this, and you'll be glad I went back in. A bunch of new files have been added since we last looked. Something serious is going down with this project.'

'Like what?'

'Documents, letters, emails, all flying around,' Cass said with a measure of excitement in her voice. 'The project heads are in a panic. That doctor they put in charge of Commander Fowler stopped turning in data a couple of weeks ago. He's gone dark; they're worried he's been compromised in some way.'

'Compromised? How could Hales have been compromised? No one else knows about this project,' said Austin.

'It doesn't say, sir. But from the correspondence, he sounds dangerous. It's as though they picked him for his unscrupulous personality and now it's coming back to bite them in the ass!'

'Shit, I'd better warn James,' Austin said, jumping back into his computer chair and opening another video call. 'Thanks, Cass. Keep me posted if you find anything else.'

No sooner had he hung up the phone than his computer screen began to flicker and the videoconferencing interface shut down.

What the…?

Austin slammed the mouse on the desk and pressed keys repeatedly, trying to wrestle back control of the computer, but nothing responded. Then the screen, still flickering, went black.

'Fuck!' cried Austin, throwing the wireless mouse across the room, smashing it on the wall. 'What a time for this piece of shit to break!'

He got up from the chair and wandered back and forth in the room, his fists clenching as he closed his eyes and steadied his breathing.

'Hello, Captain Queen…'

Austin stopped in his tracks and an icy chill shot up his spine. With a frown, he whipped around to look for the source of the voice that had made his blood run cold. Where before there had been blackness on the computer screen, now a new, lone window had opened displaying a man's face smiling back at him. Austin then saw that his webcam light had come on.

The man was older and clean-shaven, with a bulbous red-tipped nose and round, thin-rimmed glasses. His hairline was almost non-existent and all that remained was tufts of grey above his ears.

'Who the hell are you?' asked Austin, turning bodily towards the computer and leaning on the back of his chair.

'I just wanted to thank you,' said the man with a slight malicious chuckle. 'You have given me a wonderful gift through your call to the commander.'

'Creepy, British, and you know about Jimmy… I'm guessin' you're Dr Hales?' Austin growled, his face growing hot as he tensed. 'You bastard. What are you talking about? What gift?'

Dr Hales scoffed, 'Why, the Achelon translation data of course! It will help me no end with my research to know exactly how our illustrious, unwitting benefactors synthesised the enzyme.'

Goddammit, no!

Austin roared and threw his computer chair to one side, toppling it over with a crash. 'How?'

'It's simple. My people intercepted your call to the commander,' said Dr Hales. He paused, and after a moment of mock-thoughtfulness said, 'It really was a silly idea to talk about this openly through an unsecured connection.'

Yeah, but it wasn't unsecured, you parasite!

'Ta-ta,' said Dr Hales, and he promptly vanished from the screen, leaving Austin dumbstruck and fuming. The computer returned to normal, displaying its background image—the group photo of the crew of the *Magnum Opus*—as if nothing had happened. Austin clicked through the machine's file browser and found the translation data was missing.

It's gone! Ah, shit…

* * *

As the weeks went on, the experiments at TELOMER Labs took an increasing toll on James. He had become used to the bruises, bumps and scrapes, and to pushing his limits, but these new tests seemed to be designed to exhaust him and inflict as much pain as possible. So much so that James began to wonder whether Dr Hales knew he had discovered his secret. But the doctor didn't say anything to give that impression; in fact, it had become increasingly difficult to get much out of him beyond simple instructions.

I can endure; I have to endure. Now I know there's no cure, the question becomes what the true limits of my abilities are.

'Commander, if you would stand up against this

machine, please?'

'Wait, what is this one for?' asked James, examining the crude tilted table, running his hands over the smooth surface. It was a metal slab with thick arm and leg restraints and a headrest. It reminded James of some torture device, or something from Gothic horror, and he hesitated. Some of the assistants wheeled out a large device and stopped it in front of the table, locking the brakes down.

James's jaw tensed as he looked at the machine, a metre-long cylinder covered with wires and boxes and other small cylinders—a hodgepodge of advanced technology. It reminded him of his days as an intern at the physics lab after his graduation; it was some kind of high-energy particle generator.

Dr Hales gave James a stern look and motioned for him to do as he had been instructed, but James stood his ground.

'No way. I'm not standing in front of that thing,' said James, pointing at the machine, 'until I know exactly what it is and what you intend to do with it.'

The doctor groaned and rolled his eyes. 'It's nothing too strenuous,' he said, pinching the bridge of his nose. 'For this experiment I want to test your cells' regenerative capabilities.'

'Regenera— No! You're out of your damn mind,' James cried, laughing incredulously. 'There's not a chance in hell I'm standing in front of a neutron generator.'

Dr Hales chuckled. 'Oh, there's no need to worry, Commander. This is not a neutron generator; don't be silly.' His expression suddenly became serious and he raised his hand, clicking his fingers.

All at once, the group of orderlies grabbed James by the arms, holding him tight.

'What is the meaning of this? Let go of me!' James roared,

struggling to free himself from their grip. But despite his increased strength, he was no match for the hold they had on him, and realising this, he settled.

'Goddammit, Hales, you lunatic! If it's not a neutron generator, what is it?' said James.

With a sneer, the doctor replied, 'It's simple, Commander. This device is a gamma ray emitter.'

James's stomach clenched and his body went cold with dread. He redoubled his efforts to escape, groaning and straining, pulling this way and that, but still the orderlies kept their hold on him.

Dr Hales motioned with a wave and the orderlies walked James to the table. They made a start locking down his arms and legs in the restraints. Still James struggled and writhed. Before they could close one of the cuffs, he wrenched his arm free and grabbed one of the orderlies by the neck. As he threw the man to one side, two more appeared and gripped his arm anew. It took all their strength to wrestle his arm back into the cuff and lock it down.

James roared and heaved against the restraints on the cold metal table, but they were made of thick metal and quite immovable. He swore under his breath and lamented that his augmentation had not granted him even greater strength.

'This is a fucking terrible idea, Doctor,' James said, the panic setting in. 'I know we established I'm immune to cancer, but flooding my body with gamma radiation could still kill me!'

'Hmm.' Dr Hales thought for a moment, before powering up the machine and walking towards the nearby lab. He leaned into the microphone behind the glass and said, 'No, I don't think it will. And even if it does, it will show us something very important about your augmentation. I wouldn't be doing this if it weren't strictly necessary, Commander, I assure you. Now, hold still, please.'

'Even if it does…'? What the…?

'No! You sadistic bastard. Let me out of here this instant,' James shouted at the top of his lungs, his panicked voice echoing around the facility. 'I do not consent to this experiment, you hear? I do not consent!'

Dr Hales chuckled over the radio in the room as he took his seat in the lab and sealed the door electronically. 'My dear boy, it's a little bit late for that.'

The machine whirred to life and the sound intensified quickly, reaching its peak. James scrunched up his face to the side, bracing himself. There was a short, loud buzz and the machine began to power down. The whirring sound slowed and grew quieter until, after a few seconds, all was silent.

James blinked and looked around him; everything was as if nothing had happened at all. After a few moments, the door to the other lab opened and Dr Hales and his staff marched towards James.

'Was that… it?' he asked.

Dr Hales remained silent with a grim look about him, and motioned for the orderlies to unfasten James's restraints.

'I don't feel anything,' said James as he stepped away from the table and rubbed his wrists. Suddenly, his vision blurred and his stomach churned, and he was hit by such an intense wave of nausea that he doubled over and vomited on the floor. The room began to spin and he keeled over onto his side, shivering on the cold floor.

Dr Hales looked down on him as the other staff members wheeled the gamma ray emitter away. He knelt down beside James, pulling a handkerchief from his pocket and covering his nose from the stench of the vomit.

'What… have… you done… to me?' James croaked. He whimpered in pain as his skin began to turn red and blister. His vision swam and it took all of his energy just to focus on Dr Hales's face.

'I thought it prudent to start with what would normally be a highly lethal dose, about twenty-five gray.'

'You… bastard.'

'Worry not, Commander. Based on my estimates, you should stop feeling the effects of this in the next few days.'

'Funny way… of saying I'll… be dead!'

'Oh, don't be so dramatic,' chuckled Dr Hales. 'You should start to recover in the next couple of hours.'

He was right.

Two hours later and James's convulsions had subsided. He was still nauseous, but he could get up from the floor of the lab where Dr Hales had left him. His head pounded, his skin ached and the room still lurched violently around him. As he raised himself to a standing position, he held on to his stomach and doubled over again, vomiting next to the first puddle, which had not yet been cleaned up. He wiped his mouth and limped towards the door of the lab and threw himself at the door handle.

Home… must go home.

With great effort, he hauled himself through the facility, supporting and pulling himself along on any surface he could reach. He found his legs became stronger the more he used them and the effort grew less. Reaching the exit to the warehouse, he fished his ID card out of his pocket and struggled to put it in the machine. Nothing happened.

Damn radiation wiped the card.

Leaning bodily on the machine, he blindly manoeuvred his fingers to the help button and pressed it, before slumping

340

down to catch his breath. A lab technician rushed over and helped him back up off the machine.

'What's the problem, sir?' he asked, supporting James under the arm.

'I'm leaving. Card's broken,' James puffed in reply.

Without a word, the technician placed his card in the machine, opening the door. The moment the door was open, James shrugged off the man and limped through.

The next hour on public transport was excruciating and he attracted worried looks from drivers and passengers alike. Good Samaritans approached James to enquire about his health, and he tried his best to assure them that he was fine, which in itself was exhausting.

Eventually, he limped up to his house and lunged at the door, hanging on to it for dear life. He took his keys out of his pocket and tried to steady himself against the door frame so he wouldn't fall forwards when the door opened.

Just as he pressed the key into the lock, the door opened and Angela appeared in the entrance, looking confused. She looked to her left and saw James, pale and sickly, hanging on to the frame.

'Oh, James! What's happened?' she cried.

James grunted and moved around her, staggering into the house. He had barely made it through the doorway to the living room when he fell face first to the floor. The carpet was soft and comfortable, and Angela's voice echoed and faded in his ears, and as he closed his eyes everything around him went black.

* * *

James could hear a voice speaking nearby. He couldn't tell the direction or the content; it was as if his ears were submerged in water. The next thing he became aware of was something cool and damp being placed on his forehead. Then he felt the weight of the soft duvet covering him and the cotton of the pillow behind his head. He recognised the scent of the sheets, the mix of citrus fabric conditioner and another sweet musk that brought with it a feeling of safety, security... love. His thoughts returned to him and he wondered who was speaking; he wished they would stop mumbling!

He opened his eyes and he could see a red blur attached to a body pacing around the room. As his vision cleared and Angela came into focus, he could see that she was angry and grumbling to herself. She was holding her phone to her ear and she tutted impatiently every so often.

Without moving his head, James looked around the place. It was his and Angela's bedroom. Soft light filtered through the net curtain above his head.

It's daytime. How long have I...?

His neck was stiff and he grunted as he lifted his head, the damp flannel sliding off to the floor. Angela spun round, her expression changing from irritation to shock. She threw her phone down onto the end of the bed and shuffled quickly around to James's side.

'You're finally awake! Thank God. I thought I'd lost you all over again,' she said, kneeling down and caressing his cheek. 'How are you feeling?'

James grunted again. 'A bit stiff, if I'm honest,' he said in a crackly voice. He cleared his throat as she leant in to cuddle him and asked, 'How long was I asleep for?'

'Ten days. Today's the 26th of July.'

James sat up suddenly. 'Ten?'

Angela stood up and nodded. 'After you passed out, I

brought you up to bed. I called Dr Hales immediately, and he told me it was just some harmless experiment and not to worry, just to keep you hydrated. Then you developed a fever and it took ages for your skin to go back to its normal colour. Your fever only just broke the other day.'

'That bloody doctor,' James growled. 'He never told you what he did to me?'

She shook her head.

'That monster blasted me with a lethal dose of gamma radiation. The kind I'd get from standing next to a damn nuke.'

Angela gasped. 'What? It's a miracle you're still alive at all! I've been worried sick these last couple of weeks, and I could barely get through to the man. I was trying to call him just now and all I got was a busy tone.'

'The experiments have been getting worse steadily over the last few weeks. Something's changed. Anyway, what about that car?'

'The car? James... the car's gone; it went that morning after Captain Queen called and you went to the lab, remember?' Angela said, shifting her weight slightly and looking out of the window.

'Urgh, yeah... Sorry, my head is feeling all jumbled,' James said, rubbing his head and moving onto his side.

'This isn't good, James. This isn't worth it anymore. I don't care what you still need to find out. We got our answer: there's no cure, and I'm willing to live with that.'

She's right. There's more to discover, but at what cost? I became obsessed and I almost died, all to control the uncontrollable. Maybe now the only way to come to terms with this thing is to live with it.

James paused and looked at Angela. He motioned for her

to come to him, and she sat down by his side. Lifting his hand, he stroked her cheek, brushing her hair behind her ear. She smiled, moving ever closer to him, and he took in her intoxicating scent.

'I love you,' he said, barely above a whisper, as he gazed into her eyes. It was like a moment of calm, a patch of blue sky amid a raging storm. 'And you're right. I have all I need right here.'

The two kissed, their passion restrained only by James's need for recuperation. Angela pulled away slowly, moaning slightly at the effort, biting and pulling his lip as she relinquished her grip.

James felt the exhaustion of his mind and body, though he longed for more. 'I'll have to confront him,' he said. 'It's time I told him we know, and to get him out of our lives.'

'I know you have to,' said Angela. 'But he's become dangerously unpredictable. You need to be careful.'

'I think we've gone way past careful,' James replied, his voice fading as tiredness overwhelmed him once more and he closed his eyes, drifting off to sleep.

CHAPTER TWENTY-THREE
CONFRONTATION

A WEEK HAD PASSED AND JAMES, now feeling like himself again, was making his way to TELOMER Labs for his session on Monday the 2nd of August. As he arrived, he was presented with a new ID card by one of the lab technicians. He thought about refusing for a moment, but reasoned he might need it and so took it without a word and marched through the maze of laboratories. He found Dr Hales sitting at a computer next to a whirring centrifuge. The doctor's screen showed a readout of comparative DNA sequencing. James had come to recognise some of these interfaces over the many months he had worked with the doctor, but he still had no idea how to read the data.

Dr Hales heard him enter and turned in his chair to face him. 'Commander. Good to see you up and about.' He stood and walked towards James, who remained in the doorway. 'Now that you're back,' the doctor continued in a nonchalant manner, 'we can go ahead with some more advanced testing.

I have some long-term experiments planned that will require you to make some extended stays here.'

The nerve…

'Excuse me?' James snapped, crossing his arms.

'Oh, it wouldn't be long. Perhaps a couple of weeks at a time.'

James laughed, a loud, harsh laugh, and said, 'There is no bloody chance I'm doing anything for you anymore.'

Dr Hales looked at him in confusion, like he might regard an object behaving unexpectedly. 'I don't understand, Commander. Is there a problem?'

My word, he's delusional…

'Are you *fucking* insane?' James cried with a derisive laugh, throwing his arms wide. 'You almost killed me with ionising radiation. As far as I'm concerned, our professional relationship is over. There is no way I'm going to stay here while you get yourself off dissecting me!'

He stepped towards Dr Hales and came close to his face, locking eyes with him, and growled, 'Make no mistake, the *only* reason I even came here today was to tell you I'm *done.* I want my life back, free of you, your damn fool experiments and the watchful eye of the ESA!'

Dr Hales looked between James's eyes for a moment and his surprised expression broke into a smile. 'So you know then? You have uncovered a great revelation of which you understand little, and you want your pathetic excuse for a life back. How quaint.'

He stepped away from James and turned around, sitting back down at his computer. Raising his voice, he said, 'You are a hybrid, Commander. You don't really have a life. Whatever James Fowler wanted before he encountered the Achelon matters not. He is dead, and you have taken his place. This is your true life: you are my pet, pretending at a life, nothing more.'

'I understand enough,' said James, pointing to the back of Hales's head as the doctor resumed his work. 'You were placed by the ESA to play doctor, all so you could study me and gather data for Project Augment. But you can't keep me here. I know my rights.'

Dr Hales froze at James's words, then laughed. 'Ah, so the hybrid knows more than I gave it credit for.' He spun around in his chair and spat, 'Curious, how it fails to comprehend that it has no rights. It isn't even human.'

'Goodbye, Doctor.'

As James turned to leave, Dr Hales's voice echoed about the lab through the intercom system with a single word: 'Security.'

All at once a trio of guards, lightly armoured, dressed in black and holding semi-automatics, rushed to block the doorway. James spun back around to look at Dr Hales, who had now crossed his legs in his chair.

Where the hell did these guys come from?

'You are done when I say you're done, Commander,' said the doctor.

'You tell them to stand down,' James shouted, pointing at him.

Dr Hales scoffed, 'That's not going to happen. At least, not until you comply.'

James huffed and glanced at the guards, before looking back at the doctor again. 'Damn it, you're a madman. I can't see how the ESA approves of all this. There was no need for the secrecy either; I'd have volunteered!'

'How noble,' said Dr Hales, rolling his eyes. 'But I'm afraid your research is rather out of date. I no longer work for the ESA; haven't for quite some time, in fact. Let's just say I have formed a new working relationship which is far more suited to my needs.'

It was as though time had come to a screeching halt. James's heart beat hard in his chest as he stared at the doctor, his mind racing.

What? Oh, shit. If that's true then my position here just got a whole lot more precarious!

Seeing James's shock, Dr Hales continued, 'You see, TELOMER Labs was set up as a classified research and development subsidiary by the ESA shortly after the *Magnum Opus* returned to Earth, with the express purpose of studying the Achelon technology your team brought back.

'When we became aware of your... *unique* genetics during your coma, the ESA were convinced of the need to watch you up close in secret to monitor the effects of your alien genetic therapy. You were an important piece of the alien puzzle; a vessel, if you will, for some of their technology. Then, when your abilities eventually came to the fore and it became apparent what you were, that's when Project Augment was born.'

'You wanted to create super-soldiers, just like the Achelon had. Infantry that could survive in the harshest of environments and were really hard to kill,' said James with disgust. 'You were just a pawn, a pathetic lackey in their plans to sell my augmentation to the highest bidder.'

Dr Hales suddenly leaped from his chair and snarled, 'That's just it, Commander! I am no pawn. I have broken free of my shackles. The ESA, NASA... they're all pathetic. You're quite right about what they want, but what a waste it would be for such a wonderful gift as yours to fall into the hands of the military and be used to wage endless war. And you, bleating on about a cure... you're just as pathetic as they are.'

James laughed. 'And what is *your* grand plan then? Your cause that's so righteous?'

'I have a chance, Commander. A chance to do something truly remarkable. With your condition developed into a serum, I can free mankind from its greatest enemy: death itself! I could save billions of lives.'

'*How noble*,' James said, mimicking the doctor and folding his arms. 'Now who's being pathetic? You think that taking away death will solve all of humanity's problems? It will exacerbate them! Only a fool would think like that. Immortality is a curse. One I wouldn't wish on anyone.'

Dr Hales remained silent, looking at James.

'Unless…' James continued, placing a hand on his hip. 'You don't really care about any of that, do you? What is it, money? No… too clichéd. The fame that comes with curing death, no matter how it dooms us?' He paused and a flash of realisation hit him. 'Ahh, I see what it is. No, you couldn't give a shit about helping the world, or even the long-term effects such a serum would have on humanity. You're old and you want it for yourself. You are afraid of your own mortality! Is that what your new boss has promised you? Everlasting life?'

'And why shouldn't I have it?' Dr Hales snapped back. 'What a cruel joke it is that this gift of the gods went to one who clearly doesn't appreciate it. Why not give it to me? At least I would make use of it!'

'There's a flaw in your plan,' said James with a smirk. 'You need me. You don't have what you need to complete the duplication, and if I don't comply, your grand plans fall to pieces.'

Dr Hales paused for a moment and then shrugged. 'Wrong again, Commander. It's true that I had just one piece of the puzzle missing and I was hoping to acquire it through working with you. But I have recently come into possession of what I need quite independently. And unlike those imbeciles at NASA and the ESA, I do not require access to the Achelon chamber on Mars. I can replicate the augmentation process right here on Earth.

'I *was* willing to take you on as my permanent test subject as an act of mercy, but if you are unwilling to play along, then I'm afraid you and Ms Marie-Stewart are simply loose ends. And I can't have that.'

James clenched his fists and his face contorted into a scowl. His whole body shook with anger as he growled, 'You *dare* threaten her?'

'Yes, I dare,' Dr Hales replied, raising his hand and gesturing towards the guards.

At once, the three in black raised their weapons in unison and advanced further into the room, pointing them at James.

I have to get out of here. I need to get to Angela before he does!

The moment he felt one of the barrels brush against his jacket, he spun, faster than the guards could react. He grabbed the rightmost guard and shoved him aside, causing him to drop his weapon. The guard toppled into the other two, ruining their aim. James scooped up the gun and pointed it at the guards as he backed out of that lab and into another.

The man who had been in the middle recovered the fastest and pursued James into the next room. James pulled the trigger and let off a volley of shots into the glass lintel, which made the guard dive down for cover.

Taking the opportunity, James turned and ran, weaving his way through the labs, sprinting as fast as he could for the exit gangway. The disarmed man stayed back with the doctor while the two remaining armed guards continued their pursuit. They fired through the toughened transparent walls, sending small glass shards flying as the bullets ripped through. Luckily for James, there were plenty of sizeable pieces of machinery between him and his pursuers, but still he ducked low as he ran.

James could see the gangway to the right and ahead of him by three labs. He turned as he passed through a doorway and fired again in the general direction of the guards, hoping to give them pause. He heard another volley of shots come at him in return, and this time, just as he was one room from the exit, a round caught him in the side of the leg.

He cried out and stumbled to the floor. Quickly, he picked himself up again and, ignoring the searing pain and bleeding on the side of his thigh, he hobbled through the final lab and up the gangway.

He pulled out his new ID card and shoved it into the machine. The two seconds he waited felt like an eternity, but the security gate opened for him and he heaved himself through. Once he'd made it outside, he pulled the warehouse door closed behind him and waited to one side, turning the submachine gun around.

As the door was wrenched open and the first guard flew out, James came down hard on his head with the shoulder stock, sending him face first into the dirt. As the second came through, James grabbed his gun and yanked him sideways. The guard hit out at James, catching him in the chest and knocking him back. Before the attacker could bring his gun to bear, James lunged at him, toppling him to the ground.

The two wrestled on the ground as they vied for control of the weapon. The guard managed to get his finger back onto the trigger and fired, just missing James's head. Then, yanking as hard as he could, James got the weapon free of the guard's grasp and brought the shoulder stock down onto his face, knocking him out. There was a sickening crunch as the guard's nose broke, and it sat on his face at an odd angle, pouring with blood.

James lifted himself off the guard, gathered up the three weapons and threw them over the fence into the river. Then, as the two guards started to come to, groaning and writhing on the ground, he hobbled as fast he could out of the car park gate.

* * *

'Alright, kiddos, you know the drill: back behind the shield. Cass, you ready to press go on this?'

Austin stepped away from the generator in the middle of the testing room. This machine looked very different from its previous iterations. Gone was the top-mounted interferometer, and the aluminium ring filament was now fully encapsulated within the device, which was a simple box made of polished metal. It sat upon a flat trolley, which had strong metal wheels and was low to the ground. Toughened cables snaked out from the bottom of the box, leading to the control units and computer systems behind the shield. Before retreating, Austin disengaged the brakes. This was the first time the team had been able to test Cass's field geometry solutions since she'd given her equations to the engineers two months ago.

'Ready to go, Captain,' said Cass, seated as usual at her monitoring station as Austin took his place in front of the team. There was nervous excitement in her voice, a sentiment shared equally among those present. They were in uncharted waters with every iteration, pushing the boundaries of science,

352

on the cusp of yet another momentous breakthrough.

This time Cass held the control switch as Austin stared through the protective sheet at the box.

This is it, the final proof. It'll be another twenty years before we can get this thing into space, but this one right here is the true test. The last truly major hurdle.

He licked his lips, which had gone dry, and he trembled in anticipation, his skin tingling and his heart racing. He hardly heard himself as he said the words, 'Project *Aurora*, IXS-06, Warp-Field Geometry Manipulation Test One. Monday, August 2nd, 2027. Commencing in three… two… one… Cass, take it away!'

There was a loud clack as Cass pressed down on the control unit and the now familiar hum of the Austinium Generator reverberated around the room.

'Setting field geometry into position one,' said Cass as she tapped away at the computer.

'Stop the test!' came an echoing cry, the commanding voice of the assistant director.

Austin, Cass and the team looked over to the far corner of the hangar. Dr Barnes, flanked by the assistant director and six police officers, marched through the set of double doors and headed in the direction of the team.

'Christ! What're you doing?' cried Austin, stepping out from the plastic shield and frantically waving for them to stop. 'It's not safe. The gravitational shear!'

Still they kept walking.

'Damn it, Cass, shut down the field!' Austin shouted, looking back at the technician, his eyes wide with panic.

She acknowledged his instruction with a wave and pressed the control unit. Almost immediately, the thrum of the generator began to fade, throwing the clack of approaching shoes into sharp relief.

'Captain Austin Queen,' said Dr Barnes, calling over the residual noise as she motioned to her police escort, 'you are ordered to stand down and cease all operations immediately. These officers are here to arrest you.'

One of the officers pulled out a rigid set of handcuffs from his belt, stepped forward and grabbed Austin's arm, twisting it behind his back.

'What's the meaning of this?' said Austin, his face a mixture of pain and confusion, trying his best to feign ignorance. But the truth was, he knew why they had come for him. 'On what charge?'

Cass and the rest of the team came running out from behind the shield, their footsteps echoing around the now quiet hangar. The other five officers rushed forwards, intercepting the bewildered crowd and holding them back.

'You're under arrest on suspicion of cybercrime, theft and the unauthorised disclosure of classified information,' said the police officer as he clicked the cuffs closed on Austin's wrists.

'No!' Cass shouted. 'You can't take him!'

'I'd advise you to butt out, Ms Spilka. You will be able to return to the experiment shortly,' said Dr Barnes.

'You don't understand!' Cass cried in response, tears forming in her eyes as she struggled to break through the unyielding police line.

Austin shot her a glare, making eye contact, and shook his head softly. Her panicked expression morphed into one of dogged indignation.

'No,' she roared. 'You're not going down for this!' Cass looked back at Dr Barnes and said, 'It was me. I was the one who hacked into NASA's systems.'

Austin groaned and strained against the cuffs and the grip of the police officer. 'Don't listen to her,' he said, pulling towards the director as far as he could before being pulled upright. 'She had nothing to do with it; she's just tryna protect me!'

Dr Barnes looked from Cass to Austin and back again with a raised eyebrow. 'Explain, Ms Spilka. Now.'

The police relinquished their grip on Cass and let her approach. 'He's the one protecting me,' she pleaded, pointing towards the captain. 'You know I have a background in cyber security. Queen's not capable of hacking and stealing classified intel. He can barely use a computer!'

'No... Cass...' Austin grunted, pulling forwards from the police officer once more and looking at his friend with sorrow.

This time, it was Cass's turn to give him a look, but it wasn't stern; rather, it was a look of contentment. Silently, she mouthed, 'It's okay. Let me do this.'

Austin let out a great sigh and bowed his head.

What is she doing? I said I'd take responsibility if anything came back. I thought we'd agreed that!

Dr Barnes surveyed Cass for a long moment, then said, 'Why? Why would you do it? You've always been a great researcher here. You're working on the project of a lifetime. Why throw it all away?'

Cass's expression hardened into a scowl and her body trembled as she channelled the captain's prior furious indignation. 'Because I found out what you're doing to Commander Fowler,' she said, looking the director up and down with disdain. 'How dare you! He's one of the captain's friends, and a hero in his own right. It's inhumane, disrespectful and illegal. I couldn't let that go on; I had to try to do something to stop you!'

'What an *uncharacteristic* amount of backbone, Ms

Spilka,' said Dr Barnes, stroking her finger along her chin pensively. She thought for a moment, looking at the high ceiling of the hangar, before shooting Cass a glare. 'I don't buy it. It sounds like you're trying to cover for your lover here,' she said, gesturing to Austin.

'Hey, wait a min—' Austin began.

'He's not my lover!' Cass interrupted with a snort. It wasn't a lie, but Austin recoiled at the thought of the pain it must have caused her to speak that truth aloud. She gave nothing away, however; made no outward sign of the turmoil Austin alone could see in the eyes of his friend.

Without missing a beat, Cass spat, 'I just have some god-damn human decency, you stuck-up bitch.'

Taken aback, Dr Barnes frowned. 'Fine. Officer, release Captain Queen. It seems I was mistaken as to the perpetrator's identity. Please arrest Ms Spilka and get her out of my sight.'

With a grumble, the police officer undid Austin's cuffs, freeing his arms. Austin rubbed his aching wrists and made a move towards Cass. The other police officers grabbed him by the arms and shoved him backward, detaining him with the rest of the team.

He watched, as if in slow motion, while the police officer who had been holding him now slapped the handcuffs on his friend and began to lead her away. The other officers detaining Austin and the team warned them to stay put, and then loosened their formation and turned away, breaking their line and following after the other officer. One stopped to speak quietly to Dr Barnes and then moved off to catch up.

As Cass walked, bound and led by the police officers, nearing the double doors at the end of the hangar, she turned her head and looked back at Austin. As their eyes met across the widening gap, she gave a small, melancholy smile before turning away.

No… Cass!

Austin's heart ached as she disappeared from view and silent tears streamed down his cheeks.

Is this some damn fool expression of love? You knew I couldn't return your feelings, so why the hell would you do this?

Dr Barnes remained standing before them, and Austin's gaze locked on to her. He struggled to keep his expression stony as he burned with anger; not at Dr Barnes, but at himself for drawing Cass into this, enticing her with a tantalising return to her old life and her true passion. For ignoring the signs that it might be a bad idea, all for the sake of his own agenda. And now, another of his friends was going to suffer for his terrible decisions.

I'm not worthy of that kind of sacrifice. Cass, you should have moved on from me. What kind of friend am I?

'Queen,' said Dr Barnes shortly, breaking Austin out of his introspection, 'continue the experiment. I want the results on my desk in the morning.'

Austin sighed and looked at his feet. An intense need to speak his mind rose up in him, but he bit his tongue and said only, 'Yes, Director.'

The director clomped away, the sound of her footsteps echoing across the hangar as they receded, and Austin turned to face the rest of his team. Worry was etched across all of their faces and their eyes upon him felt like needles.

'You heard her,' Austin growled. 'Get this thing back on.'

Soon the hum of the machine filled the air once more, but Austin's attention was elsewhere. He gazed out of the shield with his hands on his hips, remembering all the things he had said to Cass and searching his mind for any way to get her out of custody. But every time his mind wandered back to her voiceless plea of only moments ago: 'It's okay. Let me do this.' He frowned.

Damn it, she's way smarter than I am! What good am I to Jimmy if I'm in jail? She figured that out right away; she knew this was our only option. Not only that, but she knew the Aurora *project would get shut down without me at the helm. Why didn't I see it? She's willing to get locked up so I can help save James.*

A faint scraping sound interrupted his thoughts and his eyes focused once again on the machine in the room. He glanced at his team: the engineers, the technicians and the new guy who had taken over at Cass's terminal. All continued their work monitoring the warp field's stability and the machine's power output. None could hear what Austin could.

What is that sound?

He looked back out to the impossible box and the scraping continued. With a frown, he concentrated more, staring at the floor around the wheels of the trolley.

Is that...?

The faint scraping grew louder, until it reached a low whine and blended in with the harmonics of the machine, but for that brief moment it was unmistakable: the box was moving. The wheels on the trolley turned, pushing the generator along the floor. With the greater movement, the rest of the team began to take notice, one by one stepping forward and stopping next to Austin for a better look.

The slow movement of the trolley continued at a constant snail's pace until it could go no further, restricted by the now-taut cables, which were lifted slightly from the floor and wobbling in the air.

She did it... She goddamn did it!

CHAPTER TWENTY-FOUR
ON THE RUN

'COME ON, ANGE, PICK UP!' James muttered, pressing the phone to his ear as he leaned against the cold alleyway wall.

He didn't know how long he had run for, limping through uniform grey streets, past high-rises, hotels and office blocks. Apart from the usual London traffic, this part of town was quiet. There was hardly a pedestrian in sight and no crowds to blend into. Keeping to the main streets, he would be out in the open, vulnerable, easy to track. So he had limped down side streets, zigzagging through the blocks of buildings, turning at every junction in the hope that the unpredictability would throw his pursuers off the trail.

Eventually, he'd found this alley, a dark, overgrown passage between the backs of two restaurants. There were bins placed regularly along its length and black refuse sacks piled high next to them, some spilling their contents onto the path. He could afford to stop here and make sure that

Angela was okay. He reasoned it was likely that he'd lost the two guards pursuing him soon after leaving the compound. After all, he had left them in a bad state. But there was no guarantee they were the only ones, and he couldn't rule out the possibility that Hales could track him somehow.

He'd taken a moment to examine the gunshot wound in his leg. The bullet had grazed the outside of his thigh, ripping through his jeans, and the channel it had made in his leg was deep and painful. It felt like when he and his mates used to play 'granddad' back in school, kneeing each other in the hip to cause a limp. The wound was bleeding profusely and stung horribly. He had nothing on him to tie around his leg, so as he leant against the wall, he kept his palm pressed to the outside of his jeans, hoping that would help stem the flow. With the other hand he had pulled his phone from his pocket and attempted to call Angela.

Two missed calls; no answer. He pulled the phone away and tried again, trying to keep his breathing steady.

It would have been easier to handle if Hales had simply threatened him; he could've taken that in his stride. The time he'd spent participating in Hales's experiments had given him a decent enough idea of what he could do and how much punishment he could take. He could now guess at a glance whether he was strong enough to overpower a person, and if that was a nonstarter, outpacing them was always an option. He was more capable than he had ever been; he had been forced to admit that much, even though he resented the effect it would have on his future.

But Hales had threatened Angela directly, and though she was perfectly capable of looking after herself under normal circumstances, she didn't have any sort of combat training and wouldn't be expecting an attempt on her life;

no reasonable person would. They knew Hales was a liar, reckless and ethically grey—dangerous in many ways, but ways they'd thought they could handle with a little vigilance. Neither of them had expected such a sudden, vindictive turn. It was clear something had changed in Hales's behaviour; something had happened to him that played on his deepest fears and amplified his belief that the ends justify the means. But James had no time to consider what this may be; he needed to get to Angela before Hales found her.

'Hey, what's up? You okay?'

James breathed a sigh of relief as Angela answered the call, puzzled by the apparent urgency.

'Thank God! You have no idea how glad I am to hear your voice, love,' said James. 'Listen. Where are you?'

'At work. Why?'

'You need to leave. Now. I want you to come and meet me at the place we had our second date—'

'Hold on a minute. What's going on?' Angela asked, beginning to sound worried.

'Everything's gone tits-up with Hales. I've had to leg it. I've... I've been shot,' James replied.

Angela gasped, then said in a hushed tone, 'What? I can't just up and leave.'

With panicked irritation in his voice, James interjected, 'He threatened you, Ange! I'm afraid he might send someone for you.'

'What about the people who shot you? How would it be any safer where you are?'

'They were chasing me, but I think I've managed to lose them for now,' James replied with urgency, swapping the phone over to his other ear and glancing at both ends of the alleyway. 'I'm bleeding, but it's just a scratch really.'

There was a long moment of tense silence down the phone line before Angela replied, 'Alright. I'll meet you.'

'Where we had our *second* date, remember?'

'Of course I remember.'

The phone call clicked off as Angela hung up. James sighed and stuffed it back in his pocket. He looked down at his leg again, pulling the ripped, bloodied fabric of the jeans away from the wound.

What? It's stopped bleeding already? Finally, some good news.

He turned his attention back to the plan. It shouldn't take Angela long to get to Tower Bridge from her office, and out of the two of them, she would likely arrive first. He shook his head in disbelief; why had he picked the location of their second date? In truth it had been the first thing that came into his mind as he'd thought of his plan on the spot. Their second date had been an unmitigated disaster that they'd both pledged to forget. Now remembering it could save their lives! He grimaced at the irony.

Better get moving.

James gave a final glance around the alley before starting back out the way he'd come.

Fifteen minutes passed as he hurried along main roads and down side streets, making sure to keep up his erratic movements while still heading in the right general direction. It was now getting towards the lunchtime rush and pubs were already starting to overflow, with patrons standing around in the street, laughing raucously. As he blasted past them, James felt that anywhere else his pace and blood-stained jeans would have attracted unwanted attention. But in London the speed was well within the norm for commuters, and his leg would escape attention. In fact at rush hour even

James's quick march could have been considered slow by those who had spent years perfecting the art of walking between stations. He glanced around every so often. His dodging and weaving appeared to have paid off, as there had been no sign of his pursuers since the warehouse.

As he passed a pub on a corner, swerving out into the road to avoid the punters in their business suits, he felt his phone vibrating in his pocket. He stepped up onto the pavement on the other side of the crowd, pulling the phone out as he did so, and continued towards Tower Bridge, now visible in the distance.

He pressed the handset to his ear and nearly tripped over his own feet, screeching to a halt as he heard Angela's panicked voice.

'James. I'm nearly there. I can see it,' she said, breathless. 'But… I think I'm being followed.'

The words sent an icy chill through James's body and he muttered a swear. He thought for a moment and then, trying to keep a measured tone, said, 'Right, Ange, what can you see around you? Are there any big groups?'

'Uhhh, yeah, there's an anti-xeno protest nearby. Why?'

'Listen. You're going to need to lose your tail. Head towards that crowd and work your way through, and keep moving. The more erratic, the better.'

'Okay. Stay on the line with me.'

'Of course,' said James, continuing his march along the street.

There was a long pause before Angela spoke again. 'I'm just coming out of the crowd, but it was only small and I think I stick out like a sore thumb! *Shit*. He's still following me. What do I do, Jim?'

James stopped and looked around. He caught sight of a

street sign and had an idea. 'Alright, where are you? We must be close by if we've both seen the tower. What street are you on?'

'Uhh, hold on…' said Angela. 'I'm just coming out of Savage Gardens onto Trinity Square.'

'Perfect. I'm on Seething Lane. You just keep moving towards the bridge. Don't stop for anything. How far behind you is this guy?'

'James, wha—'

'What does he look like?'

Angela sputtered, 'Umm, about two hundred yards. He's shorter than me, wearing a light-brown suit and a flat cap.'

'I'm going to put the phone down now,' said James. He pulled the device away from his ear and hung up the call before she could answer. He then quickened his pace along the road, breaking into a run.

She did the best she could, but she's right. She's tall and gorgeous, and her red hair makes her hard to miss. Especially around here. Going to have to do this the hard way…

At a full sprint, he passed a small garden outside a huge hotel, startling a few people who were sitting eating lunch on the planters. He took the first left and ran past a strange, oval-shaped building. Within seconds he had sprinted the width of the hotel and come out onto the road Angela had said she was on. He stopped at the taxi rank outside the door of the hotel and looked around.

He could see Angela walking away from him to his right, around the Tower Hill Memorial. There were groups of tourists and commuters milling about all over and it was difficult to see around them. He craned his neck, looking across the way to Savage Gardens. As he squinted, he caught a glimpse of a person matching the description Angela had given coming out of the junction. He was on the other side of the street, walking at a brisk pace.

James moved along his side of the road in the opposite direction, keeping the man in his peripheral vision. As he passed, James marched across the road and walked along a few yards behind. At the junction, the man crossed the road at a jog and slipped in between some parked cars along a thin stretch of pavement. They had barely started to walk beside the bushes when James shot forwards. He grabbed the man by the upper arms and slammed him into the metal railings that held back the plant life.

The man let out a pained shout and looked up at James with a mix of surprise and terror. Without a second thought, James pulled back his arm, forming a fist with his hand. He swung and his knuckles smashed into the man's jaw, sending him sprawling, out cold, onto the ground.

These augmented muscles are good for something at least. Probably wouldn't have been so easy otherwise.

James left the man on the ground and rushed onwards, following the street around, once again heading towards his rendezvous with Angela.

'You knocked him out?' cried Angela, altogether too loudly.

'Shhh!' James gestured, darting his head around, wary of the crowds of tourists on the bridge passing by.

Angela lowered her voice until it was barely above a whisper as she continued, 'One punch? Did anyone see you?'

'No, I don't think anyone was paying attention. But that's not important. What matters is that we've lost him.'

'So what do we do now?' Angela asked, lowering her voice still further.

James turned and leant against the ornate blue-and-white railing, looking out at the river towards the HMS *Belfast*, which sat, as ever, in its berth. The midday sun peeked out from behind a cloud, casting its harsh light across the cityscape, lighting up the ship and allowing James to make out visitors milling about on the deck.

He sighed and lowered his head. 'I don't know, Ange. But it's too dangerous to go home.'

Angela leaned beside him. 'Is… there *anyone* we can call?' she asked in earnest.

'The ESA perhaps,' James muttered. 'I could call Weber.'

Angela leant next to him, brushing her hair out of her face as a chill wind picked up, blowing along the river and across the bridge. 'What about Austin?' she asked.

'I'd love to talk to the captain,' said James. 'But I'm not sure how he could help us.'

Turning around and leaning her back against the railing, Angela stared out at the traffic, thinking for a long moment, then let out a heavy sigh and said, 'He could raise the alarm. He's the one who told you about Project Augment after all. The ESA are in on it; they won't want to help us…'

James shook his head. 'That's not quite true,' he said. 'Hales told me he'd broken ties with them quite some time ago; he's working for someone else now.'

Angela gasped and stood straight, gesturing in disbelief. 'What? How long have you known that?'

'Just found out today, love,' he replied without looking up. 'I reckon it happened around the time that car turned up at the house. That's why I think the best course of action is to call the ESA and tell them what we know. I'm guessing they're not too pleased that one of their guys has gone rogue with their research.'

'That's terrifying,' she said with a shiver. 'All that time and we thought he was just lying about the ESA, and it turns out he was double-crossing them too?' Her voice was quiet, reserved, fearful, and it was almost drowned out by the passing of a double-decker bus. She leant next to James once more and, raising her voice, asked, 'Well, where do we go in the meantime?'

James looked around at her and shrugged. 'There's a few hotels nearby. Take your pick.'

'Bit expensive!' Angela scoffed. 'You do remember we're in the middle of London, right?'

'There's a cheaper one around here somewhere as well,' he replied, standing fully upright. He looked around to get his bearings and then motioned for Angela to follow him.

The two marched back the way they'd come from the middle of the bridge, weaving between commuters and tourists. Angela held her phone to her ear as she quickly called Spider and asked her very apologetically to dog-sit for them. Spider was more than happy to do so, as she loved spending time with Sputnik. The short notice didn't bother her in the slightest, and she already had a key to James and Angela's house from previous times. Angela told her that James had surprised her with a spontaneous few days away for her birthday.

Once off the bridge, James led them on an erratic path across roads and down side streets for what seemed like forever. Eventually, they looped back on themselves and came to a small chain hotel. Without stopping to discuss it, James strode into the main entrance and enquired at the desk about a room for the night.

'You're in luck, mate. We've got a double room just vacated today, as it so happens,' said the desk clerk cheerfully.

367

'How long you stayin' for, boss?'

'Just tonight,' James replied, darting his eyes around, taking in the few people sitting about in the dimly lit foyer.

'Alright. Here's the paperwork, boss. Just sign and date, and I'll take you two up to your room,' said the clerk, placing a small stack of forms on the desk in front of James.

He picked up the nearby chained pen and set to work filling out the forms, while Angela leaned on the counter watching the small television on the far wall. The news was reporting on an announcement by ITER about their recent surprise breakthrough in nuclear fusion.

In no time, James was done and the two of them were given their keys and led up three flights of stairs to their room, which felt about as far away from the foyer as possible. The clerk made sure they were settled, told them the mealtimes in the restaurant and disappeared back down the corridor as the door closed.

Angela strolled further into the room and flumped backwards, with arms outstretched, onto the double bed, letting out a heavy sigh.

James inspected the entranceway. To his right was a built-in wardrobe and a basic shelving unit. He slid open the mirrored door, the draught clattering the clothes hangers inside. There was a small, open safe at the bottom of the wardrobe.

'Oh, good, we've got a safe,' he called to Angela, who responded simply with a dull grunt.

He took note of the usage instructions and closed the door again. On the opposite wall was a door leading to a very small but immaculate bathroom. The harsh spotlights flicked on as James opened the door, followed a second later by the noisy howl of the extractor fan. Closing the door over, he wandered further into the room. It was small, cramped, with barely enough space for the double bed, but just enough for him to shimmy between the foot of the bed and the black wooden desk which stretched the length of the wall.

Got a telly, a kettle, a complimentary box of tea… and a landline.

He shuffled around to the other side of the bed, being careful not to drag his blood-stained jeans across the sheets, and opened the thick velvet curtains a little, peering out at the view.

An enclosed courtyard, or rather an inaccessible, over-grown dumping ground. Same as that awful hotel in Tenerife… This one's cleaner, though.

'Weren't you going to phone the ESA?' asked Angela blearily but suddenly enough to startle James.

'Oh, yeah, of course,' he replied, sitting down on the bed next to the starfish that was his girlfriend. The bed rolled unpleasantly as he sank into it, the puffy duvet doing nothing to mask the discomfort of the mattress.

He pulled his phone out of his pocket and scrolled through the list of contacts until he came to the name 'Julia Weber'. He was about to press the call icon when the phone began to vibrate and chirrup with James's ringtone. Austin's name appeared on the screen, and without a moment's hesitation James swiped to answer.

'Jimmy, it's Queen. Listen, I ain't got much time here, but I got some bad news, man.' Austin's voice was breathless and carried an uncharacteristic tremble; a sharp contrast from the measured confidence James was used to, and it immediately set him on edge.

'What is it, Captain? We're not in a great place ourselves at the minute,' James replied, standing up from the bed and pacing in what little space he had available.

Austin groaned. 'I wish I'd been able to get hold of you sooner,' he said. 'I think I've put you and Angie in danger.'

James raised an eyebrow and replied, 'Well, we are in danger right now, but you couldn't have had anything to do with it.'

'Whaddya mean?'

Starting with the car parked outside their house, James filled Austin in on what had happened to him over the last five weeks, through the irradiation and to Hales's revelations about his break with the ESA. Austin listened intently, offering up the occasional grunt to show he was still there.

When James had finished, Austin said, 'I'm so sorry, man. This is my fault. If I had only called you sooner…'

'What do you mean, it's your fault?' asked James.

'Well, straight after our video call, Cass got in contact and told me all about how Hales had stopped turning in data to the ESA. I was gonna call you right back, but Hales gained access to my computer. If you're tellin' me he was watching your house, that's probably how he intercepted the call. He found out about the translation data through our conversation and then stole it from my system.'

'So that was the missing piece he was talking about,' James muttered.

'Yeah, I'm afraid I made things worse for you,' said Austin. 'My carelessness made you expendable. And to top it off, that friend I spoke about, Cass? I pushed her into accessing the classified documents, and now she's been arrested. They came for *me*, Jimmy, and she took the fall.'

James exhaled heavily. 'Listen, mate, I'm not hearing any more of this self-pity from you. It's not your fault, and I don't blame you, right? You tried to warn me, but Hales was

370

one step ahead of us, that's all. As for Cass, I'm eternally grateful to both of you for doing what you did. I'm sure if she did that for you, she's not gonna want you moping about. It's not your fault.'

'Ah, you're right. She knew what she was doing,' said Austin with another heavy sigh. 'Rest assured, man, my fault or not, I'm gonna do everything in my power to fix this.'

'What are you gonna do?'

'Well, I can't do much about Hales from here. Afraid you're on your own with that one. But I'll see what I can do about the wider problem.'

'Project Augment,' James said, parting the curtains and leaning on the glass, looking out to the light well.

'Exactly. Hey, Jimmy, you be careful. Cass told me they chose Hales to run TELOMER specifically because he's a stone-cold asshole. There's no tellin' the lengths he'll go to. Give my love to Angie,' Austin said before he hung up the call.

Fuck.

James stared at the phone for a second and then chucked it unceremoniously onto the tiny bedside table with a clatter. It slid along the short surface and dropped off the far edge onto the carpet. James rolled his eyes.

Just then, a pair of arms were wrapped around his chest, their embrace warming, comforting him. Angela kissed the back of his neck, making his hairs stand on end. He breathed a heavy sigh and slumped down next to her, burying his head in the puffy pillow so that both ends erupted like an airbag all about him.

'How's Austin doing? He sounded worried,' said Angela.

'Yeah,' James replied. 'It's not good news. We're on our own with Hales, but the captain's gonna try some things at his end to help out.'

'So I guess you're not calling the ESA now?'

'No, not yet. I'm gonna trust the captain on this. He's got contacts we haven't. We just need to avoid Hales for as long as we can,' said James.

* * *

Two days passed as Austin waited for his moment. He'd seen, through interdepartmental memos, that the facility was expecting another visit from General Mahoney and that he would be inspecting progress on their projects personally. It would not be like the previous visit, which had taken place almost exclusively in the conference room (in fact, no one would have known the general and others were even there if it weren't for the cavalcade parked outside the front entrance). Throughout the facility, stress levels ran high as the staff rushed to get their documentation up to date and prepared and rehearsed presentations to give to the NASA administrator.

The day of his arrival came, and the facility was on edge, but the visit had been planned meticulously. First, the general would meet with Dr Barnes and the administration team in the conference room, and then they would take what had become a customary tour of the labs.

Austin watched the clock on his screen intently, waiting for Mahoney's arrival. As the time ticked closer, his heart picked up its pace and he tapped his fingers frenetically on the desk, his eyes darting between the clock and the blank report document for the *Aurora* project. It was no use filling it in. He was likely to derail the entire visit with this plan, and lose his job in the process. The general already had him in his bad books, after all, and this would be like bringing a sledgehammer down onto the 'thin ice' on which Austin stood. But each time the pangs of doubt rose up, Austin was filled in equal measure with determination, strengthening his resolve. This had to be done. There was no other choice. It was what Cass had sacrificed her career and her freedom for, and it may be the only way to win them back for her. And James might escape from Hales, but what was to stop it happening all over again?

Mahoney may be a hard-ass military man, but he's still human. He's gotta know what they've been doing is wrong. If he's even aware of what Hales has been doing at all...

A face appeared around the door frame after a short knock and Austin looked up. It was Kolton, looking grim.

'The general just arrived, sir,' he said in a low voice. 'Barnes has led him to the conference room already.'

Austin gave an appreciative nod and the disillusioned technician went to move away, but hesitated. He locked eyes with Austin and his gaze hardened.

'For Cass,' said Kolton, before disappearing down the corridor.

Austin smiled. 'For Cass,' he muttered to himself. There was a dreadful sense of finality as he rose from his chair. He brushed his hand over the exposed wood of his desk, feeling the grain in the gaps in the lacquer as he moved around it.

Probably the last time I'll see this desk. Well, second to last if they let me come back to clear it out.

Pulling his hand away and balling it into a fist, he strode purposefully out of the open door and slammed it hard behind him.

The walk to the end of the department's main corridor seemed to go by in excruciating slow motion. He gave each lab a sidelong glance as he passed, taking in the sight of the teams still hard at work on the *Aurora* project. Some looked up as he passed; he went by far too quickly to notice their expressions but guessed they would be full of concern.

Most of the teams knew already what Austin had in mind. He had informed them of his plan to get Cass out of trouble and, to his surprise, received widespread support. He had, however, conveniently left out the part where he was also risking everything to help James. But would it really change anything if they knew? If they knew the truth of Project Augment and the depths to which their employers had sunk? No, that kind of knowledge would only disillusion them and lead to a widespread exodus. They could talk about Austin's leadership of the *Aurora* project all they wanted; the truth was that he felt he had very little to do with its success.

Our project, building humanity's first faster-than-light space drive, owes so much more to their talents than anything I've done.

Of course, there were those who disagreed with Austin's plan and had tried to talk him out of it, predictably citing his leadership as the driving force that was keeping the project going, as well as concerns over the effects on staff morale, which had already taken a nosedive since Cass's arrest. But Austin had argued back strongly, and they knew well enough not to try to stop him after his mind was set. With the matter decided, he'd then given instructions for what they should do if things went south with the administrator. They'd reluctantly agreed.

And so the corridor was empty as Austin approached the double doors that marked the end of his department.

He opened one and stopped, casting a last, forlorn look back at the workspace that had taken up the last few years of his life. With a grunt of acknowledgement and a small nod, he closed the door behind him and made his way to the conference room.

The rest of the journey across the facility went by much faster, and soon the weary captain found himself outside the same staff doors he'd stood before the last time he saw the general. With his heart racing and beads of sweat wetting his brow, he exhaled and pushed through into the conference room.

General Mahoney was half sitting on the circular table and speaking animatedly with Dr Barnes, who stood before him. It was a much more informal conversation than Austin was expecting to see; Leotie seemed to have let her guard down and was bobbing on the spot, gesturing with enthusiasm and smiling as she spoke. It was nice to see her in a less stressful situation for once, away from the constant barrage of deadlines, paperwork and bureaucracy that assailed her. Far from being intimidating, it seemed her relationship with the general was friendly, something which Austin had not expected. As he moved further into the room, unnoticed, his guts twisted at the thought of breaking this rare moment of calm for the director, and he hesitated.

No. This is for James. This is for Cass…

He shook off the pangs of guilt and pressed onwards at a march. It wasn't long before Dr Barnes and the general became aware of his presence and turned to look with confused expressions.

'Captain Queen, we weren't expecting you,' said Mahoney, standing from his perch on the table and straightening his jacket. 'I'll be making my way to your department soon on the tour.'

'Yes, sir,' said Austin, coming to a stop, bathed in what limited illumination the room offered. 'I hope I ain't interruptin', but I'm here on an entirely different matter.'

'What do you mean, Austin?' Dr Barnes asked, tilting her head slightly and furrowing her brow. 'And yeah, you're interrupting. Whatever this is, can it wait until the tour?'

Austin looked down at his feet and shuffled a little. He sighed and looked back up, locking eyes with the general. 'No, I'm afraid it can't wait. I'm here to talk about Project Augment and Dr Joshua Hales.'

General Mahoney's stance stiffened and, with a measure of caution, he asked, 'How do you know about that, Captain?'

'Coz it was me who got Cass to hack into the system,' Austin replied. 'I couldn't let it go when the ESA guy mentioned it, so I did some research.'

Dr Barnes sighed and rubbed the bridge of her nose. 'Oh, Austin…'

'Don't do that to me, Leotie,' Austin snapped, pointing at Dr Barnes. 'What you're doin' is illegal, dangerous and totally against the spirit of the *Magnum*'s mission.'

The silence was palpable and seemed to go on forever as the three stared at one another. Mahoney looked unmoved, while Dr Barnes's expression went from exasperation to disappointment to concern and back again. Austin remained half-heartedly pointing to the director, his eyes darting between her and the general.

'So what's your plan here, Captain?' asked Mahoney, breaking the silence. He folded his arms and continued, 'You know some names and you're incredulous… So fucking what?'

'I want you to abandon the project,' Austin replied. 'And give Cass her freedom back.'

The general scoffed, 'You have no idea what you're dealing with here, Queen. You're out of your depth. I suggest you turn

376

around and go back to your department if you want to keep your job. You'll not breathe a word about Project Augment to another living soul, or I assure you, things will not go well for you.'

Austin stood his ground and growled, 'No, sir, you're gonna stay there and listen good, y'hear? I know *all* about the project, about how you and the ESA set that damned doctor on Commander Fowler.' He paused and put his hands on his hips, half laughing. 'And I know you've got a problem. Hales went rogue and now he's in the wind, right?'

'We've got it handled,' said the general.

Austin laughed, 'Like hell! Y'all are tripping over yourselves lookin' for him right now.'

'Like I said, we've got it handled, Queen,' Mahoney snapped. 'Besides, we have everything we need to replicate the commander's condition already. He's a security risk, sure, but we don't need to chase Hales up and down England for his research. He gave us enough.'

'You ain't got shit!' said Austin, letting out a loud, harsh laugh. 'If you're thinkin' you can just shuffle your "volunteer" into the chamber on Mars and hit a few buttons, I got some bad news for ya!' Austin paused as he watched the general's expression betray his confusion, and continued, 'Yeah, we destroyed the damn thing!'

'What? That wasn't in your report.'

'I know,' said Austin with a smirk. 'Wasn't relevant, coz we didn't think anyone would be stupid enough to wanna use it again. You've got no delivery method, and the translation data is with Hales—'

'Wait, what?' Mahoney cried, his face a mixture of shock and anger. He growled and shot forwards, grabbing Austin by the scruff of the neck.

Dr Barnes gasped and rushed forwards, trying to pull the general off Austin.

'Robert! No, stop! Get off him,' she screamed.

Mahoney's grip was too strong for her and he was unmoved. He started into Austin's eyes and growled, 'What did you say?'

With a chuckle, Austin replied, 'Hales stole the Achelon data. I spoke with Jimmy, and he says Hales knows how to replicate the elysian enzyme and deliver it without using the chamber. He's got one up on you.'

The general's grip slackened and his expression sank. Defeated, he let go of the captain and stepped back. Austin straightened his shirt and rubbed his neck, while Dr Barnes moved towards him.

'Are you alright, Queen?' she asked.

'I'm fine,' said Austin, glaring at Mahoney. He spoke up, directing his voice at the general: 'Now, I ain't gonna press charges for that little stunt you pulled. So long as you agree to abandon Project Augment and release Cass.

'Look, I get why you and the ESA started this project. This technology is worth a lot of money to the right buyers, and funding is hard to come by, especially to continue researching these new discoveries. Same reason you and the other administrators are selling off things like the fusion generator schematics.'

He sighed and stepped around Dr Barnes, slowly approaching Mahoney, who watched with caution. 'And I know you don't mean to get Jimmy killed, but that's the risk right now, all because you and the others worked with someone like Hales. Face it: the experiment's dead in the water. It's time to shut it down and make damn sure something like this doesn't happen again.'

Mahoney hesitated, then said slowly, 'Do you know where Hales is?'

'No, but I know where the commander is, and that Hales is chasing him around London. Jimmy's got it handled, General. Now… agree to shut down the project.'

'I can't just—'

'You damn well can!' Austin roared, sending spittle flying over Mahoney's face. 'If you don't, I will destroy the Achelon database so you'll never be able to re-translate it. One word from me, or if anything goes wrong, and my team knows what to do.'

'Damn you, Queen,' the general muttered. He turned away and paced for a long moment before turning back to face Austin. 'Fine. Project Augment is scrubbed. It's becoming more hassle than it's worth anyway.'

'And Cass? She did nothing wrong,' said Austin.

'Did nothing wrong? She hacked into a secure federal network—'

'After *you people* conducted illegal and unethical surveillance on Commander Fowler,' Austin interjected. 'She did it on *my* orders, and it allowed me to warn him about Hales, which might just have saved his life!'

'You drive a hard bargain, Queen. What's in this for us?' asked the general, placing a hand on his hip.

Austin stroked his chin for a moment and replied, 'Things go back to normal. You get to keep me working on the *Aurora*. Hell, I'll even take a suspension if you wanna punish me. You do that, and I promise you, we'll have a drive system for you. I know it's a long-term project, but the gains will be far greater than anything Project Augment could give you. That, and the knowledge you're doing the right thing. But if you sacrifice both me and Cass, you'll lose the entire department and it'll just be another expensive project down the pan.'

Mahoney chuckled. 'Alright, Queen. We'll drop the charges against Ms Spilka. I'm gonna hold you to what you said. You're on suspension; ten months. And when you're back, get me that drive system.'

He paused and looked past Austin to Dr Barnes and said, 'Sorry, Leotie, I'm not feeling too much like going on the tour, and now I have some calls to make. I'll be in touch to reschedule.'

Without a word, Dr Barnes nodded, and the general marched off, out of the conference room. Austin watched as the door slammed, leaving him alone with the director.

'I hope you're happy, Queen,' she said, before turning on her heel and walking through the staff doors, the clomping of her shoes echoing down the corridor and fading to silence.

Austin breathed for what seemed like the first time since he'd come to the conference room, as though he had been holding his breath the entire time. As he centred himself once more, a smile appeared on his face.

Yeah… I am.

CHAPTER TWENTY-FIVE
The Hotel

JAMES AND ANGELA STAYED IN THE HOTEL for one night before moving on. Angela called the morning after their arrival to book emergency leave from work, and the two of them kept to their room for the most part. After their stay was over, Angela felt uneasy about the prospect of going home. James was in agreement and made the suggestion that they look for another hotel. He reasoned that it was probably best to not stay in one place for too long.

In all, they had short stays at another four hotels dotted around various points in the city. They racked up quite the bill, but it didn't bother them; it was more important to stay safe and hidden while they waited for news from Captain Queen.

Through all of this movement, Angela's forty-third birthday, on the 4th of August, came and went. James cast a thought back to the ring and box sitting in the back of his wardrobe at home. At first it seemed a good idea to risk the journey to get it, but after further consideration he set his mind against it. After all, such a trinket would be useless if one or both of them were to lose their lives in the process. Instead, they marked Angela's birthday with a nice meal in a restaurant around the corner from their latest hotel.

On the afternoon of the 6th of August, as James reclined on the sofa-bed of their fifth hotel room—a small, dingy affair with paint peeling from the walls—his back aching from sleeping on so many varieties of uncomfortable mattresses, his phone vibrated, shattering the silence. He scrambled to grab it from the wooden table and let out a gasp as he looked at the name that had appeared on the screen: Julia Weber. Ms Weber was the HR manager at the European Astronaut Centre in Cologne, where James and Grant had both worked for years, carrying out the bulk of their training. James had had precious little to do with Julia prior to the mission. She was a woman of very few words, stern and professional to a fault, but compassionate.

Why would she be calling me all of a sudden? Is this the captain's doing?

He answered the call before it rang off and pressed the handset to his ear. 'Commander James Fowler speaking,' he said, giving Angela a puzzled glance.

Angela, sitting on the double bed and cradling the remote, muted the television and shuffled over to James. She put her arms around him and leaned in close to the phone so she could hear the conversation.

'It is good to hear your voice, Commander,' Julia began in her thick German accent. 'It has been a while.'

'And whose bloody fault is that?' James snapped, the abruptness of his tone taking him by surprise. 'I've heard barely a peep from you lot in the last year. Now you ring me out of the blue? This had better have something to do with Dr Hales.'

There was a short pause before Julia continued in her businesslike tone, '*Ja*. He is the purpose of my call. First, I wish to convey our sincerest apologies for the way you have been treated by us since your awakening. We put Dr Hales in charge of TELOMER Labs and the Project Augment. It was his suggestion to keep you in the dark. He expressed concerns that you could be dangerous. We had no idea what your condition was at the time, and it seemed reasonable to keep you at arm's length to allow you to settle—'

'All the secrecy, the lies! Why should I trust you now?' James interrupted.

Julia cleared her throat impatiently and said, 'Trusting us is unnecessary. I am informing you that, as of two days ago, Project Augment has been terminated. It seems Captain Queen provided us—via NASA—with information about the current situation with yourself and Dr Hales.'

Ha! Captain, you marvellous bastard. That's one less thing to worry about.

Julia continued, 'We have made efforts to seize the doctor's research from TELOMER Labs. Unfortunately, there was a disagreement, which led to an altercation, and one of our couriers was hospitalised. Dr Hales escaped with his research and we do not know where he is.'

'Shit, that's terrible news!' said Angela.

James shushed her and spoke into the phone: 'It's likely he'll still be hunting for us. Angela and I are loose ends to him, so we've been moving around staying in different hotels, and while he has his research, he'll still be capable of working on synthesising that elysian enzyme and delivering it to his new employer. What are the ESA doing to track him down?'

'We have turned the matter over to the Metropolitan Police, and we will be pressing charges against him once he is captured,' said Julia.

'So they're doing fuck all?' Angela hissed incredulously in James's ear.

'No,' replied Julia. 'There is simply nothing more we can do from here. We have informed the police that he is armed and dangerous. In the meantime, I suggest you continue moving around until he is caught, and then we will be able to discuss your return to work, Commander.'

'Return to—' James began, but the call disconnected before he could continue. He stared at the phone for a long moment, perplexed.

Nearly two years of silence and now they want me to come back to work? Weber's got some nerve... At least Austin came through. Looks like it's up to me to deal with Hales somehow.

'So... he escaped but the police got him?' asked Angela with a confused look, throwing herself back onto the bed with a bounce. 'I didn't quite catch the end.'

'No,' said James. 'Hales is still in the wind but they're trusting the coppers to deal with him. So we're expected to just keep moving about hotels for the foreseeable.'

'That's bullshit!'

James nodded and chucked the phone back on the table. He walked over and stretched out on the bed next to Angela. She moved closer and rested her head on his chest, letting out a loud sigh and closing her eyes. James held her tightly and kissed the top of her head. The two rested there in their comfortable embrace for a few minutes, taking in the ambient noise of the busy city street outside their window.

'So what do we do now?' asked Angela.

James stared up at the ceiling, thinking. What could they do? They still couldn't go home; Hales was on the loose and looking for them. It was great news that the project had finally been abandoned, but that didn't help their current situation. It was only a matter of time before Hales caught up with them anyway.

Or was it? James had assumed without a shred of evidence that the doctor had continued to chase them around the city. Either they had evaded him so well that he had no idea where they were or he had given up on the chase. Hales didn't really need James or Angela anymore. Sure, he didn't like the fact that they could cause him problems, but by the way he had spoken, it seemed there was nothing James could do to prevent Hales finishing the serum.

It all came down to how paranoid the doctor was. Either way, sitting around in hotels wasn't going to bring Hales to justice. The only way to do that would be to go after him themselves.

James groaned. 'I don't know, love. But we should get going really, find another hotel...'

Angela moved her leg over James's thigh and rolled on top of him, pressing herself against him and letting out a small moan.

Softly, she kissed him on the lips and said, 'Probably, but not yet...'

Pulling away with a coy smile, she looked deep into his eyes and bit her bottom lip, allowing her hand to slide down along his body until she had him in her grasp, squeezing gently.

'I guess we've got some time,' said James, returning her knowing look, his hands slipping under her shirt and caressing the small of her back, then making their way under her trousers.

He gasped as her hand, cold yet refreshing on his skin, slipped under the waistband of his jeans. She leant forwards and kissed him as her hand found its mark and gripped tight. Waves of pleasure rushed through him as she rubbed back and forth.

Pulling his hand around to the front, he undid the button on her jeans and Angela moved her hips to allow him access. It was her turn to gasp as James's fingers moved rhythmically, tracing in circles.

Each moaned and writhed under the other's touch, kissing and biting, holding one another tightly. It seemed like forever since they had done this; the stress of moving around from hotel to hotel, unsure whether they would be caught at any moment, had put a dampener on their passion. But the call with Weber and the news that Austin had successfully dismantled Project Augment meant that the end of their ordeal was in sight.

Angela pulled her hand out of James's trousers and straddled him, taking off her t-shirt and bra. James moved to take off his shirt but found himself frozen, staring. The light in the hotel room was soft and diffused; the way it fell on her breasts and curves was an incredible sight.

With a tut and a small laugh, Angela impatiently grabbed the hem of James's shirt and tugged it upwards. It seemed to bring James back to his senses and he pulled it the rest of the way off. Their collective anxieties evaporated in the presence of the reassuringly familiar. In this moment there was no threat to their lives; there was no ESA, no NASA, no augmentation. This was no longer their fifth hotel in as many days. It was just the two of them comforting one another in the tangible expression of their love.

James rose up and they embraced, taking in the warmth and smoothness of each other's skin. Angela's hands wandered along James's neck and back, scratching slightly as he kissed her all over, making his way from her neck and down her bare chest. She leaned back as he continued kissing down her abdomen and she revelled in the attention. He lifted her up and kissed further, teasing her hips and skirting the rim of her knickers. She pushed on his hair, willing him to go even further, to put his tongue to good use. But teasing her was fun; he wouldn't give in that easily.

With a groan that said she could take no more, Angela got off James, rolling onto her back, and quickly pulled off her trousers and underwear, almost falling from the uneven bed. James laughed and watched as she got herself tangled, her face red with both the horniness and the struggle. Once they were off, she gave James an incredulous look, before jumping up and tugging at his clothes. Without waiting for them to be all the way down, she threw her leg back over him and moaned loudly, desperately, as she guided him inside her.

James's eyes rolled as he was enveloped by her, delighting in her warmth and wetness.

Collapsing down onto him, Angela moved her hips, grinding herself against James, and he instinctively cupped her ass in his hands before allowing them to wander. The two remained moaning and writhing, grinding and moving against one another, the intensity of their passion growing. They went until Angela's leg cramped, and then they changed positions multiple times, knocking covers and cushions about the room in their frenzy. Thanks to James's enhanced stamina, not a single part of the room remained untouched by their love-making.

Eventually, the pleasure came to a head and, utterly spent, the two lay on the bed, Angela on her side, caressing James's chest and with her leg across his.

An hour passed. Quickly, James and Angela gathered together what little they had with them and vacated their hotel room, leaving the bed unmade and decidedly worse for wear. They rushed along the third-floor corridor, descended the expansive staircase and moved through the restaurant at the bottom until they came out into the connected foyer. James jogged up to the check-in desk and spoke to the clerk, returning their key-cards and settling their bill. They had cut it fine for their check-out time with their diversion, pleasurable as it was, and ran the risk of a surcharge.

James thanked the clerk and turned away from the desk, putting his card back into his wallet, while Angela tried to hand him one of the two small bags they had acquired during the last week. They had done their best to work with limited changes of clothes bought from nearby shops, attempting to wash what they had in their various rooms. The experience had left them craving a fresh change of clothes at home and a return to normality, but they had to endure still further.

As he took a bag from Angela, a group of five men dressed all in black came into the foyer's main entrance ahead of them. James barely registered this in his peripheral vision and paid them no mind, but then, all of a sudden, Angela grabbed his arm.

'James!' she hissed, jolting him to a halt.

Angela's expression made his blood run cold; the colour had drained from her face and her eyes were wide and fixed on the group.

James turned to look and saw that the men were not,

as he had assumed, going to the front desk, but were making a beeline for them, dodging around the various seating areas in the foyer, drawing concerned looks as they passed. They were clothed in some manner of armour, with hardened vests, helmets, padding and other tactical accoutrements; overdressed for the occasion. Each one clutched a semiautomatic weapon to his chest. It was difficult to tell because of the black on black, but they appeared to be old MP5s, ex-police service weapons that had come into the possession of private militias after their replacement a year or so prior to the launch of the *Magnum Opus*.

Mercenaries…

They came to a halt in front of the couple. Their leader—a thickset man with a dark-brown beard, aviator sunglasses and an uncovered head—smirked at James.

'Commander James Fowler,' he said, looking James up and down. 'You are a hard man to track down.'

James scowled at the man and moved a little forward of Angela, shielding her behind him. 'And who might you be?' he asked. 'Dad's fucking Army?'

'Captain Robert Murray, and these are my associates,' said the man, inviting snickers from the rest of the squad. 'We're, uhh, private military contractors, and I'm afraid I'm going to have to ask you and Ms Marie-Stewart to come with us.'

'James…' Angela whispered from behind. 'That's not his real name. Robert Murray was an eighteenth-century Scottish mercenary.'

Giving Angela a sidelong look, James hissed, 'How the hell do you know something like that?'

'Wikipedia,' she whispered back. 'What? I was bored…'

James rolled his eyes and looked back at the mercenary.

389

With a snort, he said, 'Nah, mate. We're good. Cheers for the offer, but we didn't order an armed escort.'

The mercenary's smirk morphed into a scowl and he snarled, 'I wasn't asking.'

Then he raised his weapon, pointing it at James, and the other four followed suit, aiming at the couple.

Panicked cries rose up from around the foyer, and there was a crash as the clerk dived under the counter. Guests moved away from the group, some backing out of the hotel onto the street, while others ran screaming through the restaurant, deeper into the hotel.

Unfazed by the raised weapons but seething, James glared at the mercenary leader and raised his hands slowly, motioning for Angela to do the same. One of the mercenaries stepped forwards, snatched the bags from them and tore them open, spilling their clothes over the floor.

Satisfied the couple were unarmed, 'Robert' said to James in a low voice, 'Come with us, or I'll make you watch while we kill your woman.' He pivoted the weapon towards Angela. 'Just before I drag your corpse out of here. I know our employer would prefer you both alive, but we get paid either way. So I don't really care.'

'Such an arsehole!' Angela spat, moving out from behind James. 'How do you sleep at night?'

Robert stepped towards her, pressing the butt of the gun tighter into his shoulder and flexing his fingers on the weapon's forearm.

'Alright!' James interjected, stepping once again between Angela and the gun. 'We'll come.'

'Glad to hear it,' replied Robert as he took a step back and lowered the weapon. The others followed suit and Robert turned to walk away. 'Let's go then; we haven't got all day.'

The couple were suddenly flanked by the other mercenaries, and they headed out of the foyer towards the main entrance. Out of the corner of his eye, James took note of the decorative stone pillars either side of the walkway. There was one mercenary to his left and one to Angela's right. Robert and another man were in front of them and the last one brought up the rear.

Only chance we'll get...

As they approached the entrance doors and Robert and his companion passed through, weakening the formation, James leaned across to Angela and muttered, 'Pillar.'

He stood upright, then forced himself backwards into the rear guard, knocking him aside. Angela shoved the mercenary beside her and dived to the floor, scrambling for the pillar. Before they could recover, James spun around and grabbed the rear guard's weapon. He pulled as hard as he could on the gun, wrenching it out of the mercenary's grip.

The commotion alerted the others, and as the two either side recovered from the confusion, Robert and his companion burst through the door.

James brought the disarmed man around in front of him and held him in place. Backing up slowly with his human shield, he fired the machine pistol at the other mercenaries, catching one in the side of his armour and causing him to stumble. Other rounds thudded against the wall and smashed the glass of the doors, sending showers of debris over the assailants.

The mercenaries returned fire, amid protestations from their comrade, who held his arms up to his face. Bullets cut the air and ripped into the man James was holding. He dived to his left, behind the other pillar, allowing the dead mercenary to fall to the floor.

Blindly thrusting the weapon around the stone, he let off a couple more shots. The reply was a hail of fire, the impacts sending dust and chips of stone flying. James pressed himself harder against the pillar, closing his eyes tight and breathing erratically.

He peeked out from behind his cover just in time to see Angela bolt from her pillar. Hearing this, the mercenaries turned and opened fire on her. She screamed and ducked but continued running, making a beeline for a planter at the far end of the room. A round caught her in the calf, and she fell, screaming in pain.

'Angela!' James yelled. In the same moment, burning with anger, he emerged from the pillar and buried a burst of rounds into the chest and legs of one of the mercenaries. The man dropped his weapon with a clatter and slumped against the wall, sliding down to the floor and leaving a blood trail behind him.

The remaining men ducked down and, abandoning their injured companion, backed out of the broken entranceway, taking cover around the door frame.

Seizing his chance, James ran for the planter that Angela had crawled to. He found her seated behind the stone oblong, tying something around her gaping wound. It looked to be her formerly white cardigan, now stained a deep scarlet. As James dropped to his knees beside her, she looked at him, her eyes wide with fear and her face pale. He quickly checked her over and helped her finish tying the cardigan around her leg before giving her a sorrowful look.

'We can stay here; this is the first place they'll come looking. Let's move along a bit,' he said, pointing to a horseshoe-shaped planter further along.

They moved as quickly as they could and settled

themselves behind their new cover. Their respite was short lived, however, as the three remaining assailants burst back into the room. James peeked out from behind the planter, keeping low.

'Fan out,' called Robert to his compatriots. He pointed to the other planter. 'They're here somewhere. Be careful. Check over there first.'

'Captain,' said one, kneeling to check on the man James had shot. 'Gav's still alive. We've gotta get him to a hospital. I told you these cheap vests weren't up to the job!'

'Leave him,' Robert spat, grabbing the man by the back of his armour. 'We've got a job to do.'

'But he's bleeding out, mate!' the other protested, trying to shake Robert off him.

The leader pulled even harder on the back of the man's clothing, causing him to tumble to the floor.

'Fine, I'll make things proper simple then,' said Robert as he stepped towards Gav, the bleeding man. He pulled a pistol from his belt holster and, without hesitation, fired two rounds into the man, who fell limp.

'Now get searching,' Robert ordered, walking away from his companion, who remained on the floor, staring at the body of his friend.

There's the weakest link, right there...

James turned back to Angela and said, 'Right, I've got a plan—'

'I'm staying put,' she interrupted. 'And before you ask, no, I haven't a scooby how to use a gun. You're the soldier.'

James laughed softly. 'Good, that fits right in with my plan. You sit tight. I'm gonna take out Dickhead and his mate, but that guy...' he said, gesturing in the general direction of the door, 'he and I are gonna have a little chat after.'

'Why?'

'Because right now, I reckon he's rethinking his life choices,' James replied. 'He's just realised what kind of person his boss is, so who knows what he might feel like sharing once all this is dealt with.'

Understanding flashed in Angela's eyes and she nodded, wincing slightly in pain. 'Okay, be careful. I love you.'

'You too… Oh, and I was a pilot, not a soldier.'

Angela gave him a look as he got up and moved away, out of their cover, keeping low.

He peered over to where Robert and the other mercenary were searching. After checking behind James and Angela's original cover, the mercenaries went off in the opposite direction but it wouldn't be long before they found her. They were making their way around all the planters, pillars and seating areas, checking behind sofas and under tables and chairs, moving in the direction of the check-in desk.

The third mercenary was still kneeling by the body of his friend, sobbing quietly. It would be easy for James to subdue him; his weapon lay discarded some way away from where he was kneeling, and he wasn't being mindful of his surroundings. As James crouched behind a chair, looking at the man, he pitied him and he felt a sharp twinge of guilt for his part in killing his friend. But he'd had no choice: he'd tried to shoot to injure, rather than kill, but when the shooting started, it was either them or him, and James was vastly better trained. He'd also not banked on their leader killing his own man.

Where did Hales find these guys, the black market bargain bin? This reeks of desperation.

The one who called himself Robert seemed the most professional of the group but also the most callous. Doubtless he'd served in some way—likely dishonourably discharged—but the others? Probably just mates Robert had recruited with the promise of a substantial payday; could even be their first job together. They were sloppy, uncoordinated, unprepared. At least one thing was certain: they had no idea whom they'd been sent for.

Clearly Hales didn't tell them about my augmentation… Anyway, this guy's in no state to continue. Practically taken himself out of the equation already. I'll deal with him later.

James turned his attention instead to the other lackey. He was much closer than Robert, but there was no clear shot from this distance. James would have to get closer.

One in the leg and disarm… Should be enough.

Keeping low, he moved quietly out from the seating area and made haste towards the pillar he'd sent Angela to before. Pressing himself against the stone, he watched for Robert, who was now very close to the check-in desk.

I hope that clerk had the good sense to leg it.

James's target was busy with the seating area across the walkway. When he was sure none of the mercenaries were looking his way, James crouched and crept out. As he moved quietly around the sobbing man, he picked up the discarded weapon and hung it across his back. In the middle of the walkway, he stopped.

Better plan…

James placed a hand on the shoulder of the man, causing him to recoil and spin to face him.

Raising a finger to his lips to signal to the man not to cry out, James whispered, 'I'm sorry about your mate. Your boss seems a right piece of work; he didn't need to kill Gav. Listen, you agree to keep quiet and I'll make sure he suffers for it.'

The man paused, looking into James's eyes. After a long moment, he sighed and nodded, responding, 'Alright.'

James smiled and patted the man's shoulder before moving off towards the other lackey's position.

As he drew nearer, he lifted the machine pistol, taking aim at the back of the man's thigh as he peered behind a planter. James pulled the trigger and the weapon spat fire. His aim was true and the round instantly pierced the man's leg. As he screamed in pain, James rushed forwards, his path through the seating area clear, and disarmed him.

The noise drew Robert's attention, and James dived behind a sofa just as a hail of bullets impacted the wall nearby.

'It's over, Robert!' James yelled from behind his cover. 'Your men are neutralised. Put down your weapon and surrender.'

'Nah, mate, I'm not giving up on this job. It's worth too much. If you think you've won, why don't you stop hiding?'

James stayed put, considering his options. He knew he didn't have a clear shot at Robert, and any blind fire could rip through the desk and hit the clerk if he was still crouched behind there.

Before James could move out to a better position, Robert made the decision for him. All of a sudden there was the sound of scrambling and shouting; another man's voice, youthful and terrified.

The clerk! Why didn't he get out of here?

'Alright then, since you're such a coward. Come out or I put a bullet in this kid's head,' Robert yelled amid whimpers and cries from his hostage.

Damn it…

James raised his head above the sofa, looking over to the check-in desk. Robert stood there, holding the clerk in a vice-like grip, pressing his pistol to the teenager's temple.

'Help me! Oh, God... I don't wanna die!' the clerk cried, trembling and being held up by the mercenary.

'Yeah, that's right, keep screaming. It might just save your life, kid,' said Robert. 'You hear that, Commander? He's begging for his life now. You'd better get out here; he could be in real danger.'

With a groan, James stood and moved out from behind the sofa into the walkway. Robert was in front of him, using the clerk as a human shield.

'Right, now put down the guns,' demanded the mercenary.

Glaring at the man, James raised his hands slowly, hooking the strap of the gun behind his back on his thumb as he did so. Bringing them both above his head, he kneeled down and lowered them to the floor before standing upright again.

'What's the plan now, Rob?' asked James. 'Coppers'll be on their way by now, and we're in the middle of London, so they won't be long. Believe me, if you want to walk out of here, you'll need to let the kid go.'

Robert smirked and thrust the pistol forwards, pulling the trigger. A flash and a deafening bang seemed to fill the room as the round flew and caught James in the thigh.

It was a dull thud; not immediately painful, unlike the flesh wound he'd suffered at TELOMER. At first he didn't realise what had happened, but a moment later, his leg gave way and he dropped to the floor. The acrid smell of burnt flesh assaulted James's nostrils and the delayed reaction caught up with him as searing pain surged through his body.

Robert let the clerk go, shoving him to one side, and strutted towards James with his pistol outstretched and his MP5 slung over his shoulder.

He came to a stop in front of James, who lay crumpled on the floor, holding his bloodied leg. 'All this bollocks could've been avoided,' Robert said, looking down the barrel of the gun, 'if you'd only complied. Now, no more mucking about.'

James scowled at the mercenary, keeping eye contact despite the pain. The end of the pistol was mere inches from his face. As if in slow motion, he saw Robert's arm tense, and he reacted. He grabbed the mercenary's wrist and forced it aside just as the shot rang out, and the round embedded itself harmlessly in the far wall.

Taken by surprise, Robert tried to wrench his arm free of James's grasp, but it was no use. In a single, deft move, James pulled and threw the man off balance, toppling him. With a swift roll, James had Robert on the floor underneath him. He slammed the mercenary's wrist to the floor. The gun clattered away, sliding under one of the sofas nearby.

Robert swung his free hand at James, connecting to his jaw with a deep thud and knocking him sideways. Disoriented from the blow, James was rolled onto his back, and his assailant wasted no time in pummelling him further. Another blow, and another, and another. As the impacts kept coming, James almost burst into laughter. He should have expected this, but nonetheless it came as a surprise that he felt no pain or dizziness from the punches. Robert's fists were like a couple of pillows. A warm, stinging dampness gathered around his lips and eyes as the blows began to split his skin.

He heard a scream—it was a woman's voice—followed by Robert groaning. Suddenly, the mercenary was pulled off him. James looked up to see Angela on the floor, holding the mercenary around the neck and squeezing as tight as she could. Robert fought, pulling and scratching behind him, but still she held on.

James staggered to his feet, struggling to put weight back onto his injured and bleeding leg. He swayed and faltered at first, but quickly regained his balance. He hobbled a step towards Robert and swung his good leg as hard as he could, burying his foot in the man's abdomen. Robert let out a winded howl and Angela relinquished her grip. Leaning over, James brought his fist down onto the man's face with a crunch.

He then grabbed him by the scruff of the neck and heaved, throwing him face first to the floor. James knelt hard on his spine, causing him to scream in agony.

Seizing the MP5 that was strapped to the man, James pulled it off him, snapping the cord. Once the weapon was secured, he stepped off and backed up to sit on a bullet-riddled armchair nearby, keeping the gun trained on the beaten mercenary. He stretched his injured leg out in front of him. A quick check of the wound revealed that it had stopped bleeding, and the pain had all but faded.

After a moment, Robert stirred, rolling over with a groan and a pained expression.

'Stay down,' James demanded.

Robert looked at the gun and forced himself into a seated position on the floor, holding his abdomen. 'Who the fuck *are* you?' he asked, spitting blood from his mouth.

'Should've asked your employer that before you took the job,' said James.

Moments later, a group of armed police burst through the entrance door and surrounded James, Angela and Robert, pointing their weapons at the trio.

'Put down the gun!' the lead officer shouted.

James lowered the MP5 to the floor and pushed it towards the officer with his foot, then raised his hands. Glancing around, he saw the other officers picking up the lackey James had shot in the leg, but the grieving man was nowhere to be seen.

Must've bolted. Don't blame him… What a shitshow.

Still, 'Robert' can give us the goods on Hales.

Angela edged closer to James, putting her arm around him tentatively as the officers looked on, silently assessing the situation. It wasn't long before another officer strode over, and James could see the clerk talking frantically with still another, pointing in their direction every so often.

James glanced up at this new officer. He looked to be an inspector. On his head he wore a black turban and he was sporting a neatly trimmed beard. Unlike the firearms officers, who were clad in full body armour, this officer wore an ordinary uniform. The man stood, holding the sides of his stab-proof vest, his eyes moving leisurely from James to Angela to Robert.

'Good afternoon, I'm Detective Inspector Singh. Now, I was going to place you all under arrest, but based on the testimony of the young gentleman over there, you two,' said the inspector, pointing at Angela and James, 'seem to be the ones trying to stop the chaos.'

'He tried to abduct us!' cried Angela, shooting a finger at Robert. 'Him and his goons. We barely got out alive. They shot us! Oh, shit, I need an ambulance—'

The inspector raised his hand and smiled. 'Paramedics are outside, and once we're done here, you can be seen to.'

At a wave of his hand, a group of the armoured officers stepped forwards, dragged Robert off the floor and placed him in handcuffs. They started to walk him away.

'Sir,' said James, raising his hand. 'He has some information we need. He was hired by Dr Joshua Hales to take us dead or alive. I know you're after him too.'

'Now, how do you know about that?' asked the inspector.

Shaking off the question, James continued unabated, 'Hales is in the wind. We've been evading him for the last week or so, but this guy might know where he is.'

'Right…' said DI Singh. 'And who exactly are you?'

'Commander James Fowler—'

'Oh, you're *him*? In that case, yes, I can confirm that this Hales is indeed a suspect, wanted in connection with multiple crimes. You say this man has information on Hales's whereabouts?'

James nodded and continued, 'Yes, that's why you need to let me speak to him before you take him away.'

DI Singh sighed and looked around at the remains of the hotel foyer. 'That's not how this works. If he's got information pertinent to an open and ongoing investigation, we'll procure it ourselves. There's no need for you to get involved. In fact, it would be best if you continued to lie low until—'

'I can't do that anymore!' James shot back, slamming his hands on the arms of the chair and glaring at the inspector. 'We tried that, and Hales found us anyway. Look at the chaos it caused. His goons shot up a hotel for crying out loud. In broad daylight, in the middle of London! We're lucky no one else got killed. I won't be responsible for people getting caught in the crossfire. We need to stop running and go get the bastard.'

'Like I said, you're not—'

'You don't understand,' James pleaded. 'Let us work with you on this. Aren't you wondering how I managed to take down five heavily armed mercs single-handed?'

Angela jabbed him in the ribs.

'Alright…' James winced, glancing at Angela, who wore a hurt look. 'Double… handed?' he asked as she rolled her eyes. James shook his head and looked back at the police officer.

'What I mean is, you could use me. But we have to hurry;

this can't wait until we're back at the station. It won't take long for Hales to realise his team haven't checked in, and then whatever intel "Robert" over there has will be irrelevant. Our lead will vanish like a... erm...'

'Corpse light from a grave?' Angela offered with a shrug.

'Yes, exactly!' said James, looking at the inspector. He glanced at Angela and muttered, 'Byron?' to which she pursed her lips and nodded in approval.

The weary inspector considered James for a long moment, then turned and called the others back. They walked Robert over to James and stood holding him by the shoulders.

'Alright, fine. Let's do this here then,' Singh grumbled. Turning to face the mercenary and pulling a notepad and pen out of his pocket, he continued, 'This gentleman here says you might have some information as to the whereabouts of a person of interest in one of our open cases, a Dr Joshua Hales?'

'I'm not telling you anything,' Robert spat, a look of disgust on his face.

'Oh, come on now,' said James with a smile. 'Hales proper screwed you guys. Now two of your men are dead, one's fucked off to start a new life, and you and your other mate... well, here you are being carted away by the rozzers. How long do you reckon it'll be before your "friend" with the dodgy leg over there throws you under the bus hoping for a lighter sentence, eh?'

The inspector cleared his throat and said, 'If you give us actionable intel, it may be considered mitigating circumstances in the case we have against you.'

'Looks like I'm buggered either way, so why should I help you?' Robert asked with a snort.

'You mean you *don't* want to give a nice big middle finger to that old man?' James scoffed. 'I'm sure that's not true. I'm not your enemy here; all I've done is defend myself. Can't blame me for that. But Hales? He's fucked us both sideways.'

Robert sighed and looked down at the floor for a few moments. He laughed and lifted his head, locking eyes with James. 'Y'know what? You're right. I don't owe that prick anything, especially since I'm not getting paid now. I don't know what that doctor's beef is with you, but I don't like how all this went down.'

'You know where he is?' asked the inspector, flipping a page in his notepad.

Robert nodded. 'Yeah, I know. You promise this'll go good on my record?'

'It will be considered,' said Singh.

'Okay… So, he's operating out of Greenwich now. Got this little old warehouse on Fort Street near the industrial complex. Looks like he set up in a hurry in there. All his research, whatever it is…'

James pulled his phone out, unfolded it and noted the information down. He opened his map application and checked the location.

'Kierbeck Industrial Complex…' he muttered before looking up at the inspector. 'Yep, there's an old car place with a small warehouse on Fort Street. Looks like it hasn't been used for a while.'

Singh nodded and then motioned to the officers holding the mercenary, who then and led him away.

As he left, Robert called back, cackling, 'We weren't the only mercenaries Hales hired. Good luck getting through the others!'

'Solid work, Commander,' said the inspector. He waved for the paramedics to come over and check on the couple.

While the medics fussed over the two of them, bandaging

403

their legs and cleaning their wounds, DI Singh pulled over a chair and sat opposite James and Angela.

'So, we have his location,' said the inspector, sitting back and steepling his hands. 'That's more than we've had since the case got handed over to us, and I have both of you to thank for that. But I'm afraid this is where your involvement has to end. I'll take this intel back to the station and we'll consider our next move to catch him.'

'What? No! Why don't we just go over there now?' James cried.

'James…' said Angela, squeezing his arm.

The inspector laughed. 'A raid like this takes planning, resources. We have to gather information on the warehouse and consider our next move carefully. We don't want him simply running out the back way.'

Singh stood and looked down at the couple while putting the pad and pen back into his pocket. 'Look, I'd prefer it if you both came into protective custody. The offer is there, but it's up to you. After you've been seen at the hospital and each given official statements, you're free to go home or keep moving around, but whatever you do, just keep clear. Leave it to us,' he said, before striding away.

'You hear that, Jim?' said Angela, excitement bubbling in her voice. 'We can go *home*!'

James shook his head and leant back in the chair, exhaling heavily. 'No, love,' he said. 'We can't just leave it to the police. Their method will take too long and there's the other mercs to consider. They'll come after us just like Robert.'

Angela groaned. 'I know you want to get him, but… it's too dangerous. We need to be patient and let the police do their jobs. I got shot… *you* got shot, if you remember!'

'They're gonna spook him,' said James, shaking his

head again. 'He's evaded the authorities already. I can't take the chance...'

'Jim, please! I want to go home. We can't go after him. Why are you being so stubborn about this?'

'I'm not expecting you to come with me,' said James, drawing a further groan from Angela. 'Not with your leg the way it is. I mean, mine is getting better faster than yours; must be something to do with the muscle fibre enhancements—'

'It's not about your bloody enhancements!' hissed Angela, looking around to make sure no one could overhear. 'This is about running off half-cocked. You heard the inspector: these things take detailed planning. They've got resources we couldn't hope to match. Plus, you would *definitely* get arrested, especially since he told us to stay out of it.'

James took Angela's bruised and dirt-stained hands in his and kissed them. 'I promise you I'm not going at this half-cocked. I have a plan...'

CHAPTER TWENTY-SIX
FORT STREET

IT WAS LATE EVENING AND THE STREET LIGHTS had come on, bathing pavements in their unnaturally cool light. It was a stark contrast to the glorious, warm sunset behind the buildings. Cloaked in shadows, James peered out of a dank alleyway across the road from the Fort Street warehouse. This side of the street was largely residential, a long row of mostly terraced red-brick houses with small driveways and the odd side access for cars. It was quiet; everyone who worked in the industrial complex had gone home for the day and traffic in the area was non-existent. The warehouse itself looked in worse condition than TELOMER: windows were boarded, the gate was bound in chains and rusted debris from vehicles lay strewn about the yard.

No activity. Gotta wonder if Robert was having us on.

When James had told Angela of his plan back at the hotel, he'd expected unwavering support. It was a good plan, he told himself. So it came as a surprise when Angela flat out refused to go along with it. That was why he'd had to give her the slip while she was distracted talking with one of the firearms officers. There was only one way to end this nightmare and get on with whatever would be left of their lives after the dust settled. Waiting for the police to come up with their battle plan wasn't it. So he was gone before she, or anyone else for that matter, could notice.

It had taken him a fair while to come all the way from the hotel on foot, through the winding London streets and crossing the river into Greenwich. It was a pain; he'd left his wallet back with Angela and so couldn't take the Tube or a bus, and he worried he might be too late. There were even the dregs of an anti-xeno protest to pass through on the way, scared and weary people wearing face masks and dragging signs along the ground as they made their way home.

James trusted Angela. She'd be furious, of course, but she wouldn't let him do this alone. She'd know he was forcing her into his plan and she would groan, but she'd go along with it anyway. All he needed to do was give Hales a reason to stay put.

Can't see any security cameras. I should probably get a closer look.

James eased himself out of the alley in the dimming light and, keeping to the shadows, slipped across the street, approaching the warehouse. A large padlock fastened the chains around the main gate of the perimeter fence. Compared to the state of the high metal railings, the chain and lock seemed new, or at least used recently. The gate itself was under a street lamp; if Hales and his crew were inside and watching the entrance, it would be easy to spot James's approach, so the front gate was a no-go.

From his vantage point, James scanned the edge of the

fence, and his eyes rested on something towards the far end: a block embedded in the ground. Above the fence, he saw that the barbed-wire barrier along large stretches of the fence was rusted and broken.

Looks like they come and go through the main gate. Clever, keeping it locked up so it seems no one's here. They'd spot me in a heartbeat if I tried to break the padlock, but perhaps I can climb over.

James pulled the hood of his jacket over his head and walked with purpose under the street lamp and past the main gate. Once through to the other side of the streetlight and back in the shadows, he stopped in front of the block. It was a stone fire hydrant marker, a small concrete block with a large black H affixed to it, strong enough to take his weight. His heart leapt as he looked up, for the barbed-wire section directly above him was broken. The loose ends of the corroded wire curled apart and hung down, swaying stiffly in the breeze.

Reaching up, James gripped the thick metal fencepost and gave it a firm tug. Satisfied it wouldn't move, he quickly glanced around to make sure he wasn't being watched and then, holding the fence, stepped up onto the stone marker. Placing his foot on the bar, he hoisted himself up. After no more than a few seconds, James was over the fence and had dropped to a crouch in the yard on the other side. Ducking low under the window of the short entrance building, which connected to the larger warehouse, he pressed himself against the outer wall.

With his heart beating hard in his chest, James closed his eyes and let out a breath before raising himself up the wall to the side of the nearest window. As he peered through the dust-covered pane into the near-darkness of the room, he could just make out shapes moving: two people chatting animatedly, sentries guarding the entranceway.

Slowly slipping back down to a squat under the window, James looked out at the darkening yard.

They're still here.

He knew Hales would be heavily guarded. They would be armed, well protected, and probably better trained than Robert's miserable excuse for a hit squad. But the place was small, barely a fraction of the size of TELOMER, and Hales would need to be mobile, so his guard would be limited in size, just big enough to help him evacuate to a new location should the worst happen. Still, James would be outnumbered, and the small building, which had operated as an office space in years past, was a funnel, its connection to the warehouse a choke point, and that put James at a disadvantage. He'd never killed anyone before, but he needed to thin the herd or he'd be cut down before he could even get close.

Can I do it? I can fight, I'm strong and fast, but... could I really kill? An RAF officer for twelve years, but I was never deployed, never saw action, and even if I had, it wouldn't have been at such close quarters. Just blips on a radar, blurred targets on the ground below.

James shook his head and rubbed his face with his hands. He laughed at the idea that he was even considering it.

That's not even factoring in that it's illegal. It would be murder, or manslaughter. No matter who these guys are, they're not enemy combatants; this isn't wartime. I could very well rip and tear my way through to Hales, but at the expense of a life with Angela. At the expense of whatever's left of my humanity.

He looked around at the door. His best bet would be to draw them out and use the same tactics as in the hotel: take

410

them on in smaller numbers and disarm them.

Readying himself in a crouch, he reached out to the door with his hand and hovered his knuckle over it. His heart thumped in his ears and he swallowed, trying to steady himself.

No time like the present...

He rapped on the door and waited. A few tense minutes passed, and just as James was considering that he might need to knock harder, the door swung open inwards. The silhouette of a lowered weapon appeared first and James leapt into action.

He launched himself forwards, hands outstretched, and grabbed the gun. The force of his momentum pulled the unwary guard off balance. In a deft movement, James grabbed the man by the throat with his free hand and swung him around, out of the doorway, slamming him to the ground. With the weapon wrested from the man's grip, James spun around, anticipating the second man. He swung the rear of the submachine gun out in a wide arc.

The second guard had run through the doorway at the sound of the commotion. As he cleared the doorway, his eyes lit up in realisation a moment before the butt of the weapon connected with his head in a sickening crunch, sending him sprawling to the ground.

James straightened up and went to go inside. All of a sudden he was dragged backwards and an arm was wrapped around his neck from behind. He struggled and writhed, but the guard's grip was good. James made a show of pulling at the man's arm and choking, dropping to his knees on the concrete of the yard. After a few moments, he closed his eyes and fell limp and silent.

The guard snorted and muttered, 'He wasn't all that. Don't know what the boss was so afraid of.'

Slackening his grip, he started to lower James to the

ground. In the same instant, James opened his eyes and spun around with a clenched fist, faster than the guard could respond. The punch slammed into the man's jaw and he fell, unconscious, to the ground.

James stood up, rubbing his neck, and looked down at the guard. 'Now you do.'

Walking back towards the open door, James picked up the other weapon and tossed it onto the roof. The guard nearest the doorway was stirring and groaning, holding a bleeding gash on his head. James walked over, knelt beside him and fished in his pockets quickly and with no resistance. He found a set of keys, stood back up and proceeded through the door.

There weren't many keys on the ring and it didn't take him long to find the one for the door with minimal jangling. He promptly closed it behind him and locked it, before putting the keys in his pocket.

The room was dark, lit only by the faltering evening glow and the illumination of the nearest streetlamp. At one time, it had been an office and the main reception room for the company that used to own the premises. They had since moved on to bigger and better things, it seemed, and the place had remained abandoned ever since, judging by the smell of years of accumulated dirt and dust.

The room was far longer than it was wide, and at one end was a set of windowed double doors leading into the warehouse. James moved past chairs and sales displays, the main desk and small, discarded vehicle parts until he came to the doors. Careful not to lean up against them, he peered through one of the grimy windows. There were faint lights on inside, emanating from somewhere in the middle. But he could see no shadows, and the visibility through the glass was so poor that everything was a blur.

Shit. No way I'll stay hidden going through these doors.

He looked around the office space and spotted a doorway in the back wall, leading to a small storage area. He crept through into the room. There were storage racks lining the walls, some of which had toppled, but otherwise the room had been cleared well. At the far end was another door leading back outside to what James reasoned would have been an employee smoking area.

Perhaps... the roof?

Gingerly, he climbed over and around the fallen racks and shelves. The air was thick with dust and there was even less light here than in the main foyer. Almost none, except that provided by the small circular window in the exit.

At the end of the room, he pushed the door and wiggled the handle, to no effect. After a moment of realisation, he stopped, pulled the keys out of his pocket and tried each in turn. The last one fitted snugly in the hole and it turned with some grit. There was a soft thud; James tried the handle again and the door swung wide.

After stepping through, he quickly turned and climbed up some nearby boxes onto the roof of the squat building. On the roof was the submachine gun he had thrown up earlier and, keeping low, he moved past it towards the windows in the corrugated wall of the warehouse. There was one directly above the building he was on and it looked as though it would open wide enough for him to fit through.

He sidled up to the window, and looked through. It had been a gamble, but as he had hoped, there was a gantry immediately under the window. So he set about prising the window open, feeling around the frame until his fingers found purchase. He eased it open as much as he dared, enough for him to squeeze through. Within moments he was inside and standing on the gantry overlooking the warehouse.

The inside was deceptively large and smelled of dirt and rusted metal. Voices echoed below, talking quickly and too quietly to be discernible. The window James had come through was in one of the darker areas of the building, but still he crouched low. Below, he could clearly see a system of computers and scientific equipment, and a man with his back to him standing at one of the terminals.

Must be Hales...

The man was surrounded by more of the same heavily armed mercenaries, keeping watch while he worked. Under and a little forward of the gantry was a broken-down commercial vehicle that looked as though it had not been moved in years.

James looked down at the gun in his hands. It was loaded and he knew how to use it. It would be easy; he had a perfect line of sight. A clear shot.

Raising the weapon, he tucked it securely into his shoulder and aimed down the sight, pointing the barrel of the gun squarely at the back of Hales's head. It would only take one shot. Just the slightest squeeze of the trigger and it would all be over. Hales was a threat, there was no doubt about it, and killing him would be the easiest way to neutralise that threat. It probably wouldn't even come back to James, but even if it did, would it really matter in the long run? What was twenty-five years to an immortal?

Hales said I was a hybrid. He said the real James Fowler died on Mars. That I'm not human, just a monster. What if he's right? If I have no rights, then the reverse is true: there are no laws to govern me.

Unbound by human laws; the thought was somewhat

freeing. He thought back to the trees. Some had outlived countless empires, doing as they pleased, unconcerned, while civilisations rose and fell around them.

This whole time I've been holding on tight to what I thought were the last remaining threads of my humanity... What if it's already gone? What if I never had it in the first place?

All of a sudden, the humans milling about in the warehouse below seemed very small. James laughed internally; here he was, perched above them physically, in a position of absolute power, which he considered symbolic of his superiority. He was different from them, better than them, beyond their laws and morality. He'd felt detached before when he thought of himself as a mythological being—a demigod even—but now it empowered him. He'd made up his mind.

The window remained open behind him; he could be gone before the mercenaries even had time to react. James was no marksman by any means, but that wouldn't matter at this range. He drew in a deep breath and flexed his fingers on the grip of the gun, curling one around the trigger.

But...

A thought flashed across his mind: killing Hales all of a sudden seemed a very depraved thing to do. The doctor was defenceless. He was dangerous through his influence, but doing this would just be killing an unarmed elderly man while his back was turned.

Human or not, just because I could get away with it doesn't mean I should do it. What am I doing? How could I ever look Angela in the eye again?

Shame gripped James as he became painfully aware of his base humanness and how easy it would be to slip into inhumanity. What was he thinking? His augmentation didn't elevate him above or set him apart, but murder would bring him down to Hales's level.

I am still human. I'm just different. Hales was wrong. Nothing can take my humanity away from me, not even my augmentation. It comes from within, from the choices I make. Humanity or inhumanity… and I nearly chose wrong.

The temptation subsided. James let out the breath he was holding and pulled the gun back to himself. Hales needed to be arrested for his crimes and it was James's self-appointed task to make sure that happened.

I just have to keep him from running.

'Hey!'

James looked to his right. A guard had come up the stairs to the gantry and spotted him, calling out loud.

Shit!

Hales looked around and motioned something to the others. The mercenary on the gantry raised his weapon.

James thrust his weapon forwards and fired, the rounds cracking and popping against the walls, their sound amplified. The guard ducked down, and James flung himself over the railing of the gantry and landed on the roof of the van below. A hail of bullets flew in his direction from the other mercenaries on the ground, but James rolled back and off the van and crouched behind it for cover. He fired around the front end of the vehicle, a spray of bullets impacting the computer systems and equipment. Glass smashed, electricity crackled and things exploded internally, causing smoke to rise from them.

As quickly as he had fired, James threw himself down against the front wheel of the van, pressing his back against it and holding the gun tight to his chest, bracing for the reprisal. But none came; as the echoes faded, there was silence.

'Commander,' called Dr Hales, his surprised voice echoing through the warehouse. 'I take it from your sudden and dramatic arrival that the chaperones I sent were unsuccessful?'

'They were hopeless,' James replied, his breathing rapid. 'Had no idea what they were getting into.'

'So you killed them, and now you've come for me,' said Hales matter-of-factly. 'How ruthless. I was beginning to think the warrior instincts of the elysian enzyme had not taken hold.'

Warrior instincts?

'What are you talking about?' James cried.

Dr Hales laughed. 'You're a hybrid soldier; a stone-cold killer, Commander. The Achelon baked that into their gene therapy. You're a danger to all of us; a danger to the world, to yourself and… Angela.'

James closed his eyes. Could that be true? He'd never even thought about killing anyone before. Not until he'd come here. And not only had he thought about it twice, but he'd had to fight off the temptation to go through with it too. It did make sense; of course the Achelon would want their super-soldiers hyper-focused on battle. Ageless soldiers were valuable, and only useful if they didn't die during the fighting. So there could be no room for doubt or hesitation; those things could get them killed.

But, no… I resisted! There's no such thing; he's just trying to get under my skin.

James blinked and brought himself out of his moment of self-doubt. 'You're wrong. You're just trying to get inside my head,' he said. 'Your idiot squad aren't dead. Well, two of them are, but that wasn't me. They're in custody, and guess what? They sang like canaries. Gave you up good and proper.'

Hales muttered something inaudible, and the sound of

scuffling feet could be heard as the guards repositioned themselves.

With a small laugh, the doctor said, 'So your grand plan was to come here, to the very place I wanted you, purely on the basis of the information they gave you? And here I thought you were smarter than that. Unless... Have you come to give yourself up and become my test subject?'

'Not on your life!' James spat, darting his head warily from side to side, listening to the footsteps of the guards. 'I've come to put an end to your hunt and reclaim my life once and for all.'

Hales muttered something else, then called out dismissively, 'Yes, yes, you fancy yourself the hero of your own little story, I'm sure. You are ludicrously outnumbered, Commander. I'm afraid things rarely go according to plan in real life. In fact, more often than not, the heroes die.'

In that moment, one of the guards jumped out from behind the van with a clear line of sight on James, raising his weapon. James's eyes widened as he looked around at the commotion. Belatedly, and sloppily, he pointed the gun in the direction of the guard and pulled the trigger. The guard had already begun firing. The first few shots missed James as he pressed himself closer to the van. Rounds embedded themselves in the walls and floor around him, and his own bullets did likewise around the man, causing him to recoil.

Taking advantage of the brief respite, James launched himself forwards, scrambling beast-like towards the guard. Too late, James saw the gun rise again and heard the shots fire. The short burst of hot metal ripped painlessly into his torso in dull thuds. As his momentum carried him forwards, James thought that the bullets must have missed and kept his attention on the guard. He ploughed into the man with force, knocking him to the floor, the gun clattering away under the van. With the man underneath him, James reared up, balling his fists high above his head.

As he brought them down, there was a shout from behind, and suddenly James's vision swam and his body convulsed. Flopping sideways onto the floor, James was no longer in control of his limbs as they moved of their own accord. It was as though his entire musculature had cramped at once. Through the blur, he could just make out the wires that trailed from behind his back, pulled taut in the air as they connected to a shadowy figure standing over him.

After a few seconds, the convulsions and tension ceased. His eyes rolled back in his head and he felt strong hands grab him by the shoulders, lift him and drag him across the floor.

James was barely aware of the scraping of his shoes as he was hauled across the warehouse. Before long, the mercenaries pulling him came to a halt and forced him into a kneeling position. The hardness and coolness of the floor told him he was still inside but no longer behind the van. Small fragments of concrete and other detritus bit into his knees, and his arms were held back behind him.

A searing pain flashed across his abdomen and he cried out, the smell of burnt flesh reaching his nostrils. His breathing quickened and he opened his eyes wide. As his vision cleared, he looked down, taking in the three bloodied holes in his jacket. His head swam and the edges of his vision darkened. He felt hands grab him and hold him in place as he started to topple over. The moment of faintness passed and his vision cleared once more.

He looked up to see Dr Hales standing before him, chuckling and bouncing on the balls of his feet. Anger rose up within and James tried to dart forwards, but he was restrained both by the guards holding him down and a flare of white-hot pain from his torso.

Dr Hales stooped and gripped James roughly by the jaw, speaking in a low, menacing growl. 'See? What did I tell you? Unlike the other team you faced, my men here know all about you. You may be durable, but I'm afraid when it comes to electricity, you're just as susceptible as the rest of us.'

The doctor released James from his grip and looked down, considering the bleeding bullet wounds, as James groaned, biting back the pain.

Hales grunted. 'You'll live,' he said. 'Your lucky day, Commander. You get to be my test subject after all. Though it is such a pity that Ms Marie-Stewart won't survive the night. I do hope you said your goodbyes before you embarked on your foolish quest.'

'You dare touch her,' James roared feebly, wincing and groaning with the pain.

'Yes, I know, you'll do something or other about it… Except you won't. I have a lovely restraint bed with your name on it and I'm sure you'll become well acquainted over the decades. I think I'll call you… Subject Zero-One from now on. No need to keep up the charade that you're anything but a beast any longer.'

Hales stood up and began to turn away.

'Please,' James muttered, coughing up blood, causing the doctor to halt and look back at him.

Hales regarded James through his glasses, peering through them down the end of his nose as one would with something contemptuous.

'What was that, Subject Zero-One?'

James stared up at the doctor, his eyes watering and his face turning pale. 'Please,' he whispered. The effort of speaking now tired him. 'Spare her.'

Hales scoffed and turned away again. 'It looks like I'll have to treat you after all. You appear to be dying, and I would much prefer a live subject.' He gave one of his mercenaries a sidelong look and said, 'Bring him.'

A moment later, James was lifted to his feet, the men either side of him taking almost his full weight as he slumped in their grasp. They dragged him over to a table of broken equipment riddled with bullet holes. Another two men rushed over and swept everything to the floor with a crash of splintering plastic and glass. Assisting the other two, they lifted James by the arms and legs and laid him on the table.

James longed to move, to get up and bolt—either for Hales or the door, he hadn't decided which—but his limbs refused to move. The weight of exhaustion, the weakness brought on by the loss of blood, held them down. A realisation hit him and tears streamed silently down from his eyes: Hales was right; he was dying. There was nothing more he could do. This had been a damn fool plan and he would never see Angela again. But the worst part of it all was that he *hadn't* said goodbye to her; he'd sneaked out, and her last memory of him would be his sudden, pig-headed disappearance. He hadn't banked on this; he'd thought he could hold Hales here long enough for Angela to enact the plan with which she'd disagreed so vehemently.

Fear now gripped him; his body felt cold. Fragments of his life surfaced in his mind, images of those he'd known whom he would now follow into untimely oblivion.

I don't want to die… Not now. Not like this.

Dr Hales appeared next to him wearing a medical mask and gloves, holding his hands out before him. One of the mercenaries carried over a lamp and placed it next to James, shining its light on his torso.

'Now, to save your life, Zero-One,' said the doctor.

The rest was a blur as Dr Hales got to work, cutting James's jacket and shirt open and rubbing some disinfectant on his body around the wounds. It was a funny feeling, or rather a certain morbid humour in the situation, that the very man whom James despised was now the one saving his life. He laughed internally.

Dying on this table. Robbing Hales of the satisfaction of saving my life, thereby foiling his plans to use me as a live test subject... wouldn't that just be poetic?

As the surgery went on and James's delirium continued, guilt-tinged thoughts of Angela circled in his mind, followed by ones of Captain Queen and the ways in which he had put himself out to help James.

Whether I die here or not, Hales gets his way. I'm at his mercy now. God, I'm such a failure. I put those close to me through so much and it's amounted to nothing. What a waste...

As if coming from somewhere far away, there was a muffled clank as the first of the bullets was removed and dropped into a tray, followed shortly after by two more.

James heard the likewise muffled voice of the doctor say something about recuperation, but he could make no sense of it. His mind slipped and drifted, falling at last into darkness.

CHAPTER TWENTY-SEVEN
The Raid

HE DIDN'T KNOW HOW LONG he had been out for when he finally woke, but the sound that shook him back to consciousness was unfamiliar. A crash, amplified into an explosive cacophony as it reverberated off the walls. There were shouts and screams all around him, along with the cracks and pops of scattered gunfire.

Still lying on the table, James opened his eyes. Everything was a blur, but looking along his body he could just make out the dressings taped to his bare skin. Next to the table sat a small, bloodied bowl with three chunks of metal inside, glistening red under the lamplight.

Shadows all around him moved erratically as his vision cleared, and bright bursts of light accompanied the crackle of the guns. His mind returned to him quickly now, and he looked at the unfolding chaos around him. The mercenaries were caught in an intense firefight, diving for cover and discharging their weapons in return against some invading force. Debris littered the floor, and one of the corrugated doors at the far end of the warehouse had been torn to shreds, the inward-facing shards blackened and twisted. It was plain that the noise which had roused James had come from whatever explosion had breached the door. Half-concealed in the shadows of the night, the invaders were likewise nestled behind cover, but their force was organised and efficient. As he squinted he saw, further back beyond the doors, under some artificial light in the yard, the form of a woman, slender and with long reddish hair, standing in the midst of a group.

Angela! That means these guys must be the coppers. She did it!

Raising himself up onto his elbow, he darted his head around. Hales was nowhere to be seen, neither among the mercenaries hunkered behind their makeshift shields, nor among the few bodies which already lay scattered about the floor.

Damn him... Where's he gone? I have to find him. He's not getting away from me now.

With a great effort, James heaved himself off the table and rolled to all fours on the floor below. Great clangs, thuds, flashes and sparks rang and blazed about him as the firefight continued.

Something clattered on the floor nearby and hissed. Before long, a noxious smoke began to engulf the room. Keeping low, James spied an open exit behind where he had been on the table. It looked like it led out to the back of the warehouse. Holding his stomach with one hand, James moved, unnoticed by the fray, towards the door. Pain surged and grew once again as the movement tore at his newly stitched and packed wounds. He fell to the floor. But he was determined. He had to find Hales; he could not be allowed to escape again.

James lifted himself up once more and hobbled through the doorway and out into a narrow outer area to the side of the warehouse, which backed onto another property on the road parallel to Fort Street.

A chill came over him as he stepped out into the night. He became acutely aware that he wasn't wearing anything on his torso, and he shivered, vaguely recalling that Hales had cut his clothes off him to operate.

The sudden clatter of wood drew James's attention to the far end of the passage. A figure, clothed in white, was pushing heavy boxes against the wall and had dropped one trying to stack it on top.

He's trying to climb over the wall!

'Hales!' James shouted, his voice ringing out clearly in the night air. 'Give it up—you're done.'

The man at the end glanced around, then continued pushing another box, scraping it along the rough ground.

James started towards him, hobbling as quickly as he could manage. The pain was intense. On the palm of his hand, he felt a new dampness come through the dressing, and he stopped and pulled his hand away. It was stained a deep red.

'Bleeding again?' called the doctor, standing up from pushing the box, decidedly out of breath. 'You ought to be more careful. Why not sit down and take a load off? Quick as it is, your body needs time to heal.'

'And just let you get away? No chance!' said James, glaring at Hales.

Pressing his hand back to the dressing, he continued

onwards towards the doctor.

Hales grunted and strained as he heaved the box to the top, then scrambled up as fast as he could.

With a burst of energy, James reached the stack of boxes and lunged forwards. He grabbed the back of Hales's coat and pulled, sending the old man off balance. Hales let out a cry as he fell from the boxes and landed with a thud on the ground.

'Enough of this,' said James, crouching on one knee over Hales. 'It's over; the police are right inside dealing with your mercs.'

'Over?' said Dr Hales, coughing as he lifted himself up to a sitting position. 'You're a fool if you think this ends with me.'

'What are you talking about?' James scoffed. 'Your research is destroyed. You can't fight me, and you're going away for a long time.'

'It's true, I clearly underestimated you, and I can't fight you even in your weakened state. But do you remember when I said you were part of something greater?'

James stared at him, raising an eyebrow.

Hales laughed. 'My employer is very interested in you. Oh yes, very interested indeed, and perfectly content to play the long game, especially…' He paused, licking his lips. '… since I've completed the serum.'

James froze at his words. It was as though time had come to a screeching halt, and his mind raced.

How could he have finished it? I thought he needed me for that. Who is this employer of his?

'How is that possible?' James asked, raising his voice. 'If you already had your serum, then what the fuck was all this about?'

'Oh, I never needed you to finish the synthesis, Commander,' said Dr Hales with a smirk. 'But there are always improvements to be made, irregularities to fix, enhancements... And studying a living specimen is the best way to do that. You factor in to my employer's plans as well.'

'What do they want with me?'

'Oh, I'm sure you'll find out sooner or later,' said the doctor, and he tilted his head back and laughed out loud.

James rocked back to a sitting position and considered Hales's words, dumbstruck. Taking advantage of James's lapse in concentration, Hales pulled a scalpel out from his coat pocket and lunged forwards, embedding the tiny blade in the side of James's neck.

He cried out, falling sideways, away from the doctor. He yanked the scalpel out of his neck and spun around to see Hales scrambling up the boxes once again. Holding the fresh wound, James jumped up and tried to pull the doctor back down again, but Hales was prepared. The doctor kicked his foot out as James reached out, catching him in the face and knocking him back. The force sent James tumbling onto his back, groaning with fresh stabs of pain from his bleeding wounds.

As he reached the top of the boxes, Hales turned and flung his arms wide, looking down on James.

'Enjoy your precious time while you can, Commander,' cried the doctor. 'You may have won this night, but I will be back. Maybe tomorrow, maybe fifty years from now. After all, what is time to an immortal? But rest assured I will be—'

A blast rang out, echoing in the stillness of the night. Not from the warehouse, where the battle within had ebbed, but seemingly from the sky itself. A swift, growing whistle.

A dull thud.

And a sickening, wet crunch.

Dr Hales—his head sporting a new, gruesome orifice—stared sightlessly as his legs gave way and his body crumpled. The force of the drop broke the flimsy wood of the top box and sent the old man's corpse tumbling to James's feet.

The echo of the shot still lingered, and James looked around in wide-eyed shock for its source, but he was alone. He looked back at the body of the doctor. His arm had flopped, outstretched, towards him. His lifeless eyes stared straight through James.

He breathed heavily.

He's… gone? He's gone. But… who killed him? Fuck! Sniper!

James tried to get up, but he was still bleeding and in severe pain, so he fell. He heaved himself along the ground towards the nearest wall and pressed himself against it, panting. As he sat, his eyes began to lose focus and his vision darkened. There was a commotion at the far end of the outdoor area, and James turned his head in time to see the group of firearms officers file out through the exit door. From amongst their number, Angela rushed forwards, her hair blowing in the evening breeze.

Her face was a blur as she dropped to her knees beside him and her voice grew ever more distant as she cried, 'James! James!'

And all was black.

* * *

'Hello, Commander.'

No… Hales? No… You're dead. I saw it. Someone killed you!

James's eyes shot open and stung as overwhelming white

light poured in. A figure in a white coat stood beside him, looking down. Questions flooded James's addled mind. How could the doctor have survived? Had he imagined it all? Was he still in the warehouse and now being experimented upon?

Slowly, as his vision came back into focus, another figure joined the first. His heart leapt; he didn't need his full eyesight to recognise this form, as the blur of red gave it away.

'Angela?' he said, his voice croaky.

He blinked a few times and her face came into full focus as she leant in close, smiling her beautiful smile and wiping her eyes and moving her hair behind her ear. He let out a shaky laugh and whatever tension he had felt before was suddenly released. She was all he wanted to see.

Then the memory returned and he frowned. 'But…' he said, darting his eyes to the man in white.

He was a younger man: black hair, light-brown skin, white doctor's uniform, immaculate—and most importantly, not Dr Hales. James took a moment to look around the room. He was lying in a hospital bed in a room that was very much like the one he had woken up in nearly a year ago.

Angela was crouched beside him, holding his hand, and he had wires trailing from his arm and body to machines which dripped and beeped.

'How long have I been out this time?' he asked with a small laugh, looking back into Angela's watery blue eyes.

'Only a couple of days,' she whispered, her voice trembling. 'We found you out there next to Hales's body, and you passed out. You'd lost a lot of blood. The doctors said you were at risk of infection too. They kept you sedated while your body healed.' She leant in even closer and whispered into his ear so the doctor couldn't hear, 'I didn't tell them about your augmentation, but they were amazed at how quickly you've healed.'

'Very sorry, Ms Marie-Stewart, but I do need to check on him,' said the doctor.

Angela gave James one last smile, then nodded, stood up and moved out of the doctor's way.

James shuffled up the bed a little. 'So, I'm not dying, am I, Doctor…?'

'Dr Hussein. And no, you're going to make a full recovery. Though we did have to correct that horrible patch-up job on your bullet wounds. Quite difficult since they were already starting to granulate by the time we got to work on you. Open your eyes wide, please.'

James complied, and the doctor shone a small light into his eyes, directing him to look this way and that. Dr Hussein then stood back up and checked James's temperature, blood pressure and other vitals.

'Everything looks good,' he said, making notes on a small device. 'I'd like to keep you in for another few hours and see how you're getting on, then I see no reason why we can't discharge you. If you take it easy, you should be able to recuperate at home.' He turned to walk away, then stopped and looked back. 'You're very lucky, Commander. The amount you've been shot and stabbed, it's a wonder you're still with us at all. We almost lost you.'

'Not exactly my choice, Doc,' James retorted.

Dr Hussein simply nodded and walked away, leaving James scowling after him.

Angela sidled back into view and said with a chuckle, 'What is it with you and doctors?'

'I can't believe it's over, Ange,' James replied in a low voice. 'Just like that and Hales is gone.'

'I know! It's a big relief. Any idea who took him out? Did

one of his goons get fed up with him?'

'No,' said James, frowning. 'He was talking about his employer and all these huge, ambiguous plans he had since he'd managed to develop the elysian serum.'

'He really did it then?' said Angela, sitting down on the side of the bed and staring out of the window. 'Do you think he got a chance to use it?'

'I don't know. But he said we'd have to watch our backs. That even if it took fifty years, he'd be back. But then that was just before…' James made a shooting gesture with his fingers. 'I think either his new employer, whoever that is, didn't like him talking so much, or they felt Hales had outlived his usefulness and they never intended for him to be part of the next phase of their plan.' James paused. 'Did the police—?'

'No,' said Angela. 'They checked the surrounding buildings, but there was nothing. Doesn't look like they can get anything useful from what's left of the bullet either. Except that it came from a pretty powerful rifle.'

'That much was abundantly clear,' said James grimly. 'I wonder—'

'No. Absolutely not!'

'What?'

'We are dropping this right now! Once you're discharged, we're going home and not thinking about this ordeal for the rest of our goddamn lives. Got that? You know, I'm still mad at you for just leaving me in the hotel. You bastard. What the hell were you thinking?'

James looked down at his hands, interlocking his fingers and sighing heavily. 'I'm sorry, Ange. I really thought it was the best plan, and you weren't going for it, and the police…'

Angela held up a hand and gave a small smile. 'I get why you did it. If you hadn't been there, Hales would have easily jumped the wall and escaped. But James, you almost died! I almost lost you. I couldn't bear it if the last thing between us was you disappearing without a word.'

Still looking down at his hands, James replied, 'Yes, I messed up. I shouldn't have just gone like that, and all I could think about after I got shot was how much of an idiot I'd been.' He paused and exhaled slowly. 'But I trusted you to come through. I will always trust you—with my life, with everything, because I love you. You're all I could think about, and that thought kept me alive. I know I was reckless, but I just wanted this thing with Hales finished, so we could get back to normality and live our lives together.'

James looked up at Angela and the echo of Yula's words passed once more through his mind.

'You are to do it immediately…' But I didn't. Yet again, stuff got in the way, just like it always has done, even after I bought the ring.

He had been waiting for the perfect moment, some extraordinary event where he felt the stars align. Nothing less would do; she deserved more. After his awakening, he'd convinced himself that they needed to get through his recovery, then through the uncertainty of his condition, and then to wait until the doctor was no longer a threat and they could feel secure again. But in all that waiting, he'd nearly lost her, more than once. He could put it off no longer.

I was wrong. What Angela deserves more than anything else—more than any magical moment—is for me to make a damn decision. You knew this all along, didn't you, Yula? No more waiting, no more delays.

James's heart picked up speed and his heartbeat pounded in his ears as he began to tremble. Angela looked on at him, a slight look of confusion appearing on her face as his

432

cheeks flushed.

His mouth went dry as he continued, stammering barely above a whisper, 'T-that's why... I, I want to marry you.'

Angela froze.

James slowly pointed to a black holdall on the floor under the window. 'Did you pack that bag?' he asked.

Dumbstruck, Angela said, 'N-no... It's the go-bag you packed ages ago and we left at home, before all this with the hotels. Wh—?'

'Pass it to me.'

In a daze, Angela walked over, picked up the bag and brought it over to James. He opened the zip and rummaged for a few seconds before pulling out a small package wrapped in birthday paper. He handed the box over to Angela, who held it in both hands, staring at it with her mouth wide open.

'Well...' said James after a few seconds. 'Are you going to open it?'

At once, and in a sort of frenzy, Angela tore the paper from the present and practically ripped open the cardboard box, throwing the detritus on the floor. Tears came to her eyes as she held up the intricately carved wooden dice box.

'Oh, James... It's beautiful,' she said. 'But—'

'Open it,' said James, his eyes watering and trying to keep his voice from breaking. The tears began to flow as he continued, 'I've tried... tried so many times over the last few years. There was never the right moment, or some dumb shit just got in the way. But not this time. Not... not this time. I have a promise to keep, so to hell with perfection, I'm doing this now.'

Looking from James back down at the box, Angela carefully opened the lid, lifted it clear and placed it down on the bed. Peering inside, she saw the ring, its diamonds glinting in the fluorescent hospital lights. Her mouth fell wide open.

Silently, she put her fingers inside the recess and lifted the ring out, holding it daintily. She placed the box down upon the bed next to the lid and put her free hand to her mouth, tears welling up in her already red eyes. She stared at the ring in the palm of her hand and slowly nodded, her face crumpling into deep sobs.

She looked up at James and croaked, 'Yes!'

They had broken down in tears as Angela moved in and wrapped her arms around James. She pulled away and stared into his eyes, the tears streaming down their faces. He stared back into hers, struck by their piercing blue as if for the first time. All the hurt, all the pain that had been inflicted upon them through the last couple of years came flowing out, and they pressed their heads together.

After a long moment, their tears subsided, and Angela leaned in, kissing James, her hunger intense but matched by his own as he returned the kiss with passion and energy.

'You bastard!' said Angela playfully as she pulled away, wiping the tears from her eyes. She blushed and James could see she had gone giddy. 'You proposed to me in a bloody hospital!'

Without a further word, she put the ring on her finger and grabbed her handbag from the floor. She fished out her phone, held it up and stretched her hand out in front of it, fingers splayed.

'What *are* you doing?' asked James.

Angela shrugged. 'Well, I need to tell people that you *finally* proposed, don't I? I'll call Mum and Dad in a minute, but first I'm posting this up on the D&D chat.'

'What are you gonna say? Wait, what do you mean, finally?'

'Oh, no words,' she replied with a smirk. 'Just the picture. Everyone's been taking bets on when you were going to do it. Adrian got the closest, guessing my birthday. Spider and Jenny both thought you would have proposed straightaway when you came out of the coma. They proper convinced me you would as well.'

'You expected it?' James asked, dumbfounded and more than a little amused.

Angela laughed. 'You mean you didn't expect me to notice when you went all stiff and became a gibbering idiot whenever we went on those special dates before the mission? You know I'd have said yes wherever you did it, right?'

CHAPTER TWENTY-EIGHT
New Beginnings

Saturday 20th May 2028,
Cocoa Beach, Florida

T HE LATE-AFTERNOON SUN cast its long shadows seaward, the tops of the low beachfront premises stretching their ghostly fingers across the highway skirting the edge of the beach. The heat of the day had waned and a cool breeze blew inland; the sky was a darkening azure, with not a cloud present to mar the smooth graduating brightness emanating from the sun. Excellent conditions for a rocket launch, and a beautiful day for a wedding.

The sand had been smoothed in a wide area some way back from the leisurely lapping of the waves. Chairs had been arranged in rows, accommodating twenty guests, who sat chatting animatedly, and an aisle ran through the centre towards the sea. Cool as it was, being Brits, many were not used to the Florida heat and fanned themselves with vigour. Fancy hats bobbed up and down, and the occasional harsh laugh permeated the relative quiet of the seaside venue. Most of the locals had gone home for the day, picking up their beach chairs, towels, parasols and picnics, dressing themselves fully or simply throwing a sarong over their swimsuits and departing.

At the end of the central aisle was a delicate bamboo arch, bedecked and flanked with a colourful display of flowers. Standing before the arch and facing the waves, James jigged up and down on the balls of his bare feet. The fine sand was still warm and moved further up his feet as his toes sank with each successive bob. He wore a traditional black tux with a red silk cravat and silver waistcoat, omitting the blazer, which sat folded to one side on his chair. Despite the cool breeze, beads of sweat gathered on his brow, and he looked rather sickly with his eyes glazed, mesmerised by the movement of the waves.

Wearing a simple white shirt and black trousers, the minister stood under the archway, clutching the order of service in both hands and chuckling inwardly at James's nerves.

Plenty of James and Angela's closest friends and family had dutifully turned out for the occasion, though some had been unable to make the trek across the Atlantic and had expressed their firm disapproval of the choice to hold the wedding in Florida by way of tuts and quiet grumbles. But James and Angela had good reasons and weren't about to change their plans for the sake of a few grouches. They fully appreciated that some wouldn't make it, and in some cases had counted on it.

Both sets of parents were there, as well as Angela's sisters, nieces and nephews pulling duty as bridesmaids, flower girls and pageboys. Coming in at the last minute following a surprise change of plans was Winston, who accompanied Spider; an arrangement which raised both Angela and James's eyebrows.

A firm hand appeared on James's shoulder, breaking his

trance. He looked at his best man, Captain Queen, who, without a word, gave him a supportive nod and patted him on the back. Angela and her entourage had been given access to a bridal room, and while they weren't late by any stretch, the time seemed to drag on and on, as if the seconds grew longer with each count. But it seemed Austin's distraction had catapulted time forwards; no sooner had he removed his hand from James's shoulder than the music started, emanating from a tiny amplifier somewhere nearby.

At the sound of the first few bars, James spun round in anticipation and his heart leapt and quickened at the sight of Angela. She was arm in arm with her elderly father, whose beaming, tearful smile alone set off the waterworks for some of the now-standing guests. Her dress was an elegant white A-line shortened to just below the knee. Small pieces of red detailing complemented her hair, which was styled to accentuate its natural waviness, and like everyone else, she stood barefoot on the sand. She wore no veil but a simple tiara atop her head, glistening in the golden sunlight.

At once they processed slowly, in time with the music, with Angela holding her father up more than anything. Trailing behind came the bridesmaids in matching red dresses, and the children behind them. Dumbstruck by her radiance, James couldn't take his eyes from her. He'd dreamt of this day; not, perhaps, taking place on a beach in another country, but rather in an ancient church or even a registry office somewhere in the UK. A romantic at heart, he had dreamt up many permutations of the day, and he kicked himself for delaying it for so long.

Soon Angela had kissed her father, helped him into his seat and taken her place next to James.

Smiling from ear to ear, she leaned towards him and

whispered, 'You look like a deer caught in the headlights.'

James swallowed. His mouth was dry and all he could do was choke out a feeble, 'You look amazing.'

As the music stopped, the minister cleared his throat, drawing their attention, and began, inviting the guests to be seated. The ceremony was short, but no less meaningful. James stammered his way through the vows he had written and almost put the ring on the wrong finger, drawing an audible groan from Austin, who stood beside him, smiling. The ceremony culminated in a passionate kiss, accompanied by rapturous applause and cheering, which cast all of James's nerves aside. And so the newlywed Mr and Mrs Fowler ran back down the aisle hand in hand, spraying sand everywhere.

* * *

James and Angela held hands on the beach, standing as the cool, briny fizz gently lapped at their ankles, their toes buried in the wet sand. Together, they gazed north along the sepia-toned shoreline as the last glimmer of light from the setting sun descended below the horizon. James breathed a sigh, taking in the freshness of the salt air and exhaling the stress of the day.

A short reception on the sand had followed the ceremony, with family photos, dancing and live music provided on a steelpan drum. The celebration had ended with the cutting of the cake, three tiers of magnificent adornment encompassing the couple's shared interests—dragons and spaceships, musical notes and poetry—topped with the figures of two little astronauts.

But now the tables and chairs, the arch and the wedding decorations had been cleared away, leaving only the chaotic footprints of their guests. Angela and James's parents had retired to their hotel room for dinner, and the others were sitting around on the sand, talking and laughing, or, in the case of Winston and Spider, snogging a hundred yards down the beach while everyone pretended they couldn't see them.

'What a day! How're you two lovebirds holdin' up?' said Austin, sidling up next to James and slapping a hand around his shoulder, gripping him in a tight side-hug.

James laughed and nodded. 'We're great! I feel like the day has just flown by, though. Thanks for being here, Captain. It really means a lot, especially your being my best man,' he replied.

'You kiddin'? I was honoured when you asked me. There ain't no place I'd rather be, my man.'

'I just wish the others could've been here too.'

Giving a gentle smile and an understanding nod, Austin gazed out along the beach. His smile turned wistful and his eyes watered. 'Y'know, I'm proud of you, man…' he said, giving the couple a sidelong look. 'Both of you. After all you've been through these last few years. And I'm sure Yula would say the same thing; there was no one rooting for the two of you harder than her.'

James's eyes began to water too, and he looked up into the darkening blue sky. A few stars were just fading into view, but Mars had set with the sun.

It had always been the plan to end the wedding watching the rocket launch for the ISS carrying the next crew for the *Magnum Opus*. That was the reason James and Angela had chosen Cocoa Beach for the venue, and the launch time was now drawing near.

The window for the new mission was tight, as Mars was gradually receding from Earth and would soon be on the opposite side of the sun, making it beyond costly to reach. Conditions weren't perfect as they were, but the new crew, of whom James knew little to nothing, were tasked with an extended research mission on the surface, setting up a more permanent base, to be named Arcadia Landing. The mission would stretch over several years, with a crew changeover scheduled for when the planet came close again in 2035.

Austin was right, thought James. He remembered and cherished the time he'd spent getting to know Yula; how they had become close friends during that fateful outbound journey, and how enthusiastic she had been at the prospect of James marrying Angela. She'd secretly loved weddings; it didn't matter whose. It was something she'd confided in James once during a crew movie night in Hab-2.

In another life she'd probably have been a wedding planner.

But being an astronaut was her first love, her true passion. She'd have wanted to go back to Mars if things had turned out differently. All that humanity had learned of the Achelon as a result of the mission would have fascinated her.

Much as James had at first hated the idea of sending others to the Red Planet, despite everything—and especially now that the space agencies had been forced to drop their secretive project—the return mission represented Yula's legacy. It was another way to honour her sacrifice, to ensure that in some way it had not been in vain. At least it was this idea that brought James the most comfort.

'Don't sell yourself short, Austin,' said Angela, reaching out and squeezing his arm. 'What you and Cass did for us… I don't think we could ever thank you enough.'

'Yeah, how long have you got left on your suspension now, sir?' asked James, dragging his toes out from under the sand.

Austin shrugged and waved his hand. 'Ahh, only a couple of months. And you don't need to be thankin' me. I'm proud of what I did, and I'd do it again in a heartbeat; and so's Cass. Besides, gives me plenty of time to get reacquainted with ma pupper.'

'Aw, how is she?' Angela cooed. 'I bet she missed you something rotten?'

With a loud scoff, Austin replied, 'Like hell! My idiot brother-in-law spoiled her senseless. She didn't wanna come home with me, that's for damn sure. But I run a tight ship, as the commander here knows, so she's settling back into her old routine now.'

James laughed. 'I wouldn't call the *Magnum* a tight ship!'

The captain stood back in mock offence, then joined in the laughter. After the chuckling died down, he said, 'Still, I am excited to get back to the project at White Sands.'

'The one you can't tell us about?' said James with a wry smile.

Austin nodded. 'Just between us, progress is good,' he said. 'It's just a shame Cass left after they dropped the charges. Can't say I blame her, though; being treated like that…'

'It's really going to change things, isn't it?' said Angela, the tone of her voice a mix of worry and excitement.

'It already is,' Austin replied, folding his arms. 'I once heard Guy Furious say we were like Prometheus, stealing fire from the gods. He's not entirely wrong; the technology on that ship answers so many questions about the things we've been struggling to develop down here.'

Still looking towards the horizon, James said, 'Definitely feels like the dawn of a new age, in more ways than one. This launch, a permanent off-world base, a potential end to the energy crisis and who knows what else.'

'Your wedding too, remember?' muttered Austin, which made Angela stifle a giggle. 'And you'll probably be around to see how all this pans out,' he added, giving James a soft jab in the ribs.

'Y'know what?' James said with an air of defiance, putting an arm around Angela and kissing her. 'I've accepted that… For the moment, at least. I'd rather live in the here and now, and savour this new adventure. What will be, will be.'

Angela gently hummed the melody to '*Que Sera, Sera*', and it was Austin's turn to stifle a laugh.

James looked back and forth between the two of them in disbelief for a moment, then broke into a grin. 'Yeah, that was a bit cheesy, wasn't it?' he said with a chuckle.

'Corny as hell, my man,' replied Austin, looking down as his phone buzzed. Raising an eyebrow, he pulled it out of his trouser pocket. He unfolded it and stared at the screen for a few moments before pulling out his glasses and taking another look.

'Hmm,' he grunted with a frown.

'What is it, sir?' asked James, a worried look appearing on his face. 'Is everything okay?'

Austin smiled and looked at the couple. 'Yeah, everything's great,' he said, turning the phone screen around so they could see. 'Zhu belatedly sends her apologies for missin' the wedding. She says she'd be here, but she's indisposed.'

'Wait, Zhu? As in, Major Zhu? Haven't heard from her in ages!' said James. 'Hold on… I thought she was on the ISS. How is she texting you?'

'She had some shore leave. She's been up and down to that station like a yoyo these last few years. Finally managed to get in touch with her when she was planetside a few months ago. I told her about the wedding.'

'Oh, that's brilliant. Would've been great to see her again, though,' James said, looking back to the horizon. Time was getting short; the sky was moving further into the blue hour, with more and more stars flickering into life, as if someone were gradually poking holes in a dark-blue sheet. The launch window was drawing to a close and James worried that it might have been scrubbed.

Austin looked down at his phone again, swiping and tapping. 'Ah, it's time!' he said.

Angela huddled in close to James and the two focused their attention ever harder on the horizon.

'So, where *is* Zhu?' James asked.

Austin said nothing, but with a smile simply raised his hand, pointing his finger along the shoreline in the direction they were looking.

As he did so, a bright light, blinding in the darkness, rose up flickering and flashing, trailed by a long pillar of white smoke. Seconds later, a low rumble permeated the stillness and grew into a dull roar as the rocket soared ever higher into the clear sky.

James, Angela and Austin followed the progress of the craft as it ascended into the upper atmosphere. Another bright flash signalled the first stage separation, and the boosters could be clearly seen falling away, tumbling towards the Earth for a time, before righting themselves and descending slowly out of view, back to their floating pads.

The small, bright dot continued ever upward, until it became like a passing satellite, before fading from view, blending with the light of thousands of stars.

For James and Angela, it was the perfect end to a hard-won day; the start of the normal life they had craved for so long. They put the remaining questions out of their minds to enjoy their victory, even if it was only momentary.

But the threat of Dr Hales's enigmatic employer still loomed. Who were they? Why had they killed him? Hales had said they had an interest in James, so how long would it be before they came for him? Had the doctor truly finished synthesising the elysian serum? The worst part was that there was no way to discover the answers, until the inevitable.

The Earth itself faced an uncertain future, both with the advent of new technologies and ways of life, and the ever-growing worldwide influence of political groups inspired or led by Guy Furious. It was still uncertain how nations and governments would react in the long run. Life would change, but the question remained whether it would be for humanity's good or for ill. For all humanity had learned about the Achelon, they remained an enigma. Who were they really, and why had they come here? Where had they come from?

James's own future seemed inexorably linked with this slow march forwards. As much as he wanted to forget his endless life, beyond the bounds of mortality lay a new, exciting, terrifying path. A path he dreaded to walk; the cost was too great to bear. But for now at least, he wouldn't face this uncertain future alone.

The Augment Saga continues in Book Two:
The Shadow of Arcadia

ABOUT THE AUTHOR

Alan K. Dell is a British science-fiction author and creative person with far too many hobbies. For his day job he works as the parish administrator for his local church, where he also volunteers as a musician. His hobbies include playing the guitar, illustration, graphic design, photography, astronomy, reading sci-fi and playing videogames. He lives at home in Essex with his wife and two children.

Get in touch (he doesn't bite!):
Website: www.alankdell.co.uk
Twitter: @alandell88
Facebook: @alankdell
Goodreads: www.goodreads.com/alankdell

If you have enjoyed this book, please leave a review on Amazon or Goodreads. It would be greatly appreciated and it's a brilliant way to support authors.

MORE IN
THE AUGMENT SAGA

The Re-Emergence:
An Augment Saga Novella

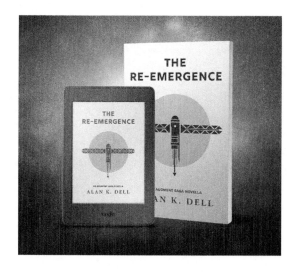

'*A great start and introduction to an interesting series*'.

'*If you are a fan of gripping duels this novella is a good read.*'

The space opera and companion novella to *From the Grave of the Gods*. Available now from Amazon in ebook and paperback. Sign up to my email newsletter and get the ebook **FREE!**